THE TREE OF LIFE MYSTERIES

THE TREE
OF LIFE
MYSTERIES

BOOK I

The Black Cube

By George Stanley

For my grandfather, Michael.
A man who wished to write a novel, but was caught by
the merciless claws of dementia before he could.
Grandad, allow me to fulfil your wish.

ACKNOWLEDGEMENTS

Writing this book has been a monumental milestone of my life so far, and it couldn't of been done without the help of my loved ones, and those who have given their time to help me with the project. My passion to write meaningful stories has only just begun, and I am thankful to God that I have been blessed with such a fruitful and unique journey, giving me great meaning, and a Heroes journey that is of now only a sapling.

I want to thank my editor, Andrew Dawson, for his incredible attention to detail; making this novel read smoothly, and see things that my untrained eyes would never see. Your understanding of the intricacies of the English language humble me greatly, and makes me realise how much I still have to learn.

Xavier Comas, and Baris Sehri, for both their incredible cover design, and their artful interior design and typology. It was such a pleasure working with you both. Your dedication to understanding my vision, and incorporating it into your design style, is something I will never forget.

It goes without saying that I thank my friends and family, the ones who supported me every step of the way. Words on this page alone will never be enough to pay my respects to you. Mum, Dad, Sis, and Nanny Pat; you guys are the spirit beneath this book, and I will never be thankful enough.

Finally, I want to thank the person who I would say had the most dramatic impact on shaping this novel. Carys Hedley, this is more than just a book for us. For us, this book was what brought us together; and as we moulded it, it, moulded us. This book in my opinion has been both inspired by us, and has inspired us simultaneously. Without you, the book may never of even been completed, and for that, I am forever thankful. I will never forget your passion for this book.

PART ONE: SONS OF THE FATHER

1. A NIGHTMARE

A six-year-old boy, Arthur, is in a dream. In this dream, he is a small, white dove, and he flies above old castle ruins. The low sun is shining brightly in the sky. The sunlight reflects off the stone below with great intensity and power, and expansive green plains can be seen for miles around. Arthur flaps his wings with joy; he swoops, glides and flutters. Oh, how he feels so free!

The grounds below him are old, they are fallen, and they are degraded. They are shells of what they used to be. Arthur then swoops down, and decides to land on top of a rocky ruin that overlooks the remains of a courtyard. Within the courtyard's centre lies a large oak tree. The tree's beauty, richness and colour all strike Arthur deeply. And like a magnet, he is compelled to move towards it. He gracefully floats down from the ruin and lands on the grass beside the trunk. As he walks his little clawed feet closer and closer towards it, he suddenly notices an *old man* appear from the side of the tree. The man is dressed in a long, grey robe and has dishevelled white hair, and a messy white beard. The man looks down at Arthur, but Arthur feels no fear. The man has the warmest of smiles, and Arthur is filled with this very warmth from within himself. The old man leans down and gently lays his hand on the grass. Arthur hops onto the man's hand, and the man lifts him up to hold him in front of his chest, cupping him carefully.

'Oh, isn't she beautiful?' the man says as he looks towards the tree, beginning to walk around it casually. 'She stands here in her glory, tall and strong; yet her surroundings die and crumble. This is why we say that trees have wisdom, as they sit and watch throughout history. They have no opinions; they just pay attention. They take what they need, and they *grow*. They shed their leaves in dark times; and grow them back in bright times. And the older they become, the deeper their roots go down into the earth. And this is, of course, necessary, because as she ages, and grows taller, she must find more spirit and fuel by going downwards; she must struggle and use all her might to continue to push herself upwards. But it is not the roots we see; no, we do not see the struggle in the dark underneath. We only see the beauty that shines in the light; the beauty of the blossom, the greenery shining in the sun. Yet the roots are just as much part of the tree as her branches, no? The tree has no choice but to use her roots, as the roots are what keep the tree alive and flourishing. You see, little dove, it is us men who think we are so different from trees; yet this is our arrogance. Why should we assume we can do without roots any more than a tree can? And what if man forget his roots? Forgets his past, forgets where he came from? Or what if man even understands and remembers, and has moments of insight and wisdom; but in his arrogance, or his fear, he pretends it is not part of him? He lies to himself, refusing to associate with such darkness. He then goes on believing and acting as if he is better than his ancestors. Man says: "Surely one would not associate with such primitive ways? These ways are old, they are dated, restricted to the savages! We can outthink these old ways!" What if we begin to believe that this darkness within doesn't even exist? And that these ways are merely ideas that we can just shed with a mere *click*. What if we do not even acknowledge it's a part of us? Surely, would this not be like a tree shedding its own roots? And would we, like the tree, not fall into chaos and destruction?

'The tree may be tall now, but would she have been as tall if she had not also gone low? No tree, it is said, can grow to heaven, unless its roots descend into hell.'

The old man continues to stare at Arthur, and stays awfully still. Arthur twists and turns his fluffy head, and then things around him begin morphing into a more modern and familiar sight.

The old man's face and body begin to transform. They melt, morph and contort. The man is no longer old, and no longer wears the grey robe. The man now in front of Arthur, is his father, Phillip. His hands, which were holding Arthur as a dove, are now trying to do up a zip that is currently stuck on Arthur's little jacket instead. Both Arthur and his father are standing outside a large supermarket.

'What are we doing here, Daddy?' Arthur asks his father, who has just managed to zip up his little blue puffer jacket.

'I need some medicine. Don't worry, it won't take long,' his father replies.

Phillip leads Arthur by the hand inside the supermarket, and they walk towards the medicine counter.

'Hello. Can I have my medicine please?' Phillip asks the lady behind the counter.

'We haven't got your medicine,' she replies.

'But I need it.'

'We haven't got any medicine for you.'

'What?!' Phillip exclaims in a deep, elongated way best described as demonic. The way he says it fills Arthur with a deep dread and terror.

'I. Need. My. Medicine!' Phillip's voice cracks and contorts; it is twisted, full of low-end bass and rumble. And as Arthur stares at his father, he notices his face is now beginning to change once again. Golden fur begins sprouting out from every pore; his nasal area becomes incredibly pronounced and looks rather feline and pouted.

Phillip lets out a mighty roar!

He aggressively shakes his body and head, baring his large teeth with a snarl. Arthur's father has transformed into what can only be described as a *man lion*. The lion turns his attention to Arthur now, and lets out another mighty roar.

Arthur runs away.

He runs as fast as his little legs will carry him. He flees from the supermarket. As he prepares to turn around to face the chasing beast, he screams himself awake.

Arthur jolts up from his bed, screaming.

'Who are you, who are you?!' Arthur yells towards his bedroom door, in the moment believing a guitar case is actually a dark, muddy figure. As he awakens and realises he's been dreaming, Arthur regains his composure. He turns his side light on.

'Mummy! Daddy!' he shouts, waking the whole Stanley family. Phillip, his father, Áine, his mother, and Jack, his eight-year-old brother; all emerge on the landing to investigate the screaming.

'Ahh, are you having a bad dream my love?' Áine asks as she picks him up to embrace him. She then puts him back into bed.

'Yes, Mummy, a horrible one. I was going shopping with Daddy, and he turned into a lion and started chasing me …'

'Ha! Did you get eaten then?' asks Jack, who has tired eyes but a smirk on his face.

'Jack, please, can you go back to bed, we've got to be up early for camping tomorrow,' Phillip says sternly.

'Okay …' Jack says sheepishly as he heads back to his bedroom.

Phillip walks into Arthur's bedroom, and sits on the bed next to Arthur.

'No!' Arthur recoils, part of him still scared his father would transform into a lion again.

'It's okay, Arthur, it's okay. I'm not a lion; look, my hands haven't got any fur.' Phillip holds his hands up to Arthur to prove it. Arthur makes a rather sad looking face, showing a slight resistance at first, but then holds out his arms as if wanting to be hugged.

'Daddy. I love you, Daddy.'

'I love you too, Arthur.'

'Okay you two, don't stay awake too long, as I don't want any grumpters tomorrow …' Áine says, as she leans around the bedroom door.

'Don't worry, I just want to talk to Arthur for a moment.'

Áine purses her lips and nods. She then heads back upstairs to sleep.

'You know, I use to get bad dreams a lot when I was your age.'

'Really? Like *really scary* ones?'

'Oh yes; they were awful! But one day, something changed. And I wasn't scared anymore …'

'What changed?'

'Well, it wasn't the dreams that really changed, but it was my attitude. Instead of being scared in the dreams, I imagined I was a hero. And as a hero, instead of letting the scary things frighten me, I would instead face the fear, face the darkness. I tried to be excited instead; I tried to see the dreams as adventures, rather than something I simply must suffer and endure. When I would see something scary in a dream, I would imagine I also had a sword in my hand Instead of screaming, I would hold my sword high and think: *Bring it on monsters, I'm not going down without a fight.* But the funny thing was, after a while, and as life went on, the nightmares stopped almost entirely, and it was only now and again that I would have them. And to be honest, I would even look forward to them! So remember these words, Arthur. If you are ever struggling with something, remember, *that what you most need is where you least want to look. In filth, it will be found …*'

'In filth, it will be found …' a captivated Arthur repeats softly back to himself.

Phillip nods, and smiles gently.

'Now, you better go and get some sleep, otherwise your mother will be angry. I will speak to you tomorrow…'

Phillip is cut off by a sudden and unexpected knock on the front door.

'What the hell? It's 10 o'clock … Go back to sleep, and remember what I said to you, okay?' Phillip smiles at Arthur and gives a wink.

Phillip is instantly suspicious of this late-night interruption. He heads downstairs to investigate. He takes a quick peek through the peephole and a sees a teenager, approximately 16 years old, black hair, holding a package for delivery. Almost without thinking, he goes to the kitchen to grab a knife. He momentarily realises how bizarre his behaviour is, as he has never once in his life intended to stab someone with a knife; it seems like such an overreaction, yet he puts the knife in his back pocket regardless. He opens the door a little, peeking his head out through the gap ...

'Delivery for number 44?' the monotone teenager asks with a blank stare, holding a small, square box.

'Isn't it a bit late for deliveries?' Phillip asks, suspiciously.

'Yeah, sorry, some deliveries have been delayed ...'

They both stare at one another for an extended period. The teenager is clearly frustrated, his eyes darting around as he shakes the box with agitation, giving the impression he is in a rush.

'Okay, well I suppose my wife must have ordered something ...' Phillip says as he opens the door fully, raising his eyebrows reluctantly, almost with a sense of defeat.

Rather than handing Phillip the box, the teenager drops it on the floor, causing Phillip to freeze with anxiety.

Two men wearing balaclavas come out from around the corner, one of them armed with a handgun, and the other with a baseball bat. They force their way into the house.

Phillip immediately starts stabbing them with his blade.

He catches the man with the gun in the shoulder and in the arm; but the other man manages to get behind the enraged father, and lands a clean bat strike to Phillip's head, knocking him unconscious. They then stuff his mouth with a sponge and tape over it. At this point, the teenager is just silently standing on the porch, watching this all unfold; but his eyes are wide and look strangely content at what they see ... The men cable tie Phillip's hands behind his back.

Áine, Jack and Arthur rush to the top of the stairs to inspect the chaos. Jack continues to run halfway down the stairs, but then freezes. He sees his father, helpless and desperate on the ground, with the men standing over him. The teenager on the porch calmly stares up at Jack, like a ghost. Jack feels compelled to look back at him, captivated. A peculiar feeling of déjà vu hits Jack, making him feel a trance-like dissociation from the chaos, albeit still overwhelmed and shocked.

Áine begins to scream frantically. Jack snaps out of it.

'Get out of my house! Leave us alone! What do you want?!' Áine shouts in a desperate panic, flailing her hands manically. She then rushes down the stairs to try and help her beloved husband.

The gunman indicates to his accomplices to restrain the screaming woman. Both the teenager and the man with the baseball bat run up the stairs, going straight for Áine. They pull her down the stairs and into the hallway beside Phillip on the floor.

'Get off me! You bastards! Please! Just don't hurt my children! Please! I beg you!'

Jack storms down the stairs and towards the men with ferocity. The bleeding man with the gun grabs Jack and pins his head pinned to floor. The man then removes his hand from Jack's face, and instead points his gun at it. The two others continue to grip Áine's arms tightly. The ringleader then turns to look her in the eyes.

'I could easily put a bullet in your son's head right now, would you like that?' the armed ringleader says to her.

Áine is now in complete shock and begins to wail, tears running down her cheeks.

'No? Well, let's start with his ears.'

The ringleader shoots his pistol close to Jack's left ear. Jack flops to the ground, clasping his ringing ears in agony. He feels a deep shock run through his body and curls up in a ball; frozen, like a turtle turned to stone.

'My baby!' Áine screams, as she instinctively launches towards her child to provide support and comfort, temporarily breaking the grips of the intruders. The man and the teenager quickly regain control of her, hauling her back up to her feet. The mother begins screaming and flailing frantically like someone possessed. The two intruders struggle to restrain the slim, petite Áine; it is obvious from their expressions that they are shocked by her strength as a powerful, primal energy courses through her veins.

Arthur is still standing and watching at the top of the stairs; although very confused, he understands very clearly his mother is being attacked. In the mother's desperation, she notices something shining on the ground. She breaks free of the grip the teenager and quickly leans down to grab the kitchen knife that Phillip used earlier. She immediately stabs the man with the gun in the throat with a savage, one-handed swing. His blood begins pouring everywhere, and he clenches his neck desperately. He then falls and slides against one of the white walls by the door, covering it in blood. The bleeding intruder squints, and slowly his hand raises for one last shot. He fires his gun, and hits Áine directly in the stomach. She staggers, then flops to the ground. Arthur begins crying uncontrollably from the top of the stairs, shouting for his mother and father in desperation even though he can quite clearly see his whole family is powerless.

'Mummy! You shot my mummy!'

Arthur runs off into his bedroom and begins screaming out the window.

'They shot my mummy!' he sobs, followed by mumbling some unintelligible words, shaking his head erratically.

Next door neighbours John and Suzy Horwood are lying in bed and have just been awoken by the gunshot.

John and Suzy are long-time friends of the family, with them all meeting one another at Oxford University. Phillip and John continued to stay close to one another and together launched a martial arts academy called The Tree of Life. Not long afterwards, John served in the British Royal Marines as a commando, and eventually went on to specialise as a conditioning and close-quarters combat instructor, teaching Brazilian jiujitsu to the force. It was true that in John's heart he had always wanted to serve in the military, and he justified the decision to Phillip by saying it could provide the academy with a sense of legitimacy, and make the business more appealing to students. During John's time in the military, he still kept in close contact with Phillip, and would come back to help run the business whenever he could. Yet that wasn't always possible as within John's two years of deployed service, between 2003 and 2005, he completed two tours of Iraq.

John and Suzy were no strangers to the children either, so much so that the brothers referred to them both as Uncle John and Aunty Suzy. Phillip and Áine even decided to make John and Suzy the boys' godparents.

At university, they all joked and, in a sense, even dreamt of living closely to each other. And this dream was finally realised following a particular phone call Phillip had with John towards the end of his second tour. John had gone through some tough times while serving which had prompted some deep revelations about his own life, and he decided it best to jump on the opportunity to be permanently discharged and help run the academy full time. The fact that upon his discharge the house next door had just gone up for sale John saw as the stars aligning; leaving him to pursue the civilian life for good.

The gunshot immediately causes flashes in John's vision, almost as if he had been expecting this moment; it prompted a feeling of strange familiarity, as if he had dreamt this moment before in a nightmare.

John immediately rushes out of his bed and puts on his nightgown. As John rushes out onto the street, he sees the two remaining intruders fleeing the Stanleys' house and jumping into a black Ford Focus getaway vehicle. John runs towards the house, and notices Arthur leaning out the window, still sobbing wildly.

'My mummy… My mummy…'

'Arthur, it's going to be okay mate, I'm here now,' John shouts up to Arthur.

As John enters the house, he can clearly see both Phillip and Áine are unconscious and lifeless. He notices the bleeding intruder, who is now completely immobile, slumped up against the wall by the door below a trail of blood. John surveys the aftermath in utter disgust. He notices the tape over Phillip's mouth and removes it immediately. John wastes no time and calls for an ambulance. He then tends to Jack, who is clearly in a lot of pain. He remains in a turtled position on the floor, shaking and in shock. John strokes the back of Jack's head to try and calm him.

'Alright Jack, there we go, you're okay now.'

Jack stares blankly, his features fixed like a statue. After 10 agonising minutes, the emergency services arrive and all are rushed to hospital.

John, Suzy and Arthur sit in the hospital with a sense of dread and anxiety whilst they wait for an update from the doctor. Beside them are a police officer and a social worker providing support for Arthur. When the doctor finally walks over to give them an update, they all stare at him like hawks, looking for clues in his body language of what news he might bring. The social worker had at this point tried to persuade Arthur to go on a walk with her, but he was having none of it. He kept shaking his head, wanting to hear the news from the doctor himself, knowing too well what was going on. He may have only been six, but they couldn't pull the wool over his eyes.

'Okay, here's what you need to know,' the doctor says uncomfortably, clearly knowing this is going to be very unpleasant for all to hear.

'Jack is suffering with a badly perforated eardrum, and from what seems to be high levels of tinnitus in his left ear. I'm afraid I cannot guarantee at this point if the tinnitus will improve or not, but for someone his age it is highly likely. Psychologically, Jack is in a mild state of withdrawn catatonia, and is currently very incoherent other than his repetitive complaints about the ringing in his ears. His father is not so lucky, I'm afraid. The hit to his head caused a significant degree of trauma and a build-up of blood in his nose. Combined with his mouth being taped, this meant he struggled to breathe, restricting the oxygen flow to his brain and increasing the levels of brain damage. He is alive; however, is suffering from heavy cognitive impairment and it is without question that he will need care for the rest of his life.'

'And Áine?' Suzy asks, with her eyes wide and laser focused.

'Yes … Áine unfortunately suffered a severe loss of blood due to heavy internal bleeding, and a badly ruptured stomach. I must unfortunately confirm that she passed away in the last hour … I am deeply sorry.'

John, filled with anger, sadness, frustration and shock, stares straight at the doctor, who walks off with his head bowed.

An intense shiver pulses through John's body as he tries to focus on his breathing. Suzy bursts into a wailing cry and buries her face into John's chest. John cradles her head, and puts his arm around Arthur, who at this point is staring at the wall as if in a trance …

2. ALL GROWN UP

Some 12 years have passed since the home invasion. It is now 2018. Since the incident, godparents, and now foster parents, Suzy and John, decided it would be best to move to another house in Oxford. Naturally, they did not feel it would be healthy for the boys to see the house of horrors next door every day. They chose a more rural location, with lots of trees and fields nearby, but still only a 15-minute drive from Oxford city centre.

Despite a nationwide investigation following the incident, the trail of the two intruders mysteriously went cold. Cold in the sense that the charred remains of one were found in a burnt-out Ford Focus; and the other teenage intruder had seemingly vanished off the radar completely. The intruder who Áine slashed in the neck was confirmed dead. He was known to the authorities as 'Jester', real name Charlie Hemsworth. Jester was known to be a small-time gangster with a penchant for conducting seemingly random and spontaneous attacks on innocent families' homes, with no clear intent to steal or gain anything of financial worth. The Stanleys were unfortunately not the first victims of this type of attack orchestrated by him, but thankfully now they would be the last. When Arthur and Jack were questioned by the police shortly after the incident, they were told that the teenager was still on the run. The police made it clear to them, in a poorly-thought-out effort to elicit some empathy, that this teenager had likely 'suffered trauma like you', and if he could be found, he could be given the help he needed to become a 'good person'. Neither of the brothers were particularly happy after hearing this from the police, or inclined to help by giving a description of the teenager (the only one not wearing a balaclava). In particular Jack, who at this point was already harbouring resentment and fantasies of revenge …

It was not confirmed by the police at the time, but they speculated that this teenager was actually kidnapped as a child by Jester from a previous home invasion. Jester then moulded him into his own personal accomplice, exposing him to acts of atrocity and evil. Although discussed by some within the press and public, nothing was certain and this was all simply hearsay. Phillip's assailant was the one found dead in the boot of the Ford Focus getaway vehicle after being severely brutalised. Who killed him and why remains a mystery. Of course, more rumours surfaced, namely that the teenager was actually responsible, yet many found this very hard to believe. Regardless, it was after this discovery that the case of the remaining teenager went cold …

Arthur, now 18 years old, has developed distinctive features: a strong, broad jaw at odds with his otherwise feminine facial features. He is of average height, yet his build, in particular his arms, is quite muscular considering he has done no weight training and at this point only occasionally trained in jiujitsu at the Tree of Life Academy. His hair has gone from a light to a dark blond since the incident. He is a good-looking young man, with many people regularly giving him compliments on his large bluey-green eyes. He had a peculiar type of stare; a laser-beam focus, yet with a softness that ensured many did not find it overwhelming or too intense.. Arthur was certainly a smart young man, albeit not too intellectual. He was more so an extremely curious and big-hearted fellow; a 'dreamer', it could be said. And he had an undying thirst to learn new things, listen to people's life stories and explore new places. He would regularly go out for long walks with no clear intention or purpose, and would often come back with bizarre artefacts that caught his eye, whether that be a stone, a lost item of clothing or a stray door handle; whatever he would find meaningful or interesting on that particular day.

Jack is now 20 years old, six-feet tall and slender. He lacked natural muscle tone and athletic pursuits were of no interest to him. Jack's eyes are lazier looking than his brothers, and they are not as large either. He wears a constant frown, whether in a good mood or not, giving the impression that he is rather sceptical. It was not uncommon for John to gently tease him about it. Jack was a little more forthright with his humour, which could sometimes border on being insensitive; and Arthur often bore the brunt. It was also not uncommon for Jack to get rather angry and resentful whenever he saw happy families walking and holding hands. His fist would clench and his cheeks would tighten. Jack often projected these feelings on to Arthur, and he got even more annoyed when Arthur didn't share his resentment. Arthur wouldn't easily be able to articulate why he wasn't annoyed, but nonetheless this very fact made his brother strangely jealous, and therefore angry. It was hard for Arthur to ever win an argument against his older brother (not that Arthur particularly liked arguing, in fact it exhausted him, but it did occasionally happen). It has to be said that Jack did indeed have the superior intellect of the two brothers; his wit, rationality and logical ability were razor sharp. This is not to say that Jack had no heart, or was cold and dispassionate. It was also true that, at this point, he truly loved his brother, even if it didn't always look like it on the surface. Rather, Jack would suppress these parts of him, focusing his attention more on his fantasies that were ultimately rooted in anger and resentment. It was these that took much of his energy. Regardless, Jack had much respect for John and Suzy. He was mature enough to realise that they gave him a normal family upbringing. He was adamant that they should not buy him anything or financially support him in any way. Instead, he preferred to be financially independent, which he managed through his freelance software development work. One of the clearest differences between the brothers was what they valued, and what drove them forward. Jack was much more financially driven, at least that's what he told everyone. Already, at 20, he was almost in a position to move into his own place. Conversely, Arthur, whilst he understood the importance of money, was more concerned with his spiritual foundations. He was focused on pursuing something he loves, and that provides him with meaning, rather than purely chasing money. For this reason, Arthur had been working as a bartender at a pub called The Rabbit for two years. Not because he cared about serving drinks, but because he wanted to listen to lots of different people from all walks of life. He was fascinated by the social interaction and seeing the worst, and best, in people on a regular basis. Bartending was definitely not something he wanted to do forever; instead, he saw it as a platform to support himself until he found his true purpose in life, of which he currently wasn't sure.

It also must be said that Arthur had a unique skillset, which was rooted in creativity. Yet he didn't have a traditional creative outlet like most, such as painting or the like; in fact, painting was his worst subject at school. What he did enjoy doing, however, was observing and paying attention. Arthur would commonly sit, close his eyes and meditate, which had actually been a habit for many years, and one which he found gave much relief to his inner suffering from the trauma. When Arthur let his imagination take him, when he let go, he learnt to enter his unconscious dream world whilst he was awake; and it was not uncommon for him to speak to characters or lifelike beings within himself. But unlike mere imagination, these visions that came to him were not always in his complete control, and could some-times be very frightening. Whilst Arthur had learnt to *somewhat* control and summon these visions, they did not always come to him voluntarily. These visions, in their most powerful form, were forced into him during power-ful seizures. These seizures were sometimes random, and other times trig-gered by something in particular. Doctors speculated that since the incident, Arthur suffered from a deep psychological trauma, and this caused him to experience psychogenic nonepileptic seizures. Along with these seizures, his entire field of vision is constantly a little grainy, a condition known as 'visual snow', not too dissimilar to the static one may see on an old televi-sion screen. Doctors also believed that this visual snow was likely a symp-tom related to the psychogenic seizures.

But these visions of his were not always scary; sometimes they were in-credibly euphoric, in fact, and after the seizure, he would walk around with a large smile on his face. However, sometimes Arthur cannot leave his bed-room for days out of terror; leaving him trapped on his bed, battling his inner demons. But every time this happens, he remembers what his father told him: he must look deeper into the darkness, no matter how scary that place may be. Arthur may have trauma, he may be suffering, but he suffers willingly, truthfully and with courage.

Arthur could also see patterns where other people could not. On his walks and meditations, he would find great beauty in feeling how all living things are connected in mysterious ways, including humans. Arthur could sometimes even read people and their desires better than they themselves could, and he could see right through people's lies. He put all this down to discovering a weird fact about how the characters inside his mind related to real people in the outside world. Whilst he understood that on some level these unconscious entities he spoke to were not *real,* per se (at least that's what he told himself to not truly believe he was, in fact, crazy), their traits and reactions would actually be identical to those of real people in the material world. So, the more he understood and related to these inside characters, the more he understood *real* people in the outside world; thus giving him an extraordinary ability to understand people on an extremely deep level. It would also make it very hard for him not to love people, even people who many others would hate. It also has to be said that this higher level of awareness and insight into human nature gave him cause for worry about modern-day culture, which Arthur began to believe was rather sick and disconnected from this spiritual underworld he was ever so aware of. He could not understand how people had no *conscious awareness* of this *unconscious world*. Regardless, he remained optimistic for the future of society, and never let his doubts interfere with living his life, or allowed them to bring others down. To put it simply, Arthur had an incredible introverted awareness, and he soon tried to delve deeper into what was really happening during these visions of his. It didn't take long before this thirst for learning caught the attention of a certain eccentric Christian Orthodox priest called Vladimir Myshkin, who was a regular at The Rabbit. The elderly priest was of Russian descent, but had been living in England for the majority of his life. He had a very laid back and easy going attitude, and seemed very different to the usual vicars in England that Arthur had spoken to. Despite his age, and having a wife and four children, the priest had a rather childlike demeanour, and had a peculiar habit of *always* ordering the pistachio souffle with his ale. The priest himself took a particular liking to Arthur, and so did Arthur to him. After many conversations revolving around Arthur's seizures and visions, spirituality and the meaning of life, the priest told Arthur that some people just have a natural ability to communicate with God. The priest went on to say that some can connect to the Holy Spirit with more natural ease, and how it is likely that the trauma Arthur suffered as a young child opened his soul for direct communication with the transcendent world of the spirit.

He told Arthur that when he himself was a young man, he was an adamant atheist. He was a chemist working for a large Russian pharmaceuticals company, so in general the people he was surrounded by, day in, day out, were of similar ilk and perspective: those being highly intelligent, highly rational types. At times on work breaks, he would discuss deeper topics with his colleagues, and the general consensus was that religion was just a mechanism for controlling people, and that was that. Ironically, at this point the Soviet Union was firmly under the iron fist of communism, where everything was controlled and ordered very much like a religion. The priest told Arthur:

'After a while, I found my job wasn't fulfilling me anymore. The people I worked with, whilst pleasant and friendly enough, were rather boring folk. They lacked much passion and enthusiasm for anything other than chemistry, and had no real curiosity about the deeper mysteries of life. For me, I was originally attracted to chemistry to try and discover how everything is made up of these mysterious compounds and elements, these fantastic atoms and quarks. It was the bizarreness and the beauty of this atomic world that grasped my interest as a child. Ultimately, I thought science at its core was an attempt to address these great mysteries of life. But my colleagues didn't seem to care about these big questions, but instead would much rather just stick to their comfort zone and just do what they were told. I must say, it was at this point in my early 20s, if I recall correctly, that a need in me for answers grew, and I became extremely curious to break out of the box I was in and branch out. At this point in Russia, to believe in anything other than the state and its vision of utopia was a crime; but for me, the state didn't satisfy my growing curiosity or answer my spiritual questions.

'And then, one night after work, I was walking to my apartment in St Petersburg when something came over me. Out of nowhere, I decided to cut through a park called Sosnovka. It was late, and this detour would actually take longer; but there was barely anyone around, and inside I was feeling highly introspective, as if something within me needed release. At the park, I stared into a pond full of sleeping ducks. Like a child, I made a silly duck sound, as if I were trying to communicate with them. I made a few more sounds, and that was when I felt the presence of someone behind me, causing me to feel rather embarrassed. I turned and saw a couple who were looking at me suppressing their smiles, as if they were trying not to laugh.

"'I'm just trying to talk to the ducks," I said to them, with a smile on my face, trying to show them I was self-aware of my silliness. And then the man replied, with a rather surprised expression:

"'Vladimir? Is that you?" All at once I was overcome with a strong feeling of familiarity, and an even stronger one of *déjà vu*. It was at this moment the hairs on my spine stood up with unexplainable force. My body seemed to recognise something, yet my mind had not caught up. I continued to stare at this familiar face, and he back at me with squinted eyes.

"'Ganya Razumikhin?" I said in a realisation. It suddenly hit me that this was someone who I had not been particularly close with, but knew from school. I only had positive and funny memories of him. Ganya had always misbehaved in the classroom. I remembered him primarily as the boy who would make disruptive animal sounds at the back of the class whilst the teacher tried to teach, and the teacher used to hate him for it. I used to find these sounds so funny, and remember having to cover my mouth to suppress my laughter. And now, 10 years later, and with a sort of divine irony, he was the one listening to me make the animal sounds instead. This immediately broke the ice, and we started talking passionately like we had always been friends. However, there was a certain look in his eye that suggested this was a man with a secret, and I could tell he was being very careful with his questions. Yet still, he was very curious about me and my life. Although his questions could be quite testing in nature, he didn't make me feel threatened in any way. His peculiar demeanour made my own curiosity grow stronger, so I decided to invite him and his partner back to my apartment for a drink.

''It didn't take long for the discussion to tilt towards the fear and helplessness we felt under the current Soviet regime. I was surprised how we came on to the subject so easily, and without awkwardness, as I had up to this point been incredibly careful to not talk about it. It seemed most folk around me lacked awareness of the depth of their own oppression, and many felt truly patriotic towards the image of the Soviet utopia. To speak ill of it was equivalent to the deadliest of sins. And it was true, communism imbued many with a sense of camaraderie that every human deeply desires; but to me, this bond was fake, and I had no wish for this type of brotherhood. I felt this bond was futile, and lacked any true human depth. To me this bond felt like a mask, preventing true love from really flourishing from within our culture.

'It wasn't long into the conversation before Ganya's apparent hesitancy was explained, and he brought up the fact that he was part of an underground subculture called "Sistema". Sistema were basically hippies that didn't believe in Soviet values, but rather those of freedom and individuality. So naturally, I got involved in this subculture, and we had various meetings and festivities, including forest walks and the consumption of psychedelic mushrooms. It didn't take long until I became more and more immersed in Sistema, and started to understand the other members and what it was really all about. The world you see on psychedelics is very much the world we always see, yet it is like you are seeing it through the eyes of an innocent and pure child. You see things for what they are, and beauty is far more apparent. But most importantly, I began to see how all the world is connected by what Daoists call "the way", and what Christians call God. And it was at this time that I began reading the Bible, and so began my journey as an Orthodox Christian.

'But the snake always finds its way into paradise, and it wasn't long before the KGB started to crack down on Sistema and its outings. Many of the members around me began disappearing, with rumours spreading about how they had been put in prison. So myself and Ganya decided that we had to escape Russia; and as you can tell, we were successful.

'I still to this day occasionally go on forest walks with my wife, and we do indeed consume psychedelic mushrooms. For me, it is a sort of prayer. My ritualistic use of the mushroom fits my Orthodox belief. We have a term called "theosis", which in Orthodox Christianity means "to become like God", or to "align yourself with the spirit of God", and therefore the Holy Spirit. And I must say, it is during my unique "prayer sessions" that I actually feel closest to him.'

After this conversation with Vladimir, Arthur felt the need to research this strange world of shamanism himself. He remembered on occasions seeing relevant books on his father's bookshelf; so, he rummaged around the boxes in the attic where John and Suzy had stored his parents' old belongings, and found many books on plant medicines, shamanism and mycology (the study of fungi). Arthur discovered that many ancient civilisations would use psychedelic mushrooms, and other plants, to connect to the ever-present world of the spirit, and as medicine to purge one's soul of darkness, to connect back to that pure and childlike foundation of the human self. It was after his readings that he became extremely intrigued to try these famous mushrooms himself. He discovered that in England, the liberty cap was the most common psychedelic mushroom available and can be picked at first frost, between September and November. And so, he made it a yearly occurrence to go out between those months to pick up enough to last the entire year.

It wasn't long before Arthur became very adept at understanding the nature of these powerful fungi, but only after a few fairly disturbing incidents and trips that taught him the hard way. For example, the first time he ever did them was by no stretch of the imagination a calm experience.

One weekend, the brothers and their godparents decided they would visit the Tate Modern art gallery in London. Initially, Arthur was keen to go, as he did like art, but he preferred more classic artists, especially van Gogh. Arthur generally found modern art soulless, and didn't even think it was "art" at all most of the time. So his interest waned half way through the trip, and he decided he would go off and explore London on his own (without telling any of the others, of course) …

Arthur left the gallery and headed for Richmond Park, a place he had always wanted to go to. He had no idea how to get around London, however he never struggled in these situations because of his seemingly natural ability to connect with people. He saw a group of art students outside the gallery and casually walked up to them with a friendly face to ask if any of them had ever gone to Richmond Park. They said that it was a lovely place, and how they all liked the deer very much. They told Arthur he would need to go from Waterloo Station, and agreed to drop him off there.

In the very short car journey to the station, the conversation became very deep, very quickly, and the students were enthralled at Arthur's understanding of art as a medium of expression of the soul; and how all good art achieves this, and how bad art does not. They could not believe he was only 16. It was true that Arthur struggled to express himself around people who had no interest in such things, but when he came across people who were very open minded, or shared his interests, he would open up and talk very passionately. The subject of psychedelics managed to find its way into the conversation. Arthur told them that he had recently been reading books about them, and had been very curious to try and pick them. It turned out the students themselves picked mushrooms, and they actually had some on them. They gave Arthur four grams for his day out in Richmond Park, along with some useful advice about how to successfully pick them.

Arthur consumed the mushrooms whilst on the train to Richmond. As he hadn't eaten that day, he began to feel nauseous quite quickly.

He made it to Richmond Park, and began roaming the large, green grounds. For a couple of hours he was in awe, in his own little world, feeling connected to all the nature around him. And then something caught his attention. As he walked across an opening with tall grass, he saw a herd of many deer running at pace across the field. The deer ran with such urgency that it startled him to a halt. He stopped and stared at the rushing herd; and then he noticed another deer, moving much slower. This deer had blood on its rear right leg, and it limped and moved awkwardly. Arthur felt his heart seize in compassion for this deer, and began moving closer towards it. As he did so, he heard wild and rowdy laughs from a group of six hooded young men that were stalking it. He noticed that one of the boys had a slingshot, and one held a blade. The lad with the blade then sprinted towards the limping animal, and did an exaggerated jump as he slashed the animal in its rear, whilst shouting 'hi-ya' like a stereotypical ninja. The group of lads burst out laughing, with one of them even falling to the ground rolling round in fits of hysteria.

Despite Arthur's normal compassion, his senses and heart in his current state were so open, heightened and aware that a deep primal instinct arose within him. He felt a deep anger, and any feeling of cowardice and self-preservation that one may normally feel in this situation simply vanished.

Arthur felt a massive wave of energy shoot into him, and without any fear, sprinted towards the lad with the blade. He took him down with a double-leg take down that he had learned from some rudimentary jiujitsu training from John.

Arthur mounted the lad, grabbed the wrist holding the knife and wrestled the blade free from his grip, throwing it into the bushes. Arthur had no plan at this point; he was just acting on instinct, disgusted by the boys' lack of respect for the deer.

Bang! A boot to the jaw caused Arthur to fall off the lad, onto his side on the grass. A wave of beatings, slaps and kicks then follow, knocking him unconscious.

You might assume that this would be an incredibly traumatic experience, especially under the influence of a psychedelic. However, this experience led to one of Arthur's fondest memories.

As Arthur's bruised and bloodied eyes widened, he felt himself being dragged by the collar. He woke to a feeling of deep euphoria; and whilst he was in physical pain, his soul felt great contentment. The mushrooms had begun taking a higher effect on him as well, with his vision now swirling and the greenery around him becoming incredibly saturated. Arthur soon realised that it wasn't the yobs who were dragging him by his coat collar but two large stags. He smiled manically at this, and felt loved and protected by the stags; indeed, in this moment, he felt as if he was also a stag, and his stag family were protecting him. This feeling was very intense, and it caused him to cry euphorically.

The two stags eventually let go of Arthur's coat collar and dropped him on a bed of leaves, in an area where many other deer formed a sort of circle around him. Arthur, now in a euphoric and mystical state, caught a glance of the two stags that dragged him, and they were both of the rare white kind. They were extra muscular, with huge antlers. One of the white stags laid on the floor beside Arthur, whilst the other licked his wounds. He continued to go in and out of consciousness for many more hours, until he finally woke up not in Richmond Park, but instead in a hospital, with a rather worried John and Suzy standing at the end of his bed, looking over him. This was just one of the moments when they knew for certain that Arthur was no ordinary boy ...

3. ISHMAEL'S SHOP

Jack and Arthur are on their way to see their father, who resides in a care home due to the brain injuries he sustained. They are being driven by John, with Suzy staying at home. The boys are sitting in the back of the car quietly, staring out of their respective windows. Arthur's eyes are wide open, and his pupils are dilated wide. He is in a state of trance and meditation, ever curious at what comes to his eye. As he stares, he begins to feel a strong sense of rising warmth within his stomach, a sudden blend of euphoric, yet still anxious energy. In his head he feels a tingling sensation, and the static in his vision begins to swirl, twist and intensify into spiralling patterns. The world around him becomes bright and gooey. Whenever he begins to feel these signs, he at first focuses on his breathing, and then on something to look at. Sometimes he can actually suppress a seizure through breathing and focus alone, if he does not desire the visionary experience. At this moment, he thought it best to not unnecessarily garner attention, or interrupt the journey, so he tries to calmly and subtly suppress the building vision without alarming John and his brother.

As the car gets stuck in traffic down a country lane, he notices a horse being ridden on the road. He tries to focus his attention on the moving legs, and squints his eyes tightly with all his might. As he increases his focus, he rides the waves of feelings that flood his body and mind. The feelings begin to calm, and he relaxes believing he successfully managed to suppress the seizure. He sits back, leaning his head on the headrest, looks forward, and notices neither Jack nor John saw him acting strangely. He takes a sigh of relief, and closes his eyes to take a deep breath in.

A powerful shockwave shoots up his spine.

His eyes slant sideways, and a buzzing sensation fills his body. Before he can even react any further, his whole body starts to convulse, and he falls into an unconscious state …

He wakes. And finds himself inside a white-tiled butcher's shop.

He looks around in a dream-like haze, yet is still completely conscious and lucid; he knows full well he just left the car and is hallucinating within a seizure. Regardless, whenever he entered a vision, he always adopted the mentality that he should treat the experience as real, and go deeper into it. 'Let it say, what it needs to say,' was his mantra.

After taking in his surroundings, he notices on the counter a sign, saying: 'Special – Fresh Horse legs - *50% off*'.

'Since when do butchers sell horse legs?' he asks the butcher, with a puzzled expression.

'Since the horses stopped running,' the butcher replies nonchalantly, as if it were self-explanatory.

Arthur frowns, and then notices a sign above a doorway saying, 'Leg storage unit'. He looks back at the counter, and the butcher has vanished.

He walks through the doorway to a five-metre corridor with a door at the end to which a butchered and bloodied horse leg is crudely taped and dangling from the handle. There is a chill in the air, and the light is a cold blue. Arthur approaches the door and picks the leg off. He holds it between his hands, and it begins wiggling and twitching. He jolts in shock, and drops the leg on the floor; it still twitching and writhing ...

Inside, he witnesses a truly unsettling sight: dozens of horse legs dangling from meat hooks, separated into two blocks on the left and right side of the room. The horse legs have the same unsettling and uncanny twitching movement to them. It was almost as if they were alive, like snakes. At the end of the room in the centre is a dark figure, who sits on a black throne, motionless. Arthur struggles to make out their features, as a layer of a black, slimy substance covers the flesh. However, even through this mushy slime, it is quite noticeable that this figure has two curved horns coming from the head, and a long, pouting face, looking quite bull like. The posture of this figure seems to be how a powerful king would sit, upright, with arms out at the side on the rests. Arthur stares at this figure, as if in a trance within a trance. He is suddenly filled with a brutal moment of heightened aware-ness and experience. Even though he is in a vision, his emotions intensify into a feeling he had never felt before. He feels fear, but it is the sort one may feel in moments of existential threat; not just fear for himself, but a fear for *everybody*. The sort of fear one may feel when they don't know exactly what they are being fearful of, but the eerie feeling of rising, hard-to-explain evil ... It was as if the current experience was on a higher plane of reality.

As Arthur walks between the two lanes of twitching horse legs, the slime on the figure begins dripping off, like water melting off ice. This powerful figure of darkness suddenly, but slowly, with a snake-like slithering motion, begins to rise up in front of him, its head and mouth twisting and gaping like an animal waking from slumber. The demonic figure then bellows deeply like a bull, steam erupting from its nostrils. It slowly adjusts its eyes towards Arthur's. As they stare at each other, Arthur finally gets a clear picture of the beast. Its body is covered in hair like a bull, yet its arms are long and black with a thick, leathery skin. Its hands are a deep black, yet human in shape. Its legs are akin to those of a black antelope, with large, sharp hooves.

'A blessed boy with gifts of underworld travel approaches ...' the bull king says, its tone deep and coarse.

'My name is Arthur.'

'Names, names, names ...' the bull says slowly. 'Obsessed with names you all are. For are names not just a self-delusion that one is unique and important?'

'But do you not have a name yourself?' Arthur asks in a rather innocent and sweet tone, with a tilt of his head and a squint of his eye.

'Moloch. Yet *I am significant*, and have a large role to play in the drama of time. Your kind, you take names for granted, but they won't last for much longer; for your spiritual core has fallen, and now individuals will no longer be unique, but just necessary sources of fuel, like fish to be eaten.'

'That doesn't sound very nice ...'

Moloch laughs slowly, and with deep, sinister tone.

'It was your kind who chose to let go of their core. What happens to them now will simply be a product of their own doing ... Alas, though, I say, alas ... For you still interest me ... I look at you now, and by that merit alone you are different ... I look at you, and I see a kindling spark, a spark that with nurturing could help trigger the great coming ...'

'The coming of what?'

'The inevitable ...'

The pair hold gazes. Moloch lowers his snout and stares deeply and intensely at Arthur. 'But that is all for now. Be gone! My flesh be shown to you in time soon to come ...'

Moloch leans back into his throne, lays his hands on the throne's rests, and opens his mouth wide.

Everything starts vibrating, and Arthur's vision goes jittery.

Arthur looks around anxiously, and is not able to focus on anything. Everything looks melty and liquid-like. The environment begins folding and twisting, becoming more unstable and chaotic ...

But then all settles.

Arthur's vision fades darker and darker; his senses in this realm becoming blunted and dull …

He awakes.

He comes back down to earth. He finds himself on his side, and in the recovery position on a patch of green beside the road, just outside Oxford city centre. He feels John stroke the back of his head with care.

'Why are we so unlucky? Why does pain constantly come to this family?' Jack mutters loudly in a negative tone, flailing his arms around rather childishly.

'Pain makes us stronger, Jack; you must accept pain and learn from it,' John replies, as he turns his head whilst still stroking the side of Arthur's head. 'Hey there, mate, how are you feeling? That looked like quite an intense one?'

Arthur blinks a few times, and sits back up and rubs his eyes as if waking up from sleep.

'Yes, it was an intense one … But I'm fine now, let's go and see Dad.'

'Yes, we will see him shortly, but I want you both to follow me first. You need to have a quick walk to ground yourself back to earth. I don't want you being all airy fairy when we get to the home …'

'What are we doing?' Jack asks grumpily. 'He's fine. Yes, he had a seizure, but he has them all the time. I'm sure he knows how to deal with them by now.'

'Your dad deserves to be welcomed with a warm energy. He may not understand us like he used to, with words and with logic, but he can still feel our spirit. So we must calm ourselves, and bring ourselves together before we see him. You may be 20, Jack, but sometimes you don't act like it; so for now you will respect my decisions until you move out of my house and get your own.'

'Oh, I don't act my age, but Arthur does? He's going to be living at your house for a lot longer than me, I can assure you of that …'

'You are both maturing in different ways,' John replies calmly. 'I'm proud of you both, and *both of you* still have growing up to do; and I will always be here to help with that.'

'Fair enough …' Jack replies, shaking his head and rolling his eyes with a hint of arrogance.

'Also, I want you both to meet a friend of mine. His name is Ishmael, and he helps run the academy. So we aren't just going to go on a random walk to waste time. He was actually one of mine and your parents' close friends when we were all at university. He's a very interesting chap; a bit weird, yet in the best possible way.'

'Is the car going to be okay here?' Arthur asks shyly, noticing it is on a narrow country road.

'Maybe, maybe not … But if it gets destroyed, I guess we will just have to walk all the way back home!' John laughs, and gives a teasing yet warm smile. 'You're all good though, Arthur, yeah?'

'Yes, I'm fine. In fact, I feel strangely refreshed. It was a very weird vision though, I can't lie'

'Good. Let's go then,' John says.

The trio walk down the lane in tandem, almost like soldiers on a march; John leads as if the commander of the troops, Jack is in the middle and Arthur is at the back.

After walking for almost an hour to reach Oxford city centre, they reach a narrow, quiet side street. Down this street lies an old-fashioned book shop, which has various brightly-coloured flowers dotted around its entrance.

'Here it is, boys. Ishmael's been running this book shop for years.'

Inside the shop, a middle-aged man is sitting behind an antique-looking mahogany desk, and is leaning forward in an engaged posture while reading a book. The man wears a pair of small, circular spectacles slid slightly down his nose, yet has an air of sharpness and fitness to him that hints at danger. His whole demeanour gives the impression that he is not only highly intelligent, but also a man of depth and wisdom.

'Ishmael, how are you, my friend?' John says, after approaching the desk in silence.

'Ahh, if it isn't John Horwood himself. It looks like you've brought friends with you,' Ishmael replies calmly, whilst looking up with a soft, warm smile.

'You've actually both met Ishmael before,' John says as he turns to the brothers, 'but I believe you would have been too young to remember.'

'Yes, it was at your christenings if I recall correctly. And how you both have grown since then … and I don't just mean physically, either.' Ishmael takes a close look into each of the brother's eyes, clearly intrigued.

'Hello,' Arthur says, whilst giving a nod and piercing his lips together.

Jack follows by greeting Ishmael with a lazy sort of wave, and then says:

'I'm surprised this is the first time we've met, especially considering you were close with our father.' He turns to John. 'Why haven't you introduced us before?'

John gives a smirk and a raise of the eyebrow to Ishmael, as if communicating an already mutual understanding.

'Ah ... Well, I actually spend much of my time at the academy. So if you both decided to train there more often, we might have already been well acquainted,' Ishmael says, in a simultaneously stern yet polite manner. 'John tells me he's been trying to get you both to come down, but neither of you seem particularly interested in the idea. Let me tell you this now, boys: you have *no idea* what you are missing out on; I can guarantee you both that. I would even go as far to say that the academy will change your life forever ...'

Jack gives a rather patronising look, rolling his eyes and gaping his mouth as if to say: 'Why does this man think he knows what's best for me?' Arthur, on the other hand, seems genuinely curious, and even a little guilty. He had trained at the academy a few times, yet lacked the discipline to be consistent. In his heart he knew this to be true, causing him to bow his head and sigh.

Ishmael pushes his glasses further up his nose to inspect the boys. He stares at them one by one, as he did before; but this time for an extended period, as if he was now really trying to look into their souls. Then, seemingly out of nowhere, and without saying a word, Ishmael leaves his desk and walks through a door behind him. Both boys look at John, as if hoping he would know where his friend had just gone. John simply gives an equally puzzled look, and holds up both hands to communicate that he has no idea either. Three minutes go by, and there is still no sign of him. So, Arthur and Jack decide to have a little look around the shop.

In the top left corner of the shop, there is a long bookshelf labelled 'Bookkeepers' favourites'. It has many classic books for sale, most being of a philosophical, psychological or historical nature. However, there seems to be quite a few books on fishing, music, and one titled *The Art of the Disc Jockey*. Arthur wanders back over to the desk and, out of natural curiosity, picks up the very book Ishmael was reading: *Aion: Researches into the Phenomenology of the Self* by the psychologist Carl Jung. Arthur begins to flick through the pages and then ...

'Ahh, so you are interested in Jung then?!' Ishmael asks, surprising Arthur with his sudden re-emergence.

'Oh, ha-ha, I'm sorry ... I just picked it up out of curiosity.'

'Ah, I see, so yes, you are definitely interested in Jung then!' Ishmael places another book down on the desk. 'Phillip is a great man, and a good friend of mine. Whilst he may have lost his body, his soul remains true. So these two books are my gifts to you; consider it a gesture from a family friend. Even when you were both just little children, he spoke about you both with such understanding, recognising your natures based on what he observed. He said that you like all things mechanical, Jack, as well as having a cunning mind. Well, a great piece of ancient engineering, and tactical genius, was the classic Trojan Horse the Greeks used to bring down the Trojans. I feel a cunning young man like yourself would enjoy this epic poem.'

Ishmael passes Jack *The Aeneid*, by Virgil. Jack flicks through to a random page while everyone stares at him, as if waiting for a reaction.

'What is this crap? It doesn't make any logical sense. It's written in a very bizarre style,' he says, after reading a few lines.

'Jack, it was written before Christ, for goodness' sake. How can you be so disregarding of something which is clearly classical and well respected?'

'John, I am well aware of the various epic poems of the past. Obviously, I'm being somewhat sarcastic. I've given a few a go, like *Inferno* by Dante, and yes, I can respect them. But frankly, I think they are written in a very nonsensical and uncivilised way and are ultimately not grounded in fact or the real world. I think it just goes to show how much we have progressed since those times. They simply did not have the accuracy we possess from modern scientific method, so they had to make up rubbish instead to convey concepts.'

John purses his lips and raises his eyebrows, thinking to himself that it isn't even worth arguing or wasting energy on debate. Arthur and Ishmael seemed to not take much notice at all ...

'And for you Arthur ...' He passes Arthur the Jungian book he was originally reading when they came in.

'Jung has always been an inspiration for our group since university. Your father and I read him the most, and I think you dabbled a bit didn't you, John? Regardless, 'aion' is Greek for *age*. Jung deducted from his research on his patients, and through his own inner psychological analysis, that as a society, we will inevitably come to a crossroads. If we take one path, we will decide to take the inner world of all things soulful seriously; that is things like dreams and religious symbols, things that are of a more intuitive nature, that are hard to pin down with logic alone. Or, we continue to pretend that these things aren't real, and carry on deducting everything by external means; that is, sourcing our understanding from pure logic, mathematics, science and, inevitably, artificial intelligence ...'

'The death of magic ...' Arthur suddenly blurts out, as if he had Tourette's. John and Ishmael turn to look at Arthur with raised eyebrows, and it is clear they are both fascinated with this statement. Jack, however, could not help but find it hilarious how someone could just say something completely nonsensical; it was beyond his understanding. Jack felt embarrassed merely being next to Arthur, and so shakes his head and rolls his eyes.

'I understand these symbols were clearly of some use hundreds of years ago,' he says, 'but clearly that was because they had not yet evolved to understand and explain things using the precision that we possess today. People like my brother think they can find meaning in such things as his visions and his dreams, but this is simply dangerous self-delusion, deriving sanity from what is clearly insanity ... No offence, Arthur; you've said to me yourself that you know you are a freak.'

Arthur stays quiet, feeling rather offended, but not quite knowing how to reply to his brother's articulate argument.

'Ahh, you see, your brother is no freak!' Ishmael says loudly, yet still calmly, keeping a cool composure. 'He may not be normal *per se*, but who wants to be normal anyway?! Your brother is an intuitive type! He lives through his soul, whilst you, Jack, you live through *your mind*. Regardless, it seems clear which path from the crossroads you have both picked ...'

'Yeah, well, he may live in his soul or what not,' said Jack, 'but he's never with us like a normal person. He's always wandering off and staring into space, and gets distracted very easily. You can't tell me that's healthy in our society. I think this alone proves my point that the so called "path" my brother is following is clearly pathological.'

'Arthur is not yet Arthur. *Arthur* is yet to be. Right now, Arthur lives in the abyss, the depths, the underworld ... He swims with mermaids, or should I say, he is *enthralled* with his very own mermaid. This fish, yes, this fish, lies within us all, and not everyone is destined to find their fish. But, young Jack, you may not know of your fish at all! One day, you will find it; and I believe it will be found through the help of your brother. But credit where credit's due,

Jack, you do raise a valid point. We live in bodies, and live within the realm of earth, and you clearly are more grounded in yours than Arthur is in his. Balance of soul and body is, of course, key. Arthur is *completely in love with his fish*; so much so that he forgets to come up and breathe on land. But when he does find his footing, his grounding, *when he finds balance with his fish*, he will truly be a man of great value. But he has much work –much fishing – to do …'

Jack bursts out laughing. Even John could not help but smile at the bizarreness of Ishmael's words.

'I'm not going to even begin to reply to what you just said, because to argue against nonsense using sense is just futile. All it will do is bring me down to your level, and you'll just better me with experience.'

'Oi! None of that!' John shouts. 'Apologize to Ishmael immediately! And say it with meaning, to his face. He's a good friend of mine, and deserves your respect.'

'Sorry, Ishmael, I didn't mean to be too brutal. I just get frustrated when people talk about things that I believe are clearly not proven, nor factual, and I just think it's dangerous for our society. I do truly believe that most of our world's problems come from a knuckleheaded belief in these childish stories and fantasies, and I'm actually very passionate about this. I understand people want to have something to believe in, as it gives them a sense of security, like a comfort blanket; and *I can* respect that to a certain degree, especially for people of lesser intelligence. But soon, the true intelligence of the human race will figure out how to connect us all together under something actually *real,* and not make believe.'

'Ishmael, we need to go. The boys need to see their father. Thank you for their gifts,' John says abruptly, clearly wanting to stop any further arguments between Jack and Ishmael.

Ishmael takes in a deep breath, and looks at Jack very seriously. Jack smirks a little, clearly enjoying this intellectual sparring match.

'Tell me, Jack, what will it be that eventually brings us all together?' Ishmael asks sceptically, and with one raised eyebrow.

'I have some ideas …' Jack says, still with a hint of a smirk on his face.

'Well, be careful with those ideas, my friend. *Because they may not actually be yours …*' Ishmael says this last sentence with a deep and sincere conviction, hinting at a concept that he had thought much about yet didn't wish to fully explain.

Jack frowns, and looks back at him as if he is stupid.

'Goodbye, Ishmael. I'll see you on the mats soon,' John says.

Ishmael nods slowly.

John and Jack begin walking out of the shop. Arthur, however, stays still, staring straight into Ishmael's eyes.

'Arthur, wait here for a second. I have one more thing to give you ...' Ishmael scurries off, and comes back to give Arthur a leather-bound book.

'What's this?' Arthur asks.

'Open it up, have a look.'

Arthur opens the book, and sees inside it is an old photo album. He flicks through the pages and sees many photographs from his parents' time at university.

'I thought the photos could stimulate your father's soul,' Ishmael says, 'revitalise his spirit, and connect him to love. He may not be here in body, but his spirit is still inside him.'

'I'll show him the photos, don't worry,' Arthur replies after a few moments, finally managing to break his fixation on the photos.

'Good. Now go, we will meet again soon I have no doubt.'

Arthur smiles, and walks off to meet the others.

4. VISITING FATHER

After walking a further 15 minutes, with Jack complaining almost the entire way at the fact that they shouldn't have left the car back on the country road, they finally arrive at the care home. Jack and John walk straight inside, yet something forces Arthur to stop and stare up at a tree next to the entrance. He notices an owl with a rather large head, sitting on a branch. Arthur finds this quite disturbing, as of course owls are rarely seen during the day.

'Arthur, come on mate, what's caught your attention now?' John says sternly.

Witnessing Arthur get distracted was nothing new to John, and whilst Arthur's spacey nature was a quirk he loved in him, it did also cause him worry and frustration at times. Yet he was still accepting, and he believed Arthur would grow to become more focused as he got older.

'An owl, look.' Arthur points up.

'How peculiar. Let's go though, Arthur, we really shouldn't waste much more time.'

The trio walk into Phillip's room, and see him sitting in his all too familiar chair at the nursing home. He stares into space blankly whilst a little globule of saliva dribbles down his mouth.

'We have arrived! How are you, Phil?' John says, with forced enthusiasm.

Phillip, with a startled and shaky movement not too dissimilar to someone with Parkinson's disease, turns to see the three familiar faces. Arthur rushes towards his father with energy.

'Dad!' he says contently, as he puts his arms around him.

'Hey, Dad ...' Jack says in a rather monotone voice, slowly approaching to sit on the bed next to the chair.

Phillip makes a sort of groaning noise, and then begins smiling quite childishly. From behind, John steps in as well, and holds Phillips's hand.

'Look, Phillip, your old friend Ishmael gave the boys some books.'

Jack and Arthur show their dad the books. Phillip clasps them with his hands, with a somewhat shaky grip, and continues to stare at the covers.

'And look at this one,' Arthur says cunningly, opening up the photo album to a random page.

The photo that he showed was quite beautiful. It was shot inside a library, with sun shining in from the end of the room, causing patterns of light to appear all over. A young Áine sat calmly at the far end of the room, with her legs crossed, looking up at the light coming in from the window above.

'Are you okay?' Arthur says, as he notices a trance like look in Phillip.

Phillip continues to stare, completely fixated on the photograph. He groans audibly, as if it is the only sound he can make. This strained sound alone is a struggle for him to produce; it was if the groan was a sort of natural expression of his internal strife, with his spirit and energy being squeezed for all they were worth. John quickly takes the photo album away from him, but it is clear something has been triggered inside. Phillip's arms begin to shake violently, his eyes begin to roll back.

It is clear he is having a violent seizure.

John immediately puts Phillip on his side and into the recovery position, where he carries on shaking and groaning violently.

'Why is he making a weird gargling sound?!' Jack asks whilst looking around frantically.

'It's his tongue! He's swallowed his tongue,' John notices.

John has dealt with swallowed tongues before on multiple occasions when dealing with Arthur's seizures. He wastes no time and slams his fingers into Phillip's mouth, yanking out the lodged tongue. Almost as soon as the tongue is removed, the spasming from the seizure calms.

And then, in an instant, Arthur notices a shift in *his* reality and perception. Everything around him begins to slow down, as if the frame of his vision was like a piece of artwork. Colours become brighter, the sun coming in from the window more radiant; and his body is filled with energy and warmth. If it weren't for his father being in this tragic state, he would have been in a state of utter ecstasy. But then Arthur looked around and realised things really were slowed down; not just in his perception, but in reality, in the physical, material sense. He felt little control of his movements at all; in fact, it was almost as if, in this moment, his surroundings were a film being played out to him. He had, of course, experienced similar feelings from his own seizures in the past; but this time he didn't fall unconscious, and instead felt very grounded to the earthly realm.

And then, suddenly, something very disturbing catches his attention out the window. He notices a dark, cloaked figure standing at the far end of the courtyard of the nursing home. Arthur stares straight into this figure's eyes, which glow a burning orange. The figure pulls down his hood, and suddenly two horn-like growths sprout from his skull, extending like a swiftly growing plant. Shivers are sent down Arthur's spine. He realises that these are the very same horns from the bull-headed demon in his vision earlier. The demon stares right back at him with a disturbing smile. A wave of fear spreads through his body. And just as the fear rises before the climax of a nightmare, he is snapped right back into the room.

'Arthur?! Arthur?!' John shouts, as he waves his hand in front of his face.

Arthur looks left and right, and frowns in confusion at what just happened. He sees his brother lean on a wall with his heads in his hands, and sees nurses putting Phillip into bed.

'Could you not hear me? What happened?' John asks.

'I don't know ...' Arthur shakes his head. 'It was like I was having a seizure, but I didn't ... Anyway, it doesn't matter.'

John frowns, and then sighs.

'Okay. Well, we have to leave your father to rest now, so let's just go home.'

The trio walk out of the home feeling more miserable than when they entered. The energy between them even felt a bit awkward.

'Why did Dad start shaking as soon as he saw that photograph?' Arthur asks as they step outside the gates.

'I don't care, to be honest. Everything that happens to us is always awful. I can't even see my own father without something bad happening,' Jack says with tense, raised cheeks, looking almost disgusted.

'Look, I'm sorry you had to go through that, boys,' John says, stopping mid walk, turning to face the brothers. 'As you know, your father is not in a healthy condition, and is on a lot of medication. It makes things like this far more likely to happen. As for the photo, Arthur, it may have triggered a kind of emotional reaction in him, and all that energy had to go somewhere; in this case, it came in the form of a seizure.'

They carry on walking a little further up the road towards the car, but then Arthur realises he needs the toilet. He had been bursting since he got to the home, but had been too preoccupied with seeing his father.

'Guys, really sorry, but I'm bursting to go to the toilet. I'll be two seconds.'

Jack shakes his head in annoyance.

'Just go in a bush,' he says.

'No, its residential; just rush back quickly, we'll wait here,' John says calmly, yet clearly trying hard not to lose his patience.

Arthur rushes back inside the home and goes to the toilet. He quickly relieves himself and approaches the sink to wash his hands. A sudden feeling of fear then arises in him once again; as if a predator or evil spirit is nearby. Arthur rushes out of the toilet as fast as he can. As he runs, he notices all the nurses and staff are frozen in time, just as things were in his father's room before ...

He knows this can mean only one thing; the dark one, Moloch, must be near ... Arthur reaches the exit, but the door is closed. He tries opening it, first by pressing the button, and then using force; but both are to no avail. He looks behind him. And that is when he sees the same bull-headed demon looking right at him. The demon's eyes glow orange, and he wears a long, black robe. In his right hand, he wields a black and shadowy whip, which has a black, spiked ball on the end.

'Hello, boy. Did I not say we would meet again?'

Arthur stares at Moloch in silence, lost for words and frozen in place. As he stares, he has a strong feeling that words would be useless in this situation.

'Your father is very ill.'

'Yes, he is ... Please don't make him suffer anymore. My brother Jack and I will do anything to help him. Could you help us?'

Arthur is surprised at himself for asking this question. He knows intuitively that this demon should not be trusted. Yet an element of weakness within him made him ask for help, a desperate attempt to befriend this beast ...

'Anything? Why do you speak such foolish words? You do not know the extent of *anything*. Why do you think it would be possible to save your father from his abyssal condition, and why do you think you should even do so? Is it not possible to merely accept his suffering?

Arthur stares back terrified, with no answer. Moloch begins laughing to himself, but then his face turns serious again.

'If it is your wish to save your father from his crippled earthly bonds, then I am the only one who can do so. But only at a cost of loyalty. If loyalty is accepted, I will indeed give my milk; for I am Moloch, and I am the milk giver.'

Moloch holds his palm up, and a dark black cube hovers above it. Arthur takes a moment to contemplate this offer, his fear still burning strong inside.

'This cube will give you access to your father's soul.'

'So, using this cube, I'll be able to speak to him one last time?'

'If you take this cube, you will indeed be able to speak to his soul, and his earthly bonds of suffering will be broken. But hear these words carefully, little one. On acceptance of this cube, you agree to loyalty to me. If your loyalty breaks, I will take necessary sacrifice …'

Arthur looks down at the ground, and takes in a deep breath of air. He then looks back up into Moloch's fiery eyes, and holds out his hand. Moloch drops the dark obsidian-looking cube into his hand. The cube does not move as you would expect, like a rock; instead, it flows with a dark, slow tracer pattern behind it, as if it is less affected by gravity.

'This cube belongs to my very own lord. He has tasked me to give it to the ones I feel worthy, to the ones who will help bring *the great inversion*. For the inevitable is to come, and it all starts with this cube. *For it is through the box that the new order shall begin …*'

Moloch gives an unsettlingly stern look, and then vanishes into nothingness in the blink of an eye.

Everything around Arthur reanimates, and he wastes no time hanging around. He sprints back to John and Jack as fast as his legs will carry him.

'So, you didn't need the toilet in the end then?' John asks curiously, looking a little taken back by the speed at which Arthur approached.

'What do you mean? I just went.'

'What?! you managed to go in 30 seconds?' Jack says as he looks at John, both of them beginning to laugh.

'What? I was worried you were going to tell me off, I thought I was gone for at least five minutes …'

Jack shakes his head, but this time smiling and not looking annoyed.

As they continued the walk back to the car, Arthur did not say a word. John and Jack chatted away, occasionally glancing back at Arthur curiously. Arthur just kept his head down, repeatedly tapping his right pocket to check the cube was still there …

5. THE BLACK CUBE

Arthur is in his bedroom, sitting on his bed in deep thought and contemplation. He is surrounded by various plants: bonsai trees, cacti and a couple of snake plants, which rest on wall shelves and along the windowsill. There is a dark oak desk by the entrance to the room, and it is here that Arthur spends many hours reading and journaling. Directly above the desk, there is a whiteboard where he writes his ideas and meditations, his feelings and the contents of his visions. Written chaotically and with large font currently is: 'Moloch??? Upper and lower worlds bridged by black cube?!'

Either side of the desk, there are Himalayan rock salt lamps, which glow bright orange, creating a moody ambience that Arthur finds relaxing. It was quite common for Jack to tease him about this; he would sarcastically call them Arthur's 'demon catchers'. The reason is that when Arthur originally bought them, he claimed they kill evil spirits. (He read this on an online review, and was more than happy to go along with it; in fact, it was this review that really 'sealed the deal' for him.) When Arthur isn't at his desk, he spends a lot of time sitting on a large red bean bag on the floor. He's not quite as focused here as when sitting at the desk, but still more than if he was on the bed; it was as if the bag was a happy medium of both focus and chill. His room is decorated in a way that suggests it is inhabited by someone more mature than a teenager.

Arthur sits on his bed while he holds the dark cube, passing it from one hand to another in a sort of tranced fascination, watching it glide to and fro in slow motion. *What is this cube?* he thinks to himself, frowning. The cube is an intriguing object, no doubt about it. It looks so sublime in many ways: its reflective, smooth rectangular edges are in perfect symmetry with each other. Merely holding the cube give's Arthur great pleasure, of a sort he can't quite comprehend.

Arthur puts down the cube to his left on the bed; and is immediately struck by a compulsion to pick it up once again and feel its weight. He picks up the cube, and once again puts it down. He does this five times before shouting to himself:

'Stop! Think about this, Arthur! You are stuck in a cycle!'

And then goes on to think, *How can this cube be an object of goodness; how can it be? The demonic entity was surely not one from the light, with his sly smiles*

and manipulative cunning, so why should I trust such an object? But even someone pure such as Arthur cannot resist the temptations of the cube. Arthur
notices something peculiar when he holds the cube in his hand: an increase
in brain activity like he's never had before. Thoughts, sensations, stimulations,
knowledge, emotions, fantasies, imagery; all of a distractive and invasive nature, all feeling as if they were not coming from him, but were instead being
forced inside him. It was as if he was put on a rollercoaster of pure consciousness, one of which he had no control. Was this cube a tool to be mastered,
then? And with responsibility, mastery, focus and discipline, could be used
for good? Arthur felt it was a double-edged sword: in the right hands it
may be incredibly useful, but in the wrong hands incredibly dangerous …

It didn't take Arthur long to differentiate between the 'data' of the cube
and the more natural and organic connection he had with his own soul.
When he held the cube, Arthur was certainly not used to the sensations;
he had always been far more familiar with listening to and feeling his own
self. But when holding the cube, it was like he had plugged himself directly
into an alien supercomputer pumping him full of knowledge; knowledge
Arthur hadn't learnt for himself. In a way it felt like cheating; the knowledge lacked solidity as it hadn't been learnt from his own personal experience. It then suddenly occurred to Arthur that if Jack were to get hold of
this cube, with his already-tilted temperament and disposition for acquiring endless amounts of information, the cube may possess him with a sort
of addiction. Arthur therefore decided it best to keep this object far out of
reach of his brother, as he feared the consequences …

Whilst the 'feed' of knowledge from the cube seemed almost random,
Arthur could not deny it certainly felt good to learn more about everything.
Yet he was struck by what his father told him when he was younger: 'Knowledge for the sake of knowledge is a shallow fruit. It is far better to have
less knowledge, but be able to use the knowledge you do have effectively,
in your efforts towards the Good. It is not what you *think* but what you *do*
that matters. Be careful of unearned wisdom.'

'What are you doing?' Jack startles Arthur with his unexpected entry
to his room.

'I'm sitting on my bed. Why are you so curious?'

'You're not just sitting on your bed though, are you? I saw you holding
something, and you were staring at it like a baby to candy.'

'It's a rock I found back at the home. I thought it looked cool.'

'Why are you lying? You never lie. And I can tell you are lying, so something must have happened.'

'Jack, you always mock me for the things I see and experience, and you call me crazy; so if I told you the truth about this rock, you wouldn't believe me anyway.'

'Yes, I mock you, but only because you are very weird sometimes, and I get a bit worried …' Jack pauses, and gives his brother a sincere look. 'I promise to listen to you this time.'

Arthur pauses for a second in confusion, thinking to himself something seems off about this, as Jack would never be this nice and agreeable unless he wanted something.

'Okay, fine. But promise, you'll try and be open minded?'

'I promise.'

'A demon gave this to me.'

Arthur shows Jack the black cube; being careful not to pass it to him by keeping it close to his body. Jack seems mesmerized and is more interested in the cube itself than the fact it was given to Arthur by a 'demon'.

'Give that to me,' Jack demands, sharply turning his gaze towards Arthur with cold, penetrating eyes.

'Why are you so obsessed with this rock?' Arthur says. 'I'm usually the one picking rocks off the ground. You're never interested when we go out for walks.'

'Oh my god, Arthur, why are you lying again? I'm not an idiot. You just said you got it from a demon …'

'I didn't think you believe in demons?'

'Yeah, well, I know that you do; and that you also believe a demon gave it to you. Now, although I don't believe these things myself, it's obvious to me that you believe a demon gave it to you, and whilst that obviously is just a figment of your imagination, it's still real to you, and therefore to state it's just "off the ground" is a lie from your delusional perspective. So, give it to me and stop bullshitting.'

Arthur realises his options are running out here. Jack is the older brother, and whilst he isn't quite as built as him, and not as fit either, he is taller. He knew Jack would eventually just try and take it by force, and Arthur senses his brother is not going to take no for an answer.

'Okay, fine, you can hold it,' Arthur concedes. 'But let me warn you, you are going to experience something you haven't experienced before. Your mind and body will feel things you are not used to, and you will not be in control as long as you hold the cube.'

'Whatever, just give me the cube, Arthur.'

Arthur cautiously passes the cube to Jack. As Jack wraps his hands around it, his pupils immediately dilate; he takes a large gasp of air, and then freezes in a state of shock. His hand is glued to the cube with a vice-like grip, as if the muscles contracted involuntarily. Arthur lets this process continue for a little while longer, but then Jack begins to shake violently. Arthur quickly realises he needs to pull the cube out of Jack's hand. He yanks it away from him. Jack flies backwards and flops onto the floor like he has just been punched by a professional boxer. Arthur approaches his brother lying on the ground and tries to wake him up by gently slapping his face. Jack's eyes open, and then a heavy and sudden onslaught of tears stream down his face. Just as quickly as he fell to the floor, he jumps back up and runs to his room, all still whilst crying.

'Oh no,' Arthur mutters under his breath.

Worried for his brother, he hastily follows Jack to his bedroom.

Jack is lying on his bed, his face buried into the pillow. He is no longer crying, but is immobile and silent. Arthur feels it best to leave Jack for a bit, as he knew the experience was going to be a lot for him to handle. Even if it was true he didn't know exactly what happened to him, he intuitively knew his brother's frame of mind would cause a reaction of some sort.

As Arthur waits for Jack to regain his composure, he finds himself walking around Jack's room with deep curiosity. This was, of course, not the first time Arthur had been in Jack's room, but he had never really observed it properly or given it any deep thought like he usually does with his surroundings. This is likely because on some level Arthur felt someone's room is a very private place, and to analyse too deeply would be on some level an intrusion of privacy. Arthur was certainly aware and confident of his abilities to get a lot of information about someone through his perception of even the subtlest of things. Knowing his brother's character, it was difficult not to smile at the uncanny representation of Jack's personality displayed by his room. Jack had an intense interest in machines, computer networks and all things clockwork. On the shelves were various cogs, gears, sprockets and pieces of computer hardware that for some reason Jack considered the epitome of beauty. Most of the time, Jack could be seen sitting on his glass desk playing hours of chess against other players online. It was true, Jack was an extremely gifted chess player and regularly won local and online competitions with ease. Suzy was always saying that he should pursue it professionally, which Jack would rapidly dismiss by saying something along the lines of: 'Most chess players don't understand that the real chess game is life itself. They are just a bunch of losers who need to broaden their horizons. They need to instead apply what they learn from chess to life.' And Jack wasn't just saying this out of delusional arrogance; he was applying his intelligence and industriousness to creating various software that he was already making money from. His main interest was systems analysis; and he had designed multiple staff intranet networks for many small businesses. However, when either Arthur or his godparents would ask him about his work, he would answer vaguely and give little detail; which did indeed arouse a little suspicion. Jack's room was very orderly and tidy as well; everything was placed in a way that may be considered obsessive compulsive, although it was more likely that Jack was simply a very conscientious person.

'I saw Mum and Dad …' Jack says suddenly, leaning up and resting his back up against the bed board. This surprised Arthur, causing him to jolt his shoulders.

'Really?? Tell me exactly what they said and what you saw.'

'I can't believe this is real. This is the sort of stuff you see all the time, isn't it?'

'I don't fully understand what this cube is or what it does, to be honest, Jack. I just know it's powerful, and is a tool of some sort. You can see now why I didn't want to give it to you, can't you? Now tell me, what did Mum and Dad say?'

'Okay, well, don't get me wrong, Arthur, I still don't believe in any of this, and I'm not taking its "meaning" or what not seriously. Whatever that cube is, it is clearly some sort of technology that simulates dreams. I don't know where the hell you found it, but it's obviously very powerful and not something we should be using. But, I know you are interested, and it was quite intense, so this is what I saw …

'I was in this black room, or maybe it wasn't a room … I don't know … Anyway, it was very black, but still light at the same time; all I could see was Mum and Dad in the distance, and I screamed for them. They came closer to me, and I gave them both a hug and started crying for what felt like five minutes. They both said nothing, but just kept hugging me and stroking my head. I noticed Mum was fine, but she looked concerned … And then she said something that, for whatever reason, made me feel really uneasy, and that was the last thing I remember before coming back into consciousness.'

'What? What did she say??'

'She said: "Only I can speak to you. Your father is only partially here; he cannot speak as his spirit is torn between two worlds. You and Arthur must go and speak to him. *The Father must be rescued.*" It was how she described dad as "The Father" which I found unsettling, and I have no understanding at all why it made me feel like this. She never described him like that, and it almost felt like there was more to that statement. Honestly, I'm not sure how to explain it; she looked at me in a way she never did, a look of such depth and knowing … But yeah, that sort of stuff happens in dreams, doesn't it?'

Arthur looks left and squints his eyes in contemplation.

'That is weird that she said, "The Father"; it's almost like she wasn't even just talking about Dad, but was referring to something … broader? Hmm, okay, well, let's think about this. She said his spirit is partially here, and torn between two worlds, and then goes on to say we should speak to him. Now, if we even for one moment take what she says seriously, even if it's just for fun's sake …' he looks at Jack with raised eyebrows, '… then she is letting us know it is actually possible to speak to his spirit. Now, this is where I have to tell you more about what the demon told me. The demon told me that this cube will give us access to Dad's soul. I know you may think it sounds crazy, but I think we should at least try. Look what it did to you? It clearly has powers of some sort …'

Jack pauses, bites his lip, then sighs.

'Well, it's worth a go, isn't it?' Jack says, reluctantly.

Arthur smiles ecstatically and claps his hands together.

'Yes, Jack! Okay, well, maybe if we combine his body, our bodies and the cube all together, we can bridge the gap …'

'Okay, okay. But we do this alone. John and Suzy aren't to know about this. We break into the home tonight, and you follow my lead. Understood?'

'Is it really a good idea to not tell John? Surely he would understand …'

'Are you joking? I can't even believe I'm having to say this: if we tell John we are going to see Dad with a cube given to you by a demon, he's not going to be overly enthusiastic is he …'

'John's open-minded, you know … But fine, whatever, we sneak in without anyone knowing. I hope you know what you're doing ..'

Jack laughs with a sort of pride. 'There's lots you don't know about me, Arthur. This isn't my first time breaking in somewhere, that's all I'll say …'

Arthur is slightly taken aback, but he can't say he's surprised.

6. THE BREAK IN

Arthur and Jack decide to mount their 'infiltration' (as Jack so enthusiastically described it) at 3am. Jack saw on a History Channel programme that the most effective time to launch a 'raid' was early in the morning; although Arthur was keen to show his scepticism that the same logic may not apply to a nursing home …

The boys approach on their bicycles, then dump them in a bush at the side of the home's car park.

'Okay, now we are here, how do we get in?' Arthur says as he scours the building.

'There's only one way to get in places like this … The roof.'

'You've got to be joking, who do you think we are? Assassins?'

'Arthur, as your older brother, you've got to trust me. A crazy person like you will secretly enjoy this, I promise.'

Arthur smiles sheepishly. He is morally conflicted: he's very excited by this whole 'mission', but also knows what they are doing is technically illegal and they shouldn't be doing it.

Jack leads Arthur around to the back of the home where there is an area for rubbish disposal, with two large bins in an enclosed space.

'We can use these bins to get to the roof,' Jack says. 'Aha, what did I say? How cool is this?!' He says as he climbs up on the bin, giving a large grin.

Jack gives Arthur a hand up on to the bin, and they both move up on top of the first floor.

'It is cool yes, I can't lie,' Arthur admits after looking around for a few moments. 'But we are here for a reason, so let's not get distracted. We should try and get down there to the courtyard. We can go to his outside door, can't we?'

'Are you seriously the one to tell *me* to not get distracted?' Jack teases, giving a frown.

'I can actually focus when I want to, you know. Normality just bores me. Anyway, come on, let's just find an opening.'

Jack shakes his head and rolls his eyes, and then they spread out to try and find an opening of some sort to the courtyard. For a nursing home, the security is surprisingly good, and large fencing surrounds the top of the roof preventing easy access inside to the courtyard. Arthur then stumbles across a partially opened skylight looking down into a corridor.

'Reckon we can get in here?' Arthur says with a concerned expression.

'Oh, yeah, for sure we can; just give me one second.'

Jack walks off around the edge of the roof, as if looking for something. Arthur squints suspiciously, then his mouth gapes open as he becomes increasingly concerned.

'Aha, look what ya boy has got.'

Jack shows Arthur a large brick.

'What on earth are you planning to do with that …?'

And before Arthur can say or do anything else, Jack throws the brick into the skylight, smashing it violently, and glass shatters onto the carpet of the corridor below.

'Decoy. Come on, let's go.'

'And you call me the crazy one?! I thought we were going to be quiet and stealthy?'

'No time to waste now! Come on, let's jump down!'

Arthur cannot believe what his brother has just done. Before he can fully process what just happened, Jack jumps down and lands perfectly into the corridor.

'Come on, quick!' Jack 'shouts' in a whisper from below.

Arthur realises he has no option now but to jump. As he lands, his knees buckle and his face hits the glass on the ground, causing a large cut on his cheek; blood immediately starting to run down it.

Before the boys can even do or think about their next move, they turn around to see a tall, slender, white-haired old woman staring right at them. She is holding a Zimmer frame, and by the way she is looking at them, it is quite evident that she is lacking cognitive abilities; she does not, however, look at all concerned at the sight of the bloodied glass and bleeding teenager on the floor in front of her. The boys and the woman stare in silence for what feels like an age to the brothers. The woman then looks to her left towards an open door.

'My room!' the woman says in a playful tone, like a young child seeing a puppy. Both the boys quickly rush inside her room and enter the en-suite bathroom immediately. As the boys wait, they hear multiple rushing footsteps in the corridor.

'I can't believe the staff have only just come now, that window smashing sounded like a jet engine taking off,' Arthur says under his breath.

'Shh, listen to what they are saying,' Jack replies.

The boys strain to hear to what is being said out in the corridor through the walls of the bathroom.

'Martha, what on earth has happened, are you okay?! Is this your blood?' a large male nurse worriedly asks.

'Brick.'

Martha, the old woman, points at the brick on the floor.

'Martha, did you see who did this? Did you see someone come through this window?'

'It was Bertie. Bertie threw a brick at the window, he's a dreadful man.'

And then suddenly, a naked man comes walking out of the room opposite Martha's. His face is bright red, and it is clear he is angry and confused. It is also clear from how he reacts to being accused by Martha that they have a history of tension.

'You fucking bitch whore, I did no such thing!'

'Bertie, come on, let's get you back to your room, we need to let the others try and get back to sleep.'

'You silly man,' Martha adds.

'You too, Martha, let's get you back into bed.'

The staff convene and decide it is best to call the police. The larger nurse escorts Martha back to her room and attempts to put her to bed, all while the boys still listen intently in the bathroom next door, trying their best not to make a sound.

'Do you need to go to the toilet, Martha?'

'No, I don't. I want to sleep.'

'Okay, remember to push the red button on the side if you need us. Sleep well.'

The large nurse leaves, and the boys breathe a sigh of relief. Before they can even think about their next move, Martha opens the door to the bathroom and looks at the boys with a penetrating stare, as if she knows why they are here; not with a stare of clarity and rationality, however, but more of a trance-like, intuitive understanding. She then makes a 'come here' motion with her finger. The boys walk towards her, and she points at the sliding glass doors that lead to the courtyard.

'Your father,' the old lady says suddenly and mysteriously, all whilst holding her two hands over her heart.

She then bows deeply to the boys, smiles and tucks herself into bed to sleep, as if she had done her duty and could now rest.

'How on earth?' Jack says in shock.

'Sometimes, some things happen that do not make sense to us. There is a mystery to many things Jack, and it is this very mystery, this magic, that gives meaning to all things. Come on, let's go to Dad.'

Jack was about to reply, but before he could, Arthur is leading the way to the glass door that connects to the courtyard. They exit the old lady's room, and tiptoe across the courtyard to their father's door, swivelling their heads to check no-one is watching.

'It's locked,' Arthur says desperately, after trying to open the door.

Jack smiles, expecting this situation and, in fact, looking forward to it.

'Ah, well, thankfully I've come prepared ...'

Jack shows Arthur a sophisticated-looking lock pick.

'There really is much I don't know about you, isn't there?' Arthur says with a worried expression.

'Well, you have your mysteries, and I have mine ...' Jack says with a devilish smirk.

He continues to pick the lock. Within 10 seconds, the lock clicks and Jack slides the door open. He faces Arthur and takes a bow like a magician would after performing a trick, all whilst looking incredibly pleased with himself. Arthur can't help but smile. If he was to be completely honest with himself, he was indeed impressed. The boys head inside the room quietly, sliding the door closed behind them, slipping in between the crack in the curtains.

Phillip is sitting in his chair, asleep.

'I can't believe our own father continues to live like this. How is this fair, Arthur? You say you believe in a higher power, but how could a loving higher power let a man as lovely as our own dad suffer like this?'

'I don't know. But I am also not God, and do not understand his ways. What I do know is that everything is connected to something larger, something mysterious, something magical. I understand that I do not understand, yet I am humbled by this mysterious magic nonetheless. Let us not judge our dad's situation, as I have a feeling we are about to learn something when we go inside to meet him in the realm his soul lingers.'

The boys decide to waste little time. Arthur brings out the black cube from his pocket and puts it inside the hand of their father. The brothers then proceed to wrap both their own hands around their dad's, joining and connecting their energies under the cube's power.

7. AND IN THEY WENT

The room starts to melt, and everything becomes vivid in a way that neither of the boys had experienced, not even Arthur with his intense fantasies. Everything is vibrating in a way that things perhaps always do, but only now is it being perceived ever so clearly. The room feels alive: light refracts through the air as if being shone through liquid, and the outline of everything has a saturated tinge to it, as if it were in some way simulated by something greater. The boys' and Phillip's hands are now completely glued to the cube, and their bodies along with their hands are frozen like stone. It seems as if this frame of reality has been slowed down to such a degree that they have stepped outside of the space-time continuum altogether. And, sure enough, things did now begin to change. Everything in the nursing home room was becoming unrecognizable, morphing into brightly-coloured, cartoon-like dough. The boys felt inside them an injection of pure energy, shooting from the base of their spine right up into the centre of their brains. It felt like they were strapped to a rocket ship taking off; and all they could do at this point was hang on. They have no other choice but to accept what is happening to them. But then, things begin to calm. The vibrations begin to slow and materials return to their normal nature.

If they did indeed travel through a sort of hyperspace, they now reach what could be called a destination. And it is an incredibly beautiful sight. They are surrounded by lush green hills rolling into the distance. It's pleasantly warm with a gentle breeze. A small, white stone bridge glistens in the distance, and rises over a large lake that leads right up to where they stand. There are peculiar-looking trees which stand very tall and thin; not of the sort we see in our earthly realm, but still very organic and natural-looking. These trees have a weird feature of swaying elegantly in the gentle wind (presumably because of their lightness). The boys look around at all this in awe. The entire landscape is very earthly in many ways, but still has an element of dreaminess to it.

'Arthur ... Where are we?' Jack asks nervously with a stutter in his voice as he looks around.

Jack is a man of the earth; a conscientious, grounded fellow. Frankly, right now, he is out of his element. Arthur, on the other hand, is relaxed and loving every moment of this alternate reality. He feels very much (even to his own surprise) at home in this plane. Arthur looks around excitably, his arms out to his side like an aeroplane. He's in a playful mood. He takes in a large breath of air like it is some sort of sweet, delicious nectar.

'The air is so sweet, isn't it?! Breathe it in, Jack!'

Jack closes his eyes in an attempt to relax, and takes a deep breath in. He finally lets out a playful laugh.

'Ha! Oh yeah, it is!'

Whilst Arthur watches his brother laugh and smile, he is filled with a kind of joy that makes him tear up a little. He is not used to seeing his brother act in this child-like and playful way. It must be said that Arthur does worry about Jack sometimes, and has observed elements of resentment within his brother's spirit. Arthur can, of course, understand why given what happened in their early childhood, but what worries him is how he sees Jack uses this resentment as fuel for his life. But now, and for the first time since Arthur can remember, his brother looked genuinely happy; the previous nervousness upon entry to this realm had now turned into genuine euphoria.

'What is that thing walking towards us?' Jack says whilst pointing towards a peculiar-looking creature in the distance.

Arthur squints and tries to make out the coming beast. The creature stands around seven-foot tall and has fur like a lion, along with a golden mane to suit. The shape and stature are more like man, however. Neither of the boys feel worried by this creature's presence, and the movements seem very calm and joyous. In fact, the boys feel a compulsion to run towards it. As the beast comes closer, the boys notice a warm smile on its face.

'Do you think that's …?' Arthur says with an almost overbearing excitement, his pupils dilating as his eyes light up.

'Welcome to my soul, boys,' a familiar voice says.

The boys rush as fast as they can towards what they now know must be their dad, tears instantly streaming down their faces. As they cry into the luscious fur of their 'soul father', Lion Phillip himself starts to cry as he embraces them tightly with his paws.

'I cannot tell you how happy I am to finally see you both,' Phillip says. 'Yet, never did I have doubts that I would. I have been waiting for such a long time, you see; but now, I can rest at last.'

'I can't believe we made it here to see you,' Arthur says through his tears. 'It's beyond magical …'

'It is *beyond magic,* yes. Yet still, this place is only transitionary. My soul will stay here until my earthly body dies.'

'Where will it go after you die, then?' Arthur asks, looking worried.

'That is not for me to decide, but my form here is light and content; and this alone fills me with calmness, and for that I am not worried. But boys, my boys. I have much to tell and show you. Now it is time I complete my duty before I pass, and I must tell you, *I will pass* when I complete this duty …'

Both the boys feel a sudden sadness, but also an acceptance; as they know that their dad is doing whatever he is doing for the best. They never really believed they would meet their own father again, and to do so now has filled them with a deep bliss that will never leave them. Both the boys then give their father another hug.

'Will we ever see you again after you pass away, Dad?' Jack asks sadly whilst looking down at his feet.

'Ahh, well you see, Jack, to answer that question is not so simple. I could simply say yes, but that would not be a complete answer. All I will say is this. The life we live on earth is not the end; what comes next is something words can never do justice. I can say them, but all they will do is alter and deform the reality of the truth. The truth is to be felt, and one day, in this life or the next, you will feel the truth.' Lion Phillip, in front of the boys, gets down onto the grass by the lake and sits cross legged. The boys follow suit, and stare intently at their spirit father.

8. THE VISION

'**My** sons, I must pass a vision on to you. For it is this vision that I have been waiting to tell since I lost unison of my soul and body. For now, my soul in its totality remains trapped in limbo; and that is the realm you see me in as of now. But when I tell you what you need to hear, my duty will be completed, and I will cut the connection from my body on earth.

'Firstly, I will start by saying that I know of the dark one you spoke with Arthur, and I know of the cube which gave you access to my soul. This cube has done its job now, as you have gained access to me; so now you both must take responsibility of it, until its next purpose makes itself clear. But, my sons, do not allow its tendrils to coerce you into the making of dark fruits; for it is dark fruits that seem beautiful on the surface, only to sprout poison after they have been digested.

'I will begin by saying this: there are forces at play that lurk in the undergrowth of our civilisation, and whilst these forces helped give you access to me, do not fall prey to their games. What I have done was at great risk, but necessary to convey my vision. Yet still, the dark ones tease and entice you with low-hanging pleasures and fruits; they make you grip their fruit so tightly that you forget what it was like to be free of this grip. My children, I tell you, a good grip is important, but what is more important is to be able to flow between gripping and not gripping, like a phoenix constantly dying and being reborn. If there was to be an ultimate value, it would be to grip onto *the very process of gripping and letting go.* For any grip held too long becomes closed to anything new and fresh, as the new is needed for our progression and redemption. Yet to have no grip leaves you lost in the ocean with nothing to guide you. And here is where our problem lies: what *do we* hold on to? How do we ground ourselves in helpful truths? We must believe in something to grow, otherwise we are like a ship in the ocean with no compass, and no direction. And in this empty ocean, in our desperation, we are at the mercy of the dark forces that lurk below the surface, constantly trying to seize our attention by shouting: "Believe in me! For I will set you free, and I will show you the way!" For that is the nature of all so-called 'truths'. The truth will set you free, they say, but what is the truth that is true, and not just a *relative perspective?* Oh, they will shout that their truth is the truth, and others will come along and shout in support. But how do we really know what to act out in life, what to believe in? And how do we really know what is north and what is south, what is up and what is down? Where is our compass now, my sons? Where is it? For even the smartest of us modern folk can speculate on what to do, what is best, what to value; but no single modern man can compete with the wisdom of our ancestors, for it was the continual struggle of our fathers and mothers, and the games of love and war, dance and adventure, over the generations, that gave birth to the wisdom of the ages. And it is true that this wisdom remains ingrained in our souls as a spirit, and some may call this *the Holy Spirit*. This spirit remains inside for those who have eyes and ears to see and listen, and modern folk may now even call this spirit *common sense*. But what of those who do not have access to this spirit, or refuse to listen, or lack the ability to hear and to see it? How long will it be before the spirit inside evaporates, like alcohol leaking from a bottle? For we must not just have spirit, but a body to keep it safe, like a mother to her child. For now, the time has come where the teachings and wisdom gathered over the generations, from all the world's kingdoms, must come together and form a *world tree*. And even the tree, with its solid foundations, is never complete; like the phoenix rising and falling, it must grip and un-grip. Just as with us all, it is in a constant process of growth, of death and rebirth. It is known to some as the philosopher's stone, and to Christians as Christ. Yet still, it is through this image of phoenix, of Christ, of grip and un-grip, that our tree can continue to grow upwards towards the light; and it is only through this process that the tree will not become bitter, will not become tainted, will not become corrupted by anything other than *truth itself.*

'It is the dark one who tempts us to hold onto something so tightly, and it is he who prevents us from redeeming ourselves and letting go. It is the dark one who prevents us from shedding our dead branches, yet it is also him who prevents us from gripping anything at all. For it is he who lacks graceful flow, and it is he whose lack of grace destroys things completely and utterly, preventing any chance of *salvation.*

'But now I must share a vision from him. For if we do not furnish my Tree of Life, we will be corrupted and boxed in by the dark one's unholy lack of grace. We must look around us now, and see what grips people's spirits. For when we look around, we see people's spirits gripped by false ideas;

ideas that seem sweet and tempting on the surface, yet have bitter and false cores. These ideas spread through technology; networks upon networks of endless information and data, stimulations of all kinds, low-hanging fruits that capture our most precious life force. For we are being forced against our will into many trances that prevent us from being *whole,* trances that make it easier to feed us lies. Through this kind of hypnotism, we can so easily be tricked into selling our soul to the shadows, leaving part of us behind, pretending to ourselves that it should be cut off. But here is the problem: it is only the whole man and woman who are free to make their own decisions, and it is only they who acquire *free choice.* The man who leaves his soul behind will be at the mercy of the one he gave it to. So, therefore, it is the duty of man and woman to set themselves free, and to become *individuals.* For the dark one fears nothing more than for us to become *who we are.* How long will it be until these forces trap us completely in a never-ending trance, a never-ending loop, a dark *black box* of infinite horrors and suffering? A womb where they feed us through virtual and technological umbilical cords, as if we are unborn life; cords we will have no choice but to accept because we have been forced to know no different, as the decision to cut off our roots has already at this point been taken. *An unborn knows nothing outside the womb, so why would a society trapped in one know any different?*

'I say this: Do not let the forces masquerading as God on earth dictate and capture your souls; for they cannot know how you should channel and order yourselves. For that is only the job of *you,* the master and captain of your soul, to gather your inner entities together, within your own pantheon, and listen to what they say *as one.* But what can we do now my sons? If it is only the individual and their conscience that should be captain, then how do we guide them towards this spirit without ourselves being evil tyrannical kings who "know best"? Well, we give them a compass and a map, and then it is up to the individual to choose and become *who they really are.* We give them guidance on how to arrange the inside life forms, within their soul, and how to help the inside 'life' become friends and lovers, like Greek gods in a pantheon, working together in harmony. Now they have at least some grounding and understanding of how to operate within, how to be a *good captain.* And they will feel the benefit, because of the love radiating from within, which is a natural consequence of inner *wholeness.* But I must stress that guidance is needed for our new generation! But it is simply that: *guid-*

ance. For it is the dark one who says, "All must go to this island!" But what if I do not want to go to that island? And what if that island does not please the gods inside my soul? It is the uniqueness of every individual that *redeems* civilisation.

'So what if dark forces appear and tell us all: "Go to this island only. It is for the best, we promise. You must go to this island. Trust us, as we are so smart, we are experts, we are your masters. *Obey!*" And what of the ones who refuse? The disobedient souls who don't share their masters' taste and seek fulfilment from different islands, what then? The masters punish them, brutally. They enjoy punishing the disobedient souls; they see their actions as good and justified, as it is, in their eyes, for 'the greater good'. So, of course, they enjoy it, this sweet justice in their hearts. And why not? For they may say: "For the ones we rule are clearly selfish; because we, their masters, are trying to help them with our generous feeding of fruits. *Just submit to us, and all will be okay ...*"

'So, you see, my sons, the arrogance of those who play God. It is only when we submit to the greater transcendental forces, the spiritual forces, that we become humble on earth. For when we realise that we, man, cannot control everything but must be humble and meek to the wills of the *greater forces*, then we begin to live more in harmony with them; and, ironically, live with more strength. But what of these *greater forces*? Where is our connection to them? Where is our representation of these sacred patterns and symbols? Is our great father dead? *Is God dead?* No. God lives. Yet is forgotten. His spirit is there to be rescued, but for that a great task must be underway ...

'For it is now that I pass the duty I received from the angels, and this is my baton to you. You must rescue the wisdoms of old; you must rescue these symbols, these things that show us *who we really are,* these things that help us learn the true nature of our soul, and therefore reality. Do not let future man lose connection to the sacred! These are the things that keep us connected to what is *meaningful.* For we, as a species, must realise that within every man and woman, there is indeed something special, something sacred, something that cannot be defined by mathematics or science. Inside lies something *sovereign*; and the human soul must be celebrated, otherwise we are sure to fall prey to the machines. If we do not celebrate the existence of the soul, it is sure to evaporate like a spirit from a bottle. We must never allow our soul to be eaten completely. We must fight for the survival of the human spirit, for the time has come to introduce the sacred back into our new Tree of Life.

'I have planted the seed already for you, my boys, but the tree is young and fragile; it needs much furnishing and love for it to grow high towards the light. But let me tell you this: I am happy and optimistic, and whilst I have visions of dark futures, the ones I have of a brighter future are stronger. For I have a vision for this Tree of Life. I see souls from all over the world dancing in harmony, all connected by a general world tree, a Tree of Life; and with this *general* connection, there will be a *general love* of all dimensions. Yes, there will still be pain; but it will be one that is understood and accepted. Now, with the connection of the tree, all can at long last feel a love of being connected by something, whilst still maintaining all our beautiful individual differences.'

The boys approach their spirit father, and hug him for as long as they can. They begin to feel the fur slowly dissolve into nothingness. And before the boys can even process what has happened, they find themselves back down to earth in the nursing home. As the boys continue to stare at their father's shell of a body, he takes his final breath of air on earth and collapses into the chair, passing away.

PART TWO: ROOTS

1. MAT TIME

It is 1995. Phillip Stanley is lying in his Oxford university halls, asleep. His room is what you might expect of a student: a desk, books, some clutter and mess, a couple of empty beer bottles; certainly nothing terrible compared with other students. Next to Phillip's bed is a pre-packed drawstring bag ready for his Brazilian jiujitsu training. Inside is his uniform, or Gi (and of course his blue belt), along with other essentials such as his mouthguard, tape, flip flops and a prefilled water bottle. Phillip, at the time of university, was known for sleeping a lot; in fact, his closest friends gave him the nickname of 'The Sloth'. Phillip was not ashamed; he loved sleep, but what he loved even more was the *dreams* that came along with it. Next to his bed, he always kept a diary at hand to record his dreams, which was always the very first thing he did when he woke up.

Phillip was self-aware enough to know that he also had a habit of oversleeping, so he spent extra care before bedtime preparing his clothes, bags, etc. to speed up the morning process and make it as painless as possible. It didn't help that he had a tendency to go to bed late. Phillip loved reading books, and approximately 50 were piled on top of each other on his desk. The night before, he was up until 4am reading *The Brothers Karamazov* by Dostoyevsky. Phillip had been extremely captivated by this book in ways he couldn't quite explain. He had a habit of constantly recommending it to all his other friends, telling them 'how loveable Alyosha is'. Yet at this point he hadn't even finished the whole book yet.

And then comes a loud knocking on his dorm door.

'Phillip, come on, its 9.30; we've got to get to the gym.'

Phillip stirs in his bed, realising he must have set his alarm to a later time. Usually training is at noon, but on Saturdays it is earlier at 10am.

'Oh shit,' he groans. 'Okay, sorry John, I'll be two seconds …'

Despite being in a rush, Phillip still grabs his dream diary and quickly, in shorthand, scribbles down some key notes that he would expand on later: demon, violet, cross, lion, bull, mud. He then grabs his jogging bottoms, T-shirt and jumper, which he's laid out ready, and throws his drawstring bag on his back. This was not the first time John had to wake up Phillip to go training; it was a recurring joke between them, in fact; but it was also true that John was getting a little annoyed by it. John was naturally, it seemed, more conscientious than Phillip; more organised, with better time management. John's room was generally tidier too, although Phillip's room was not messy by student standards. Still, both John and Phillip were good friends because of their many similarities: notably, both were smart, open-minded, had an ability to think abstractedly and could admit when they were wrong without holding on too tightly to their egos. Phillip may have lacked John's conscientiousness, but he made up for it with more openness and curiosity. He was also very empathetic and compassionate. John took a cold, hard, pragmatic approach to philosophy (which he was studying); a stoic, some may say, albeit with a spiritual element and an open-mindedness to the concept of God. Phillip was more dreamy, more of a feeler than a thinker. These were their dominant characteristics, although both were well-rounded in their thoughts and feelings. This balancing of temperaments worked strangely well and made them almost inseparable.

Occasionally, John's girlfriend, Suzy, would make joke about how the young men were secret gay lovers, asking John if she should be worried at all; to which he would always reply sarcastically: 'I love it.'

The two hurriedly walk towards the academy, not really saying much to each other as they are focused on getting there as soon as possible. Saturday's class was an open-mat session, rather than the more typical teaching of technique, so they were not *too* worried about being late. Open mat meant anything goes, whether that be drilling a certain technique, sparring, chatting or just watching. They were social, chilled out sessions. Most of the time people just got in as many rounds of sparring as possible. The natural high you get after doing multiple rounds of 'rolls' sets you up brilliantly for the rest of the day. This is why the pair had no time to waste! They arrive through the doors at almost exactly noon and are casually greeted by a few of their teammates; however, both know how easy it is for them to get distracted by conversation, so they decide it's best to head straight to the mat.

'Flow roll to warm up?' John asks, quickly rotating his head around to warm up his neck. It is clear he wants to get straight to the sparring.

Phillip nods. They slap and bump their hands, then begin; manoeuvring around each other, looking for opportunities and entries, expending little energy at this point. At the open mat there is always music playing, with the owner and head instructor of the academy, Dean Simons, recently investing in a powerful, high-end sound system. Many at the gym wondered why he had invested so much in multiple subwoofers and speakers dotted around the gym as if it were a nightclub. The music generally playing was bass-heavy and repetitive deep house and techno. Some loved it; others found it annoying, however. Dean insisted that the repetitive beats and rhythms help focus and contribute to inducing a flow state. It was not uncommon to see Dean running to and from the mats and his state-of-the-art CDJ-500 decks. He personally took control of the decks on Saturday open mats; but every other day, he would pick a volunteer to sit out of the class and hop on the decks instead to do so-called 'deck-jitsu'. Dean felt he could control the intensity of the sparring sessions by the music that was played. He would regularly say: 'I'm a BJJ-DJ'; this became a running joke within the academy, and he was commonly referred to by his students as 'DJ Dean'. Phillip and John loved this type of music, and regularly spent long periods of time after class talking to Dean about dance music and events and raves that were going on around the country.

Phillip swiftly catches John's back with a seatbelt control (under one arm and around the neck) and, after a grip-fighting struggle, submits John with a rear naked choke.

'You're getting so good at taking my back, it's actually annoying …' John says whilst crossing his legs, tilting his head and panting heavily.

'Well, you know what they say, you wouldn't turn your back on life, so why would you turn it on me?' Phillip says cheekily.

'It's not like I gave it to you willingly; sometimes life just stabs you in the back without warning.'

'That's why you need eyes in the back of your head.'

Phillip tilts his head on its side and gives a bizarre expression with his tongue sticking out.

'Ha, well, if only life was that simple …'

'Well, you are right, life certainly isn't simple; but, as we have discussed, it definitely has a divine structure, I'm convinced of this. I just find it so funny how the wisdoms of the jiujitsu mat run parallel to the world of the outside too.'

'Yes, well you try and tell Suzy that.'

'What do you mean?'

'I don't know what's happened, but since starting university she has changed quite a bit; don't get me wrong, she's still Suzy, it's just we tend to argue more over the pettiest of things, and I feel there's a weird tension between us.'

'Oh really? When you're debating politics, or not even that?'

'It's not obvious that it's a political thing. It seems more psychological, like there's an integral part of me that she is for some reason now having issues with. I just try and be myself, and I always have done. I don't want to pretend I'm being someone I'm not, but it seems that she doesn't like parts of who I am. She never used to feel this way; something has definitely changed recently ...'

'Okay, well, what sort of things does she not approve of?'

'It's not really *things,* it's more my actions, my spirit. Okay, so for instance, the other day I was cooking, and she came up to me and said, "Why are you moving with such rigidity?" I was genuinely confused when she said this, and thought she was joking, but she really did seem annoyed at my movements. As far as I am aware, my body's movements have not changed that dramatically since I met her two years back, so why on earth is she now expressing her annoyance with them?'

Phillip can't help but laugh at the thought of John being mocked by his girlfriend for how he moves while cooking. It was so silly in many ways, but the funny thing is that Phillip knew what she meant. This rigid, almost mechanical movement was noticeable in John's jiujitsu style too; it was very ordered, almost robotic, and generally was more orthodox and predictable than Phillip's style.

'Okay, John, I don't need to tell you that I am by no means an authority when it comes to relationships. However, I have noticed from my own observations that tension between men and women in relations of any kind are always prevalent, and in fact to be expected, even cherished. The reason I say this is that if there was no tension, then where is the progression? There is always a degree of awkwardness and pain when two forces meet, even with inner forces. Take jiujitsu, for example: when Dean teaches us a new technique, it causes tension within us because it's new, unknown; 'cognitive dissonance', if you like. We can either run away from the challenge and complain how it's too much to deal with; or, we can really try and dig in to the problem and engage in the conflict. Before we know it, the battle inside our minds has already begun, and when we re-engage battle next time, maybe after a good night's sleep even, it's like our unconscious has already recruited troops and begun to push forward.'

'Is this going anywhere?' John interrupts with a smile, as if to say, 'Yeah, I like what you're saying but get practical.'

'Okay, look, you and Suzy are two polarising energies: she provides a more feminine energy; you, a masculine one. At first, you simply feel the attraction because of unconscious factors; it heightens your emotions, grips you in its tendrils and sucks you in like a mad rollercoaster of love. At this point, you aren't getting annoyed at each other's differences because all you feel is bliss. You are enjoying the opposite energy without any ego or meddling; you both feel complete, a coming together in harmonious unity.'

'Coming together …? That's quite funny.'

'Easy tiger, but yes, that is synchronistic and beautiful in many ways, I will admit … Anyway, let me carry on my analysis. Now, as I have stated, this is the first stage, the 'honeymoon stage', as society likes to put it. Over time, however, the differences between you both become more obvious. As we are all human, there's a lot of stuff about us that frankly isn't good or desirable. And the significant other is there to point out your flaws so as you can be a more complete individual.'

'Are you saying my rigid movements aren't desirable and Suzy is there to "correct them?"'

'Ha, no, I'm not quite saying this. I love your rigid movements. But let us be honest here: rigid, solid, structured movements are clearly masculine to anyone with a degree of common sense; people are always looking at how someone moves when judging them, whether they admit it or not. Look at our boy Charlie Cartfield, one of the most openly gay guys you will ever meet, and everyone loves him for it. It is, however, clear he's gay by the way he moves. His movements contain a higher degree of flow and lightness, almost as if the feminine energy is finding form through his movements. Not to say this is always the case: femininity can be expressed in many ways. It may be the case that in Suzy's natural efforts to connect you to your feminine side —that in a relationship is her unconscious duty, as yours to her masculine side — she expresses her annoyance at your obviously mechanical and masculine movements in an instinctive way. She likely didn't take much time to really think consciously about it, but said it more out of natural jest, or better still unconsciously projected, albeit with an undertone of a heightened annoyance, which I can only assume means there is something deeper going on which she hasn't fully expressed yet …'

'Such as?'

'No idea.'

'Oh well, that's helpful.'

'Who do you think I am? Inspector Morse?! Okay, well, if we want to find out what's really on her mind, maybe it's a good idea we all meet up for drinks and have a chat. There's probably something going on that she hasn't felt like bringing up yet.'

The two had been so involved in this conversation that they did not realise how much time had passed. This was a regular occurrence at open mats: both would go in expecting a solid hour of sparring, but instead do a round or so and end up talking for much of the remaining time. They both found it so much easier to talk after sparring, as if it made their brain more efficient but also loosened up any ego or primal restraints or underlying tension between them. It was as if an energy exchange had taken place; similar to a man and woman talking after sex for the first time, which comes far easier and with less doubt and fear of judgement.

Dean sees the boys chatting away and jokingly shouts across the mat:

'Are you bellends gonna do any jiujitsu today, or just talk bullshit the whole time?'

Both Phillip and John have a great relationship with Dean, who has a significant soft spot for both the lads. They had a natural talent for jiujitsu, and when they weren't talking psychology or philosophy, or any other such subject, they were highly dedicated and both were improving rapidly. Whilst they were both clearly talented, this growth came down to their work ethic and discipline. It also helped that they were such good friends on a similar wavelength. They were very good at communicating ideas and concepts related to jiujitsu. They both acted as catalysts for each other's growth, on and off the mats.

John and Phillip manage to put the brakes on the talking, and get a few more rounds of sparring in. Dean approaches them at the end of the session.

'Bloody hell, lads, I haven't seen talking like that since my old man mistakenly drunk a whole bottle of cough syrup.'

'Ha, yeah, you know us too well. John's got relationship issues so I was trying to give him some deep Phil Stanley insight.'

'Fucking hell, John, I wouldn't be taking relationship advice from that virgin if I was you,' Dean says, with a wink at Phil.

John and Dean burst out laughing.

'I would tell you to shut up, but you'll break my arm. I'll have you know that they use to call me "Big Deal Phil" back at school parties.'

'More like "Phillatio",' Dean says whilst continuing to laugh at his own joke, with John quickly following suit.

'For fuck's sake ...' Phillip says whilst looking down, shaking his head, accepting the roasting from his instructor in good spirit.

'Jokes aside, lads,' Dean continues, 'there's a really cool event near here I wanted to tell you both about. Deep house and techno, I think, kind of underground psychedelic stuff though. It's in Bagley Wood near here. I think it's a bit of an arty kind of setup, though, a hippy and spiritual element to it. Not sure exactly what, though.'

'Oh yeah, when is that?' Phillip asks with excitement and intrigue.

'Next Saturday throughout the day, so I guess if you go, we won't have to suffer your verbal diarrhoea here on the mats.' John and Dean start sniggering again.

2. A DRINK

John and Suzy are together in John's university halls room getting ready. In typical fashion, Suzy is straightening her hair with a mild but very real sense of urgency (it was already 7.45 pm and they said they would meet Phillip in the student union at 8pm) and John is bobbing around in his boxers, dancing to the deep house music coming through his hi-fi system on his desk. The room's layout is the same as Phillip's (as they are in the same building) but, as mentioned before, John always kept a very ordered and clean room. The books were stacked neatly, and no loose containers or rubbish were anywhere to be seen on the floor or on the surfaces. If John did have a vice of any sort, it would be snacking; he loved eating for the sake of it, and if it were not for his intense and regular training, he would surely be overweight. For this reason, he has a small fridge kept under his desk containing a secret stash of chocolate and other sugary treats. Whenever John brought up to Phillip his excessive sleeping habits, and called him a 'sloth', Phillip would immediately fire back and call John a 'fat bastard'. John continues to bob to the beats, and then grabs some chocolate from the small fridge.

'Can you please hurry up, and why the hell are you eating chocolate now?' says an annoyed Suzy, looking him up and down in frustration.

'Why does it concern you so much? I'm just having a good time minding my own business, eating my chocolate, dancing to my beats. We both know it will literally take me two seconds to put some jeans and a T-shirt on, but with you it will take another 20 minutes.'

'I'm literally ready, John.'

'Well, you're literally not are you; you're still straightening your hair …'

'Can you stop talking to me like that, John, otherwise I'm going to burn my hair and it's going to be your fault.'

'Talking to you like what?'

'Just being a dick in general.'

'Don't lie, we both know you like it when I'm a bit of a dick.' John then proceeds to go up behind Suzy, who is still straightening her hair, gets her under a seatbelt control, then nibbles her neck in a playful, sexual way.

Suzy and John are lovers, and both very sexual in their nature, and they would often have sex to dissolve tension and re-tie bonds that may have been undone from the conflict. Suzy at first does not resist John's playfulness, and in fact enjoys this interlude; but then quickly resumes the job at hand and remembers her original annoyance.

'John, you're going to make me burn myself! Can you not see I'm holding a pair of bloody hair straighteners!'

'Yeah, but danger's kind of fun, right?'

'Oh my god, you are such a freak. Can you just shut up for, like, five minutes and sit on your bed, eat your chocolate and leave me in peace?'

John laughs to himself and puts on his T-shirt and jeans (which did, in fact, only take 30 seconds or so). Suzy, frustrated, but also smiling to herself, continues straightening, but then a knock on the door is heard. John squints through the peep hole and sees Phillip standing there with an eight-pack of bottled Corona beer.

'Oi, oi, I thought we were meeting you in the SU?' John says as he opens the door.

'Well, I thought we could do a little pre-drinks before we head down, plus I knew it would take you guys half a millennium to get ready. By the way, Suzy, I hope you don't mind me third-wheeling you guys tonight, it's just John and I thought it would be nice to have a drink just us three.'

'Oh, don't worry, you're not third-wheeling tonight,' Suzy says with a devilish grin, putting down her hair straighteners.

'Erm, he is third-wheeling tonight, what do you mean he *isn't* third wheeling tonight?' John says, frowning in confusion.

'Ha, well, as you boys decided on a last-minute drink, I also made my own last-minute decision …'

'Which is?' John asks curiously, albeit with an element of frustration, as he did really want this to be just the three of them.

'Well, I want to introduce Phillip to my friend, Áine,' Suzy says whilst looking over at Phillip with the same cheeky, devilish grin.

'So, just to confirm, Suzy, you're hooking me up with this friend of yours, Áine?' Phillip says, even though he already knew the answer.

'Well, I wouldn't say hooking up, but I would say I've invited her with the knowledge you are both single, and with an insight that you and her are both lovely, and I thought there would be a good chance there could be sparks and chemistry.'

In a way, Phillip felt a little awkward about things like this. He had a view that human interaction is best done in a natural, fluid manner; and whenever he wanted to speak to a girl who he was attracted to, he didn't want it to be 'forced'. Phillip believed that whenever an interaction was too planned, it missed that natural spark of flow and spontaneity that keeps things smooth, pure, genuine and raw. It was sometimes to Phillips's detriment that he regularly fluctuated between states of intense natural flow and instinctual action to being stuck in his head and over-analysing. To Phillip, the more a situation was built up as a 'big deal', the more his ego and rational mind would start planning things to say and ways to behave, rather than simply allowing the essence from his self to *flow*. Situations like being hooked up with a girl just seemed very unnatural to him. In his earlier school years, Phillip dabbled with casual sex, as most boys do. However, recently he had developed an inner discipline and realisation that this was not what he wanted. He was a sensitive and deep individual, and what he actually wanted was a real connection that would last; not just based on sex, but practicality, personality and friendship.

'Oh yeah? So, she's a nice girl then?' Phillip answers robotically, and Suzy laughs instantly.

'Yes! She's an amazing girl! She's studying classics. Very smart, but a bit weird as well; perfect for you …'

'Phil is in! Don't worry mate, I got your back for this one, I'm gonna big you up proper style,' John says, as he gives Phillip a soft and playful punch to the stomach. Phillip then goes straight over to the bed, sits down and cracks open a bottle of Corona. The three then all give each other a knowing look and smile; and then something shifts, as if the tempo of the vibe just merged with one of a higher vibration. The three instantly become more positive and excited, and then Suzy and John crack open a bottle for themselves.

'Okay, let's get this party started!' John says as he turns up the music.

'Hey, you know there's this party on Saturday at Bagley Wood, Suzy; you up for it?' Phillip says whilst turning to look at her.

'Oh yeah, John briefly mentioned this; it's kind of an arty vibe isn't it, a bit hippy? Áine would be well up for that, you should ask her to come,' Suzy says whilst smirking playfully.

'Jesus, I haven't even met this girl yet, you're really trying to set me up, aren't you!'

'It's a match made in heaven, that's why! She's quite, err, spacey … I mean, she's not *crazy* crazy, but she's a little scatter-brained. She's the sort of girl who likes LSD and psychedelics and stuff. Spiritual, that's what she is, spiritual. Fairly sure she keeps a dream diary like you too. You could both exchange dreams! How cute would that be? Dream buddies!' Suzy laughs to herself once again, pleased with her matchmaking abilities.

Phillip, whilst excited at how this girl does actually sound interesting, can't help but cringe a bit at the expression 'dream buddies'.

'Sounds like a winner to me, mate, maybe she can sort us some stuff for the party on Saturday? Would love to try acid. You've never done it before either, have you Phil?' interjects John.

'I've done low doses of mushrooms a few times, but never properly had a full-fledged experience. They were all still quite enlightening though. However, I've had equally spiritual experiences whilst meditating, and taking MDMA at a rave can be pretty spiritual and psychedelic. But it's more euphoric than psychedelic, I guess …'

'I'm actually surprised I've never done any yet, seeing how interested I am in psychology and philosophy,' John says. 'I was speaking to Dean about his tripping experiences, and he told me he once did DMT at an ayahuasca ceremony in South America. During the trip he was told by the spirits he was destined to be a teacher of some sort. And look where he is now …'

'Yeah, some of the experiences I've heard can be insane, DMT especially. Apparently, a trip can feel like a lifetime, but in fact it only lasts about 10 minutes.'

'That's what scares me about taking stuff like that, I just don't like to be out of control. You hear stories of people killing themselves whilst tripping if they have a bad one,' Suzy says suspiciously, frowning with uncertainty whilst looking from John to Phillip.

'From what I've read about them,' Phillip says slowly, and with one raised eyebrow, 'and from my own understanding of my own experiences, set and setting are very important, so we must make sure we are around people who love us, and know us, to our core. What seems to be the case on psychedelics is they strip you back to a very pure and raw form of the self, where ego is reduced significantly, and in some cases, on high doses, ego may be killed completely. What you are left with is unfiltered consciousness. To put it in a different way, it seems psychedelics may induce a childlike innocence, where the rational and intellectual insight of "what I am" and "what this is" are reduced, and instead, raw emotional connection to novel *experience* is increased dramatically. Meditation, when practised correctly, can have similar effects on ego control and reduction. Think back to when you were a child and saw something like fireworks for the first time; that euphoria is in a way awe being expressed, and is why we say "awesome", for it is something new and exciting for the senses. The right hemisphere of the brain is overloaded, as the experience is new and novel. The experience has not yet been assimilated and digested, analysed and criticized. The experience is still in its rawest, most pure, *truest* form. It is being experienced through the mind, body and soul in a totality.' As Phillip says this, he is conscious of trying not to sound too pretentious and arrogant, yet he still felt he had a decent understanding based on his own experiences, insights and readings.

'You sound like you've done them a fair few times from how you describe them!' Suzy says in a light and teasing tone.

'Who's that guy at our gym who loves them, Phil? You know, the Muslim fella?' John asks curiously.

'Oh yeah, Ishmael I think his name is; I rolled with him a few weeks ago, actually. He's a little weird – nice, but very intense; clearly smart though. You can tell he has taken a lot of drugs …'

'Oh, for sure he has. When I spoke to him, he told me how he's had lots of intense and ego-shattering experiences. He takes them in combination with his prayer and Islamic practices, which I thought was interesting. I didn't think Muslims could take drugs.'

'I think it depends on the interpretation,' Phillip says, 'many Muslims don't consider psychedelics "consciousness inhibiting" like alcohol, but instead see them as "consciousness intensifiers", to bring them closer to God, instead of further away like alcohol.'

'Oh, interesting. He was telling me how the ancient tribes had a focus on staying grounded after many of their psychedelic rituals. They would engage in manual labour of some sort, or tasks that engage their bodies to a great extent. He said that for him, training jiujitsu had this same grounding and sobering effect. He believed if it weren't for the jiujitsu, it would be easy for him to become disconnected with reality and slip into a confused, chaotic, unstructured and undisciplined frame of mind.'

'That is so true though; I find my mind is so much clearer and focused after jiujitsu, It is very grounding for sure, isn't it? Do you reckon that's why we dance to music? Because the music loosens up our mind, reducing our resistance, opening up our energies, and the dancing is a way for the energy to be transferred without it getting blocked?'

'I have no idea, mate. But it does remind me of something … Suzy, I told Phil how you got annoyed at my movements the other day; do they still piss you off?' John says with a cheeky smile on his face, looking over at Phillip as if to say: 'Remember what she said the other day.'

Suzy rolls her eyes at this jab from her boyfriend.

'Okay, I don't mean to be rude, but I know what you boys are like; you'll talk for days if I don't stop you, and I said to Áine we would be down in the SU by now …'

The group down their beers as fast as they can and head straight downstairs to the SU to meet this new friend of Suzy's …

3. MUSIC OPENS LIBIDO

The group eventually walk through the doors of the student union. Whilst they are not completely drunk, they are excitable, jolly and full of energy; all ready for a good night. The bunker-like student union was only built in the last couple of years. The bar runs down an entire side of the building, to the right as you walk in, with a seated section being separated from the dance floor by metal railings. At the far end of the building, there are multiple sofas with tables in between them; and in the middle lies the large, open space for the dance floor. When John and Phillip first saw this design, they were pleasantly surprised; they did not expect a university like Oxford to have such a large space designed solely for dancing. Most student unions are instead more like bars than clubs. Some students may have preferred a more conservative style, but Phillip, John and Suzy loved it as for them dancing was always the best part of the night. Perhaps the university picked up on the lack of notable clubs in the local area and thought they could capitalise.

Directly parallel to the bar, in the middle, stands a large DJ booth, with a familiar face behind the decks …

'Talk of the devil!' John says whilst squinting, making sure his eyes did not deceive him.

'No way is that Ishmael … There's more to this guy than meets the eye …' Phillip says following a stunned laugh.

'Wait, that's the guy from your jiujitsu class? The one who loves acid and stuff?' Suzy asks whilst looking confused.

'Yes, that's the guy. It wouldn't surprise me if he's off his face right now whilst he DJs,' Phillip says as he smiles to himself. 'So where is this friend of yours, then?'

'Oh, so now you're interested …' Suzy says as she flicks her finger at Phillip. 'I'm not sure, I said to meet at the bar; wait, I'll give her a call now,' Suzy says as she begins fumbling on her Nokia 2110 mobile phone.

John walks to the bar to order some drinks for the group. Phillip leans over the metal railing that separates the bar seating area from the main dance floor. He watches the large crowd of people dancing, and gently taps his hand against the railing to the rhythm of the bass beats. He always found this type of music, that is, music with a repetitive bass beat, to be very trance inducing. For him, it was incredibly relaxing, yet energy inducing; an oxymoron, some may say. Phillip was often in a trance-like state, whether that be whilst reading, meditating, listening to music and dancing, or even during jiujitsu. Whilst not all typically relaxing, he found each activity, in different ways, helped calm his mind to a more contained and focused pace which helped keep his thoughts under control and observation. The common thread with these things is that they all required degrees of *focus,* and this focus required practice. Many friends of his didn't like the repetitive music he, John and Suzy enjoyed; but what John and Phillip had commonly discussed was that the more instrumental and minimalist the music was, the more focus would be required to truly be *immersed in the musical journey.* They believed that music itself was a practice, and a process that required training to really reap the fruits. Phillip noted that many of his friends, when immersed in a certain set and setting, where the music was more *felt* with higher volume, energy and increased awareness, suddenly appreciated certain music styles they had previously professed to hate. Phillip believed this was also true with many spiritual and mystical experiences, which can be related to musical patterns. Phillip commonly spoke to others about his thought that music could in some way be a spiritual language of the soul; and whilst we have different spoken languages on earth, all can understand the language of music as it speaks to any soul. It is no surprise, then, that the beat of the drum or the whistle of the pipe has been used for thousands of years in tribal traditions and rituals; helping to induce trance states, relaxing our conscious egos, activating catharsis, and ultimately helping to release trapped spirits *within our unconscious.*

What happens next is a defining moment in the lives of each character, and one they would continue to joke and talk about for long after.

As Phillip continues to stare at the dance floor, looking like a young philosopher of sorts, John returns with some drinks and passes Phillip a cup of vodka and lemonade. Suzy returns from her attempts at contacting Áine, with a slightly worried expression.

'Okay, so I couldn't get through to her by phone, however I have received a slightly bizarre text saying: "HE Tol"… I have no idea what that means, but I have a feeling it's not good, and I'm actually a bit worried for her.'

'He tol?' Phillip repeats with a confused look.

'I don't understand why you would even bother trying to send messages on those devices,' John says as he shakes his head. 'It's just such a poor way of communicating …'

'Well, I did try calling her first!'

John sighs in exasperation, and then looks up to the ceiling.

'Why are you worried, then? I have the feeling there's something you're not telling us.'

'Okay, fine …' Suzy looks guiltily at Phillip. 'I didn't want to say it at first, but Áine technically still has a boyfriend …'

'Boyfriend? You mean you've set Phillip up with someone who's still in a relationship?' John says in a tone of shocked disbelief.

'Look, it's actually a bit more complicated than that, and I didn't want to cause drama so I didn't say anything at first … But yes, she technically still has a boyfriend, but he's not a very nice person and has been really manipulative and controlling. So, I thought it would be good if she gets out and meets other boys, so she doesn't feel so reliant on this dickhead,' Suzy says whilst exhaling, relieving herself of pent-up tension and a truth that she's been struggling to hold in.

Phillip pinches his forehead and then looks back up to say: 'It's fine. It is what it is, we just have to make sure she's okay.'

'I don't mean to be a judgemental prick, but there is a pretty well-built tattooed bloke who I just saw walk into the girl's toilets. I'm not a betting man, but maybe the message means something along the lines of: "Help toile—" John is cut off before he can finish.

Suzy and Phillip are rushing to the girls' toilets to investigate.

'Shit …' John says as he watches them rush away, shaking his head once again, knowing intuitively this wasn't going to end well.

He follows reluctantly.

As they all approach the toilet, a group of three girls rush out looking stressed and flustered.

'A big bald man just stormed in! A girl is getting choked in there!' a well-spoken blonde girl from the group says with wide-eyed shock.

'That's my friend, Áine!' Suzy replies frantically.

Phillip decides to intervene.

'Hold on, look, calm down. It's not my business, and I'm not involved. I don't know this guy personally, but I think it's better to not get security involved before we absolutely have to. Let's be honest, none of us really understand their situation, so it's easy for us to judge and want to be heroes,' Phillip says, scouting around for reactions whilst trying to remain measured, calm and rational, resisting the temptation to be a chivalrous hero.

'He's choking a fucking girl, Phil,' John blurts in stark contrast to Phillip's measured approach.

'Fair comment. Fine, let's take a peek inside and make sure he's actually the threat she says he is. If he is, it's game time,' Phil says as he makes eye contact with the blonde, who looks back at him mouth agape.

They all go inside together, John leading and Suzy watching over the situation at the tail. They initially lurk behind a wall at the entrance, edging their heads around the corner to catch a glimpse of the action inside, from where an intense, sharp exchange echoes around the room.

'Who the fuck is this guy Phillip then, ay?!' the large, bald, tattooed man shouts with a strong cockney accent; all whilst he holds Áine's mobile phone in front of her, showing a text from Áine that mentions Phillip.

'I don't even know him. My friend mentioned this guy to me, said he was nice,' Áine replies in a soft, calming voice with a thick Irish accent.

She does not seem scared, but she does seem a bit worried. It is obvious she is no weakling, but it is also clear to see she is uncomfortable and knows it's in her best interest to keep the situation from escalating.

'Yeah, well, think about it. I am your boyfriend still, so why do you think talking about other guys is a good idea? Do you take me for a mug? Remember what happens when you mug me off? Yeah, now you remember …' the man says with a devilish look on his face, whilst grabbing Áine's ponytail, exposing her neck.

'Let's take a break, Brian. It's just too intense, and I need to think about us, okay?'

'You don't need to think about anything. Just let me do what I want to you, and do what I tell you, and be a good little puppy dog for me? How about that?'

Brian then puts his hands around her throat, ready to dominate Áine sexually by putting her into a submissive state. Part of Áine wants to submit, but another part, her conscience, doesn't. From an onlooker's perspective, and to the three spying on this action, this relationship seemed abusive and controlling; the kinky side of their relationship was clearly being used for more than just play within the bedroom. It was being used as a form of control that was not *fully* consensual, with Brian taking advantage of Áine's more primitive, instinctual libido and potential complexes. Brian was not allowing her to harmoniously balance her instinctive, animalistic side with her more human and spiritual conscience. As was as if her wholeness was trapped within fragmented sub-personalities, and only he held the key. In some devilish way, this was enticing to Áine. It seemed 'naughty' to fully let herself go, to fully submit to a clearly beastly man. She could not deny that she found this thought incredibly arousing. But whilst one part of her felt in the grip of this instinct, another part, her conscience, still knew it was not a good idea to be held captive by this person who, in all honesty, she barely knew. If she was being honest with herself, she would admit to being attracted to Brian for possessing such 'beastly' traits of power and dominance; and she did have a great desire to try and tame him, to harness his libido and energy, to show him compassion and kindness, which he seemed to lack. During this attempt to dominate Áine, however, her conscience was the victor; Áine pushes away Brian's hand and shoves him back, letting him know in no uncertain terms how she feels.

'I said, let's have a break! Just leave me alone for a bit, okay!'

As Áine makes her stand, it is clear from Brian's face turning red and his fists beginning to clench that the group needed to interrupt before things escalated. Phillip decides to make a move and show himself. John and Suzy pull their heads back and continue to listen, unseen.

'Hello mate, you alright?' Phillip says casually and calmly, as he walks out from around the corner, whilst staring Brian in the eye.

'Who the fuck are you?' Brian replies aggressively.

'I'm Phillip,' he says calmly, albeit with intense eye contact.

Brian stares back at Phillip, assessing him. Brian's first feelings are that of hate and fury; with every fibre of his being, he wanted to crush this male threat who was in contact with his girl. But even with the confidence that comes with being man of his size and build, Brian felt an element of fear and caution. This was possibly due to the way Phillip conducted himself, with his strong eye contact and calm demeanour. This is unusual for Brian, as he is normally a very dominant man. What shocked Brian was how he felt around Phillips's presence, and he couldn't quite explain the uneasiness.

'Why is your name popping up on my girlfriend's telephone?' Brian says, clearly in a volatile state.

Suzy walks out from around the corner. Áine is immediately reassured by her friend's presence, and no longer feels the same level of unease as she did before.

'Hey, dickhead, if you've got a problem then talk to me. I set Áine up with Phillip, you wanna know why? Because you are a controlling, abusive prick. And guess what? I don't want my friend with a controlling, abusive prick,' Suzy says with a fire and feist that shocks both Phillip and John. John nods along with an expression as if to say 'that's my girl'.

'Aww, look at you, getting girls to set you up on dates with girls who are already taken. You are pathetic, mate. You can't even score a bird yourself so you get some bimbo to help you,' Brian snarls at Phillip, his aggression partially extinguished by Suzy's fire. What now remained was more of a general disgust at the situation.

John walks out from around the corner.

'Okay, so two things, big man: firstly, Phillip isn't pathetic; secondly, don't ever call my girlfriend a bimbo again, or I'll tear your ACL.'

'You're gonna what, mate?' Brian says in a sarcastic tone whilst giving a condescending laugh.

It is true that Brian did not know that ACL meant the anterior cruciate ligament that supports the knee joint, which infamously is extremely painful and takes a long time to heal if torn. John and Phillip, since meeting each other at the start of university, have already developed a sort of bond where they can communicate almost telepathically. They are always on or near the same wavelength because of how deeply they understand each other. Phillip immediately knew from the reference to the ACL that John was flirting with the idea of getting Brian in a 'heel hook' (a jiujitsu leg lock that targets the ACL). Whilst many people throw threats around like this, Phillip knew John would happily make good on it, especially if it could be justified. John had personally told him how desperate he was to try out his jiujitsu in a real-life situation; and, lo and behold, here they were with a bullish and arrogant boyfriend who deserves a humbling. John and Phillip turn to each other, communicating with looks only. John gives Phillip a sort of smirk as if to say, 'Should I do it?' and Phillip replies with scrunch of the nose as if to say, 'Not a good idea.'

But John just couldn't help himself. He suddenly and dramatically, like a Ninja, rolls on the ground, directly into the heel-hook position, and sweeps Brian off his feet and onto his back, with his leg firmly under John's control. John begins to apply pressure, and Brian begins to writhe and scramble, not knowing this is the worst thing he can do, as it will just make a tear more inevitable.

'Oh my god!' a conflicted Áine cries.

On the one hand she wanted to support her boyfriend, but on the other she wanted him to suffer and felt he was getting what he deserved.

'Don't tear it, John! God damn it, why did you have to go for a heel hook? A choke would have sufficed,' Phillip says, rolling his eyes, yet unable to suppress a cheeky smirk.

Suzy, observing the carnage unravelling, signals for Áine to leave the toilet and stand outside with her until the situation calms down. Áine stumbles across the floor and out of the toilet, allowing the boys to finish their business.

'I'm going to fucking kill you, motherfuckers!' Brian screams whilst his ACL is at near-breaking point.

John is being careful to not apply too much pressure, but still keep Brian on the brink of pain to teach him a lesson.

'Okay, that's enough,' Phillip says, mounting the side of Brian to assume a side-control position; Phillip swiftly grabs Brian's collar with a baseball bat grip to put him in a choke. Brian continues to flail and strain, but against two trained jiujitsu practitioners he has little chance of gaining any control.

Brian's movements calm and his body goes limp.

He falls unconscious.

Phillip and John put him in the recovery position.

'Let's get the fuck out of here,' Phillip says, knowing it would only be a few seconds before Brian wakes up.

The boys rush outside the toilet and run past the girls, ushering them to follow them towards the dance floor in hopes they could blend in with the crowd when Brian Re-emerges. The girls reluctantly follow, carried away by this chaotic drama unfolding. Ishmael is still DJing up in the booth; from his elevated vantage position, he can see the entire dance floor very well. He notices the familiar faces stumble onto the dance floor from the toilets. As a DJ, it is his job to read the energy and tone of the room and adjust the music accordingly. Being an intuitive-mystical type as he is, he immediately notices the body language of the group and realises something is not quite right.

The DJ box beside Ishmael has a panel inside it that controls the lighting of the room, and something inside him tells him that he must lower the lights. Ishmael decides a dark and ambient red tinge is suitable, followed by a deep house track containing an intense, low, melodic bassline. This adds another level of darkness to the vibe, all whilst making everybody on the dance floor move with greater intensity.

'Oh my god, shouldn't we leave?!' Suzy says with a panicked expression, whilst trying to look normal by dancing awkwardly along with the others.

'Yeah, we should probably leave … You guys do know Brian works the door here?' Áine says nonchalantly, yet to realise what this would mean for John and Phillip.

'Please tell me that's a joke …' John says, looking at his girlfriend with raised eyebrows and a tilted head. 'Oh look, he's stumbling out of the toilet now. Aaaand, there's a bouncer rushing over towards him …'

The group watch Brian talk to the bouncer. The bouncer, with a stern expression, shouts down a radio to his colleagues.

'Okay, we need to get the hell out of here; every bouncer in here is going to know what's just happened,' Phillip says, nodding towards the bouncer with the radio. 'Let's start making our way through the crowd. We gotta keep our cool though, guys, we don't want to arouse any suspicions.'

Once again, Ishmael notices this shift in movement from his jiujitsu pals. After a moment of contemplation whilst looking around and stroking his beard, he makes the connection between their and the bouncer's movements and concludes that the lads may be in trouble. Ishmael feels compelled to help his jiujitsu 'brothers'; He quickly mixes into a climactic part of a song, which gives way to intense strobe-lighting effects that makes it more difficult for the bouncers to track the group. After some light pushing and shoving, still not trying to make a scene, the group reach the door to leave but are stopped by the doormen.

'Guys, sorry to stop you leaving, but we've had an assault taking place in the club tonight. One of our staff was attacked in the toilets here; have any of you seen anything?' a tall doorman asks with a thick Russian accent.

'No, nothing, sorry,' says Phillip.

'Sorry mate,' says John.

'I'm so sorry to hear that! I didn't see anything either,' says Áine.

'That's so horrible! I hope you catch the bastard who attacked him,' Suzy says whilst subtly glancing ironically over at her boyfriend.

The doorman frowns and looks at them all suspiciously, but decides to usher them out, ladies first. As soon as Áine and Suzy cross the threshold of the door.

The hearts of both John and Phillip suddenly drop.

'Those are the fucking cunts who attacked me!!' Brian screams from across the club, pointing at the group.

He starts limping towards them as fast as he can. The two doorman who were standing in front of Phillip and John lock eyes with them; they are suddenly different animals, now both in predator mode. Before they can act, Phillip gains control of one of the doorman's wrists, pulling it across his body to expose the tricep, which he drags with his other hand, freeing up a space to pass. Subtle, but effective. Phillip walks outside, then turns to faces the doorman to get his attention.

'Come on then, good sir, show me your skills,' Phillip says politely whilst clapping his hands together.

He engages a kick boxing stance to ready himself for combat. This is typical of Phillip: a warrior, but also a gentleman. He always shows respect to his opponent, whatever the circumstances. Phillip is no fool either; he knows that doormen and bouncers enjoy a good fight. They may act like they just want peace, but even the most by-the-book bouncer will pounce on any excuse to fight. Phillip believed it best to use the minimum necessary force for any given scenario. John had a different interpretation of what constitutes minimum necessary force.

This situation was no different.

John grabs hold of his doorman and throws him over his hip using a Judo move known as *O-goshi*. The doorman hits the hard floor with a thud, and John follows up with three rapid strikes to the face. He then notices Brian hobbling towards him; so he swiftly makes his own exit as Phillip distracts the other bouncer outside.

Suzy and Áine are still standing by watching this drama unfold. John sprints towards them and grabs his girlfriend by the hand, as if to signal an evacuation.

'Áine, go with Phillip, I'm getting Suzy out of here.' John shouts to Phillip to take Áine to safety.

John and Suzy sprint off down the road into the university grounds.

'So much for "in this together"…' Phillip mutters to himself. The rest of the security team begin piling out of the club in numbers. Phillip and Áine know there's only one thing they can do, and that is to run for their life.

'Get away from my fucking girlfriend, you prick!' Brian shouts, limping towards them as fast as he can. Phillip swiftly drags a bin from his left, and it trips Brian over; the other bouncers struggle to suppress their amusement, while Áine blushes at this humiliation of her now ex-lover.

'We need to move. Let's try and lose them through the campus grounds,' Phillip says calmly, but with conviction.

They both sprint off as fast as their legs will carry them. As they run, they hear the faint screams of Brian:

'Whore! You whore! You fucking whore! Enjoy your time with bitch boy, you whore!'

Brian shakes his head, spits on the ground, then sits down on the steps, clasping his knee in agony. He looks up and around at the other bouncers, who give one another looks which say: 'Shall we?'. After a quick verbal exchange, the bouncers give chase …

4. ENERGETIC SYZYGY

The newly-acquainted pair rush through the dark streets of Oxford centre, adrenaline coursing through their veins. They look back to see two burly six-foot units sprinting behind them at full throttle with faces etched with anger.

Already at this point, they seemed to have formed a natural bond. They were running as if in tune with one another; both their direction and pace seemed to intertwine and connect as if they were one being. This was rather peculiar, as they had barely uttered a single word to one another; yet both noticed this intuitive bond.

One thing that had already struck Phillip was how fast Áine could run. She was naturally an athletic type, albeit relatively small in height. Áine was also, to Phillip, and he could not hide his feelings here, incredibly beautiful. Her light blonde ponytailed hair and her exceptionally large brown eyes both seemed to induce a trance-like state whenever he was caught in her gaze. It was not *just* her eyes or hair that he found attractive, but more how her spirit seemed to animate them; how her movements caused her hair to flick, and how her stare pierced and cut deep into his soul.

Much of the time, Áine's body language alone could make many men and women feel stupid, as she would answer their questions with a subtle shift in body positioning or eye contact, but still in way that was filled with compassion and understanding, rather than arrogance and condescension. The similarity in facial features between Áine and Phillip was uncanny; they both possessed feline jaws and cheekbones. It was also undoubted that they shared a certain *fire* in their spirits. This is what they both intuitively sensed in each other, and what brought them together in natural synergy. This fire within their souls was not visible but felt in both their presences, and sensed when gazing into their eyes. And it was true, these two gave off a strong, powerful vibe whenever they interacted with people for reasons they could not quite fathom if you asked them.

After five minutes, the couple stop running to catch their breath. They look around, but there's no sight of their chasers. They have stopped directly outside the famous Bodleian Library, which at this time of night is closed. Regardless, the library is well lit, and the pair can't help but notice its beauty.

'Maybe we could hide in here …' Áine says softly and mysteriously, whilst making firm eye contact with Phillip.

'I would love to sneak in, but I'm not sure how …' Phillip pauses for a moment, and turns to squint at the library. 'Only one way to find out though, right?' he smirks.

They sneak around the outside of the building to see if they can find a way in.

'Look! A cleaner,' Áine says after peaking through a window with a childlike smile. Once again, her trance-inducing eyes glisten as she looks at Phillip, who holds her gaze for a little longer than before …

The pair continue scouting the building until they see a slightly opened door. They both look at each other with euphoria and giddiness. As they sneak up to the door, they peak in and notice the cleaner at the far end of the library mopping the floor. They assume a classic burglar's stance, keeping their bodies low and tiptoeing to make as little noise as possible. They creep over towards the left side of the library, where there are some wooden pillars and a barrier slightly above ground level. After some quiet exchanges, they decide to hide face down on the floor behind the barrier, which is just high enough.

'What now?' Áine whispers.

'We wait. It won't be long until that cleaner is finished.'

'Are you sure about that?'

'Err … Well, I hope so. I'm already getting uncomfortable down here.' He pops his head up. 'Shh! He's coming back this way!'

The cleaner slowly makes his way towards the entrance. As he reaches the door, he turns his head for one last time, slowly, calmly and with precision like an owl. As the cleaner turns, he notices a small black shoe sticking out from behind the pillar.

'This great library is more than 400 years old. During that time, men and women of all kinds have used this space to make breakthrough discoveries, some of which have led to permanent advancements in human civilisation. Some people may say that this very space is sacred, special, and to be treated with the utmost degree of respect. And whilst I may just be her caretaker, I take great pride in keeping this building in the greatest of conditions, so students can continue to help move humanity forward. Now, may I ask, what are you two doing to move humanity forward?' the well-spoken caretaker asks, his words coming to him so smoothly they that could be scripted.

Áine and Phillip slowly raise themselves off the ground. They feel ashamed an embarrassed, yet can't help but smile at the caretaker's humbling words.

'Hello there, Sir. Look, we are really sorry, we didn't mean to sneak in here like this, it's just ... Well, basically ...' Phillip struggles to form an excuse, so Áine decides to cut in.

'We were getting chased by my crazy ex-boyfriend and two large bouncers and were quite honestly scared for our lives; so we decided to sneak into this library to escape.'

'Yes, exactly,' Phillip says as he nods towards Áine in appreciation.

The caretaker, aged around 60, is unusually smart for a man cleaning a library. He has groomed grey hair and is wearing a well-ironed, stripy blue shirt neatly tucked into his trousers. He holds himself with deep conviction and meaning; it was if he knew exactly what he was doing at all times, and had everything under complete control.

He walks over towards the pair to inspect them more closely. As he looks at them both, his eyes squint with a deep curiosity. He continues to make slight grunting sounds, as if having some inner conflict in deciding what to make of the situation. Phillip has a fleeting moment of intuitive doubt whether this was genuine or merely an act. He couldn't put his finger on it, but something just didn't add up about this mysterious man.

'Whilst I believe you were escaping these ... people ... I also believe you two had other intentions when you walked through those doors. Intentions you may have not discussed openly with one another, but intentions that remain true deep down regardless. Yes, I may be old, but I was also young once. In fact, I met my wife within this very library. I dare say, without the obvious coincidental irony, that we also came through those doors with the same 'intentions' that you both clearly possess.'

'Oh, look, we aren't together like that. I only met her tonight, and we honestly just thought this would be a good place to hide,' Phillip says whilst looking rather awkwardly towards Áine hoping for back up. She instead looks down at the floor in embarrassment.

'Oh, don't bullshit me like that, lad! I find it rather rude. I would much rather you tell the truth and it be unpleasant than to lie and it sound sweet. As I said, I have also been young once.' The old man looks up towards the ceiling. 'And what I would do to relive those days ...'

The caretaker continues to stare silently as if reminiscing about some surfacing euphoric memory that suddenly popped into his conscious awareness. He takes a big sigh and looks back towards the pair with increased seriousness.

'Okay, look. I want you both to have the experience I had when I was a young boy. This library is a magical place, and you both seem … alright … So, just this once, *and just this once,* you can stay here for the night.'

Áine and Phillip instantly smile with excitement and surprise, both trying their hardest to hold back fully expressing themselves; they were certainly not expecting this!

'But look. If you leave any kind of mess, or if there's just one book out of place, I'll report you both to the university, and mark my words, you do not want that.'

'Thank you so much, Sir, this is truly kind of you. Sorry, I didn't introduce myself; my name is Phillip, and this is my friend Áine.'

'Hello,' Áine says with a warm smile and a slight wave.

'Hmm, yes, you do both seem alright. Well, I would recommend you use this time here wisely; you might even learn a thing or two.'

The caretaker begins to make his way out, and then abruptly pauses in the doorway, frozen like a statue. He stays still for a while, causing the couple to exchange confused looks.

He turns to face the pair once more, this time with raised eyebrows and a serious expression.

'Your holiest son will be called Arthur.'

'Excuse me?' says a confused Phillip through a squint, tilting his head.

'God bless.' The caretaker gives a mysterious smile and then leaves swiftly, closing the door behind him.

'Why did he just say my holiest son will be called Arthur? Why would he say that? It's just so random.'

'What?' Áine says as she laughs.

'Didn't you just hear what he said? He said my holiest son will be called Arthur …'

'I didn't hear him say that. But I can see in your eyes that you heard it, and I believe you did. Something's telling me that there is something going on in the depths here, something spiritual … I can feel it … I mean, what caretaker would allow two random students into the library on their own at 3 am? I'm not complaining, it's amazing we have this place all to ourselves, but it just seems too good to be true. Something seems very dreamlike about this place, like a kind of magic exists here.'

'Yes, I agree. And my intuition is also picking up on something weird, like a sort of spiritual presence … Maybe the library is haunted or something,' Phillip says with a degree of seriousness, as if he was suddenly a little scared.

'Well, sounds like we are going to have a fun night then! Let's go and find some ghosts!' Áine says with a playful smirk.

They enthusiastically walk around the library with no clear goal or intention; both are enjoying the situation for what it is. As Áine moves around, she puts her arms out at her side mimicking the wing of a bird, trying to express her feelings of freedom. Phillip walks behind, eyes wide and head on a swivel, clearly taken back by the beauty of the empty library.

Phillip thinks to himself, *I've been here to study many times in the day, but why is it when there's no one here, at night, the excitement and beauty of this place just seems so much more intense?'*

'Hey, Phil. Can I call you that? I mean, Phillip just seems so formal,' Áine says.

Phillip laughs.

'Of course you can. In fact, I prefer Phil to Phillip, I just never bother to correct people.'

'Okay then, *Phil*. You want to know a little secret?' Phillip smiles in anticipation.

'So, I was actually really excited to meet you tonight. And I didn't expect to meet Brian out either. Whilst it's ended up being a very … interesting … night, it's not quite what I had in mind. Suzy was telling me all about you, and from how she described you, I was really interested straight away, which is weird because I'm usually quite standoffish until I really get to know someone. But there's just something about you that I'm really fascinated by, and I can't quite put my finger on it.'

'Well, look, I really respect your honesty there; most people wouldn't be that honest, as it is something that seems to be becoming less and less common these days. I must admit, when Suzy was telling me about you, I didn't know what to think; I thought you were just some girl wanting a bit of fun or something …' Phillip gives a withdrawn laugh. 'But now that I've seen you, I know that you're actually quite a deep girl, and obviously very smart as well. I can just see it in your eyes, in the way you move, the way you talk, the way you … Umm … it's hard to describe rationally. I like to think I have well-developed intuition, and that I'm the sort of person who is genuinely interested in people's souls; not just the mask they show to the world, but the actual depths of the person. And when I look at you, there is this *depth*, and this depth radiates through all your actions; and I must say, *I like it.*'

Áine, flattered, blushes and looks down at the floor. She feels even more attracted to him now he's articulated his feelings.

'Well, I kind of had a plan about tonight and it's clearly changed quite a bit. What I originally had in mind was something … a little different. But I think we could maybe still improvise …'

Phillip, intrigued, raises his eyebrows and tilts his head, wondering what trick she has up her sleeve. Áine gives a playful smirk to Phillip, making strong eye contact, and then rummages through her bra to try and find something. She pulls out a small bag with two red pills. Phillip stares in mild disbelief, as if the potential of what could come tonight is suddenly flashing through his mind. *Is this really a good idea?* But still … It would be such a memorable night. How many people could say they've done ecstasy in the Bodleian Library! A story for the grandkids, for sure …'

Phillip sighs deeply. It seems he's already accepted the fact he can't get away from this.

'This probably isn't a good idea. But fuck it. One for the bucket list,' Phillip says whilst holding out his hand for Áine to give him the pill.

'One pill for Phil. And one pill for Áine,' Áine says as they chink their hands together as if toasting with a glass of wine. They both swallow with a degree of struggle, laughing to each other throughout.

The pair walk around the library on their own for a bit. Both have taken MDMA before, so they are aware of its effects, and the slight apprehension before the 'coming up' phase. So, it seems natural for both to wander around on their own and gather their thoughts and ground themselves before things get … weirder.

They both browse through various books, and Phillip ends up stumbling into the 'classics' section. Phillip very much enjoys reading myths and legends; he finds the stories very enlightening and feels they help him understand life, and himself, to a large degree. As his eyes scan the shelves, he sees all the usual suspects: Greek, Egyptian, Nordic.

He jolts in shock as he hears something fall to the ground.

He looks behind him and notices a book mysteriously on the floor, even though he was not even near it. He is caught off guard by this; his heart rate increases, and he at once feels the presence of something that he cannot explain. A compulsion to read this fallen book arouses within him. He picks up the book and reads the title: *44 – Arthur – King of the Tree.*

Phillip had read variants of the King Arthur myth as a child, but as a young man he had not really given them much thought or attention.

The mysterious caretaker said about how my holiest son will be called Arthur, pops into his head. *King of the tree though?* Whilst Phillip's memory was not his strongest asset, and he was no expert on King Arthur, he had never heard of any relation between the tree and King Arthur; and this notion made him even more intrigued. To his mind, King Arthur was all about Camelot, Merlin, the sword in the stone, the knights of the round table. Nothing about a king of a tree. Phillip opens the book to the first page and sees a large, vibrant picture of an oak tree, with its roots on full display, as if the picture showed beneath the earth. In front of the tree, a young man with brown hair sits in light-plated armour of high quality in a position like the buddha would, as if he were meditating. On the knight's chest plate is a picture of a tree, almost identical in shape to the tree behind him. Beneath this image, on the book, a quote read:

'For Arthur is for the age, but his tree for the ages. He and his variants will come and go, but his tree will always show, when England and the world are in times of sorrow. But how far down does sorrow grow? I just do not know. We await the king's return, and he must arrive quick! Let this king allow the tree to be watered, as she is so thirsty. The tree must grow high and strong! It must go on! Hail, Arthur! King of the tree!'

Phillip's heartbeat is racing even faster than it was before. He is in a mild state of shock at the bizarre chain of events. Intrigued, he flicks to the next page, which reads: 'For the readers of this work, I intend not to prove but only to express. I wish to express what my soul desires to burst onto these pages. What my soul compels of me is no easy task, as I am but only one man. It is not my duty to change the world with my vast campaigns or fighting, but instead to plant seeds that may lead others to do things I am not capable of. As what is the real task of life if not to plant seeds in people's souls? For these seeds, if well attended, will later flourish within imagination in the light, in the awareness of consciousness. Does not all life start with a seed? And does the fact that I can use the word *seed* to talk about many things not prove the nature of the *way*? Is that not the real task of any artist, to plant seeds? This book is my magnus opus, for the expression of my words here is less out of need for approval, but more so out of duty for my fellow humans, who I love with all my heart. For I have been observing since my inception on this earth; I have been observing people, cultures, art, intentions, love, emotion and the depths of reality itself; and by reality, I mean my self, as what is reality if not within me? *Cogito ergo sum.* One thing I know to be true, and with no argument, is *whatever is the nature of self is truth*. But not just the self of *mine,* but the collective self of *ours.* One can choose to put more energy into questions like these if one so desires. But what if we are told to no longer ask such questions? What if we are told to leave these questions to those only at the top, in charge of the kingdom? Oh, but is it not the right of every man and woman to find the meaning of life within their own self? Imagine the arrogance of those who do not trust us with such inward journeying! As if those in charge were too scared to allow the individual access to the power of *the god within*. But who can blame them? As if the individual becomes God, then it will be no easy task to control 10 billion of them! But what if I told you that we could help people connect to this god inside them? What if I told you that one day, the king of the tree will return? And when he does, he will plant the Tree of Life, and all will taste its fruits that will once again connect them to their divinity. To the readers, I say, this tree must be planted with great haste! Currently the soil is still fertile, but soon the ground will rot with the flesh of trampled and tortured men and women. If we keep waiting, keep waiting without any structure and guidance, then we are destined to fall. *But we will not! We shall not!* We will not fall because I have witnessed something. I have witnessed that within the souls of many, there is a growing *fire*. There is a fire for the liberation of the soul; a growing desire for a place for men and women to go, to find this liberation; a place men and women can go to escape and overcome petty trivialities such as *death*. Let us laugh at how we fear such trivial matters, as our ancestors likely are from within. For our ancestors wait within this realm, this realm of the gods. What if this realm is always within us? And all our ancestors, from every dimension, lie in this world of many dimensions? Time is an irrelevance in the realm of the gods.

'Oh, but what childish things you talk about,' they say. As if they write off any thought for higher matters as mere childish fantasy. But let me tell you, my readers, these child-like fantasies are the root of all good in the world, but, *admittedly*, also of all evil. But these fantasies only act as a source of evil when they remain in the dark; for when we look at them with integrity and, more importantly, when we shine the *inward eye of light* upon them, we then become honest with ourselves about their contents. But what of this topic of shedding light on feeling? Emotion is merely thinking that has yet to be unpacked and assimilated, a strongly-concentrated spirit you might say; and only when we take time for our bodies to digest these emotions, to open Pandora's box, to process them, to look at them, can we understand the root of what they are trying to tell us. Anger may be seen as a devastating emotion, but when we shed light on its source, using our mind's eye, only then can we reveal the secrets of what it is trying to say. But all these things require at least some help from the mothers and fathers, to give their children guidance to captain their soul towards meaning. Where is such a place for children to find these things? Where can man now go to worship such holy practices? I look around myself and see the destruction and ridicule of all things holy. I just see endless worship of machines that function for what exactly? To merely keep us *breathing*. And what good is breathing if for no greater purpose? You might as well be dead. People see no other choice but to write off all classic tales as mere childish fantasy, archaic and irrelevant. And it is true, the church of the old Father may be dead. But I believe his spirit remains trapped in the undergrowth. But this chase for greater purpose is where our very problem lies, my readers. Within everyone's soul is a search for meaning, and it is the duty of us, *the guardians of the Tree of Life*, to make sure we help our fellow humans gain from its fruits; as it is with these fruits that they will find their meaning. *Have we forgotten that even such a tree exists?* That very sentence may seem insane to many, and dare I am one of them! But let us all fear not, because I know in my soul, and in my heart, that the return of the king is nearby. Let us hail the coming king! The king of the tree! King Arthur!'

Phillip's hands begin to sweat as he finishes reading the preface of the book. In his stomach, he feels an intense rush of energy; everything around him feels far more sharp and real, as if he were looking around in high definition.

He is overwhelmed with emotion and feels an urgent need to sit on the floor.

He flops to the ground, knocking many other books to the ground, and without care throws the prophetic book onto the lowermost part of the bookshelf.

Whilst he was reading, he forgot completely about the ecstasy tablet he took; he confused the intense feelings of coming up with his emotions during reading. These emotions triggered by the reading in their pure form were very real, but were no doubt further heightened by the drug. He was still confused at why the words he read resonated with him so profoundly, in ways he currently could not grasp fully. It was almost as if he was reading the words to himself, *from himself*, like a message from his soul demanding some sort of action. But what action exactly was something he did not yet know ...

After taking some moments to regain his composure (if you could call what he achieved 'composure', given he looked like someone who had just suffered an electric shock), he suddenly felt an intense and powerful urge to find Áine. He desperately wanted to share what he just read, to solidify and share his feelings; and he generally just wanted to connect with another human in his current state. It was extremely clear to him now that he was starting to feel the boost of serotonin that come along with the drug, and his empathy levels were in the need of immediate human contact and connection. He got to his feet as quickly as he had sat down, and begins speed walking frantically to try and find Áine.

'Áine?! Are you here? I'm really starting to feel it now ... Fuck ...' Phillip says in a drug-fuelled haze, cursing quietly to himself to express the great levels of energy and excitement he was feeling.

Phillip rushes into one of the main wings of the library like a man possessed by a demon, and stares ahead. And then, and in contrast, he sees an angelic sight indeed. Áine is sitting in front of large stained-glass windows, calm and composed. The sun is starting to rise, and beams of light are shining through the windows, illuminating the whole room in an intense, golden light. Behind the window, the branches of a tree are swaying in the wind, causing light to ripple and refract through the window in majestic and intricate patterns all over the room. He is in awe at this sight and is suddenly, and once again, emotionally overwhelmed. This very image would never leave his memory; it would, in fact, be a source of great motivation and solace for his future self whenever he was experiencing times of pain, adversity or struggle. Phillip's apprehension and anxiety evaporated in an instant. He now felt like he could relax and there was no need to rush or worry. This moment made such an impact on him that he takes a photo with a disposable camera he keeps inside his leather jacket so he could remember it for years to come.

He walks over towards Áine, with not a single thought going through his head. He touches her on her back whilst leaning down to sit on the floor with her. Immediately, Áine calmly touches his wrist, as if to signal she desired more intimacy.

She put her hand into his.

The pair locked gazes with their now heavily-dilated pupils, intense golden light from the window shining on the sides of their faces. Without any conscious input, their heads move closer together. They begin to kiss passionately, starting slowly until gradually the energy builds, and builds, and builds …

They lose complete control over their bodies, their hands gliding all over each other's skin. They continue to touch each other with great intensity and passion. Bathed in the sun's golden brightness, they begin to make love.

5. WHAT GOES UP MUST COME DOWN

The couple writhe ecstatically, completely unaware of the outside world. They are lost in each other, sharing energy in blissful synergy. Any fears, responsibilities, worries, any connection to the material world, melts away. Unaware of time, they continue to make love for nearly three hours until the thought suddenly occurs to Phillip that opening time must be fast approaching. .

'We should probably get out of here,' Phillip says, coming to his senses with a degree of sobriety and clarity.

Áine nods, and the pair look down the hall to visualise their exit. What they see, however, does not give them any comfort …

'Oh no!' Áine says whilst slanting her eyes towards Phillip, jaw slacked open.

At the entrance of the library wing, they see a few female librarians making a commotion. They are peering around the corner, clearly looking at the couple, wondering what to do.

'Come on, let's go,' Phillip says with confidence.

'But where? the only way out is to go past them!'

'Then let us go past them; we'll give them a nice smile, say good morning, and we will be all good. Trust me, Áine, doing everything with confidence and belief has been working for me so far.' Phillip gives Áine a wink with hint of cockiness.

Áine clearly has her doubts. She can't help but think this confidence is fuelled by the lingering effects of the MDMA. They both stand up. Phillip grabs Áine's hand and begins leading her with authority towards the wing's entrance, like everything is completely normal.

'Good morning, guys, how are you all today?' Phillip says as he walks past the staff.

The librarians look at the couple with disbelief and confusion on their faces. It is obvious by their dishevelled appearances what had been going on. Their dilated pupils added to the level of crazy they must have been giving off.

'See, what did I tell you? Everything with confidence,' Phillip says whilst smiling as they kept a lively pace of walking.

'We aren't out of the woods yet, though, and I honestly have a bad feeling about this. Did you see they all had radios?' Áine says with a doubtful look.

Phillip looks similarly worried. *She might be right*, he thinks.

The couple reach the entrance, and to their surprise, no one is there. They walk outside, and just as Phillip is about to take a sigh of relief, he sees two police officers standing there, along with one of the bouncers from the student union.

'Shit!' both Phillip and Áine mutter in unison, which would be comical were it not for the circumstances. It was at this moment that any feelings of euphoria, love, adventure or excitement from earlier instantly evaporated. They were now very anxious, despite still not being completely sober, yet both felt comforted by still being with each other, as if the night had already created a powerful connection that acted like a drug of its own. Phillip locks his gaze onto the two officers, and they stare back and the tension grows. It's clear from the officers' faces that they are both a little amused at the two dishevelled creatures squinting like vampires in front of them. Their smirks made Phillip feel little more relaxed; perhaps they won't be too bad to deal with.

'Phillip Stanley?' the officer asks.

'Yes, that's me,' Phillip says reluctantly, knowing it's in his best interest to save what little energy he had and avoid resisting.

'I am arresting you on suspicion of assault. You do not have to say anything, but it may harm your defence if you do not mention when questioned something which you later rely on in court. Anything you do say may be given in evidence. Do you understand?'

'I do, yes.'

'Okay. I'm also letting you know that your friend John and his girlfriend are at the station now being questioned.'

'If that is true, I also need to be there. I was a witness to the whole event, and believe I was also the cause. My name is Áine McCarthy, and this whole incident was triggered by this boy who I was seeing; he was being aggressive towards me in the club toilets. The boys were just looking out for me, and I appreciate it deeply.'

The officer looks at Áine with interest. Phillips's assumption was correct; this officer wasn't just a robotic, by-the-book type; he seemed genuinely interested in the truth and glad to hear Áine's heartfelt perspective on the matter.

'Okay, well, you better come with us as well,' the officer says as if he already knows where this is going but still must go through the motions.

Áine and Phillip are driven to the police station. They are escorted in by the two officers, although Phillip is not handcuffed. Phillip found this a little odd, and thought to himself that maybe they simply did not see him as a threat as he was careful to not argue or show any aggressive behaviour.

Before Áine and Phillip can even reach the station's front desk, they are surprised by a familiar trio who emerge from a side corridor. Behind an officer is Ishmael, who is followed by John and Suzy. The officer draws the attention of his colleagues and slides his finger across his throat in a cutting motion, shaking his head. The three officers begin talking.

'What the hell?' says a confused Phillip, the waves of euphoria he was feeling not too long ago rushing back to him.

'Don't worry, guys, I've sorted it all out. You're no longer under arrest,' Ishmael says with a warm smile on his face, knowing his news will bring nothing but relief and joy.

'Are you an undercover policeman or something? And weren't you the DJ back at the SU?' Áine asks, looking extremely bewildered.

Ishmael laughs.

'It's kind of a long story, but it turns out our friend Ishmael has had some dirt on big man Brian for a while,' John says.

'I've had an eye on him for some time, yes,' Ishmael says. 'I originally felt bad getting involved or saying anything because I didn't want to cause any drama; but over the past few months, Brian has been building a bit of reputation, and the incident with you, Áine, was the final straw. His behaviour has until now just been written off by the SU staff as aggressively flirtatious, and we all just accepted him for what he was.'

'What? A misogynistic cunt?' Suzy says with a snarl.

Ishmael purses his lips in agreement.

'Well, yes, it's hard to disagree with that. However, it's always a grey area with these incidents, isn't it? Many times I've witnessed girls who will put the blame on the man to purposely destroy their reputation, knowing full well what they are doing by playing the victim to something that was always mutually consensual. However, it was becoming harder and harder to give Brian the benefit of the doubt. Many of the girls he's been with have been coming back and telling the club what he's done; but most of these claims were vague, and the girls were drunk at the time, so no one really took them seriously. But recently, this one girl Melissa claimed that she was raped ...' The group all look at one another with raised eyebrows, and Áine shakes her head and looks up at the ceiling with welling eyes. 'So, the doormen, knowing of these previous claims, didn't take her too seriously. They had almost become accustomed to these accusations, adopting a 'here's another one' kind of attitude. If I'm being honest, the bouncers somewhat respected Brian for his ability to attract women. They saw him as a player, and they actually even looked up to him; this is why they all defended him so viscerally.'

'Seeing as Ishmael is close with management there, he was able to point police in the direction of CCTV proof of Brian's behaviour,' John continues. 'We aren't completely out of the woods, because we technically still assaulted him, but we have evidence, and therefore grounds to stand on now, that we used "minimum necessary force" to protect Áine from harm.'

'Oh, well, thank the lord and all that's holy for that. I was already beginning to feel suicidal from the lack of serotonin,' Phillip says whilst exhaling from relief.

Ishmael, John and Suzy all look at each other knowingly and smile to each other.

'What the hell have you two been up to?' Suzy asks mischievously.

Áine and Phillip look at each other a little embarrassed.

'We'll tell you about it later ... but let's just say it's been a crazy night,' Phillip says.

With sudden enthusiasm, Ishmael, as if being struck by an idea, says:

'Well, how about you all come round mine and talk over a joint? I'll make it really chill for everyone, get some nice euphoric beats on, put on some incense. Tonight's your night, guys.'

'Yep, well up for that,' John says.

'I won't smoke but, yeah, sounds good,' Suzy says.

'I guess we have a plan,' Phillip says. 'Áine?'

Áine looks at Phillip with a smile, and then at the rest of the group:

'Is the pope catholic?'

They all laugh and make their way out of the station.

6. ISHMAEL'S AFTERPARTY

The group walk into Ishmael's house. They are all surprised to see that he lives on his own, and by how nice his place is for student accommodation. Knowing how Ishmael enjoyed psychedelics, they were not surprised by the décor and vibe of his place. Hung up on the walls of the living room were multiple mandala rugs, which looked Persian in origin. What first hit the group when they walked in, however, was the distinct smell of incense. Whilst none was burning as they walked in, it was obvious he used it regularly; the smell seemed to be embedded into the furniture itself. John makes a passing comment about how he liked the smell, and Ishmael immediately scurried to a cabinet underneath his television where he kept his 'herbs of all sorts', as he put it, and lit up multiple incense burners around the room. It was a very pleasant place to spend an early morning, and considering all present hadn't slept yet, they all felt remarkably positive, calm, mellow and still not in desperate need to go to bed yet. It must be said, however, that this group were no strangers to late nights (technically more like early mornings) and all enjoyed the altered sense of reality (you could say delirium) that came with sleep deprivation. However, Áine and Phillip were in a far different state to the others, as they were now coming down off the ecstasy that they took back at the Bodleian; and whilst the group knew they had taken ecstasy, they were still puzzled as to why, where and when they had done so.

Regardless, the group rest in the pleasant atmosphere, which Ishmael so masterfully prepared for such occasions. Multiple Himalayan salt lamps give the room a gentle red glow; and incense smoke diffuses through the rays of subtle sunlight finding their way through the gaps in the curtains, which looked majestic to those in the room.

'Does anyone want to roll the joint? Or do you just want me to?' Ishmael says as he looks at the couples cuddling on the two sofas.

No one responds for a few seconds, until John quips:

'I think the silence says it all, mate.'

Ishmael smiles. He is quite glad to roll the joint, as he enjoys the process.

It was true Ishmael was a very empathetic and compassionate soul; when looked at you, it seemed as if he were seeing more than most do, and that he was always trying to see the best in people. Many found Ishmael quite weird for this very reason, however, and awkward to talk to because of this very piercing stare. His deep love for humanity was very present in his personality, but only obvious to certain people. More rational, objective, grounded and 'normal' people might clash with Ishmael because of how 'spiritual' and 'out there' he was. It was true that our group of four were not particularly normal per se, and all of them were more open-minded than most people, but even they found Ishmael's level of mysticism more than what they were used to. Phillip, however, was becoming more and more intrigued by Ishmael; he was already curious, from the few interactions they had at the jiujitsu academy, but since seeing him this morning, this had grown to new heights, and Phillip wanted to get to know Ishmael even more.

'Oh, and how could I forget?' Ishmael says as he finishes rolling the joint, walking over to the speaker next to the television to put on some chilled-out deep house which complemented the carefully curated ambience.

The group pass the joint round, not saying anything at this point, until Suzy finally breaks the silence.

'Soo, what happened with you two tonight?'

Everyone gives a laugh as it was clear all were thinking the same thing.

Phillip retells the night in detail; from how they sneaked in to the Bodleian Library, to the strange occurrence with the mysterious caretaker, to the book that he stumbled across (which at this point was also news to Áine), and finally, of course, to the quite literal climax of them making love as the sun began to rise. Phillip tried to convey the beauty and emotion he felt in this moment, but no matter how good he was with words (and he had a talent for storytelling) he still could not quite convey the profundity of this night which affected him in a deeply personal way and which he would always remember. The group all listen intently, with Áine occasionally chipping in with added details and slight adjustments.

'Well, can I just say, I believe this match made in heaven was down to me. I should start my own match making company, shouldn't I?' Suzy says after the story finishes, with a smug look on her face.

John is quick to recount his and Suzy's night.

'Jesus … Well, that certainly beats our night. It wasn't long before one of the bouncers caught up with us. The bouncer grabbed my wrist like I was some sort of naughty school child, and within 10 seconds a police car rocked up and we were both given the whole police spiel and put in the back.'

'And this is where I become involved,' Ishmael suddenly chips in.

John gives a slight laugh and continues with his account.

'Aha, yes. As we were sitting in the back, I see Ishmael running towards the bouncer and then briefly talking to him—'

Ishmael then cuts in.

'Yes, this bouncer is called Frank, and he is actually one of the more friendly ones who work there. Anyway, unlike the other bouncers, Frank and I regularly talk to each other about our thoughts and feelings on Brian. I am no fan of talking about others behind their backs; however, as I'm sure we can all agree, Brian is an exception. I am sorry, Áine, but you know it's true.'

'Oh, I'm not going to argue about that. Tonight has just made it so obvious. Before, I think I was just lonely and he was all I had ...' Áine says in a way that makes the others feel a little sad. They were surprised a girl as nice and as deep as Áine didn't have more friends than she did.

Ishmael continues to recall the events.

'So anyway, as you two were in the back of the police car, I basically told Frank that I had spoken to the general manager, Subu, about the CCTV footage of Brian being aggressive towards multiple girls in the club, and Subu told me to release the footage and let the police know. Subu is no fan of Brian; he was waiting for an opportunity to get rid of him, and lo and behold, a situation presents itself. So, after I gave Frank the lowdown, I let the officer know the story, and he said to come along as well to the station. As soon as the officers knew the situation regarding Brian, it only made sense to let you fellas off the hook regarding the assault inquiry. However, they will likely call you in again for a formal statement and to ask some questions. But hey, at least you are both here relaxing, and not spending the day in a cell.'

'Yeah, fuck that,' John says.

'John, I've known you for about two years now, and I know for a fact you would have loved to tick 'spending a night in a police cell' off your bucket list,' Phillip interjects smirking at John.

'Been there, done that already, mate.'

'I'm not even going to ask,' Phillip says through a laugh, realising he should have known. 'Guys, I just want to say something that's been on my mind, if, you don't mind ...' Phillip says with incongruous seriousness, summoning the group's attention immediately. 'Just after Áine and I dropped the pills in the library, I came across that weird book. Well, the book kind of left an impact on me in a way that I don't fully understand. When I was reading the words on the page, it felt like it was not fully … Well, real. It's hard to describe what I'm trying to say, but it was like I was reading my own thoughts … Or, more like my own soul … Anyway, what I'm trying to say is that this book prophesised about a return of a king; King Arthur, specifically. Do you remember how I told you how that caretaker said my holiest son will be called Arthur? It just seems too much of a coincidence …' The group look genuinely weirded out by this. 'Yes, exactly. Super weird … Anyway, the book went on to prophesise how this new king would return "the Tree of Life" to the world, and restore some sort of balance. The book described this new king as "the king of the tree".'

'You should have picked up the book and taken it with you. I would love to have a read of it myself,' John says.

'Hmm, yes, but my mind was all over the place; as I said, I literally started coming up off the pill right after reading the preface, and then went to find Áine.'

'I like the thought of a return of a wise king, though,' Áine says. 'These days all our leaders are just so one dimensional; they are either logical like a machine, lacking the essence that makes them human and relatable; or, they are honest and human to some extent, yet incompetent blathering idiots. We might as well have either machines or a chimp making the decisions for us, because that's basically what the leaders act like now,' Áine says with a sudden enthusiasm and passion, like this was something she had given much thought.

'Well, yes, and I think they think they are being logical and rational,' Phillip says, 'but they lack any understanding of their own humanity, their own biases; and many of our leaders ignore their intuition and deem it to be "irrational". They don't realise that beneath their "mechanical processes" lie biases based on their personality and temperament. Regarding the chimps, well, I personally would rather a chimp than a machine, because at least I can predict that a chimp will be a chimp; machines give me snake vibes. Anyway, let's be honest, all of us are flawed, and that's part of the human experience: making errors and learning from them. I just feel that there is no leader that represents the spiritual side of man and woman. It feels like we have a leader for the logistics of everything, but where is our leader for the real purpose of us, a leader for our higher meaning?'

'Yeah, well, it's a dangerous game though, isn't it, having a leader that leads us to "a higher purpose",' John says. 'There have been many examples of them in the past: Hitler, Stalin, to name a couple. They believed, or at least the people believed, that they were leading them to a higher spiritual cause, and the illusion alone got everyone to jump straight on board. But look how those turned out … Honestly, the only person to lead us should be ourselves. But then again, I suppose if a leader can set an example of discipline, and taking responsibility for what you know is best for *you,* and *your own conscience,* then I suppose that is a good thing.'

John sits back looking quite pleased at his rather rational and grounded contribution to the conversation.

'Yeah, that's a very good point, John; it is a dangerous game indeed. But could there not be a leader that is generally relatable to everyone, one like you said? A leader that unites the left and the right? Maybe we could have a king *and* a prime minister. One for spirit, one for material.'

'Well, Phillip, we do have that, and she's not a king, she's a queen you sexist pig,' Suzy chips in sarcastically, with a smile on her face.

Suzy considered herself a feminist to a certain extent, but not an extreme one by any means; in fact, she was a member of a feminist group at university and thought many of the members were girls with issues who used feminism to disguise their resentment and bad history with men. John was all too familiar with her thoughts on this, as he regularly received the backlash.

'Yes, it is true we have a queen, but let's be honest, what does she represent? I know she represents the spirit of whatever the UK is, on a symbolic level, a figurehead if you will. But the way things are going, it is like the monarchy is dying, and whatever they represent seems to be as well. Not to say it will completely die, but it seems to me that whatever it does represent needs an upgrade. Does it not make sense that a new, modern monarch emerges, one that represents the culture and spirit of the current generation? I mean look, I'm babbling here, and I know it sounds far out, but I look around and see structures becoming weaker and weaker. I mean, let's say the Queen represents whatever Christianity is in England, but what is at the very core of Christianity? I feel like most don't even really know what it is in a true spiritual sense; they just follow it like sheep.'

'Mate, you are getting deep here. Don't get me wrong, I love it, but are you sure it was just pills you and Áine took?' John says with a slight chuckle.

At this point Phillip notices Ishmael being very quiet, leaning back in his chair with faded, stoned eyes, listening with great intent. This spurs Phillip on to continue his stream of thoughts.

'Look, I've read enough Jung to know that all the world's religions have a sort of core, a core of all things. It seems to me that all religions are connected by similar and recurring symbols. Jung would call these connections archetypes; and religions call them gods, the Yin and the Yang, Christ, Shiva, etc. Anyway, all these 'archetypes' are to be found within ourselves, and out there in the universe! It's like these archetypes are the very fabric of reality, just in symbolic form rather than the mathematical form that the physicists of today prefer. But to be honest, I prefer to look at them as gods, and I think most humans do, because they are just far more relatable. We can connect to these gods, these processes, or simply our very nature, by putting ourselves in trance states by dancing, praying, meditating, taking drugs, whatever. The point is, if we don't connect to our human condition, we are sure to be taken over by the machines!'

After listening to Phillip's ideas carefully, Ishmael decides to give his input.

'I love what you are saying, my brother. And I too see much resistance and wars caused by the inability to understand one another. I see this with many of my Muslim brothers; they do not understand that at the root of all spirituality lies a constant, a bedrock, from where all the world's religions ultimately stem, a collective transcendent reality if you will. And all the world's religions are simply different ways of connecting and living by the same source energy, Allah, whom I also believe can be found within us all. What I find fascinating is your mention of the Tree of Life. I am not sure if you know, but the Tree of Life is the only symbol used by all the major religions. And it is no surprise, because trees are everywhere and are used metaphorically to describe much about the nature of reality. Look at lungs, plants, road networks, neurons: it's no coincidence they are all similar in structure. But tell me, Phillip, do you think it's possible that we could see a new messiah, a new king, one that represents the *general spirit* of all around the world? A new Muhammad? A new Jesus? Is this what you are saying?'

'Honestly, I do not know, Ishmael; I'm just rambling on about my feelings whilst on a comedown right now; I probably wouldn't take anything I'm saying too seriously. But what I can tell you is when I read that book in the library, it hit some sort of nerve deep within in me, in a way I can't explain.

And yes, I get these feelings that there is some sort of movement, some sort of energy building. We go to raves, we feel that energy; I feel people want to have something that helps them understand what they feel at these spiritual experiences, but other than some drugged-up veteran hippie in the corner, there seems to be a severe lack of wisdom in our cultures, a lack of spiritual understanding. It's like in our modern day and age, we have so much scientific knowledge and understanding but so little wisdom of how everything connects, of what the bigger picture is, of what the bigger meaning is. We are just so objective, so detail orientated, but we always miss the bigger picture. I feel our ancestors were in many ways wiser than us, even if they were less "smart" than us.'

'So, this return of the king you read about, you think he could be the one to connect us back to our spirituality?' Áine asks with great interest; being an intuitive girl herself, she felt herself to be alien to many other people, and for this reason she did not often engage in conversations with groups of people unless she felt comfortable enough to do so, or if she felt the group were on her level. She was someone who was greatly connected to her 'spiritual side', and she would make many connections and have insights that others would miss. It was for this reason she was most often misunderstood, and others would either not listen to her, or fail to understand her observations and feelings towards things; many would also call her crazy. It must be said with Áine, that whilst she had extremely strong emotions and inclinations towards things, it was not always easy for her to express exactly how she felt. To observe Áine alongside Phillip, it would be hard not to see them as a well-balanced couple for this reason: both were intuitive, but Phillip helped her articulate much of what she felt intuitively. When it came down to raw intuitive sensitivity, Áine was always faster to notice some subtle energy or shift; with Phillip, it would require more filtration and analysis, with the result being a more refined, more rational representation which was easier to articulate. Yet it seemed that Áine *felt the whole* more than Phillip ever could, regardless of her trouble articulating it.

'As I said, I have no clue, it's just an idea,' Phillip continues. 'But one thing I do think is that we are in desperate need of meaning, a common point of reference to find purpose and value in our life, and I believe that comes from a connection to something greater, a voice inside us that leads us to our higher purpose. I feel deeply passionate that there exists another divine realm beneath all our noses, and we so easily miss it because we spend so much time distracted; focusing instead on details and numbers, getting distracted by small branches and forgetting the main vine that connects us all together. We forget to look inside ourselves and find out what really matters; but it's always with us, and even familiar to us, so familiar we *take it for granted*. I just feel that in our countries, this way lacks representation, and all policy seems to be based on ideas that they think will be best for us, rather than something far deeper; at least that is where it seems like it's going. I don't know, maybe one day there could be a place people could go; a place people could connect to the spiritual world, to find their meaning, to find out who they really are; and at the same time, find out more about reality itself, as we are part of reality at the end of the day.'

'So … a cult, basically,' John laughs. John's face was slightly red, however, and a very intense feeling ran through his head, as if he were very much engaged and connected to what Phillip was saying but didn't want to fully admit his interest.

John felt it was important to bring Phillip's far-out ramblings back down to earth with a joke (that also contained potential truth). And, of course, it was necessary to play devil's advocate here, bringing light to the potential dangers of such ideas.

'Ha, well, yes, you could say a sort of cult; but it's not like it would be a place where people were told such and such and forced to follow certain rules due to some charismatic cult leader's pathological need to control and dominate. Maybe more like a club, or, I don't know, a church, a community centre, an academy! I'm rambling again, but somewhere people could go to connect to themselves and others, celebrate their humanity, seek wisdom and counsel, meet friends, dance! Feel love, learn wisdom from individuals with experience in life … I don't know … I mean, John, we train jiujitsu at Dean's academy pretty religiously; we wear weird robes and coloured belts, we have a weird handshake, but we don't call that a cult, do we?'

'Well, it's pretty debatable. It does feel like a cult sometimes … Not that I am complaining, I love the culty vibes, but at the end of the day it's just jiujitsu; it's not like Dean is stepping into spirituality, getting us to do weird rituals, read lines of scripture and put pig heads in our neighbour's bed to get our next belt promotion.'

'True, but he does make us run the gauntlet (a ritual in jiujitsu before a belt promotion where the individual must walk through a tunnel of people whipping their back) ... which, if I had a choice, I would probably pick the pig head ...'

'What you were saying back there, Phillip, about the place people could go to connect to their humanity, for some reason that reminds me of the Eleusinian Mysteries, in Ancient Greece,' Áine says with a sudden spark of curiosity.

'Oh yes, I have read about this. Doesn't new evidence suggest that they were likely doing psychedelics at the ceremonies? I believe I read that they would ingest this sacred spiked wine that contained ergot; ergot being the precursor to LSD,' Ishmael adds.

'Yes, that's what I was just going to say; I find it so interesting, because many classic historians are all so quick to write off the possibility that the Ancient Greeks, and philosophers such as Plato, would go to these sacred ceremonies and trip, basically. During these trips, these ceremonies, they would become 'initiates'; and they were taken on a journey involving puppetry, music, dance and all kinds of theatre that would ultimately give them a transcendent experience and certain insights to lose their fear of death.'

'I knew it! It just makes so much sense. I get this feeling sometimes, whenever I'm at a music event; a feeling I can't quite explain, but it makes me feel like my soul is freer, like I am more real, and have more clarity over my life,' Ishmael responds.

Suzy cannot help herself but laugh at all the things she is hearing.

'Okay, so basically what we are all saying is we should start a jiujitsu Jedi LSD cult ... I think maybe start with the jiujitsu academy idea first lads, and then keep the LSD thing on the back burner. Think it will be a bit of a hard sell,' she says with light-hearted sarcasm and doubt.

Suzy was aware that John and Phillip had previously discussed how amazing it would be to own their own martial arts club. She also knew that Phillip regularly gets carried away with all these ultra-creative and out-there ideas, and as much as she enjoys listening to them, she thought it important to be realistic as well. In a way she felt like it was her job to bring him back down to reality.

'How amazing would that be though, Phil, to have our own academy,' John says.

'Beyond words, mate. We have to get our black belts first, though,' Phillip replies whilst laughing, knowing they both had many more years to go before they achieved any kind of level where they could start teaching jiujitsu.

'We will get there. We just can't give up,' John says in a more serious and passionate tone. The lads look at each other as if to convey the message in a deeper and more meaningful way, as they both felt like this could be a reality with enough determination and hard work.

'Ishmael, you in on this too? Three black belts are more powerful than two, and a brain like yours could really add some dynamism,' Phillip asks as Ishmael stares at him, smiling, and then slowly nods with excitement at this proposition.

As Ishmael ponders at this idea, he imagines what the academy will look like and starts to feel warmth throughout his body, as if the future were in some way living in his very imagination and it was well within his grasp to achieve in reality. A chain reaction leads to him thinking of all the steps needed to realise this dream, and then suddenly, from nowhere, an idea comes to him.

'Well, if we are going to be working together in the future, it only seems right that we get to know each other a bit better, and I have an idea if you are all interested.'

The group suddenly perk up and turn their heads towards Ishmael in excitement.

'I was going to bring this up earlier, when Áine mentioned the Eleusinian Mysteries. But this weekend, I'm DJing at a festival in Bagley Wood, and funnily enough they've called it the Bagley Mysteries.' Phillip immediately laughs at this but is not quite sure why.

'It's not a standard type of rave, it's more of a hippy, arty kind of vibe, but it looks really cool and unique actually.'

'Oh, I'm pretty sure I've already heard about this. Didn't Dean mention this festival to us earlier, Phil?' John asks.

'Yes, he did indeed, and I was already up for going. I think this has just sealed the deal.'

'I'm coming too!' Áine interjects with a sudden enthusiasm.

'Okay, fuck it. But is it going to be the sort of festival where everyone is tripping on psychedelics and they are playing that weird, wobbly trance music?' Suzy says reluctantly. 'I'm not sure I want to commit to doing them at a weird festival, and I don't want to be pressured into taking them either, guys, I'm just saying that now.'

Suzy had been to many festivals before, but more orthodox and commercial events, and hearing the word 'hippy', put her off a little bit.

'Well, yes, I am sure a lot of people will be on psychedelics, but you will have fun regardless. Just come and enjoy the vibes, have a few drinks; there will be plenty to enjoy, even if you are sober!' Ishmael says. 'Plus, I am DJing, so it will be impossible to not have a good time. I've actually got a lot of new music I'm going to be playing for the first time too. I think it's unique, you're going to love it … Oh, and I have a cool friend who is going too. I think you guys need to meet him, especially after having this conversation today. His name is Adam. He is a depth psychologist, I believe, a student of Carl Jung; so Phillip, you are bound to get on like a house on fire. He is currently leading an experimental team here at the university. I believe they are conducting research into alternative therapies for various psychological conditions, and part of the research is using psychedelics and rituals to treat psychological conditions; so, it is no surprise he is a regular at these types of events.'

'How did you meet this guy, out of interest?' Phillip asks.

'At a festival, believe it or not,' Ishmael says, and they all laugh.

'Of course, silly question really. But yeah, I would love to meet him. Who knows, maybe I can even join his team of researchers after I graduate …'

'Funny you say that, because he usually brings members of his team with him to these kinds of festivals and gatherings, especially new members who haven't done any psychedelics before; he's very experienced in taking them, so he usually guides new members of his team through their trips and keeps them safe and grounded. He believes it's important all his team understand the psychedelic world first-hand, as he doesn't want them merely having a purely detached, logical and scientific understanding of what they do; he wants them to actually understand the experience themselves, which makes sense really, considering they will be working and treating patients experiencing this themselves.'

'Sounds like a hippy with a PhD to me,' Suzy says suspiciously.

'Oh, come on Suze, he's leading up a team at Oxford University; you really think they would just let some random hippy junkie do that? He's obviously a serious academic,' John says with a sudden passion and fire that catches the rest of the group a little off guard.

'Jeez, chill, I was kind of just joking ... But yeah, you know my thoughts on psychedelics; I am just very sceptical whenever anyone is super into them or worships them like they are the holy grail or whatever; there's other, safer ways of gaining wisdom. And as for treating psychological disorders, it just seems like a very grey area to me. Just go on a long walk or go travelling, or even a meditation retreat or something; it's still a trip, and you will still learn something about yourself and your life, just without the flying Mars bars. There's safer ways to achieve the same results. Just my opinion.'

Phillip tilts his head whilst listening to Suzy explain her scepticism towards psychedelics; thinking how he cannot help but agree with her common sense and grounded view. Phillip had not done psychedelics many times, and never at high doses. He had never had a bad experience, but he could certainly understand how they could be psychologically destabilising, especially if used incorrectly and not shown respect. However, Phillip also passionately believed society lacked a connection to the spiritual world, and believed without this the world around us would continue to become more and more cold, mechanical and bitter. He thought that if it were possible for psychedelics to be safely incorporated into society under a systematic approach, by people who understood the human soul, they could provide a portal for many to realise there is more to reality than meets the eye. And whilst they were certainly not the only way, they were indeed *a way*. One thing was for sure, though: Ishmael mentioning this man Adam had sparked an intense feeling of excitement within him, and he could not wait to meet him in person.

7. THE FESTIVAL

The day of the festival finally arrived. Ever since the group confirmed they were all going to go, excitement had built. They'd been to lots of music events before, but this one, from what they had been told, had an edge, and was quite different to what they were all used to. And so, it was natural that some (Suzy mainly) were a bit unsure if they would have a good time. That's not to say that Suzy was not open-minded; she enjoyed going out, experimenting with certain substances and trying new things. But she was more a creature of orthodoxy and status quo when compared to the others. Perhaps it is more accurate to say that Suzy was the most averse to taking risks out of the group. She provided an essential backbone of normality and common sense, as John, Áine and Phillip could all be described as some-what unorthodox characters. John was the most stoic and bold, Phillip the most creative and intuitive, and Áine the most mysterious and dreamy. Yet still, the novelty and *mystery* of this Bagley festival had, in a way, added an edge and another layer of excitement. Phillip was particularly excited, for a unique reason. Secretly, he felt attending an event like this with his new girlfriend could take their relationship to the next level. But deep down, however, he also felt a little vulnerable … He felt vulnerable because he had never felt this way towards a girl before, and this connection he so recently developed with Áine had happened so fast that he hadn't fully been able to grasp his feelings. He was somewhat scared that after sharing what could potentially be a magical day, his feelings could spiral out of control. Whilst this thought did cross his mind, he was somewhat ashamed and weakened by it, feeling rather pathetic and emasculated. After all, he *had* only known Áine for a week, and as much as he felt he could see right into her soul al-ready, he rationally knew it takes far longer to really get to know all of a person's dimensions and depth, and to fully develop trust. Yet still, this edge, this slight danger, added to the excitement for him.

John, whilst also excited, was a little apprehensive that Suzy would not enjoy herself, start complaining and affect the vibe of the group.

Two days before the festival, he even brought this up with her, saying: 'I know you aren't sure about this festival, Suze, but please just try and have a good time, and don't lower the vibe.'

She was particularly offended by this, replying: 'It might not be my usual type of festival, John, but I'm still getting to spend time with my friends on a day out, so obviously I'm going to have a good time and be happy. I can't believe you would think I'm going to be some sort of grumpy old woman constantly complaining ... Surely you know me better than that by now?'

John then quickly apologised and realised that what he was thinking didn't quite make sense, as Suzy was always conscientious enough to not allow her inner emotions affect others. Regardless, for some reason, he couldn't help but get the thought out of his head, probably because he was so desperate for this to be a great day out for all of them.

Áine had been particularly quiet about her feelings towards the festival, but inside she was probably the most excited of all the group, even more so than Phillip. Áine did not want to say it to the others, for a reason she could not quite explain, but she regularly attended these types of festivals, often going on her own. She would sometimes make new friends with strangers, which might be odd to some as Áine seems like a very introverted type. However, she in fact has no real problem approaching or interacting with people she gets good feelings about. However, she never really made any long-lasting friends at these events, and part of her felt saddened by this; she really did want to make strong, lasting bonds and to have friends she could rely on. Áine had an intoxicating, free-flowing charm which caused many to label her as a 'free spirit', or a hippy. She did not consider herself a hippy by any stretch of the imagination; however, she could not deny that she enjoyed being referred to as a free spirit. Because Áine was a regular at these more niche, arty festivals, she was also a regular consumer of psylocibin mushrooms, and it could be speculated that this led to her somewhat dreamy, spacey character. However, it is also true that since a child she had always been very much like this, and it is likely that it was her very open-minded nature that led to her interest in trance-inducing substances in the first place. And so, because of Áine's 'expertise' in this area, she was fully ready for this festival; in her little beige festival rucksack, she had multiple bags of dried mushrooms, with which she was ever so excited to surprise her newfound friends, albeit a little nervous to see how Suzy would react ... And indeed, she did feel these people really were her friends, and not just the ones she would casually meet and not talk to again. For once, she felt she had found a group who she really wanted to stay close with; and for this reason, she felt that this festival was a milestone moment.

The group are in Ishmael's van on their way to the festival. Ishmael is at the wheel, wearing orange-tinted sunglasses, a black T-shirt and jeans and a large straw cowboy hat. The group have already joked how they love his look, a sort of Iranian cowboy. Being an eccentric type, though, it suited Ishmael perfectly, and the consensus of the group was that, of course Ishmael would wear a cowboy hat to a festival.

The festival starts at noon, and they are due to arrive about 30 minutes later. Outside, the sun is shining through the trees with a beautiful afternoon radiance. The group are transfixed by the light blending and streaming through the cracks in the woodland, as if they are half-asleep. The sunlight warms their faces as they stare wide-eyed like children.

'Do you mind putting some music on? We need to get the party started! Maybe put on some of your new music, the music you mentioned the other day.' John says suddenly, picking up on the oddly quiet and somewhat apprehensive atmosphere.

'Oh, but we have to be patient!' Ishmael replies. 'If we play my music now, it won't be a surprise for when I play it during my set! And trust me, you will not have heard anything like what I'm going to drop ...'

'Well, you've definitely got me excited to hear it now, mate,' Phillip says. 'But no, I do get what you mean; I suppose when we get there and start hearing your music on the sound system, it will just hit us harder and be even more euphoric.' He looks over at John and smirks. 'But ... maybe you can at least give us just a little clue to how this music will be *different*. I mean, is it still your usual house and techno kind of vibe? Or have you gone for a completely different style?'

'Ahh, very intuitive of you, Phil. Yes, I have gone for a different sound this time. Well, not *completely* different, but more like I've tried to fuse two genres together to create a modern, yet classical sound.'

'Classical in the sense of classic house and techno, or actual classical music?' Phillip asks with a raised eyebrow, and then notices a smug look on Ishmael's face. 'No, you haven't, have you ...?'

'Whoa, wait, have I missed something there?' Suzy says, confused.

'Okay, well, I could be wrong, but what I think Ishmael has done with this new music of his is combine classical music with electronic music ... Am I right?' Phillip asks with his eyebrows raised, his head tilted and his mouth slightly ajar in anticipation.

'Yes, you are correct, Phil. I have always been a fan of classical music, and I just think it is a shame that most of our generation do not appreciate it. To be honest, I can understand why: its old school, requires more focus, not as 'catchy'… However, I just believe in the importance of not letting classical music die. The power of the classical instruments in an orchestra is something that can induce awe in the heart of any man or woman, young or old. However, the power, control and range of sounds we can create with electronic equipment must be respected, and is indeed the future. But what seems appropriate to me, and almost synchronistic, is the fact that beauty is always somewhere in between classic and modern, new and old. And I believe this formula applies to music as well; it is, in essence, *the way*, and not just for music, but for *life*. But today, and either way, I'm excited to know what you guys will think when you hear what I've done.'

'Whoa, that's deep! I love it, and I cannot wait to hear your tunes! I really enjoy listening to classical music too, especially when reading. I mean, I couldn't tell you all the names of the composers, but I still love the classical sound,' Áine says enthusiastically.

The van reaches the entrance to the festival, which is a basic, drive-through checkpoint of a small gazebo covering a table with a cash register and various wrist bands scattered across it. A short girl with blonde, braided hair, stands next to it looking particularly relaxed and content, and genuinely seems happy with her simple job.

'Hey, how's it going? You look very happy today,' Ishmael says as he pulls up his van.

'I am happy! How could I not be?! The vibes inside here are already so contagious. Everyone I speak to is excited and warm, and it is rubbing off on me! I love it!' The girl looks through the window where Áine is sitting and lets out a gasp. 'Oh my god … Is that you, Áine?'

Áine is a *little* taken back, but she is not as surprised to see her old friend here as her friend is to see her.

'Oh my, what a lovely surprise. Guys, this is an old friend of mine, Jess. We met a while ago at a similar event.'

'You guys look like you've got history,' Phillip says, realizing there is some interesting tension between this girl and Áine, although he cannot quite figure out the reason behind it.

'Oh yes ... We have been through an interesting journey together,' Jess says as she gazes at Áine, her face blushing a little. 'I would love to tell you the story, but I will probably get told off for taking too long ... All I will say is you guys are lucky to be spending the day with this beautiful soul. It is rare to find someone as warm and kind as this girl. Anyway, have a lovely day, guys, there's already an amazing energy in there.'

The braided girl takes their tickets and then gives them all a wrist band. She then locks her gaze intensely on Áine, blowing a kiss and bowing slightly, her face still slightly flushed. This was picked up on by the group and made them all very intrigued to know the history of these two.

'So how do you know her then?' Suzy asks with a curious smile.

'We met at a similar festival a while back and went through a quite intense bonding experience ... I will tell you guys more about it later, but yeah, it was quite intense and weird and left an impact on both of us. It is strange because I have only met her once, but if you were to look at us you would think we were lifelong friends, wouldn't you? To me, there's something beautiful about that, but also, it makes me feel a little weird ...'

The group, appreciating Áine's introversion and privacy, leave it at that and do not probe any further, albeit with their curiosities piqued at this point.

Ishmael finally parks up his van and they all eagerly jump out.

Phillip and John have decided to both wear black jeans and T-shirts that represent their academic and spiritual interests: John's features the stoic philosopher Marcus Aurelius wearing sunglasses on a black background, while Phillip wears a white T-shirt depicting a large, colourful mandala on it, which he thought would be much appreciated at a festival like this. On some level, he was hoping it would spark conversation with other people. Their clothing is in contrast to the style of the girls, although they weirdly complement each other. Áine has gone for a more liberal look, with loose-hanging, green 'hippy pants', with various mandala patterns and a matching light hoodie. Suzy has gone for double denim jacket and jeans with a white T-shirt underneath.

And so, to the group wander into the festival, into the depths of the greenery, with the sun still shining and flickering through the cracks in a way that seems more vivid to them than it would on any other day. Various other groups of festival-goers wander in beside them, wearing all kinds of clothing, most of which is brightly coloured. There was certainly a spiritual theme to the style of dress. Phillip, who considered himself a 'spiritual' yet also analytical person, took particular note of this and thought to himself: *I wonder how many people here have a genuine interest in the spiritual world, and how many are simply here for the ride? Then again, just being here for the ride is also spiritual, no? What even is spiritual? How can I pin it down? Clearly the spiritual is not merely intellectual and rational, but more of a felt nature ... But why is it that this clothing becomes cool in the first place? I suppose at some point it snowballs in popularity and becomes cool because everyone's wearing it, but at its root there must have been something that resonated within the soul of that very first trendsetter, something felt, yet not quite logically tangible.* Phillip stops himself from analysing any further; he realises that it would be easy for him to get carried away with this train of thought, and he knows it will bring him out of enjoying the moment and make him seem distant and distracted. Phillip was no stranger to these moments of inner analysis and streams of consciousness; in fact, he enjoyed them and they made him who he was. However, he did have to stop himself on occasion, and it was not uncommon for him to receive comments from others about him not being 'present'. These moments of intense inner analysis made him seem locked in his head rather than in his body; they also made direct action harder, essentially causing a sort of *paralysis by analysis.*

The group approach the first designated area of the festival: a large, open, circular space with lots of places to sit down designated by lush rugs on the floor, once again with mandalas on them. At this point, distinct low frequency beats can be heard from the stage area further along. This circular communal area has various smaller speakers as well, but they are playing more ambient, gentle music. To the left is a separate, smaller section containing various food stalls and some portable toilets. Fairy lights are intricately laced around the communal area, spiralling around multiple poles embedded into the ground and above their heads, which when dark will become a ceiling of lights (there is a general chatter among the group of how beautiful they will look when night falls).

The group decide to sit on one of the rugs first, as it seems very chilled out and a good place to make base before they enter what they assume to be a more chaotic area. There are also strong, distinct smells of incense burning, although it is not obvious where they are coming from.

The group instinctively wander over to one of the rugs on the right side of the circle and sit down to settle in.

'Okay, this is actually quite nice. I was expecting to be overwhelmed by the stench of dirty hippies by this point. My only criticism currently is they decided to put the toilets next to the food vans … That is a bit weird, you must admit,' Suzy remarks light-heartedly.

'Thank God! She actually likes it, she likes it everybody!' John says, followed by a slow, sarcastic clap.

Áine, Phillip and Ishmael try to restrain their laughter to avoid being insensitive or rude to Suzy. Suzy does not take John's overreaction badly at all, but in fact laughs to the surprise of the others. It is clear she is doing her best to enjoy herself and not let her own perceptions negatively influence the group.

'Well, we haven't even begun yet! I didn't tell you this, but I'm actually a regular at these sorts of festivals. I was even planning on going to this one …' says Áine, turning her head to guiltily look at them all, her face flushing somewhat.

They all stare back, as if expecting her to say something else.

'Go on, I know there's something else you want to say,' Phillip says in a very caring and soft tone, assuming that on some level she feels guilty about whatever happened with the braided girl from earlier. Áine instead stares straight at Suzy, as if to focus her guilt on her.

'I'm sorry, Suzy …' Áine says, her guilt peaking.

8. THE FORBIDDEN FRUIT

'**Y**ou've brought magic mushrooms, haven't you?' Suzy sighs, with a reluctant acceptance in her voice, like she is not surprised and thought it was only a matter of time.

Áine brings out a pouch of mushrooms from her little beige bag and passes them round the group; the boys immediately lean in with excitement to take a closer look.

'Okay, well, I thought I was going to have to find some myself for you guys, but now you've made my life a little easier,' Ishmael says with a smirk on his face, knowing this moment would happen at some point today but not expecting it to be this early.

'Guys, you have as much fun as you want. Do the mushrooms! I want you to. I'm going to have a great day either way, I'm already loving it,' Suzy says briskly, with a slightly forced warmth.

'I reckon if you just take one of those little ones, you'll get a nice little high,' John says with a degree of caution, but also humorously, causing the others to laugh.

John very much wanted his girlfriend to be in this with them. He had already decided he was going to trip, but knew he would feel awkward if his girlfriend was not on the same level. Not only that, he knew that it would play on his conscience if he left his girlfriend to her own devices in the 'sober' world. But his desire to take the plunge was winning the battle with his moral conscience, and he knew this. He also knew, from his knowledge of the drug and its effects, that his conscience would be heightened after taking it, which could potentially lead to a bad trip. The others see this struggle expressed on John's face, giving subtle smiles of recognition to each other. If the others were also being honest, they very much wanted Suzy to at least do a little bit, so they could all be in their soon-to-be-altered state of consciousness together. Thankfully, however, Áine was no stranger to these types of circumstances and had become an expert of making others feel comfortable and relaxed when it comes to psychedelics. She and Ishmael had both witnessed people having bad trips and, more importantly, both had their fair share themselves; giving them both an understanding of what to expect if things did indeed start to go south.

'I want you to know that as much as I would love you to trip with me, Suzy, I also want you to make your own decision. All I want is for you to enjoy today. But I will just say this: if you were to do any, I would stay with you the whole time, always by your side. And John has got a point; you only do have to do a little bit,' Áine says, suddenly quite intense and sincere, looking right into the eyes of Suzy with an aura of kindness and understanding.

Suzy holds the gaze with Áine for a few moments.

'This has just reminded me of my friend Adam; he messaged me this morning saying he's looking forward to meeting up,' Ishmael says. 'I have already told him about you guys, and he said he would love to meet you all. So, Suzy, you will be in some of the safest hands if he joins us. Not many people can have their first trip guided by a depth psychologist.'

Suzy looks around to see all their faces staring right at her, eagerly awaiting her response.

'Well, for fuck sake … I haven't really got a choice now, do I? I will do *one* of them. But only because I trust Áine.'

The whole group begin to shout at once with great excitement, clapping their hands and cheering ecstatically. Other groups nearby look over to see what all the fuss is about. It may seem like an overreaction, but having Suzy willing to join them on their trip was something the group was thrilled by. And so, Áine hands around the mushroom pouch, and they all consume varying amounts, with Áine saying she has got 'loads more' if they want more later.

The group then decide to walk around the festival and explore, whilst they wait to start feeling the effects. They venture towards the main stage area, from where the low bass frequencies are coming. It is in a similar configuration to the chill-out area, but with a less pronounced circular shape. It's more of a natural opening, which gives the feeling of being 'among the trees'. In the middle is the DJ area, with the stage looking like a Greek temple, with various columns standing tall. A large banner at the top says 'The Bagley Mysteries' in a bright neon green with Grecian font. The surrounding woodland is dotted with various animal sculptures: polar bears, tigers, lions, various monkeys and bats (hanging from the branches); and, for some bizarre reason, the organisers decided to put a life-sized giraffe halfway up a tree, as if it got stuck during an attempted climb, much to the amusement of onlookers.

The group feel the music vibrate in their chests, and all are immediately filled with a warm and comforting feeling. The music is deep, euphoric, yet also chilled, with a warm and pronounced bass that can be felt vividly and intensely inside all bodies within the stage area. It was a type of house, close to being psychedelic or electronica, with a liquid feel that could be observed in the dancers' movements. It was as if those dancing were merely electronic conductors for the music, receivers for the *vibrations.*

As the group begin to dance and flow, Phillip looks around curiously with squinting eyes, entering one of his deep thought streams: *Is the dancer really in control right now? Or is the music? Or does the answer lie somewhere in between? It is hard to tell at this point how many people around me are under the influence of drugs, as at this point it is still early in the festival, so it is to be expected that most will still be relatively sober. One thing is certain, though, everyone around me is affected by the atmosphere to some extent, and the simple gathering of people under the music is enough to create an inescapable feeling of blissful ecstasy; I'm definitely feeling it, aren't I! I suppose, in a way, it can be justified as opening up our energies by tapping into the instincts that have evolved from mankind's days as animals through to tribal cultures; the natural empathy circuits are being triggered to a massive extent, and it is hard to not feel like you are part of a sort of tribe, a family. We forget that, in terms of evolutionary timescales, tribal cultures were not at all that long ago, biologically speaking anyway … Something us humans all too dearly require is a feeling of belonging, a feeling of togetherness, a feeling of unity under something. And in this case, the something is the music, and the faces around me show that they are desperate for it and soaking it up … Even Suzy is letting go now: she looks like she's in the moment and very relaxed … It's interesting as well to watch people's style of dancing, individual to individual, and how this seems to naturally correspond with their personalities. Hmm, it sort of reminds me of when John mentioned Suzy getting annoyed at his movements. It seems clear to me that whilst it is easy to laugh at this, and to write it off as irrational or childish, I do think it contains merit, as if there is some sort of reaction between two different substances. This continuous clashing process or battle is essential for any type of spiritual growth, and that applies on both the individual and relationship level.'*

Phillip turns his gaze to stare at John dancing.

When we look at John dance, we can clearly see elements of rigidity, focused aggression, order, composure and precision. All a direct expression of his nature, his self. It's a beautiful thing, really, the music inducing a trance state that has diluted his ego to a degree where only the depths are left. It is no surprise to me that when we watch a dance coming from a place of pure egoless expression, we are naturally captivated because it is only the most timeless, pure parts of the personality that remain. When we dance with the self-examining eyes of our ego, it is easy to be a little embarrassed and intimidated. We aren't really letting go and being ourselves, are we? I wonder if I'm dancing well right now … I'm definitely flowing well with these thoughts; my body feels pretty loose too, so I guess I must look pretty loose … Anyway, I guess it is natural when we witness this pure spirit, whether that be in speech, dance, writing, art or any act of true self-expression, that our ego tries to diminish the show, or to reduce it to something it is not, to make it feel better; as it may be afraid to look at it's very self for what he or she actually is. But I guess it's there to try and spot the flaws, like a sort of self-regulation system … Either way, I like seeing people show their whole self; it's beautiful, even with all the flaws, the imperfections, the vulnerabilities it contains. It is indeed a powerful show, and may make others gravitate naturally, regardless of whether that person is friend or foe. Being oneself is a powerful force of attraction to any human being. For when we show the world who we really are, and take off our mask, we are at our most vulnerable to attack. But this is where we have our power. Do not let them reduce us to just a mask! Dance with strength and courage, I say! Into darkness, with your light burning bright! Let the dance give you clear vision, protection and fight! Holy shit, Phillip, calm down your thoughts and focus on your body now, your brain needs to chill out for a bit, mate …

Áine bobs and floats around angelically, with soft and subtle movements with her hands and head. Her eyes look up towards her forehead, as if she is in a dream of sorts, or at least in a deep meditation, in which it was obvious she was well practised. Phillip dances closely beside her, with a style just as relaxed and open but with more power and conviction but less grace and finesse; the masculine equivalent, if you like (although still with more flow than Suzy and John).

At this point, and without them even realising, Ishmael had gone up behind the DJ decks. He was not yet DJing, but bantering with various other faces he recognised, presumably fellow artists getting ready to begin their sets. At this point, the group's dancing calmed for a moment, as if they all at once felt a shift in themselves and in the world around them.

'I'm definitely starting to feel something … Does anyone else think light seems … sharper?' John states above the music, looking at his friends beside him.

'Maybe, it's hard to tell; today the light has seemed a little more vivid than usual for me anyway. Maybe let's go back and sit down over in the chillout zone for a bit,' Phillip replies, as the group head back.

Ishmael spots his friends move from the DJ area, and realises it is likely because they are beginning to feel the drugs kick in. He cannot deny that he is also starting to feel an energy in the pit of his stomach, and he all too well knows what that means ...

Áine and Phillip silently lie on one of the rugs, facing upwards towards the sky, their hands in each other's, looking very calm and relaxed together. John and Suzy are sitting up, their faces inches away from each other, conversing quietly and looking very intimate.

'I just can't put my finger on it. I don't know if I feel good or not ...' Suzy says with uncertainty and a touch of fear.

'Just relax, babe, enjoy the feelings; you are going to have a lovely experience. I'm here for you, okay? We're in this together.'

As John finishes his words of comfort, he caresses the back of her head softly. Suzy embraces John, and they hold a passionate cuddle for several moments.

Phillip sits up as well, and Áine does too. They both look over to see John and Suzy cuddling in silence; Phillip and Áine's eyes lock with a sudden intensity, and then Phillip gently pulls Áine's head towards his, and they begin to kiss slowly but passionately.

From the opening of the mainstage area, a straw cowboy hat can be seen bobbing towards the group.

Ishmael.

And he walks with two others. The first is in his early 20s, wearing a black T-shirt and blue jeans. His face has a sort of pleasant, childlike radiance and he gives off a friendly but somewhat vulnerable vibe. His looks around wide-eyed at the greenery. To the side of him is a slightly older man, around six-feet tall; early 30s or late 20s, it is hard to tell exactly. His face is quite angular, with a strong jaw, yet also has a feminine quality, making him not look too aggressive yet not too passive either. From just his movements you can tell he has great maturity, composure and confidence, yet he seems laid back rather than arrogant. It is easy to understand why the younger man to his side may feel at ease because of this man's leadership qualities. He also wears a wooden cross around his neck, which catches Phillip's attention immediately, as it is a sign of his spiritual connection. Phillip notices Ishmael with these new people out of the corner of his eye, and stops his kissing at once, turning to look towards them.

'You guys look all very loved up over here!' Ishmael says as he approaches. 'This is my friend Adam I was telling you guys about.'

'Oh, it is so amazing to meet you! Sorry … We have all taken some mushrooms and I am beginning to feel a little like liquid …' Phillip begins laughing to himself. 'Sorry if I'm not as composed as I should be, I really respect your work, if you know what I mean …' Phillip says with childish innocence, coming across a little nervous and embarrassed.

Adam at first does not respond to Phillip, but instead silently sits next to him, pulls out a bottle of vitamin water from his rucksack and passes it to Phillip with a smile.

'I wasn't expecting you to be feeling *solid* and composed right now. If you are starting to feel like *liquid,* it makes sense you drink some!' Adam says confidently. 'This drink contains electrolytes, so they should keep you all nice and hydrated through your trip. Here, take them.' Adam passes around multiple bottles to the group, which they gratefully accept. 'It is lovely to meet you all. Ishmael is a close friend of mine, and I trust him dearly; he tells me this group of yours has such a deep sense of love to it, and it didn't take me long to work that out myself!' Adam smiles, clearly referring to the cuddling and kissing he saw as he approached. 'I would like to introduce you guys to one of the new members of my research team, James. It is a little rite of passage I like to do with new students to initiate them into my team; that is, I guide them through a psychedelic trip. Of course, I do all I can to bring about a most productive and positive trip. Well, I try my best anyway; whatever needs to come out, will. Whether that be good or bad energy.'

At this moment, our group all look over at Adam's student, James, who can be seen caressing a medium-sized oak tree to the right of the rug where they sit, rolling his hands over its bark.

'Hey, James, meet these lovely people, they are beginning to enter your world,' Adam says.

'Sorry, guys, I'm still here; it's just I feel so connected to nature!' James says, and then laughs to himself innocently.

The rest of our group cannot help but understand James's attraction to the tree and smile back at him, wanting him to join them on the rug.

'Yeah, come sit with us, mate! There's space for you too!' John says with uncharacteristic compassion.

'Oh, why thank you. You lot seem so nice!' James replies, and then flops himself down onto the rug, leaning on his elbows by his side, with a rather large smile on his face. He looks at the others with such warmth, openness and willingness to connect.

'That tree has such a life to it, doesn't it? You were really feeling it, weren't you?' Áine says knowingly.

'It was calling me! I felt its pull! I love trees!' he replies.

'There is something about mushrooms and nature … I just don't know what that something is, but there is definitely something …' Phillip adds, beginning to feel extremely contemplative.

'That something is *divinity*,' Adam says, smiling with sincerity, his eyes showing a calm intensity, although still with a vulnerability and meekness to them; it was a look that can only be described as showing a sort of all-encompassing spiritual love.

At this point, Suzy and John were still close by each other's side. Suzy hadn't said much; John, realising this, made an effort to focus more of his love on her, to provide comfort. As quiet as she was, she was captivated by Adam; something about him made her extremely curious: the way he sat, the way he spoke, the tempo of his words; but more so, what he meant by 'divinity'. If she had not been in the state she currently was in, she may have written off this comment as a well-meaning delusion.

'What is divinity?' she asks suddenly, breaking her silence. All eyes turned to Adam for a response to this profound question, as if without question he was an authority on all things deep and mystical. This might seem odd considering he had only sat down, but he had such a strong presence that seemed almost ethereal and otherworldly; something about his movements triggered innate feelings, something warm inside that made all around feel attracted to him in a subtle, unconscious way.

Adam looks around at the faces staring back at him and takes a few moments to see if the answer comes to him.

'I'll show you,' he says suddenly, standing up and walking towards the centre of the circle.

When he arrives at the centre point of the area, those surrounding him looking over at him curiously, he faces the sun (which at this point is at its highest point as it's just gone noon). As he looks up, the sun shines brightly against his face, and naturally he closes his eyes. He puts his hands out to his side, slightly away from his body, and turns his palms to face up. He takes a few deep breaths, and enjoys the feeling of sunshine on his skin, a slight smile appearing on his face.

He drops to his knees and moves his hands onto his knees, clasping them together.

Adam had only been here for a few moments, but already many people nearby were beginning to look and point with great curiosity. Phillip is the first to walk over and join him; he kneels to the left of Adam, clasping his hands and closing his eyes. Áine, John, James and Suzy quickly follow suit, all captivated by this bold action. The underlying compulsion to do so was felt strongly, but not fully understood by any of them. John briefly thought: *I'm not sure what I make of this fella. He's giving me vibes of both Jesus, and Charles Manson ... Fuck it, I'm on mushrooms ...*

Ishmael had mysteriously disappeared at this point, but this fact went unnoticed.

So the group kneeled together beside Adam, facing the sun, bathing in meditative bliss. Any feelings of anxiety, nervousness, fear or apprehension were dispelled. Instead, they felt an energy build within their stomachs, a feeling of complete freedom within their souls; they felt like they were masters of themselves, and that they could do anything. Everything felt so clear; there was so little confusion, so much understanding. At this point, the group were having a powerful impact on those around them, and others began to kneel with them. It started with the odd person, but then entire groups began to kneel with them. It got to the point where even people in the main stage area could see this shift happening, and some would come back and join the kneeling. All were facing the sun in ceremonious and unified glory. After about 20 minutes, there were about a hundred people kneeling, a bizarre but beautiful sight indeed. During this time, some would stop kneeling and assume more casual positions, couples would engage in intimacy and people came and went at will.

And then, Adam stands up at the front of the crowd, smiling, and says: 'Does anyone fancy a dance?'

Smiles break out across the faces in the crowd, a yes that did not need to be uttered but only felt. It seemed that everybody within this now large group had developed a sort of psychic connection; they had built up spirit from the inside, and they all felt the same way. Now they wished to convert this newfound energy into *movement*. So, Adam led them into the main stage area, which was a sight indeed. How on earth did this one man have so much power and leadership over strangers? It was an awe-inspiring mystery.

Those already at the main stage, seeing this group enter, gape in surprise and fascination at the sight. There are even looks of jealousy, suspicion and even resentment. As soon as the crowd enters, the energy increases tenfold, and the air feels electric. Everyone is ready to dispel their built-up charge, to channel their life force into movement. It is at this moment that Ishmael appears on the DJ decks. Phillip, Áine, Suzy, John, James and Adam all begin cheering ecstatically. They feel almost disconnected from their bodies, the world around them like a beautiful dream; light was brighter, the air felt thick and sweet, and sound seemed to vibrate with frequencies that didn't even exist to them before. And because of this, they had completely forgotten about Ishmael while they were in their trance. Well, apart from Adam … He didn't seem shocked at all at Ishmael appearing up on the decks. It is still not certain whether what happened was planned by Adam and Ishmael, or whether it simply came together organically. Either way, Ishmael was ready to unleash his new sounds. As he takes over from the previous DJ, there's a brief moment of silence before he begins playing while the excitement builds.

The first song begins with intense orchestral strings, the intensity rising. A subtle, rhythmic bass enters, building with the strings until a euphoric crescendo is reached.

The pressure is released.

The crowd goes wild, but not a chaotic way; the movements are still fluid, but the tempo is now faster, like a little boiling water bubbling over the pan. This intensity simmers for another half an hour.

Around the main stage area, the vibe has now become a little weirder. Many people are now crying; not with sadness, but because they are overwhelmed with a deep and spiritual awe. Friends look at each other seriously, shaking their heads in disbelief. Others even walk off into the woods and try to stay standing by leaning on the trees, as if they simply cannot handle the energy that has been shot into them.

9. THE PROPHECY

The following experience was a landmark point in the lives of the group. Afterwards, things began to get progressively more complicated for all of them. In some ways you could say their lives became simpler because their destinies had been brought to light, their paths had been illuminated, and this gave them direction and purpose.

Up to this point in their psilocybin trip, things had been relatively normal (as much as it can be during a psilocybin trip) and enjoyable. Both Phillip and Áine were laid back people, and Áine was no stranger to the drug, so you would *expect* in general it would be smooth sailing. That was, however, until the ante was increased …

As soon as Ishmael began his rather intense DJ set, and after Adam had brought his 'army' to the dance floor, the festival really began to get going. People started to reach peaks on various substances, and there was a general climactic energy for several hours culminating in chaotic scenes.

As soon as the music reached full intensity, people's inhibitions loosened even further and different groups staying together became a thing of the past. Everyone now mingled and talked to each other as if there were no barriers between them. That is the ones who could still use their mouths to communicate, anyway …

The music had everyone focused on the dancing, and for around an hour all the group were dancing together. They regularly exchanged loving smiles, hugged each other relentlessly, and took many photographs of them all together. Everyone was just loving the experience.

After the first hour had passed, Áine felt like it was a good time to ask if anyone wanted more mushrooms. She once again brought out her bag and handed it around the group, with James, John and Suzy all taking some more. Phillip gave her a puzzled look as to why he wasn't offered any.

'Let's go to one of the rugs, I want to show you something,' Áine whispers in Phillip's ear. 'Guys, we will be two seconds,' she says to the group, whom give casual smiles and thumbs up in return.

Phillip and Áine re-enter the circular zone and see that people are much more scattered, with many of the rugs mysteriously missing and people sitting on the grass instead. They manage to find a rug for themselves, albeit a little more dishevelled and dirtier than it was before.

They both lock gazes and share a few moments where they just smile at each other without speaking.

'I've really enjoyed today with you,' Phillip says with a warm and sincere look, a slight squint in his eyes, the dimples on his cheeks showing strongly in the sunlight.

Áine looks down and blushes a little, smiling to herself. She looks back up at Phillip.

'So, I came over here because I just want us two to do this … I made us a little treat to share,'. Áine says excitedly and with a hint of mischief.

She rummages again through her bag and brings out a small flask.

'Why do I get the impression that there isn't orange juice in there?' Phillip smiles.

'It's some mushroom tea I made. Admittedly, it is extraordinarily strong, and maybe contains a few extra ingredients … It will hopefully send us to another dimension. You ready for this?'

Phillip takes the flask and has a look inside. He takes a few sniffs. The liquid is dark black like the night, with a surprisingly thick viscosity for 'tea'.

'Half each?' Phillip asks.

'Pretty much. I would say drink just over half as you are heavier than me; that should bring us to the same place then.'

Phillip stares once again into the flask. The liquid seems alive swirling and waving like a living, breathing organism. Staring into this black liquid was like staring into an abyss, directly into the unknown; and this excited Phillip greatly. He gives the flask a quick twirl with his wrist and takes a large couple of gulps, looking inside it again to inspect how much he drank.

He passes the flask to Áine, and she quickly drinks the rest.

'This is going to hit us like an absolute train isn't it …' he says after a sigh, looking at her whilst tilting his head down, frowning. 'Come on, let's ground ourselves in the music, it will keep us centred.'

Phillip stands up with a burst of energy, as if he was forcing himself to be conscious and active against the coming waves of lethargy and liquid psychosis which were beginning to bare down on him.

As they re-join the rest of the group, they notice faces are a little less happy and a bit more serious.

'Is everyone feeling good?' Phillip asks as he walks towards them, opening his arms wide, and forcing a smile.

'Suzy has gone in quite deep and has lost her footing,' Adam says casually and quietly. Phillip looks over at Suzy and sees her head swivelling around manically, no longer dancing.

'Have you not got any tricks or methods to get her back grounded?' Phillip replies.

'Don't worry, Phillip, I am watching. I will step in if I need to; however, for now I'm going to give you guys space and will continue to guide you subtly.'

Almost immediately after Adam says 'space', John attempts to comfort Suzy by putting his arm round her. This doesn't go down well; she pushed the arm away like he was some repulsive creature that had landed on her, and it seemed at this point she didn't even recognise that John was her boyfriend. John himself wasn't looking great: his face was making bizarre contortions and contractions, and clearly he was trying his best to hold himself together. He was feeling quite overwhelmed with everything; like he couldn't stay focused on everything being under control like he usually did.

'You got any ideas?' Phillip asks Áine. 'I just want to try and help her before we start feeling the effects from the brew and become incapable of helping anyone.'

'I think keeping her in the dance area is a good idea for now,' Áine says as she stares forward in a laser-beam trance, clearly trying her hardest to summon her rationality, 'but if she gets worse, we should take her on a walk in the forest. We could maybe try and distract her with something, to break her thought loop.'

After hearing Áine's response, the word 'distraction' began to echo inside Phillip's mind. He seemed to not be able to control it; it was as if the word connected itself to something and was waiting to find form. He closes his eyes and tries to focus. Five seconds pass, and his eyes open with sudden force. He walks over just past Suzy, who is now beginning to show small, yet real, signs of fear on her face. Phillip at first ignores Suzy completely, and then he looks up at the tree where the model giraffe is placed and begins to point at it.

'Oh my god! There's a giraffe stuck up a tree! We must help him!' he shouts with force and conviction, causing others around him to squint upwards and inspect this giraffe for themselves. 'Hey, you! Have you seen the giraffe? I think he needs our help!' Phillip says towards Suzy, now catching her attention.

Her head looks up and she sees the giraffe for herself.

'We have to save him! How can we save him?!' Suzy says desperately, sounding close to tears, her eyes are wide and sad.

It is clear every bone in her body feels a compulsion to save this giraffe at all costs. It is almost like the energy and suffering she was feeling previously has now refocused on this giraffe; providing her with a goal that she can reach. John looks at Phillip with a confused face. He is still just about rational enough to understand that in reality there isn't a giraffe up a tree, but a part of him really *wanted* to believe, to play the game and take part in this fantasy.

Adam is standing on the outskirts of the stage area, watching events unfold. His face is curious; he squints and strokes his chin, looking impressed with how Phillip was dealing with the situation. Adam has his arms behind his back, stance wide, as if what he is paying attention to is part of his work and deserving of his attention and focus.

'How can we reach him? He's so high up on the tree!' Suzy says with a childlike innocence.

'Phillip, get on my back,' John says.

Phillip responds with an uncertain look, his legs beginning to feel very unstable and relaxed. But he naturally plays along, and bends down to allow John to climb on his shoulders.

'Climb up us and save the giraffe!' John shouts towards Suzy.

She immediately clumsily climbs up the boys. By this point most of the other people in the stage area are staring with a variety of different expressions, a few shouting in jest messages of support for saving the giraffe.

'Someone needs to catch him!' Suzy shouts, realising she only has enough reach to give the giraffe a slight push. Áine sees this and offers to stand underneath the landing area for the giraffe. Adam quickly follows her. The thought did cross his mind that a falling giraffe figure could be dangerous. He didn't want either of them to be completely squashed by a giant fake giraffe.

Ishmael is, of course, completely aware of the bizarre happenings from his DJ booth and tries to imagine what possible track would suit a giraffe rescue.

He mixes in a track with an intense build-up that matches the drama of the climb, thinking that he would quickly cut to the drop when the giraffe was 'saved'.

Suzy finally starts pushing on the giraffe, which moves a little but not quite to the point of falling. The crowd around begins to ooh and aah.

Suzy gives one final push.

The giraffe falls.

The crowd goes ballistic, clapping in excitable ecstasy. Ishmael times the bass beat to come in almost perfectly at the point when the giraffe is caught by Adam and Áine. Suzy climbs down with the help of John and Phillip, and Áine passes her the giraffe. Suzy stares at it and hugs it tight, stroking the back of its neck. She holds it up in the air as a sort of prize and begins crying violently, her face bright red and streaming with tears. She begins parading it through the crowd, with others desperate to touch it, as if worshipping a religious icon. John follows behind looking very confused and overwhelmed, clearly in way over his head at this point. Yet within him, his instinctive duty to protect his girlfriend remained strong.

When the task had been completed, Phillip and Áine both sighed with a deep breath and looked at each other with an expression of shock. They moved towards each other and embraced deeply.

'This is really intense ...' Áine whispers in Phillip's ear, her voice trembling slightly with fear.

'I know. We have each other though,' Phillip says. 'Let's stay by each other's side from now on. Come on, we better get to somewhere where we can lie down.'

The couple walk away from the stage area, holding one another up with their arms wrapped around each other's waist.

After only a few steps, things around them begin to look *very* different. Everything is bent out of shape, and it's as if they are walking on a sloped surface. The ground rises and falls, conflating and contracting. The grass, the trees, the sky all merge and bubble; they break into cogs, puzzle pieces, spirals.

Even Áine had never experienced anything like this. This was a completely new world, and she was becoming quite scared.

Around them was a self-transforming world of constant flow and shift. They were in utter awe of their liquid surroundings, trying not to give in to astonishment.

And then their earthly attachment dissipated entirely, and they entered this new dimension completely.

Flickering strings of white light all around,
Foaming liquid on the ground, soft touch, pleasant still;
Light vibration in the air, sounding high, sweet and fair.

The couple are crawling on all fours like children, feeling gentle sensations on their knees from the soft, velvety liquid. Mouths gasping open in astonishment, confused yet calm. This place makes them feel nothing but warmth, love and safety.

They turn their heads and see a great spirit, tall and radiant, approaching slowly. The spirit shines with mighty brightness and has glowing, crystal wings that fold neatly on its back, face doused in such a light that makes the features hard to see. Its form is rather human in its dimensions, with legs and arms, yet it is not of flesh but instead made up of thousands of multi-coloured and spinning crystal-like cubes, turning and rotating in on themselves, shining with various colours.

An angel.

The couple are on their knees staring in debilitating awe.

The angel approaches, then stops in its tracks.

Áine and Phillip are lost for words.

The angel, slowly and calmly, puts a finger on its lips, holds for a few seconds, and points up towards the heavens.

It dissipates into a white and golden mist, along with everything around them.

Áine and Phillip fade into a new environment. This time high up in the air amongst the clouds, floating as if unaffected by gravity.

They look down.

London.

The streets look eerie, quiet, empty, with only the occasional car on the road.

DONG! DONG! DONG! rings the bell from Big Ben.

People emerge onto the streets, yet in an oddly robotic and ordered way; a way that looks very *un-human*, in fact.

In a blink, they appear on the ground, in an alley.

They look at each other, mouths wide open.

'What ... was ... that?' Phillip says.

Áine takes in a deep breath.

'This is it,' she says, shaking her head. 'This is the experience I've always wanted. This is it. This is it.'

'I have a strong feeling within me right now, one that's hard to explain, and one that I've never felt before,' Phillip says, his eyes intense and serious.

'What we saw back there; that was an angel, Áine. An angel, an actual angel …' He shakes his head, purses his lips and looks down in contemplation. 'I think everything we are seeing, or about to see, is something that we *have* to see …'

'You think we are being shown all of this for a reason? By a higher power of some sort?'

'Yes, Áine, I do.'

She raises her eyebrows, and Phillip responds with a disbelieving nod.

They walk out of the alley, and onto the street. Streams of people walk quickly beside them, in single file. The faces are blank, lacking life, essence, emotion and *soul*.

'Something's not right here,' Phillip says. 'Have you noticed how they are all moving with such composure and rigidity? No one has headphones in, and no one's doing anything individual or unique. And look …' he waves his hand out, '… there's no filth or rubbish anywhere; everything is so clean and orderly. This doesn't feel like London at all,' Phillip frowns suspiciously.

'Yeah, so weird. I mean it is so clean, so … That's a good thing, right? I don't know …' Áine says with a conflicted expression.

'No, I understand, I feel the same; but it doesn't feel right … Anyway, let's keep walking.'

The couple continue to walk through the streets of London, but no one so much as glances towards them.

'Either these people are robots, or we are ghosts,' Áine says.

'I think both may be true to some extent …' Phillip replies with a raised eyebrow.

'Whoa, you see that? What is that?' Áine asks, pointing to the back of someone's neck who walks in front of them with a look of slight disgust mixed with curiosity.

Phillip squints.

'It looks like some sort of external implanted device …'

They are staring at what looks like a metallic black S on the neck.

'I don't know what to make of that,' Áine says.

'I do.' Phillip frowns, and shakes his head. 'Come on, let's go down here.'

As they continue down another side street, their attention is caught by an incongruously animated man, who briskly, and even a little aggressively, speed walks across the road. His head is on a swivel, and his features look rather panicked. He wears a grey hoody, with the hood up, and is carrying a black, tactically-styled backpack.

The man heads down into an underground car park.

'Come on! Let's follow him!' Phillip says as he points.

They follow the man into the car park, and they see him approach a grey, electric, boxy Toyota with a dent in its door.

The man fumbles around for his keys. But he cannot find them. He looks more frantically, tapping his pockets, but to no avail. He takes off his backpack to look in there instead, but as he does, a large, black, electric BMW 4x4 pulls in to the car park. The man stays calm and looks towards the car, its headlights shining on his face. At this point, Áine and Phillip feel confident enough (by virtue of the fact no one has looked at them) that they have been made invisible by the angel.

They edge closer to the action.

Six officers dressed in black tactical gear wearing red-tinted goggles jump out of the car.

'Hello, Sir,' the squad leader says in a monotone manner. 'We will now check your box as we are registering no signal coming from your form. Take the hood off, and turn around to face the wall.'

The man takes his hood off slowly, staring the officer in the eye.

'Turn around.'

The man turns around reluctantly.

The officer goes closer, and pulls down the fabric of his hood to inspect the back of the man's neck.

Disgust briefly flickers across the officer's face.

'Do you have an exemption for not having a box?' the officer asks.

'I don't need an exemption for living as God made me,' the man replies with a considered and precise tone, speaking truth to power.

The man at the front nods to the others behind him to initiate an arrest.

The outlier takes a few quick steps back and pulls out a carbon fibre rod with a bulb on the end from the bottom of his rucksack. He pushes a button on the rod, and a bright white flash comes from the bulb.

The officers are momentarily blinded, and the man flees.

One of the officers rushes to the boot of the BMW and brings out a slender-looking rifle. The gun looks electrical in nature, with sparks of charge emanating from the end of it. He wastes little time in lining up his shot, and he manages to shoot the running outlier in the back, causing him to convulse violently on the floor …

… And just as if they were watching a film at the cinema, the environment fades, and Áine and Phillip are transported elsewhere once again, but this time to a far more sinister looking place …

They appear in an all-white cell illuminated by blinding fluorescent lights. They see the same man as before, who is naked in the corner of the room. He has his face between his knees, looking absolutely exhausted.

Four officials enter the room. They are dressed in white lab coats and wearing bizarre white latex masks. These masks wrap tightly around their heads, and they have small slits for the orifices, including one carved into the shape of a smile for the mouth area.

The officials grab the man under his arms and drag him out of the cell, down a black corridor. The outlier is almost lifeless and doesn't resist.

Áine and Phillip follow, intrigued, silent and feeling extremely unsettled.

The man is led to another white room and tied down to a bed with multiple leather straps across the torso, limbs, head, and neck. The bed is shaped like a person, with padded parts for the arms and legs. He is buckled down securely, and then another sort of rubber wrapping with multiple small holes is secured to his head. The wrapping allows him to breathe, but only just. The man starts to panic, taking several large and struggled gasps of air along as he groans and screams.

'I can't watch this. This is awful,' Áine says as she walks out the room.

Phillip feels the same about this evil in front of him, but he has a strong feeling that he must keep watching, and that the angel is showing him all this for a reason; so he continues to watch reluctantly.

One of the torturers goes over to a small cupboard and picks up a thick piece of cloth which is wrapped around the outlier's face and secured in place with another strap.

They begin to pour water over the cloth, time and time again. After removing the cloth, the man would spasm as if having a seizure, flailing, gargling and struggling. Occasionally, he would even lose consciousness, but that didn't deter his tormentors; they would just take off the cloth and wait for him to regain consciousness, and again begin to water board him. The man would scream and writhe, but he was completely helpless.

After a while, drained of energy, the man stopped screaming and instead emitted a constant flat, monotone moan of agony.

Phillip couldn't look for most of it: he bowed his head and put his hands over his face, tears streaming down it. This was by far the worst thing he had ever seen, and he was utterly sickened by the malevolence.

Phillip is startled to feel the presence of a man standing behind him. He turns to look, expecting the man to say something to him, feeling the rush of adrenaline that comes when being sneaked up on. A part of him believes this person was actually looking into his soul, but then he reminds himself that he is invisible and immediately relaxes.

The man has chiselled cheek bones, a protruding jaw and slicked-back, jet-black hair. He wears an all-black suit and tie, black leather gloves, black boots, and a red shirt; all perfectly tailored, making him look very smart. A prominent armband is wrapped around his left arm. The background to this armband is red, and inside it is a black hexagon, with three black lines that go from corner to corner, making it look like a three-dimensional cube. At each corner is also a black dot. The man looks slightly smug, only noticeable on close inspection of his eyes, which squint ever so subtly, and his mouth, which carries a slight smirk. As Phillip looks at this man, he is hit with a negative energy; a sort of cringe, an intuitive knowing that this man is deliberately hiding behind a mask.

The suited man walks over to the end of the tortured man's bed and the tormentors edge away.

The suited man takes off the bound man's mask, allowing him to breathe easily.

The bound man gasps with relief.

'Thaat's it, shh; it's okay,' the suited man says as he strokes the man's cheek. 'Hmm, yes, I know you're feeling a lot of negative feelings right now, aren't you? You must understand, this is exactly what I want; I want to break you, and I am not going to deny this.'

Áine leans around the door to listen, intrigued by this man's words.

'I'm sure you understand that we are doing all this to you for a reason; and whilst you may disagree with our ways, we really are doing it for everyone's benefit. But you will never see it that way, I'm sure. I will not also bore you with the details of our vision, as I do not hold you in high enough regard; people like you will never be open-minded enough and will always be stuck in such archaic ways of thought. Regardless, and I'm going to be honest with you here, unlike many others I do actually enjoy inflicting pain on my enemies. The average modern man will deny this fact, but that's simply because they are not as developed and mature as I am. Most simply don't have the intelligence, the vision or the honesty that I possess. For much time, man has repressed his instincts, but the truly great men of the past embraced the finest pleasures; the pleasure of inflicting pain being the finest of them all.

'Now, you may have already heard of me. I believe your organisation refers to me as "Sickle". It's hard to deny the truth in my surname actually, as I am the blade that cuts down chaff, cuts off the filth, making room for new growth in our kingdom. I am a higher man, you see, a superior man, and you and your academy will experience my true power, the power you have yet to feel with full effect … Now, regardless of the pleasure your sufferings bring me, this is but an added bonus on this occasion, as I do require you to actually tell me something. But before I ask you one very specific question, I want you to fully understand the fact that I honestly have lots and lots of time, and I will, with pleasure, if necessary, continue to watch your struggles for many weeks on end. So now, knowing this fact, I want you to really think about giving me the answer to this question.' The man pauses whilst staring the bound man in the eye. 'Where. Is. Arthur?'

'How has my once great country sunk to such depravity that it commits these acts of evil on its own citizens …' the bound outlier manages to say with a strained groan.

Sickle forces a sarcastic laugh.

'We always have! Oh my, oh my. Look, friend. Most people are pathetic, they are weak, and they have no real worth. Weak people are here for no other reason but to be led by those who willingly take power. The years have added up, people are now weak, and hence a new order is inevitable. It's very simple, it's been the same since the dawn of time! Now, our order is on a one-way trip upwards, but as you know, we rely on our genius to instil a culture that provides sustenance for all, and that sustenance will be delivered quicker once my people and I recover the object that is in your leader's possession. Admit it, friend, understand that there are now new parents of the world, and we want to provide care for everyone. It's simply how things are going, and you need not fight the inevitable.'

'You have people wearing horror masks pouring water over my face, making me feel like I'm drowning. Loving parents would never do such things,' the outlier says with a sudden burst of energy and spirit, still with a groan but managing to gain a degree of articulation.

Sickle laughs again, in the same sarcastic way as before.

'Loving parents do what is necessary for the well-being of their children! And you are in the way of the delivery of our next update. So you are, of course, a means to an end, and I am simply doing what is necessary! The only difference is some would feel shame in doing what is necessary, whilst I feel pleasure instead, because I know for a fact that what I'm doing is for the greater good.' Sickle looks down and purses his lips, taking in a breath of air. 'Okay, so where is he?' he says quickly, with greater menace.

The outlier says nothing but stares back, his face blank and stoic.

'Okay. If you insist ...' Sickle says, as he begins to walk out of the room.

He turns back before exiting, and says, 'You tell me where Arthur is, and all this stops. Pretty simple, really.'

Sickle gestures to the masked torturers to continue, and they waste no time in resuming the simulated drowning.

This sinister world then begins to evaporate into blackness as before, and the screaming fades ...

... Áine and Phillip re-emerge in a forest.

The sun is just rising and a layer of mist blankets the woodland floor. As the pair peer around, they notice smoke rising in the distance. They see a great oak tree, with around 50 people gathered around it. Some are sitting, others standing or wandering around.

'It looks like some sort of gathering,' Phillip remarks as he squints to try and see more clearly.

'There's a tension in the air, I can feel something. Those people, they are here for a specific reason,' Áine replies with a focused stare, as if she was in a trance.

As the pair move closer towards the gathering, they see people talking amongst themselves, some casually and some intensely. There are couples and families here too, with children who all seem rather well behaved, staying close to their parents; no screaming or shouting can be heard. Some of the families are eating sandwiches, and one man even cooks steaks on a grill over the fire. An odd sense of humility is prevalent among this group, and the faces are serious and melancholic.

Phillip and Áine walk to the very front of the circle by the fire, and see across from them a man intently listening to an old lady. The old lady has a hunchback and looks frail. As this man starts talking himself, she nods and looks down at the floor; her eyes tear up, and the man puts his hands on her shoulders to comfort her. He looks her in the eyes and says something softly. The lady looks back at him with a large smile, and he smiles back.

This man stands out from the others in a few ways. Firstly, he is quite young, in his late twenties or early thirties; and secondly, he has the confidence of a born leader. He is actively looking around, carefully observing to make sure everything is in order. He also moves with conviction and purpose and has a strong presence; yet he doesn't come across too dominant or controlling. He wears a black leather jacket, and his face is sharp and slender. His expressions are soft yet deep and sincere; and his eyes are large, captivating.

The man cooking steaks is joined by a middle-aged woman, who brings a stack of wooden plates and bowls, and behind her another lady who looks in her late twenties who brings a bowl full of bread rolls.

'That's Suzy, for god's sake,' Áine says with her mouth slacked open in disbelief.

'No way! She does look like an older Suzy, though, doesn't she ...' Phillip replies with a sceptical squint.

'I'm telling you for a fact. *That is Suzy*. One hundred per cent!'

The man cooking the steaks briefly turns enough to reveal his face to Phillip and Áine.

'Okay. That's John,' Phillip says with a tilt of his head, pursing his lips. 'Wow, okay, this is weird ...'

Both of them stand in shock, shaking their heads in disbelief. They watch in silence as the food is passed around, some accepting it whilst others decline.

'Okay. Well this is clearly a vision of the future, isn't it?' Phillip says.

'Obviously, Phillip ...' Áine says with a dumfounded expression.

'Ha, yes, but it's just mind blowing to see, isn't it? My point, anyway, is everything we are being shown is clearly for a reason, and it all somehow relates to us. My question is, why aren't we here with them?'

Áine opens her mouth to reply, but is simply lost for words.

After all the food is passed around, the man in the leather jacket walks towards the fire and starts announcing to the gathering:

'It is a pleasure to return to my hometown of Oxford, and it is nice to see some familiar faces here as well. Today is a day where we can all return to ourselves; we can express our humanity that is being restricted, being controlled, being oppressed and therefore repressed. Today is a day where all of you, my fellow brothers and sisters, my fellow humans, can speak in truth and allow your darkness to surface. It is a time to allow the dark voids inside to be filled with light and truth. In a time of lies, deceit and darkness, where only the approved can be said without penalty, this is a time when you can speak your mind without worry. I say be honest with each other, and have no guilt of wrongdoings or mistakes of the past. For we are humans, and we are the redeeming race, so redeemed we shall be! Do not let others say you cannot be human, for the human is beautiful, and we must love the self in its entirety; in its dark and in its light. We live today in a culture adrift of its roots, with no understanding of what it means to be human. But *here* is a place where you can embody the spirit of humanity; and together, we can rejoice. Times may be unstable now, but let me tell you all, this is just a time of cleansing, a time of mass redemption, a time of suffering before we rise to the new Aion. Around us, we may see the masses crumble, argue, and tear itself apart. But we, we will be ready. We may not yet be large in numbers, but our legacy is growing, and the ones that seek our destruction are becoming nervous. A family based on truth, and rooted in love, is always stronger than even the largest of families based on lies and falsehoods. They say love is the answer, but what does that mean? It has been said that love must be taught, but I believe it must instead be found. Look inside and find the mystery, find the size of life in all its glory, and you will feel an awesome fear. But of this fear you will not be, because when you accept it, *you will become it*. Look on the inside, and you will find God. And when God is found, you will fear death no more.' After the man's speech, various voices can be heard saying 'Amen', and some others 'Amin'.

'Now, let's begin! I and others will be wandering around the ceremony today, so if anyone wants to talk or needs help of any kind just look for the wooden cross around our necks and we will give you guidance and counsel. May God burn brightly within your souls, and I wish you all the best of luck finding him today. Now please, follow me. I will bring out the light.'

'This is all feels so familiar, but I haven't seen any of this before,' Áine says as she shakes her head to herself.

The leader walks away from the fire and people around follow, along with Áine and Phillip. The man moves to a more open area, with fewer trees and foliage. He stands in the middle of this area, and everyone circles around him. He closes his eyes, bows his head and holds his hands together, looking as if he is about to enter prayer.

His lips start to move under his breath.

'Michael, Leader of Angels, defender against wickedness in high places, and to whom this sword belongs. I request now its light, for reasons of truth and beauty, and to help spread the Holy Spirit of the Lord, so all can see the truth of God in these dark times of lies, inversion and distortion. Amen.'

There's a white flash and a sword and scabbard appear on his waist.

This scabbard is crystal clear, with a slight tinge of blue. Inside it is a sword shining with multicoloured brightness.

A spinning cube of six colours: red, orange, yellow, green, blue, indigo.

The man rips it from the sheath, which vanishes as if it were of ghostly form. The rotating cube within the sword is now shining with the six colours even brighter, which refract through the mist and illuminate much of the surrounding forest.

He strikes the sword's blade down into the soil, gripping the handle with both hands.

He closes his eyes.

The cube spins even faster.

The cube reaches an awesome speed, and the colours all merge together, releasing a powerful violet.

The powerful violet glow radiates from the cube, illuminating the forest and everyone's faces, which are relaxed yet captivated, calm yet focused.

'It's beautiful!' Phillip says, looking around in awe at the all-encompassing violet.

'Look, the mist is even dissipating!' Áine says.

Phillip frowns with intrigue, and then takes a closer look at the faces around him. He sees tears run down mothers' cheeks, fathers embracing them and their children tenderly. Some drop to their knees in front of the light, others calmly sit down cross-legged, soaking it all in as if they were bathing in it, and a few rock backwards and forwards on their knees in a state of intense worship.

Phillip shakes his head and squints.

'The violet is causing some sort of shift in these people's consciousnesses; it looks as if they are suddenly becoming more ...'

'Aware?' Áine says.

'Yeah, something like that. But it's not really making me feel any different, other than feeling awe at the aesthetic changes and seeing the effects on the people here. I mean, it's quite moving in that way, but the light itself isn't really affecting me like it is them.'

'Well, we aren't *really* here are we, so we are likely detached from this reality in some way.'

Phillip laughs, and says, 'I'm almost starting to forget this isn't *our reality*.'

After 10 minutes or so soaking in the violet rays, many of the gathering begin to disperse in different directions, staying within the general glow yet not in such close proximity to it. The leader stays close to the glowing cube and sword, but he is no longer touching it, leaving it to spin on its own. Much of the gathering are swivelling their heads around, wide-eyed, faces full of intrigue, looking at the trees and the foliage with heightened awareness and perspicacity as if they were on a drug of sorts; yet not dissociated or detached, but focused and grounded in reality.

As the ceremony continues, various areas start engaging in different activities. In one direction, a group of men and women grapple playfully with each other on mats, working on technique, sparring and rolling and using various martial arts to get one another in holds and submissions. In another direction, people are beating deep rhythms and melodies on handheld drums around a fire. Artists are here too, with one man standing by his canvas to the side of the great oak, , holding his brush near it and staring curiously at the tree through the smoke from the fire.

Phillip walks further into the forest. People are doing their own thing: some read, some sit in silence and some write in their notebooks. Phillip continues walking and sees some others by a river, the glow here still penetrating yet not as strongly as at the epicentre. They are staring meditatively out at the water, soaking in its naturally calming sound.

Phillip then notices Áine waving at him from a distance, trying to get his attention. As he walks up to her, he notices she is anxiously looking around.

'I can feel a tension. I can't explain why, but I feel I can predict that something is going to happen, and it's not a good feeling …'

'Now you mention it, I can feel it too. I've felt it in dreams before, when you know something scary or nightmarish is about to appear, and you feel a kind of eerie apprehension.'

'Yes, exactly. But it's not just that, I keep getting paranoid that something is emerging from the forest. I just feel like this gathering isn't safe.'

Just after Áine says this, she and Phillip stare out into the surrounding forest. In the distance, they see small black blobs moving around.

'Oh my god, I can't watch this. This is like a bad dream unfolding, and I can't wake myself up!' Áine says abruptly, now knowing danger is imminent.

'We just have to understand that the angel is showing us these visions for a reason. They may be uncomfortable to watch, but it is important we learn from the teachings. Burying our heads in the sand will not do us any good in the long run. I have a feeling this is the final vision until we get brought back anyway. Don't worry, Áine, we will be okay.'

Phillip holds Áine's hand to provide some comfort.

She shakes her head, and pulls her hand away.

'Suzy and John are here, Phil! It might be a vision, but didn't we agree that this is actually real! As in, this is the future … Shit, look, they are coming closer!'

They both stare into the forest as the black blobs take shape. There's 30 or 40 men, all wearing gas masks, dressed in long, black trench coats, with tactical vests full of various pieces of equipment and ammunition. Armed with various rifles (gas launchers, slender taser rifles and dart guns), the men are wearing armbands with the same clearly distinguishable three-dimensional cube/hexagon insignia as Sickle from the last vision.

Shortly after Áine and Phillip see this emerging force, many others at the gathering begin noticing too. But before the majority clock on to what is happening …

Bang-cackle-sizzle.

A blue, electrified projectile is fired from far away, moving through the air like a lightning bolt, coming from the direction of the approaching force.

The violet glow stops.

'Move up! Quickly!' a man towards the front of the advancing force shouts.

Screams of terror ring out. Parents clutch their children and others run off as fast as they can. The leader of the gathering is knocked back and onto the floor by the shockwave of the projectile, which hit its target of the cube within the sword's hilt, knocking it out and onto the floor. The leader lifts his head up, dirt covering his face. He looks around in a stunned daze, his vision blurry and his ears ringing.

Future John and Suzy rush towards the leader, but before they can reach him, two darts hit their necks and they fall to floor unconscious.

'Oh my god! Phillip!' Áine cries, clutching Phillip in distress, burying her head into his chest.

Phillip takes a deep breath, trying to stay composed. He sees a familiar figure approaching …

'That's the same bastard we saw in the last vision … Sickle, I think his name was,' he says, pointing in disgust.

Sickle is surrounded by an advancing squad, some firing gas canisters nonchalantly at the escaping ceremony goers and others giving chase to those who sprint away into the forest, hunting the screaming families as if they were prey.

Sickle picks up the fallen cube up from the ground and holds it tightly, staring into it. It glows in the six colours, although they are faded now.

He passes it to one of his squad members beside him, who inserts it into a peculiar, metal-rimmed, glass box. The cube hovers within this box's centre, and metallic electrodes fire plasma into the cube, making its six colours flash and fluctuate between bright and dim.

Sickle puts his boot on the leader's chest, and points a handgun at his face, staring down at him with a smug, contempt-filled look.

'Arthur, we meet once again! And how I enjoy our ongoing drama. Honestly, I do! It gives me great pleasure! For all this is just necessary drama, predicted drama, even; but it is in this final drama, that *my father* shall reign true, in the end. His time has come, and this time it will not be fleeting, but his reign shall be the longest it has ever been, and you *must* accept this.'

Sickle puts his boot over Arthur's face. As Phillip watches this in horror, he can't help but repeat the name 'Arthur' in his head, thinking back to what the old caretaker said back in the library: 'Your holiest son will be called *Arthur.*' The thought alone is too much to bear, so he puts it to the back of his mind to focus on the unfolding drama in front of him.

'Get used to this feeling, little one,' Sickle continues, as he smears his boot across Arthur's face, as if he were a bug. 'I admit, you are a leader for the souls of your race, but the souls that once commanded themselves will be continually pressured to the point of submission again, and again, and again. Over time, the light and spirit of the ones who cling to their souls, as if they ever had right to them in the first place, will be smothered like your face is right now.' He lifts his foot from Arthur's face. 'You like metaphors, don't you?! So how about that for one!' Sickle laughs to himself.

'Your arrogance will cause your downfall, just as it did with your father,' Arthur says after coughing, his face showing little fear.

'Stand up!' Sickle demands, brushing off Arthur's comment as if he were a child.

Arthur stands up and looks over his shoulder to see John and Suzy on the floor.

'Oh yes, don't worry, they aren't actually dead yet.' Sickle gestures to his men to pick them up and carry them back.

Arthur shakes his head, almost in pity, and then says, 'You have it all worked out, don't you? Your machines, your networks, your programming, your control of people's basic necessities; you think so highly of all these things, and you think they are enough to trap people forever. Maybe this is true in your father's hellish box of Terra Daemonum, but on earth, souls are still connected to the one true Lord and can be forgiven and achieve salvation, no matter how much trickery or deception you use. You believe mere material can trap people, but this, again, is your arrogance; and this will be your downfall. You truly believe you can restrict people's belief to only what they can see and touch? You truly believe you can distract people with your lies from the true purpose of life, which always lies in pursuing *mystery*? You talk to me now with such spite and bitterness, such smug contempt, as if I am a naïve child, and honestly you may be correct: I am a child, I am humble, and I am naïve. But I am only these things because I am humble in the face of the true greatness that I do not know, knowing there are mysteries and workings so profound that no mere mortal could fully grasp them. It is this that you, and your father, do not possess; and it is this that will always be your downfall.' Arthur's voice holds steady and true as this flows out of him. He shows no fear at all.

Sickle sarcastically claps his hand on the handle of his handgun.

'Anyway ... I will see you again, very, very shortly. Goodnight, Arthur.'

Sickle bows his head and curtseys like a court jester, then pulls out a handheld dart gun with his free hand. He shoots Arthur in the neck, whose body collapses to the floor moments after. He orders some of his men to take him away.

The world around Phillip and Áine once again begins to fade and morph, and they are brought back to the golden white dimension of the angel, who stands with his back turned away from them. Áine and Phillip this time float rather than crawl on the stringy liquid matter; and all fear from the previous visions are vanquished by the mere presence of this angelic spirit.

The angel turns around to face them, and pushes its arms out to the side, its wings spreading out wide and glowing even brighter. The golden white stringy plane fades into darkness, and it seems they are now amid a void in space. The primary angel still floats beside them, but now other smaller angels fly around too.

These lesser angels whizz around like worker bees and start casting golden beams and orbs of light into a huge, centralised spot in the universe. This light swirls and crashes into various rays. It looks like golden star dust, leaving glistening trails behind it. It builds and stacks quickly, weaving it-self like an intergalactic cobweb, eventually forming a fantastic image of a tree, with huge galaxies of light as its branches and specks and fountains of light falling from its canopy like golden rain. Its roots descend into darkness deeper than Phillip and Áine can see.

The angel floats closer towards the awestruck Phillip and Áine and shoots its hands down, with golden light streaming from its arms like galactic water slides. Phillip and Áine are pulled into these streams of light and slide down them. They can't help but laugh like children, as this is way beyond anything they have ever experienced. In front of their eyes, lesser angels actively craft what looks like a small planet made of blue water. They slide down on this golden stream towards its surface with a growing fear they will be plunged straight into the water! But as they approach, an island forms, and they land gently on its surface of soft white sand, laughing to each other manically. They gaze up to the sky, burnished with bright gold and orange from the huge, glowing tree, now separated from them by a thin atmosphere. Within this atmosphere they can hear a beautiful, harmonious hum radiating from the tree. The hum echoes and reverberates through their bodies. Within this hum, many high-pitched angelic voices can also be heard; layers upon layers of unintelligible words are spoken; and whilst this language is un-known to our couple, it feels familiar to both of them. The sound is simple, but powerful. It is only occasionally and fleetingly experienced on earth in moments of harmonious musical beauty. The sound is all encompassing, as if it were the archetypal sound of everything; the vibrational essence of life itself. This moment felt very euphoric for our overwhelmed couple, and they both stay still.

The archangel then lands beside them, lies casually on the sand and proceeds to literally form a 'sand angel', as if wanting put Áine and Phillip at ease. Our couple look at one another surprised, and giggle like infants at this angel's silliness. The angel then stops, leans up and points towards the tree. As the angel points, the couple feel thoughts emerge that aren't their own. A voice in their heads says: 'Look at the tree. The inversion is about to begin.' So, the couple look back at the tree, and the tree begins to rotate anti-clockwise gradually, and as it does the hum changes in frequency. It becomes much lower darker. The sound itself scares Phillip and Áine, but the angel casts much light around them to prevent the dark energy entering their hearts; and because of this, they still felt warm and safe.

By this time the tree has fully inverted and is now root side up; the golden rain of space dust, and buzzing angels around it, can no longer be seen or heard; their angelic song is finished, and the tree is completely black and looking rather burnt.

The angel holds out a hand, and a window in front of them appears. Inside the window appears a magnification viewpoint directed towards the very top of the tree, with the top now being the roots. The spiralling, chaotic tendrils do not look beautiful like the glistening branches, but rather disgusting.

In the centre of the roots, a dark, demonic figure is seen hovering. This figure has horns and bullish snout. The demon turns and drops a small black cube inside the tree's roots, and the tree goes up in flames. As the tree burns, a huge black box inflates around the burning tree, locking it inside.

With one simple swipe of the angel's hands, the tree and all its surroundings dissolve, and the golden stringy realm returns once again. Áine and Phillip stand up, golden white moisture dripping from them. The angel once again approaches them, and holds out its hand above them. Golden light streams out of it, and a strong golden aura pulsates from the heads of Phillip and Áine. A ghostly form begins to wrap around their faces, and their heads are transformed into those of a lion and lioness. Phillip has a large, enveloping mane and strong, focused features. Áine has large, black eyes expressing gentleness and compassion.

'You are the spirits that will birth the return of the Holy Spirit. This is your task, as it was for many before you in times past. Like the beginning of earth itself when the glaciers melted, I hereby associate this spirit with you, and all the blessings accordingly; as is it this that is commanded from my Lord in heaven.

'Young ones, your journey is your own, and struggle will come, this is true. But fear not, because we are watching, and I say have faith in your fruits, for choice is still yours and yours only; but we in heaven have faith in you both, and so should you in thee. For it is from your seed of birthing child, Áine, that you shall bring new Aion to the world. And your seed of labour, Phillip, that you shall do the same. So allow these words from above to enter the depths of your souls, and allow them never to leave. Allow our faith in you, and have faith in the Lord above, and therefore gain access to the mighty spirit that you will return to earth. Do not fear the inversion of the tree, for it is you who will set the wheels in motion and therefore restore the divine order. Goodbye lions. Blessings be with you.'

10. AFTERGLOW

Phillip and Áine awaken from their vision and are now back at the festival.

As they open their eyes, they see the ticket girl, Jess, beside them, watching them both closely. They are on one of the festival rugs, and the fairy lights above the area now glow strongly under the moonlight.

'Hey, guys. How are you both feeling, would you like some tea?' Jess says in a loving and caring voice.

Phillip blinks his eyes a few times and looks around the festival grounds through a squint, already rather grounded and comfortable being back on earth and not feeling as dissociated and uncomfortable as one may think for someone who had experienced such profundities.

'As long as it is normal tea this time,' Phillip laughs, managing keep his humour, as he raises his eyebrows and takes in a large gulp of air.

'You have no idea what we have just experienced, Jess ...' Áine says slowly, shock and disbelief in her voice. 'We met this amazing and beautiful angel, and it gave us this "blessing of the lion", and it showed as all these visions, and I just can't describe how crazy they were. But they were really beyond belief, and were as real as night and day! We saw depictions of the future; John and Suzy were even there! We saw some terrible things ... This angel, though, this angel made me feel safe. It was pure love, and I think it was trying to help us! I am in shock, Jess; you don't understand how crazy it was ...'

Before Jess can reply, Adam comes in from behind them. He has a pipe hanging from his mouth and is now wearing a long, woollen coat. Hanging over his arms he also has two woollen jumpers. He sits down on the rug and hands a jumper to both Phillip and Áine.

'You guys went in very deep, didn't you? I have only seen this type of trip once before, and the person did not come out the other side in one piece. It is a miracle you both seem so well put together.'

'We witnessed a prophecy,' Phillip says. 'May I outline to you what we witnessed? I need to get it out before I forget the details. You may be able to shed some insight on it as well. Firstly, this wasn't a normal trip: I believe we crossed over to a sort of transcendent world, another dimension. This angel we saw, it seemed straight from the Bible, and it showed us many things. To put it simply, it showed us visions of what we believe to be the future.

We saw London: it felt tyrannical, as if everything was controlled. People lacked emotion or spirit and were forced to have what they called "boxes" on their necks. We saw someone being tortured by this horrible man called Sickle, who was interrogating them to find the location of this leader called Arthur. We then saw this very Arthur in a forest with a group of people. I believe this was a sort of organised ceremony or ritual. People were gathering around this powerful, violet light that came from this cube in a sword; and people were dancing, reading, wandering, training in martial arts, drawing and painting. I have no idea what it all means, but maybe you can shed some light on it? This Sickle and his men then stormed the ceremony. They had gas, darts and all other kinds of ways of putting people to sleep. This leader, Arthur, was put to sleep by Sickle after having a conversation. They spoke like they were already acquainted, and clearly this all goes far deeper than I can even begin to understand ... The angel then showed us something on another level, something outside of human understanding. It showed us this huge, cosmic tree, floating in the universe; it was the size of galaxies, but I don't even know if size existed in this realm. This tree then inverted; it turned upside down, with its roots facing up, and on top of it stood this horned, bullish demon holding this dark cube, similar to the one glowing one inside the sword yet as black as night. The tree began burning, and was then trapped inside a massive black box. At the end, we were given some sort of spiritual blessing. The angel gave us what it called 'the spirit of the lion'. Once again, I have no idea what that means, but it said we have a special task.'

Phillip says this rapidly and with much energy; he barely took a moment to breathe or pause. He felt within him a desperate need to get it all out before he forgot.

Adam stares deeply into Phillip's eyes, focusing intensely on his face, whilst taking puffs from his pipe as smoke wafts around his face. He puts his pipe down to the side of him and takes a deep breath.

'That's a hell of a trip,' Adam says as he exhales. 'I'm going to start by saying this. I am first and foremost a pragmatist when it comes to my research. I am a scientist, and I am always careful about making large and abstract assumptions about the nature of reality. I wish to continue to be taken seriously by the university, and if I were a mere spiritual guru or other shamanic-like personality or something along those lines, I would not be respected in my field. With this said, to my core, and to my purest nature, I am a man of faith. The depth of my being believes in something greater out there, and, unlike many others in my field, I am always open to accept that things are stranger and bigger than what is accepted as fact by the scientific community. I am also a man of subtlety, and I am always looking for the signs and deeper meanings of the world around me. For I believe humans are creatures of story and drama excites us greatly, even if that drama can be painful. In my appreciation of story, and as an analytical psychologist, I am always trying to see the greater metaphorical meaning of things; I believe symbols speak louder than any words ever could. Nature herself is not stupid, and it is for that reason that our dreams speak through vague symbols and abstract visions. But it is not to the ego that the dream speaks; it talks instead to the soul ... usually, anyway, but I will not go into that ...

'This vision you have witnessed; you may not understand what you saw on a conscious level, but the essence will be in the totality of your being. The essence will be in the parts of you that aren't available to access immediately. The information will be there, and the energy absorbed from this vision will continue to affect your behaviour, motivations, emotions, in ways you will not be fully aware of. In terms of bringing these images to light, it is not up to me to directly tell you; instead, you must both find out for yourselves, as it was a message directed at you two only. However, as a therapist, I can help you down this path, and provide you with insight into the archetypes of the collective unconscious. An understanding of the archetypes will provide you with bedrock and structure when trying to make sense of the greater unconscious and nature of reality, inside and out. In short, I can help you interpret what you saw.

'From listening to your vision, there are a few stand-out, symbolic representations. The tree seems very dominant. The tree is a common representation for the self archetype, with many ancients having similar world trees, or trees of life, to represent the totality of everything; some may say this everything in totality is God, and it is this image of the self, and our relationship with it, that determines our relationship with *everything*. This self can be seen in the human and is seen in times of purest expression. It is the Christian doctrine of man being made in God's image that is the image of the self. And it is the Orthodox notion of theosis, that is to become like God, to make the unconscious conscious. For the self in its purest form is Christ;

and it is the duty of us as good people to try and maintain Christ's purity as much as we can. Within this self is not just the spirit of the father, the spirit of logos and truth, the known world as we currently see it; but also everything we do not know. The self contains pure potential and feminine chaos. Many forget that within us is not just pure order and light, but also chaos and madness. It is the unity of order and chaos inside us, and our relation to this synergy, that allows us to act and flow with the world and ultimately live in harmony with reality and live meaningful lives. And this brings me on to the cube. What if the cube engulfing the tree symbolises the trapping of the tree, preventing it from growing further into chaos by keeping it in a box with no potential for new understanding? It seems the tree is being cut off from the great mother and not allowed to expand. This poor cultural relation to mysterious chaos is causing the energy to turn into shadow energy; because we do not accept or believe it exists. This black cube may be the satanic image at work, trapping the tree inside the known world, arrogant in its own knowledge, not accepting anything new and fresh. No new life coming in from outside the box; everything is trapped within. Imagine the tree has been cut off from revitalising itself, cut off from the new, and merely stuck in the old.

'This now brings me on to the inversion of the tree. I believe this may be a representation of what Jung might have called 'enantiodromia'. It is essentially the phenomenon of things being inverted when pushed to extremes. We can see this in politics as a horseshoe, or unconsciously as projection. If we imagine the world as a place of balance between two poles, we always want to be as close to the centre as possible; if we go too far either way, we are straying too far from the opposite, and this makes it angry as it is receiving no love or appreciation of its energy. People by their nature are either closer to the great mother, chaos, or the great father, order. And this defines their political temperament. With any marriage, both the husband and wife need to constantly allow themselves to come together, mating in physical and spiritual harmony, exchanging energy and allowing their essences to mix into a wholeness. It is this flow of energy we Christians call the Holy Spirit; with this spirit birthing new life which we call the son. The totality of this quaternity is the self, which Christians worship as the cross, and as Christ. This very marriage also happens on a universal, more collective level. If any part of the quaternity is not allowed to be expressed in the culture, the archetype is repressed and then projected as a shadow opposite. This is known as shadow projection. We must allow the totality of the god image to be expressed through the individual; if culture puts restrictions on this expression, it will prevent the individual from being whole, and being him or her self. Because of this, the individual will go on to develop many dangerous complexes, which leads to evil in the world.

'To conclude, I believe that what this angel may be trying to communicate is that it is somehow up to you two to return balance to the inverted tree and free it from this black, shadowy box, where it is not allowed to grow any higher. Regarding what the spirit of the lion means, or what a lion-headed icon represents in general, it is hard to say. Lions are obviously strong, and I would expect you now have both been given some sort of strength blessing. Maybe the gathering was of worshippers of the new age of Aquarius, age of the spirit; where the fish of Pisces leaves the water, grows wings and begins to fly. Maybe in the future many will begin to see that humans need a reconnection to the spirit; and in this vision, it showed one of the early budding religious groups who believe in the coming of this new age.'

Adam continues to hold firm eye contact with Phillip after his analysis and goes on to take another puff of his pipe.

'This all makes so much sense,' Phillip says, shaking his head and putting it into his hands. 'You are articulating so well what I feel intuitively but struggle to say.'

'Yes, I have felt these things too,' Áine adds. 'But I see and relate to these things more in my head. When I listen to music, I have insights into patterns but more in pictures and images. Throughout the vision, I kept getting strong feelings build inside me; and it was sometimes very frustrating because I didn't fully understand how or what I was feeling.'

'There is something in particular that keeps running through my head, and it's giving me chills just thinking about it,' Phillip says. 'The spiritual leader in the vision, his name was Arthur ... Do you remember the caretaker in the Bodleian, Áine? He said that's what my "holiest son" would be called. And then I stumbled across that crazy book, saying how King Arthur would return and rule again. It all just seems so connected, and it's a lot to take in.'

'Caretaker in the Bodleian library you say?' Adam asks with a knowing expression. 'That would be old Julius, a wise chap. He tends to keep himself to himself; yet he has an edge to him. Those eyes of his, I've seen them in clients before after they have a breakthrough trip, or have a powerful spiritual revelation, such as losing a loved one. Yet Julius has these eyes constantly. In fact, the eyes I see in you both now are those I eyes I talk about; they are the eyes of divine children.'

'Thinking back now, we did think he was odd at the time, yet our minds were a bit distracted at that point, weren't they?' Áine says, looking over with a smirk at Phillip, who blushes and looks at the floor.

'As curious as I am about what you two were up to at the library, I will save that story for another time,' Adam says with slanted eyebrows. 'For now, you both should rest and have a nice, deep sleep. You two have had an extremely powerful experience; and I believe the magic will still be present for a few days. Unconscious forces are still present for some time after revelations like this; so, keep an eye out for signs and signals; much of the time answers come after rather than during. We should also go and pay old Julius a visit first thing tomorrow. He may be a piece in this puzzle and could help you both figure out your next move. I'll meet you both at the library at nine o'clock tomorrow.'

'Okay, that sounds like a plan. I can't lie, I'm starting to feel very tired now, actually; that was a hell of a ride ...' Phillip says as he rubs his eyes.

'I almost forgot! Are Suzy and John okay? What happened to them in the end?!' Áine asks with sudden haste.

Jess, who had been quiet up until this point, smiles; she had been waiting to let them know what happened to their friends.

'They are fine, sweetie,' she says. 'Ishmael finished his set soon after you two began to "lose it" and took care of them for the day. It was quite hilarious because me, Adam and Ishmael felt like parents looking after a bunch of unhinged children. When Suzy and John "came back down to earth" again, they were awfully worried about you both, but Adam reassured them that he would keep a watchful eye on you both. They sat with you both for over two hours and were very loving towards you both, making sure you were both comfortable. In the end, they had faith in Adam to take care of you and went back to Ishmael's house along with James. They were both very tired themselves from the looks of it.'

'I'm surprised James left your side, Adam; he was glued to it the whole day!' Phillip says with a chuckle.

'Ah, well, I also put my faith in Ishmael to take care of him; he is one of my students, you know.' Áine and Phillip both laugh whilst shaking their heads.

'Of course he is,' Phillip says. 'He didn't tell us that though, he just said you were a friend of his.'

'Ah, well, we try and be as subtle as possible about our group. It's definitely not for everyone, and it's still quite taboo for some people. I believe he already had an interest in both you and John since he spoke to you at the jiujitsu academy you train at. He let me know you may be potential students for my team, and here we all are at a festival. If any of you were further interested in doing more research with myself and my team, the window is now open for you to join. Consider today your rite of passage.'

'It would be an honour, Adam, thank you,' Phillip says with strong eye contact and great sincerity.

'Now, let's all go home! It's been a big day. I will give you both a lift back if you want. And Jess, I can take you back too if you're done here,' Adam says as scrapes his pipe ash into a metallic, portable container.

11. JULIUS

Adam, Phillip and Áine arrive at the Bodleian Library. They walk in and approach the reception, with Adam at the lead.

'Hi there, how are you doing today?' Adam asks the receptionist. The receptionist has a stern look to her and does not immediately respond to Adams's question, but instead looks behind him to see two familiar faces.

'Are those two with you?' she asks with a cold frown.

'Yes, these are two of my students. We would like to speak to old Julius. It's on matters regarding university research.'

'They aren't coming into the library. They are both trouble-making criminals who broke into the library the other night. I don't know why you are with them, but you should both be bloody ashamed of yourselves!' the receptionist says as she shoots a look of disgust at Phillip and Áine.

'Ah, yes, they are indeed young and foolish; but were we not all once the same?' Adam replies.

The receptionist sighs deeply.

'Okay, fine. But I'm going to give him a call first. He's downstairs, and I want to first confirm that you aren't up to any funny business. I won't lie, Adam, this isn't the first time I've had trouble with students from your team. What on earth are you teaching them?'

She gives Julius a call on the phone.

'Hi Julius, I have a peculiar group who want to see you. It's that weird professor Adam Shephard and two of his students.' She looks up at Adam, as if she wants him to know what she thinks of him. 'Yes. Oh yes, there are two others with him; they are those pesky kids who broke in the other night. I can send them away if you'd like? Yes. Oh, really? Honestly, it's fine, I can send them away if you'd like … Yes … uhm, okay, I'll send them down now.' She puts down the phone and gives Adam an annoyed look. 'He actually wants you all to come down and speak with him for a reason I cannot fathom. Down that corridor there, third door on the left, and then down the trap door inside,' the receptionist says rather sharply, and then looks down at her computer immediately.

The trio walk off in the direction they were told.

'What a cold, old bitch,' Áine says as she looks back at the receptionist.

'Ah, she's okay, I've seen many people like that. They get old and a bit bitter; she's obviously missed out on many things in life, and now knows it's too late to redeem herself. This understanding plays with her soul and produces a degree of shame. But from my analysis, her heart is still strong and warm,' Adam replies as he pushes open the door to the room with the trap door.

In the middle of the room is indeed the trap door. Adam bends down and attempts to open it, but with no success; it is locked securely. He then gives several knocks in rhythmic succession: 'tap-de-de-de-tap-tap, tap-tap.' The trap door immediately unlocks itself, and then Adam pulls it open. Phillip and Áine look with intrigue at Adam, who replies with a shrug and his hands facing up as if he were just lagging the taps.

They all head down a steep ladder that goes down to another staircase, which leads further underground. They then follow a short passageway to a room that has many tools and equipment like a workshop, yet still feels very homely. A large, stone-hearth fireplace is in the centre, and a fire roars inside. Facing the fireplace is a large, green leather chair. It has large sides on the head rest. In the corner is a double bed, with a simple bookcase to the left of it. On the wall above the bed, in the centre, is a metallic head of a dragon, and underneath it many swords of different styles. To the right of the bed, another cabinet can be seen, with two doors with glass inlays. Inside the cabinet are many colourful crystals, along with various flowers and containers.

A familiar voice is heard coming from the chair facing the fire.

'You all came much sooner than I expected,' Julius says.

He stands up from the chair and points to other smaller leather chairs that surround the fire. Julius and the group arrange their chairs to face each other in a tense silence. After sitting down, Julius does not say anything for a while but simply stares, analysing them and the situation. He then picks up a half-full glass of beer that is on the table beside him. He holds the glass up in the air, and the golden liquid lights up brightly as the light from the flames refract through the glass.

'What do you see? I want each of you to give an answer. Starting with you, Adam,' Julius asks in a slow and sombre tone.

'A test,' Adam replies.

'Good answer. Now, Áine, what do you see?' Áine stares deeply into the glass and feels herself slip into a light trance as she does.

'I see an hourglass, with the beer inside representing time. I see the liquid slowly dripping out. I feel the need to act, the need to do something,' Áine replies with a calm and slow-paced voice.

'Very good, Áine. And now, Phillip, tell me, what do you see?'

Phillip focuses on the glass, squinting his eyes slightly as he does. Something then catches his attention; he notices the beer's bottle on the table. He does not say anything but instead stands up, grabs the bottle and refills Julius's glass.

'How very kind of you; thank you, Phillip.'

'My pleasure. And now to answer your question with my words. I see, like Áine, leaking spirit. I see a boat that has holes in it; I see the need to refill this boat with spirit. I see, floating in that beer, a demoralized crew. I see inside this glass a crew that no longer is taking care of their ship, and because of this, the ship is sinking.'

'Indeed, Phillip. What a fantastic analysis. Now, the question posed here is how do we return the spirit to our sinking ship? Please, do not answer this. Allow me first to explain something to you all.

'I have, as I previously told you both, been working in this library for many years, and over these years, various mysterious occurrences have shown themselves to me. You both may have felt something mystical about this place when you both were here, am I correct?' Áine and Phillip nod in response to this. 'These feelings are no stranger to me either, but I do generally keep them to myself, as I of course do not wish to look crazy to my colleagues around me. Yet, when I wander the halls of the library, it is not odd for me to see these books fall from their place. This first started happening about seven years ago. At first, I thought they must have just been misplaced at a poor angle. But this just kept happening, over and over again. It got to the point where I began to feel scared in the evenings; not greatly, but enough to get my attention. It then occurred to me that all these books had similarities. They contained a common theme: *trees*.

'I then began reading these fallen books and realised that they did not exist anywhere else. I frequently researched the authors, and it turns out that the authors were not even real; there is no trace of them anywhere. And then, five years ago, I came across one fallen book, titled: *Et Amor Librorum in Arboribus,* which is Latin for "Love among books and trees". And on one quiet night, I read the tale. It told of a hero named Arthur, who had just rescued a damsel from a horde of goblins. The couple were chased by these goblins, and they took refuge in an ancient library. In this library, Arthur found a book. And in this book, it described how to kill goblins. The book said that to defeat goblins, a sword must be wielded by a man who has recently had the love of a woman under the light of a tree. So, Arthur made love to the damsel under the golden light of a tree that came in from one of the library's windows. He then went outside and slaughtered all the goblins.

For some reason, this story had an impact on me. When you two both came sneaking in here, I immediately thought of that tale that I had read. I know I told you that I had done a similar thing when I was younger, but that was not true; I did not feel it would be easy to explain my real reasoning behind allowing you to stay, as it was irrational based on my hunch about this tale. Either way, I felt I made the right decision in letting you both stay.'

'That is amazing,' Phillip says, his mouth ajar in surprise. 'Because that tale, that is like a mythical version of what actually happened when me and Áine were both here that night. But Julius, please, one thing has been bothering me. Before you left us that night, you said, "My holiest son would be called Arthur". Only I heard you say this, not Áine. What was the meaning of this?'

Julius holds a stare with Phillip for a few moments and then looks down at the floor in contemplation.

'Do you believe in God, Phillip?' he asks with a serious tone, catching Phillip off guard.

'I never used to, but the more I see of life, the more I believe there's more to this whole thing than a big, black, cold space, so yes ...' He looks to the side and frowns, as if reflecting upon what he just said. 'And if I'm being honest, this is what I've always said to myself; but now, upon further reflection, after the events I've seen in recent visions ...' he turns to Áine, '... I can't help but believe.'

'Well, I believe in him too. And there are moments where I no longer feel in control of my body. I feel in some moments a spirit of a higher power flow through me. And in that moment where I said those words to you, I said them out of an uncontrollable compulsion. It was like the words left my mouth without my control. As soon as I walked through the doors, out of the library, I frowned to myself, reflected and tried to make sense of why I had just said what I said. I have still to this day puzzled over why I said what I did. But I feel now it is clearer to me: your holiest son *will* be called Arthur; as it is God's bidding for it to be so.'

After Julius says this, a period of silence follows; all present seem to be in deep reflection.

Adam breaks the silence.

'So, these fallen books, how many have you read?'

'As of yet, 43. I keep all the fallen books under the floorboards, over there under my bed.' Julius turns his head and points. 'I believe the 44th was read by someone else, am I correct Phillip?' Phillip stares back with intrigue, signalling for Julius to continue. 'I'm not sure if you remember, but that book, you placed it quite clumsily into an empty shelf at the bottom of one of the "classics" shelves. *Arthur, King of the Tree*. Am I correct? Well, I saw it one evening and immediately knew it was you who had placed it there. I believe this library is trying to tell us all something.'

'And what do you think it is trying to say?' Phillip asks.

'As I said before, the books have a common theme of trees. Among the books, there are regular suggestions of a need for a tree to be planted. I believe the books are suggesting that this is a metaphorical tree and they are referring to the religious symbol of "the tree of life". I do not also doubt that there may also be an *actual* Tree of Life in some spiritual plane; yet, at the very least, it exists symbolically, and it is this tree that represents all life, including all higher and lower planes. The tree of life is *everything*.' The eccentric man suddenly looks to his left and opens his mouth slightly, like something has caught his attention.

'It is all coming clear to me now. Your holiest son, Arthur, he will become the leader of a spiritual revolution; he will lead a new Tree of Life, a new spirit; he will lead humans into a new age. But he will not plant the seed; no, he will be its nurturer when it is a sapling.'

'The books told you all this?' Áine says, looking captivated, yet a little confused.

'Your son, Arthur, will grow the tree; but it is up to you to plant the sapling. However, the sapling only needs to be planted in spirit, as you must base this around a tree that has already long existed. A great oak tree planted long ago ...' Julius goes on to say, ignoring Áine's question.

'I have felt an energy growing for many years, a shift, if you like,' Phillip says. 'But I have never been able to understand these feelings. I have felt like civilisation has been on the verge of a great change, a revolution of sorts. But the fear I have had along with these feelings is that this change will not be great but terrible, dystopian in its nature.

'When I read that book, the 44th one as you described it, it felt like it was articulating my intuition on paper, and it gave me the weirdest of feelings. It made so much sense, yet made no sense at all ... But Julius, you are telling me I must plant the seed for a future cultural rebirth, yet I am only one man. How on earth am I to do such a thing?'

Julius squints his eyes and strokes his chin for a few moments.

'You are a martial artist, am I correct?'

'I have no idea how you know that, but yes.'

'Then this now makes sense. Allow me to get book 24.'

Julius walks over to his bed and begins manoeuvring it to expose some floorboards. He then rips off some of the boards and reaches his arm underneath, scrambling around clumsily trying to feel where this book may be.

'Do you need some help, Julius?' Adam asks with a degree of concern.

'No, I'm fine. It's just in quite deep, I haven't read this one for such a long time.'

Julius finds the book and gives a sigh of relief. He walks back over to the trio, sits down, and blows a layer of dust off its cover.

'This was the first fallen book I read. It is called *Samurais of the Maple Sapling*. It tells the tale of a group of compassionate samurais. These samurais had begun regularly meditating on order of a daimyo named Shiba Yoshimasa. This was a general practice of the samurais living under the bushido code. Shiba believed meditation would make the samurais underneath him strong-minded and fearless in battle. And it was true; the samurais did become fearless, more fluid, more deadly, more relaxed and more feared on the battlefield. But something strange also happened ... A samurai named Popori Sagara began to experiment with his wife by making brews of different types. Well, he would test the brews that she made for him. His wife had many different brews for all occasions. If Popori was injured in battle, she would use a particular brew to help healing. If he was sad, she would have a brew to raise his spirits. The name of his wife is never mentioned in the book, however it was noted that she was very resourceful and creative.

'And one day, whilst Popori was meditating in the lush garden of his Shoin-Zukuri house, she gently tapped him on the shoulder with a new brew she made. Inside the brew was what the Japanese called the "laughing mushroom", which we know as the "magic mushroom". Popori drank the brew without questioning his wife about what was in it and carried on meditating.

It didn't take long until he found out that he could focus much harder and deeper than he had ever been able to before. He felt his mind reach a state that usually took him many hours to achieve by meditation alone. He then opened his eyes to look at his garden around him, and he immediately felt a smile come to his face and began laughing at the radiant colours and beauty. Popori felt like a child again, like he was looking at the world with fresh eyes. He began wandering around his garden wide-eyed, and he slid his hand across the many petals as if he could sense they too were alive like himself. Popori began thinking differently too: he began to view his life from a different perspective and started to question many of his past decisions.

'It was not long before Popori gave other samurais his wife's special brew, and they too began having similar revelations.

'Out of these samurais, a splinter group then formed. This splinter group started questioning much of the bushido code they were told to follow. Their own meditations with the special brew had given them certain spiritual insights that did not completely align with the standard samurai bushido code.

'So, one day, a group of seven gathered in secret for a ceremony. They planted a Japanese maple tree in an opening in a forest and promised each other that this would symbolise the start of their very own jujitsu and meditation academy. They believed that together they could start a new form of bushido that was more at one with the spirit they had accessed in their meditations.

'And so, they gathered resources together, in secret of course, until eventually they began the academy. Many other samurai joined, who also felt that this form of bushido code was much more aligned with their beliefs. The academy grew and grew; and in the end, there were 24 members, known as the "Grey 24".

'Their unique form of bushido practice gave them such insights that they were even deadlier in battle and could predict any plans or attempted challenges from any enemy. It was said that they developed powerful clairvoyant abilities and vision. However, it wasn't long until the daimyo found out about the Grey 24, and naturally saw them as a threat and a disgrace to orthodox bushido. Orthodox samurais were sent to raid the academy, killing most of the splinter samurais; but some managed to escape and blend into civilian life. Shiba burnt the entire academy to the ground. But somehow, the maple sapling was not destroyed and kept on growing. In the final chapter of the book, the story talks of a mysterious figure named Asa. Asa was the son of Popori, and he promised to fulfil his father's dying wish; that he would spread his father's form of bushido through all the land, but would do so in spirit and in secret. He promised his father that the spirit of the maple sapling would grow and become strong, until its branches stood above all that lived in Japan.

'I must go on to say to you now that these books are dense, and indeed interconnected with each other, and most people these days don't particularly like reading that much, out of sheer laziness if you ask me … However, and thankfully, I *have* read all of them, and I understand how they interconnect. Now, as I mentioned earlier, it is not your duty to plant a physical seed, but instead a spiritual one; yet, it *is* important you build your academy around a sacred rock, which is said to be the seed itself, of a very old and sacred oak tree. If you can find the tree, you have found the rock, which will be at the base of its roots.

'Within this rock surely lies Excalibur, no?' Adam asks curiously, with a subtle smirk, seeing a clear parallel to the King Arthur myth.

'I do not believe the sword will simply just be waiting there to be taken,' Julius replies cautiously, with a slightly suspicious glance. 'But it very well may appear there again one day. Even if it were there now, only the chosen one would be able to remove it; and I do not believe that one has been born yet …' Adam winces back at Julius, and a weird tension forms between them; subtly, and only for a moment.

At this point, Phillip's jaw is ajar, his heartbeat rapid, and his breath deep. He even starts seeing visions flash through his head of limitless potential, along with massive budding energy and excitement growing in his stomach.

'How do we find this tree then, Julius?' he whispers intensely.

'The fallen books are general and vague,' Julius says, suddenly becoming louder and more serious. 'The characters and the symbols are consistent through the aeons, yet the details never so, and always ever changing. So keep your eyes and ears open; the answer will come in due time to those who are chosen to receive.'

This conversation had a profound impact on Phillip. Even though it left him more confused than before, with more questions than answers, it gave him a feeling of closure, and even a solidification in regards to starting a jiujitsu academy. He had, of course, been flirting with this idea for a while, albeit half-heartedly; but now, with all that he had experienced in the last couple of days, he had both the spirit and the reason to pursue this necessary next step in his life. And whilst he wasn't sure at this point what to make of this old man's ramblings and fallen books, since experiencing and seeing what he did in his and Áine's vision, he was willing to believe anything was possible …

So, that same day, in the evening, he gathered both John and Ishmael together in a local pub to let them know his seriousness on the matter of starting an academy.

'So what do we actually need to get it done?' he asks as he gulps his third pint of Guinness.

Over the first two pints, Phillip had spent a great deal of time articulating what Julius had said earlier, and highlighted specifically the story of the *Samurais and the Maple Sapling*. He also articulated the contents of his and Áine's vision. John had already been told much of what happened by Suzy (who had already communed with Áine) so was not surprised to hear Phillip's account. At this point, John was a little dismissive of what he and Áine experienced during their vision, sceptical to say the least, and wrote it off as mainly a temporary period of extreme drug-induced psychosis.

'Well, black belts, ideally … Not to mention funds …' John replies sceptically, as he leans back on the red pew in a stained-glass booth.

'Um, you know, it's obviously ideal to have black belts,' Ishmael says, striking a more optimistic tone, 'yet there's some academies who don't actually have any active blackbelts and still teach. We will all be well into our purple belts when we finish university, won't we?'

'Really? There are academies with no black belts and they can still teach?' John asks with frowning eyebrows.

'Yeah, they're obviously cheaper, but they do exist,' Ishmael says as he nods with pursed lips.

'Okay, well, if we aren't going to be black belts, we will need something else to make people want to train with us, something unique, some sort of extra selling point …' Phillip muses as he strokes his stubble.

'Oh no, this isn't your cult idea again is it?' John smirks sarcastically.

Phillip laughs, and says, 'No, no, but seriously; Dean uses high quality music with his powerful speaker system, and we have you, Ishmael, an awesome DJ at our disposal. Maybe we can even get Adam involved and …'

'No, Phillip, you're not going to bring mushrooms or drugs into this are you?' John says, wary of Phillip's more abstract ideas.

'All I'm saying is that maybe, for certain people we get to know, we could provide certain holistic events that provide a unique sort of therapy for those with traumas, or people who want to ponder certain existential questions or what not … Come on! It's unique, and it's interesting! News could spread through word of mouth, and the academy could build gradually through a trusted network of loyal members brought together by a close bond! I'm not talking complete rubbish here, am I?!'

John raises his eyebrows in mild shock and takes a large gulp of his Stella. However, Ishmael looks extremely interested, leaning forward on his elbows with squinting, smouldering eyes, nodding slowly whilst listening.

'I think it's an amazing idea,' Ishmael says.

'See!' Phillip says as he nods at Ishmael while looking at John.

John shakes his head and looks up at the ceiling.

'You know what? I'm annoyed I actually feel so attracted to this idea, even though my mind is telling me it's fucking crazy.'

Phillip stands up and claps his hands rather wildly, causing others in the pub to look over at him.

'Boom, baby! It's on! We are starting a martial arts academy! Ha! Yes boys!'

Phillip holds his drink up to make a toast.

'Wait, before we toast, we need a name to toast to,' Ishmael says.

Phillip ponders for a few seconds, but then it comes to him.

'The Tree of Life. We should call it the Tree of Life,' he says softly and intensely whilst nodding, the name appearing in his mind as if planted there by an external force.

'To the Tree of Life Academy!' Ishmael shouts, standing up and raising his glass high in the air.

'To the Tree of Life Academy!' Phillip and John follow simultaneously as they all chink their glasses together.

The next steps of their life were now clearer than ever before. They were all filled with motivation, drive and *duty*. Now they all had a goal to reach for, and this made them all work and train harder than they ever had. Yet, along with these feelings of excitement and responsibility, there was also a kind of sadness; a kind of sadness that a soldier may feel before going into battle for the first time, knowing full well that the war must be fought, but also knowing that their lives would never be the same again …

PART THREE:
GROWTH

1. HARRY SICKLE

The night of Phillip's death was tumultuous for the Horwood family. A phone call from the police at 4.25am came as quite a shock, especially when it brought news of a death *and* an aggravating trespassing accusation. When John arrived at the care home, he wasn't particularly angry with the boys, and actually rather respected them. Even Suzy's overwhelming feeling was not that of disapproval at the brothers' behaviour but sadness at Phillip's death —although it was at first glance somewhat suspicious that Phillip passed away the same night the brothers visited him. It was confirmed by police that he passed from natural causes, and it had not come as much of a shock to the care home staff, nor John or Suzy, seeing as his condition had been deteriorating rapidly over the last year especially. John specifically brought this matter up with Arthur in an gentle and curious way. Arthur replied, 'He said what he needed to say, and he finally let go of his body.' John was happy to accept this without much question.

In many ways, the Horwoods and the brothers had already done their mourning in the years after the incident. The Phillip they knew died a long time ago, and they could not deny that their melancholy and grief was tinged with relief. None of them wanted to see Phillip as a shell of his former self. Nonetheless, his death caused a major shift in outlook for them all. A large element of their lives up until this point was dedicated to making Phillip as comfortable as possible. They'd never say this was a burden, however a load had certainly now been lifted from their shoulders.

The energy which had been freed up from within them all was now ready to be redirected.

As soon as John saw the cube (and he did see it in the care home when being called there by the police, even though Jack thought he hid it in his pocket) he intuitively knew immediately of its evil, yet decided he would for a while stay quiet. Memories of the conversations he had with Phillip and Áine started ringing bells in his head. On many occasions Phillip had passionately spoken about this cube he saw in his vision and thought extensively about what it was or its symbolic implications. After multiple discussions and making links to concepts such as possession, all they could ultimately conclude for sure was that it was no doubt evil.

John knew both the brothers like they were his own sons and immediately knew it would be Jack that would be more likely to be seduced by such an artefact.

For a while, John made it his mission to listen in to the brothers in secret; he regularly heard Arthur express his worries to Jack about his obsession, saying things along the lines of: 'I'm worried it's going to hurt you. We need to stay away from it until we figure out what it is.'

It was after eavesdropping that John felt compelled to approach Arthur and find out more. On a day that Jack wasn't in the house, he went into Arthur's bedroom to question him. As he walked in and looked at Arthur, Arthur immediately knew what John was going to ask about.

'How long have you known about the black cube then?' Arthur asks guiltily, sitting on his bed with his hands in his lap and his back against the bed headboard.

'What exactly happened that night, Arthur? What did you both do with that cube?'

Arthur took a deep breath, and then said, 'We used it to go inside Dad's soul. We went into a spiritual world that wasn't like earth, and Dad appeared as a lion. He spoke to us as if he knew the future. I didn't fully understand everything he said, but it was powerful, and I will never forget it. I now know that I must help grow his "Tree of Life". But I still don't really understand what he meant by this; did he mean he wants us to help grow the jiujitsu academy? It just felt like he was talking about something much deeper …'

John gave Arthur a serious stare, and then took a deep breath in contemplation.

'I'm not sure if your father ever mentioned it to you, but when we were younger, he had a powerful vision with your mother. He was convinced he was shown the future. In this vision, an angel showed them both many things of a prophetic nature. They saw a future London, and it was much darker and less human. In one of these visions, they were shown a demon on top of an inverted tree, and this demon was holding a black cube. As soon as I saw Jack hold this cube, I was immediately stunned and knew that this was the beginning of what Phillip had always described.'

John recounts to Arthur the wisdom of the old caretaker, Julius, and recalls the prophecies of his fallen books. He then tells the story of the Grey 24 and the Japanese maple sapling; and how Phillip felt it was his job to plant a sapling, and it was his children's job to grow it.

'This caretaker also said something that puzzled me and your dad for a long time,' John continues. 'He said that Phillip's "holiest son will be called Arthur". When Jack was born, Phillip was hesitant to call his first child Arthur. He felt that it would be unlucky to do so, and he wanted to make sure he was in control of what he called his son. However, leading up to when you were born, he and Áine had been thinking about names for a while, but they kept coming back to Arthur. It was as if they couldn't avoid it, like your name was a big elephant in the room.'

'I'm glad they chose to call me Arthur though, I love my name, actually,' Arthur says with a smile and a modest laugh. John then gives one in return and continues.

'So anyway, Phillip, Ishmael and I decided that we had to start *something* together. At the time, we were all friends because of jiujitsu. So after we graduated from Oxford, we were only a few years off training from our black belts, but we started it before that anyway … As you know, we were successful in our mission, and now have a semi-successful jiujitsu academy. The plan, however, was always to grow the academy into something much more. Your father became obsessed with the idea that we humans were losing our connection to the spirit inside us, the spirit that defines us as humans. He became convinced that machines were gradually replacing everything that makes a human, human; and he believed that, in the future, the Tree of Life could be a place that represents and celebrates humanity, keeping alive everything that we value as a human species. Your father was never quite sure of how he would do this, but all he knew was that for him, jiujitsu and martial arts kept that connection to the instincts inside alive like nothing else. But he always knew that the academy could become much more than just martial arts; he believed that it would go on to become a spiritual hub of inner worship and connection, a place where people would go to connect to the divine and find meaning for their lives, and that this could be done through various practice and ritual, and with the right people to help provide guidance. At first I thought he was quite crazy, and the beginnings of the academy practising this kind of stuff was frankly bizarre and even a bit messy. But, we actually found a way of making it all work …

'Looking at it all now, Arthur, I honestly believe it is up to you and Jack to innovate the academy. I am not losing complete hope in your brother, he's incredibly smart, but I worry that he may be too smart for his own good …'

'Well, if I'm going to eventually take over the academy, I have to start training more. Sorry I haven't been training that much recently, I know there's no excuse.'

'Train at your own pace. Just know that you are still young, but are also talented in various ways, and with time could become a great teacher, and I don't *just* mean for jiujitsu. You have a natural talent at helping others understand themselves, and that, in my eyes, is the most important thing of all. You are extremely intuitive, and that can only be taught to a lesser extent. You will find out very soon what the Tree of Life is really about.'

'Thanks, John, I appreciate how supportive you have been to me and my brother. I honestly don't know how I would have been able to hold myself together if it wasn't for the love of you and Suzy.'

Arthur and John embrace each other for a few seconds. Arthur then pulls back and looks John straight in the eyes with a sudden revelation.

'This demon. I think I know who he is, I've seen him. He's called Moloch, and he was the one who gave me the cube in the first place. Looking back now, I was stupid to trust him, and now I'm scared that Dad hasn't peacefully been united with Mum. I'm scared Moloch has trapped Dad's soul somewhere ... And now it looks like the cube may have possessed Jack's soul too. I don't know what to do John ... I'm scared I'm going to lose my brother as well.'

John holds Arthur's hand to provide some comfort.

'I made a promise to your father that I would always look out for his family if anything ever happened to him; and I intend to keep that promise. Let me tell you this: I will do everything in my power to try and keep your brother from falling into the hands of evil. I'm going to start keeping a close eye on Jack, don't you worry.'

So, John decided to regularly follow Jack at night to see what he was up to. He observed him go to a certain house, number 33, located in the heart of Oxford. It got to the point where Jack would visit this one house almost every evening. At first John assumed he was visiting a girlfriend; but it soon became clear to him that Jack was not visiting this house for pleasure. Every time, without fail, Jack would bring his laptop and his rucksack, and moved in such a way that made him look suspicious.

John's instincts were sounding alarm bells, and he didn't quite know why. Something was telling him the black cube was somehow involved.

He would sit down the road in his car and stare at the number 33, meditating, hoping to see *something*. If John was being honest, he didn't know exactly what or who he was hoping to see. All he knew was that he needed to find out the exact reason why Jack kept visiting this house.

Eventually his curiosity became too much. By this point, he had noticed that Jack routinely entered and left this house at the same times. He would enter at precisely 8pm and leave the house at around 10pm, never being later than 8.10pm, but never earlier than 9.50pm. So one day John decided that he would sneak in through the back of the house at 9pm; hoping to catch Jack and whoever else red-handed at whatever they were doing.

On one rather grey and rainy evening, John decides to make his move. He waits in his car until 9pm, and then approaches number 33. The house is rather large and detached and has lots of dead plants outside the front, with a rotten and crumpled low-hanging vine hanging down over the porch. It could have been a beautiful house if well cared for, but it was clear the owner had neglected it. Outside is a three-series BMW, but even that looks like it had never been cleaned.

John prepares himself to climb over the gate to the left of the house, but as he approaches he notices it's already open, so he enters and makes his way round to the garden. He edges slowly with his back against the wall, making sure no one is there. He peaks around the corner and sees a long, bland garden with a poorly-attended, patchy lawn.

He can't see anyone.

John keeps his body low and shimmies his way deeper onto the lawn, lurking amongst the shadows. As he inspects the back of the house, he notices all the windows are blacked out apart from one. On the very top floor of the house, there is a singular window in the attic extension. Inside, John notices a subtle yet deep, dark red glow emitting from the room. His eyes squint in curiosity and a strong, sharp burst of anxiety floods his stomach. Immediately his instincts flare up and fear kicks in. But John remains calm; his discipline allows him to detach and remain focused. As he does, he notices that his fear is replaced by anger.

What a disgrace it would be if I do not honour my best friend's life, if I allowed his son to be taken by evil, flows through his mind in an aggressive tone.

He decides to waste no time and proceeds to find a way inside. He approaches the back door, tries to open it but finds it's locked. He looks to the right and notices the kitchen window looking onto the garden isn't fully closed, so he pulls it fully open and cautiously climbs through.

With careful leg placement, he manages to avoid knocking over several potential kitchen items which would have alerted those in the house to his presence. As he enters, he looks around the kitchen and notices the state of the place. The bin is overflowing, food stains are on the walls and there are even chicken bones on the floor. John winces in disgust, and then is suddenly curious: who exactly would own a house like this and live in a state like this?

Reminds me of a few student houses at university. My bet is this is the spoilt son of wealthy parents. No discipline and lacking any real responsibility, he thinks to himself.

At this point he is suddenly hit by another wave of apprehension. He finds all the lights being off quite unsettling and unusual. Nonetheless, he continues to head up the stairs to the first floor, and that's when he notices a low-pitched humming sound coming from the attic. The sound is subtle yet very distinct; a sort of rumbling. If the sound were any lower in frequency, it would likely be inaudible.

John's apprehension builds until he can no longer bear it. He decides to confront it by climbing the last flight of stairs with pace and aggression.

Fuck it, he says to himself as he clenches his jaw. He rushes up to the attic and bursts through the door.

John sees Jack and an older man lying on the floor in parallel to each other, both in an unconscious state. The other man has black hair and strong facial features, with a tight masculine jaw and chiselled cheek bones. John is immediately surprised by the look of this man; even lying on the floor he looked particularly well-groomed, not what John was expecting by any means.

Computer wiring scattered chaotically around them hooks them up to an electronic helmet that has at least 20 individual cable connections. In between the two lies the black cube in a metallic cage, which also has several wires connected to it. A dark, deep red gently radiates from it, as if some sort of energy has been activated from within it. The wires all run along to a processing unit, which itself is connected to a bulky computer to the left of a large metallic desk.

John walks towards the desk, on top of which lie two monitors beside each other. On both screens a program is running called 'Spiral Siphon'.

On the screen is a highly detailed and dynamic fractal animation. John controls the mouse and moves it around the screen. As he does, he notices a translucent box in the top right corner. When he goes to hover the cursor over the box, the font becomes opaque and bold to reveal the name 'Jack Stanley' and on the other, 'Harry Sickle'. He squints with curiosity. *Why do I know that name?* he thinks, a feeling of familiarity coming over him. John clicks on Jack's name and sees two options pop up: 'Terminate' and 'Enhance'. John frowns and then looks behind him at the unconscious duo. After a few moments of contemplation, he moves the cursor to click on terminate.

From behind him he hears a large gasp. John turns to see Jack writhing and beginning to come to consciousness. John immediately rushes over to Jack and assumes a full mounted position. He looks down at Jack in fury and slaps him hard across the face.

'The cube is evil, you bloody idiot!' John shouts, his face reddening with fury.

'Get off me!' Jack screams as he begins flailing wildly.

John puts his left arm around Jack's head, applies his body pressure on Jack's right elbow, pinning it across his face, and then grabs Jack's wrist with his hand behind the head. He then sits up with Jack held in front, his right arm controlling Jack's other wrist.

He whispers into Jack's ear, 'You are not going to fall into a dark life. I promised your father I would always be here for you. And I will. I will treat you as my own son.' After realising he's helpless, Jack stops writhing and begins to calm. 'Now, here is what we are going to do. We are going to leave this place, go back home and discuss this.'

John releases Jack from his control.

Both stand up and face each other, staring in tense silence.

'You have no idea,' Jack says, the edges of his lips tightening in contempt towards John. 'The cube is a game-changing piece of technology. Harry and I have managed to create a program that captures the intelligence of the human mind. We have literally been mapping the unconscious human psyche into raw data. I believe that, with this cube, we can finally unlock the full potential of the brain. Do you know what this means for humanity? We can finally program ourselves however we wish by modularising specific neural channels into electronic data. Therefore, we can override circuits that we may not want to be active, such as fear or sadness; any negative emotion can be controlled at our own desire. We can finally cure evil in the world; no more scum like those who killed my parents.'

'You are playing with fire; you have no idea what you're dealing with. We are not smart enough to reprogram our humanity, like we are mere instruments to be fiddled with. You are striving for perfection before you have even achieved completion. Who are you to decide what you should feel at any given point? That is not for your ego to decide.'

'I thought you cared about me. If you did then you would understand that this is my future. I am driven to show people the potential of this technology. I am already growing up and finding my feet in the world, and I have found my passion. Who are you to shoot me down so dispassionately?'

'You are an amazing young man, Jack, and I cannot believe how intelligent you are for your age. I believe you could do amazing things for the world, and that's why it would break my heart to see this satanic cube possess someone with so much potential.'

'This satanic cube?' Jack replies with a condescending look. 'How can you believe in that crap, I thought you were rational? Let me guess, Arthur told you he got given it by a demon.'

'You speak of rationality? How can you still cling to such a narrow view of the world considering you yourself used the cube to enter your own father's soul? How can you dismiss spiritual matters so casually yet believe you possess the intelligence to reprogram our nature however you like? Surely a man of your intelligence would crave a deeper understanding of the human spirit, an understanding that it is more than just numbers and data?'

'Do you want me to be completely honest, John? I don't care what you think. You have always been stuck in the past. I see many people like you who refuse to allow us to move forward as a species. You cling desperately to archaic tales and stories that are clearly made up by people with psychosis. Surely you understand that only through innovation and technology can we finally overcome our own bodies' limiting factors? I don't understand why you are so against self-mastery? I'm going to wake up Harry now, and let me tell you, he isn't going to be happy that you've snuck into his house.'

'Wake him up then. I'll let him know how much of a shithole his house is. Maybe he needs to realise that before he reprograms the entire human species, he needs to get his own house in order first.' Jack rolls his eyes, and then goes over to the computer to wake up his friend.

The black-haired man awakens.

Unlike Jack, he does not gasp or writhe at all. As he leans up, he calmly looks left and right with a mildly confused frown. The man looks at Jack then points at John as if to ask, 'Who is this guy?'. He analyses John for a few moments, squinting with curiosity.

'You want the cube, don't you?' the man says, after taking a moment of contemplation.

'Whilst I admire both your and Jack's ingenuity, I'm afraid I cannot allow you to continue using this piece of technology. Jack's father had a vision of it long ago, and it is for certain evil. You must understand, I am acting out of love,' John says calmly.

'You seem like a good man. And although you broke into my house, I can overlook that. In a way, I respect such a bold action. Allow me to introduce myself, my name is Harry.'

John and Harry make strong eye contact, tension growing as both take stock of the situation.

'Nice to meet you, Harry, my name is John. I'm Jack's godfather. I've been looking after Jack and his brother since the loss of their parents,' John says with as much politeness as he can muster given his underlying feeling of contempt.

'Oh, Jack has already told me about what happened. An absolute tragedy. Sickening, really. Imagine if we could have stopped him being assaulted in the first place? Wouldn't that be something?' Harry says smugly, clearly enjoying the fact that he knows John's opinion with differ.

John frowns, suspecting Harry is trying to lead him down a dead end.

'I have just had this discussion with Jack, and whilst I respect the fact you are trying to help progress the human species, the wisdom I have acquired over my life gives me a strong feeling that this road will not end well. I have always respected people's desire to make the world a better place, but such invasive and extreme methods are never the way.'

Harry stares at John with exaggerated astonishment, mocking him. It made John feel distinctly uneasy as he realised this was not just a hopeless dreamer but a potentially dangerous individual. A primal instinct, a gut feeling and the eerie tingle travelling up his spine, told him that Harry had a deeply troubling spirit. A wave of ominous apprehension came over him.

'Animals. So many animals. Savages, in fact,' Harry says shaking his head, with a smirk on his lips. 'The instincts pose a problem, John, a great problem.

Old hardware needs updating. Imagine a mass overcoming, a mass detachment from such old toxic feelings and emotions. This is not far away for us now; we can finally overcome ourselves, truly be free from the burden of this savage body we are cursed with from birth. We are like caterpillars waiting to burst forth and fly! Allow the machines to rise and give us wings! Like butterflies!' Harry enters a sort of trance, as if hypnotised by his own words.

'And what if it is not a butterfly that comes from this? What if it is in fact a moth that you create? And this moth forever suffers, having an unquenchable thirst for light, which it lacks deeply from within.'

'Very abstract, John. I didn't realise you were one for poetry. From how Jack spoke of you I thought you would be a bit more … simple.'

'You think you're so clever, don't you? I'm afraid I have to leave your house now; it's just all this mess is making me feel like I'm in a chimp's bedroom. Now, I'm going to cut out the pleasantries and say it how it is. We can do this the simple way, or the hard way. Either pass over the cube, or I will take it by force.'

'I'm not sure if you've figured it out yet, but I'm not going to let you take it,' Harry says sarcastically with a sigh, tilting his head and raising his eyebrows. 'You might not know it, but this operation isn't just between me and Jack. We have a team of people working around us.' Harry finishes talking with the same smirk as before, and this time winks at John.

John frowns.

'Mango,' Harry says as he looks at John.

A door bursts open.

Three men with stun guns emerge from a bathroom. They storm towards John and open fire, hitting their target and causing John's body to seize and spasm. They hold their stun guns on his spine whilst they restrain him with buckles and handcuffs.

'Now, as I was saying, Jack and I work as a team, but we are soon going to be an official business!' Harry smiles with enthusiasm. 'And every business needs to thoroughly test and refine its product. So today, you get to be one of our product testers!'

Harry walks over to the computer whilst his men connect the electronic helmet to John's head.

'Hmm, let's see. Let's upload this set of code I've been working on.' Harry starts typing and accessing code on the computer.

'Fuck you!' John shouts.

One of the men stuns him in the throat, and John's body once again spasms, his face clenching in contortion.

'And ... Here we go ...'

Harry presses a button on the keyboard, and John's eyes roll back. His body becomes limp and lifeless. The cube starts glowing ever so slightly more, and the humming reverberates even deeper, yet still quietly, causing everything around to vibrate.

All the men other than Jack stare at John with smug pleasure. Jack instead purses his lips and looks around cautiously with fleeting glances.

'He will be okay after, won't he?' Jack asks softly.

'Yes. He will be fine. He just won't be bothering us any longer,' Harry replies.

2. AN AWKWARD AFTERNOON

John and Jack return through the front door of the Horwood home at 1pm the next day. Arthur's ears immediately pick up on the two entering the house, so he decides to walk to the top of the stairs and look at them both through the bannisters. He sees them both looking rather calm and emotionless, which makes him curious.

'Where have you two been then?' Arthur asks as he walks down the stairs.

'We went on a walk and discussed some things, and then met up with a friend of mine; we stayed round his for the night. Had a few drinks,' Jack replies whilst looking up, rubbing his hands together slowly as he does.

Arthur continues to stare at John, hoping and expecting to receive some eye contact, but John gives none back at all, seeming distracted and uninterested.

John and Jack enter the kitchen together, and Arthur follows closely behind. Suzy stands over the kitchen counter and starts to dish up pasta and meatballs.

'Don't even start. I'm not going to speak to either of you until this food is on the table. But if you can't tell, I'm not happy.' Suzy says with a forced calmness.

The boys all sit down at the table. Immediately, Arthur notices an awkward tension in the air and Jack looking around frantically in a weird manner.

Suzy brings the food to the table and also sits down.

'Right. I'm going to make myself very clear,' Suzy says in such a way that it seems rehearsed. 'I am not an idiot, and I know something is going on behind my back. You don't think I haven't noticed you leave just after Jack does?' She looks at John with venom. 'And Jack. I understand you have your business aspirations, and I am proud of what you are doing. I understand you need to do what you need to do, and I also respect you are quite a private person, so for this reason I have made an effort to never ask too many questions. I would be lying if I didn't say I have my suspicions and doubts, but I have until now kept these to myself. But John, you clearly are hiding something from me, and either way it's starting to become disrespectful because we are meant to tell each other everything, and to not tell me is essentially saying I am a child who can't handle the truth. Your "just going on a quick walk" excuse simply isn't going to cut it anymore. I want you both to tell me right now exactly what happened last night.'

'We went to my friend and business partner's house; his name is Harry. We had a few drinks and spoke about our plans for the business,' Jack replies casually, as if it's not a big deal.

Suzy at this point is staring at her husband, expecting some input from him. Instead, John is twirling spaghetti around his fork rather slowly and mechanically, fully focused on only that and nothing else. She frowns and looks at Arthur and Jack to see if they have also picked up on the odd behaviour coming from him.

'John?!' she says, now extremely annoyed, looking over at Arthur to see if he knows something she doesn't.

'Yes, are you okay?' he replies, looking as if he suddenly had awoken from a trance.

'I'm fine, John. Are you okay? Have you listened to anything I have just said? Or have you just tuned me out like I don't deserve to be listened to? Can you not see I'm very serious right now, and it's actually making me a bit emotional.' She shakes her head, looking very confused. 'Why are you acting weird? Why?!'

Suzy is on the edge of tears, feeling a creeping sense of dread, knowing something very serious is happening yet having no idea at all what it actually is.

'Oh, I'm sorry,' John replies with a fake, detached smile. He turns back to face his food and carries on slowly eating.

Suzy stares at her husband dumbfoundedly. After a few moments of this intense staring and contemplation, she stands up, grabs his plate, and throws it aggressively at the kitchen worktop, meatballs and pasta flying everywhere.

She comes back to the table and sits down again.

'My food,' John says softly, staring forward blankly.

Suzy beats her fists repeatedly onto the table like an enraged chimpanzee. Glasses spill, pasta and meatballs fly everywhere.

'What is happening?! Tell me! Tell me now! Tell me!!' she screams.

'Maybe it's private, Suzy, you don't have to know everything,' Jack says with unexpected aggression.

'Excuse me?! He's my bloody husband! Of course I deserve to know! If you don't tell me what happened tonight, I'm kicking both of you out of the house!!'

At this point Arthur hyper-focuses on John. He squints and stares at him like a hawk, trying to gain as much information as possible, summoning every ounce of intuition and intelligence he possibly could. It did not take long for him to realise that John's odd behaviour was related in some way to the black cube, and the very thought sent butterflies through his stomach.

'It's the black cube,' Arthur says suddenly, and with conviction. Jack gives a mocking laugh; it's hollow and does not sound genuine, and his face is also beginning to turn red.

'What have you done to my husband!?' Suzy screams at Jack.

'I didn't do anything,' Jack replies.

'Why are you lying?! You always lie!'

'Nope. Not lying. I didn't do anything.'

'But you know who did,' Arthur says calmly, 'and you know what happened to him, so by concealing the truth, you are lying.'

'Oh, please. Can everyone relax, he's literally just eating his food,' Jack says nonchalantly. 'I don't even know why you think he's acting so weird. He's literally just sat down and suddenly everyone's freaking out and accusing me of being a liar. How about we ask him how he's feeling before we jump to conclusions; John, how are *you* feeling?'

'Yeah, not too bad, just really hungry,' John replies in a weak, monotone voice.

'You think you can trick me like this? I know my husband; we've been married for 15 years ... What have you given him?'

Suzy puts both her hands on either side of John's face and turns his head towards hers, forcing him to look directly at her.

'John?! Are you there?' Suzy's words start to tremble, becoming ever more frantic, tears streaming down her face.

'Yes, I am here. Hello, Suzy,' John says, again with a detached monotone voice.

'You're not, though! Tell me your name! Do you even know who you are?

'I am John Horwood.'

Suzy's demeanour shifts again. It is one less of anger and now more fearful. She looks very confused and clearly overwhelmed. Arthur notices Suzy's struggle, and is also hit by a wave of sadness and frustration. He stands up and uses his head to signal Suzy to follow him into the living room next to the kitchen.

Suzy does so, crying into her hands as she walks.

Arthur enters the living room and shuts the door behind him after Suzy enters. He was fully expecting Jack to listen in to the conversation, but at least it gave the illusion of privacy and space for Suzy. Arthur gets Suzy to sit down on the sofa then sits in front of her with crossed legs on the carpet, looking up at her.

'Okay, Suzy, you need to listen to me. I think I know what's causing John's weird behaviour. You know of my seizures, and you know of my visions. Well, in my visions recently, I have been seeing a demon; his name is Moloch. I know this sounds crazy, but you need to trust me.'

'I trust you! I trust you! Please, just tell me everything you know!'

'Okay, well, this demon gave me this dark cube the day before Dad died. At first, I wasn't sure what to make of it, but now I know it is evil. The cube provides some sort of connection into other realms; it contains a power which I don't fully understand. Jack has become gradually attached to this cube, and I fear he is doing something with it that is dangerous. A few weeks ago, John told me he was aware of this cube from a long time ago; he said my mum and dad had a vision of this very demon and the cube. John then said he would keep an eye on Jack, and for the last few weeks he has been following Jack in the evenings. Those walks he says he's been going on? Really, he's been following Jack. Where exactly I don't know, but I fear Jack is up to no good. My intuition is telling me that Jack has weaponised the cube in some way or another. I have had a feeling that he's been involved in what he calls a "business" for a while, yet I fear he is actually involved with a sort of gang. I think John, while investigating Jack, has ended up being a victim of this cube's power in a way I can't comprehend. Suzy, I am so sorry, I don't know what we can do, but this is what I believe to be the truth.'

Suzy's eyes look up at the ceiling and a fresh tear runs down her cheek. Her eyes level with Arthur's, and her face turns serious and focused, as if things have become suddenly clear to her.

'I know what we have to do … But first, I have to tell you something …' Arthur frowns in curiosity at what she has to say.

'That vision John told you about, the one your parents had at the Bagley Mysteries festival. Well, that was a big day for all of our group; in fact, it changed me, and it changed the way I look at life. We all took psychedelic mushrooms, and I had quite a scary experience. I was scared for a long time after that day; however, I feel it has opened my mind and built me as a person. Your parents, though, they had an experience that was simply on another level. They had a complete out-of-body experience, and they were shown what they both believed to be the future. Since that day, both your parents, John, Ishmael and a psychedelic researcher at Oxford University called Adam decided they would start an academy for mystical and shamanic research and practice. That academy is the Tree of Life.'

'Yes, I know. John has already told me about the real purpose of the academy, it's not a mere martial arts academy, is it?' Arthur asks.

'Only on the surface. The martial arts help provide cover for the other activities at the academy, as well as giving members a good level of grounding, discipline, focus and keeping their bodies healthy.' Suzy then brings her thoughts back to John, and looks down with a sigh, rubbing her forehead. 'But yes, I do feel that the academy may be able to help John. I remember John telling me once that there was a certain ceremony at the academy which helped a man who was paralyzed from the waist down walk again by stimulating a form of neurogenesis that allowed new neural connections to form. This man went from barely being able to speak, and being bound to a wheelchair, to almost making a full recovery. I don't know much about the details, but even if there's a slither of a chance we can help John regain connection to his former self, it's worth a try. Some of the stuff the academy achieves is frankly mind-blowing, and I'm just sad it couldn't get more recognition. Who knows, maybe one day the academy *will* grow into something quite special.'

Arthur and Suzy decide they will at once take John to the academy. They stand up and walk towards the door, and hear the pitter patter of footsteps walking down the corridor.

'I knew he would be listening in,' Arthur says, shaking his head.

'Yes, well, he's staying here whilst we take John. He's already caused enough trouble,' Suzy replies.

3. A SECRET EXPOSED

After some effort, Arthur and Suzy persuade John to get in the car because 'Ishmael and Adam need some help at the academy'. By this point, Suzy had already made a swift phone call to Ishmael to make him aware of the situation, going into one of the other rooms of the house to tell him about the 'peculiar details' of the situation to avoid triggering any suspicion from John. She also said she would be coming to the academy immediately, and that he should make emergency preparations for John's arrival. During this process, John was constantly complaining of being too tired, and how he just wanted to sit on the sofa. This resistance from John further confirmed Suzy and Arthur's suspicion that something was seriously wrong with him, as laziness was severely out of character. Suzy was also adamant that she would be driving, which never happened usually, and for once John strangely did not resist. This did not go unnoticed by Arthur and Suzy because John usually took great pride in being the family's 'designated driver'.

So, the three of them left to go to the academy, leaving Jack at home. From the back seat, Arthur stares out of the car window and sees Jack standing by his bedroom window. Arthur feels a little disturbed by the image ...

Suzy drives at pace to the Tree of Life Academy. It is located outside the centre of Oxford in a rather secluded area surrounded by many trees. Within the tree boundary is a large, open field, which surrounds the academy on all sides and extends behind it for approximately half a mile. At the front is a battered metallic fence covered in ivy with a crooked gate. Past the gates stands the training hall itself. It is nothing special to look at; it is mainly made from red brick and has a triangular corrugated iron roof that is common to many urban British warehouses. It is quite modest in size.

Suzy pulls up directly in front of the hall's doors, and before all inside the car can exit, Ishmael and Adam rush out of the hall to greet them.

John is actually the first to exit the car, and he does so with surprising speed and urgency.

'Ah, there you are!' Ishmael says enthusiastically.

'I don't understand why you need me here right now. I was quite comfortable at home,' John replies.

'Oh, our apologies to interrupt your evening, but we really do need your help,' Ishmael says.

'Yes, I'm so pleased you have made it, we are in desperate need of your assistance. How about you follow us inside?' Adam says.

Ishmael makes strong, confident eye contact with Suzy, trying to reassure her everything is going to be okay. Adam begins walking inside but stops when he realises Ishmael is still standing still. Ishmael. noticing Arthur is in the back of the car, looks over again at Suzy, who gives him an intense nod in reply.

Ishmael looks over at Adam with a knowing glance.

'He's here,' he says softly.

Arthur gets out of the car and both Adam and Ishmael walk towards him.

'It's lovely to meet you, Arthur, my name is Adam.' They shake hands.

'Lovely to meet you. Did you know my father then?' Adam smiles, and gives a soft chuckle.

'Yes. Me and your father became very close at university. I was once a researcher and lecturer there, and he was my finest student.'

'I thought I was your finest student?' Ishmael asks playfully.

Adam winks at Ishmael.

'Your father was a great man, and I loved him dearly. Yet now is the time that you too become great.'

Arthur frowns in confusion at the meaning of this.

'As far as I'm aware, you have only trained occasionally in the dojo, am I correct?' Adam continues.

'Yes. And I have been thinking about this a lot recently; I think it is a bit disrespectful to my father how I haven't been training. He always encouraged me to, but for some reason I never got into it.'

'Well, just so you know, Arthur, I am not a jiujitsu teacher. In fact, I am not even a martial arts teacher of any kind. For that, you have John and Ishmael, along with some of the other experienced students. Like you, I train occasionally, but I provide instead … a different type of training. And today, you will find out what exactly what I mean by that.'

The group enter the hall. Inside is much more beautiful than the outside. The walls are a clean white and most of the floor is covered in white mats. There are also some black mats attached vertically to the walls. The day is drawing to a close, so the sun is low and shines through the windows basking the hall in a golden light. The hall is virtually free of clutter. There are Japanese maple trees in each corner, and on the right side there are two doors for the toilets and showers for each gender and some cubby holes for the students' belongings. On the walls are paintings that look very Japanese in style: a deep blue circular swirl on a white background and a yin yang symbol, both watercolours.

An class of approximately 30 students is in process. Many are sparring, but others are leaning against the black mats on the side, all soaked in sweat. A man with a brown belt and a white gi is standing in the middle of the mats observing the students who are sparring with their partners. The electronic clock then bleeps to signal the end of the round, and the sparring finishes.

'Okay, guys, I'm afraid this class is going to end a little early today,' Ishmael announces to the class as he steps onto the mat, quickly taking off his shoes. 'But for the blue belts and above, we are hosting a special advanced class down in the basement. Please stay if you would like to join.'

The white-belt students congregate at the cubby-hole area and begin changing into their casual clothes. The rest stay still on the mat.

'I put word round that we would be having an emergency ceremony for the initiated members to join; they all know John is in trouble,' Ishmael says softly to Suzy, which Arthur overhears.

The class stares at the white belts; it is clear they are being pressured to leave, and an awkward tension grew. Not one white belt decides to stay for a shower, and they all change with urgency.

Once all the white belts finally leave, about 20 students remain. Suzy leads John over the mats with deliberate care, as if looking after an elderly relative, towards a door at the right corner of the hall; her sense of urgency was obvious, not even taking his or her shoes off (which is usually considered a sacrilege when walking over the mats). This is noticed by the students, confirming their suspicions of the severity of the situation.

Adam walks to the centre of the mat and begins making an announcement; Ishmael is sitting down crossed legged behind him, and he gives Arthur a look as if to say 'sit down with me'.

'As many of you know, my brothers John, Phillip, Ishmael and I once had a dream. We had a dream of building a sacred place to better oneself. A place of worship of all that is meaningful. A place where we could connect to the things that matter in life. A place where wisdom of the past is upheld, respected and acted upon to fulfil one's full potential. A place that allows us to disconnect from the distractions of the outside and reconnect to the beauty within. A place of healing, of guidance, of understanding of all that is spiritual, and ultimately a place of building love. We may have lost Phillip, but today we bring back his spirit with the addition of his son, Arthur. Today we celebrate death, with *rebirth*. But I must stress that today is not a cause for celebrations; today is a day of work and healing, because today we must help John, for he is unwell.'

Adam and Ishmael turn to John, who stands by the rear door, looking rather fragile and weak, as if feeling uncomfortable and emasculated.

'What is going on?! I want to leave,' John says in a rather panicked tone.

Ishmael quickly stands back up and walks over to him, with Arthur following behind him.

'Look at me, John,' Ishmael says, grabbing John's shoulders. 'You are not yourself. I have only seen you for the best part of 10 minutes, and I can tell you are disconnected from your soul; Suzy herself noticed this almost instantly. You must try and trust us; we are your family, and we love you.'

John looks over at Suzy, whose eyes swell and water, and she looks down at the floor in distress.

'He's right, John,' Arthur says as he lightly touches John's arm. 'I fear you have a type of mind infection. I fear it is the product of the black cube we spoke about.'

'What do you mean, black cube?' John replies.

Arthur and the others look at each other worriedly.

'Come John, follow us,' Adam says softy.

'No! I won't come! I will not!' John stamps his feet with childish anger, like one who is having a tantrum.

'John! We are trying to help you!' Suzy says as she runs over to John and holds his face between her hands, tears now streaming down her face.

'Get off me!!' John screams in a deep voice filled with anger, as he pushes his wife away. Adam and Ishmael, along with a couple of the higher-ranking students, try to gain control of him, but he continues to flail and scream like someone who is possessed by a demon. Arthur watches this unfold and feels rather scared. A new feeling then arises in him, one of losing control. It had been John who for half his adult life had been a father figure to him, and to see him this way was just awful. This stoic man of order reduced to a chaotic mess.

Ishmael and Adam finally manage to restrain John by pinning both his arms behind his back using a kimura grip. They begin walking him carefully to the far end of the hall towards a door, which some of the students hold open for them. Suzy walks behind them too and looks back at Arthur to signal for him to also follow. The rest of the students follow behind Arthur.

Through the door, a large and beautiful oak tree appears with a large open field behind it. The tree's leaves are incredibly vibrant and green and the trunk is dense and mighty. As Arthur crosses the threshold to this outside space, he stops in bewilderment to stare at it. Within him a feeling of familiarity arises, and he suddenly feels a warmth in his stomach.

The signs of a seizure build within him.

He falls to the ground and starts to spasm.

Suzy rushes to comfort him. Adam and Ishmael look back in confusion.

'Go! Keep going downstairs and carry on with it! I'll take care of Arthur; he will be fine,' Suzy shouts to them as she holds her hand behind Arthur's head, stroking his face with the thumb of her hand.

Adam and Ishmael continue to take John into a shed on the right side of the tree. Most of the students also follow, with two staying behind showing concern over Arthur.

'Has this happened before?' one of the students ask.

'Yes, he has a condition caused by trauma from his childhood, the incident that killed Phillip and his mother, Áine. He will be fine, but they are very intense on his soul.'

'Of course, I am sorry.'

'It's fine.'

Arthur feels his consciousness leave his body. He even looks down at his own spasming form, flinching at the sight. He turns around to look at the tree, with its colours looking even more saturated and vivid than they did whilst in his earthly flesh. As he stares with a deep awe, a translucent figure of his mother steps out of the bark. The ghostly yet angelic Áine glides towards him, looking sad, with tears streaming down her cheeks. She continues to glide until she's face to face with him. For about five seconds she just stares in silence.

'Save him,' she says with bright watery eyes.

Arthur feels his dead mother's hands clasp around his, her eyes widening, staring profoundly into his soul. Electric waves of spirit flood into him, as if he's being injected with a powerful drug.

Arthur's soul re-joins his body.

Suzy stands above him, holding his hands.

'Mum! Mum!' Arthur cries out like someone still dreaming.

'It's okay, Arthur.' Suzy says as she embraces him.

'I think Dad's soul is still trapped,' Arthur says.

Suzy holds eye contact with him for a few moments and tries to think what this means.

'It's okay. Let's not dwell on what you saw right now; allow time to work with you.'

And so, they venture through into the little shed that is beside the tree. Inside, and to Arthur's surprise, there are no stairs or ladders that lead underground in sight. Instead, what they see is a kind of shrine with a golden, metallic Tree of Life icon connected to a grey-stone bricked wall. To the left and right beside them are a few plant plots with flowers of different varieties, and in the corner, a pot for an incense stick (which is not burning at this point).

'This is the secret passage we use to access the underground academy; it closes itself automatically to prevent it from being accidently left open. You now understand that what we do here is in fact quite secretive.'

Arthur touches the tree icon, looking fascinated.

'I'm not blaming you, but why didn't you and John tell me about all this? This is such a massive thing.'

'As you are Phillip's son, we can't be seen to give you special privileges. Like everyone, you must go through some degree of initiation. You have up until now not been ready to experience what we do here; but now, with what's happening with John, the time has finally come …'

Suzy reaches up to the icon and pulls it down along the wall like it is attached to a sort of mechanism. The icon moves in the shape of a Christian cross.

'Stand back,' Suzy says with a sharp and authoritative tone.

A stone slab beneath them slides across, revealing stairs to the underground.

They venture down the stairs, the other two members still following behind. At the bottom, they enter a large room with a round table, which has an open centre, all of which lies below hanging roots stemming from the great oak above. The ceiling has stone beams entangled by the tree's roots in a stunning combination of structural engineering and natural chaos. Most of the roots gravitate towards the centre of the open table, as if attracted to this spot, where a bright white rock resides. Around the table are 24 chairs. There is a gap cut out of the table, giving walking access to the middle.

Suzy beckons Arthur with her fingers, raising her eyebrows over towards the rock in the centre.

Suzy signals the two initiates to leave, and they walk through two large double doors to the left of the room.

Arthur approaches the table and looks into the centre. He sees the white, muscular rock sprouting from the ground, with a slit at its apex. Arthur is lost for words; everything feels clearer and more vivid, as if in high definition, like his vision during his recent seizure.

He walks through the gap in the table and looks above at the surrounding roots in awe; a strong feeling of cosiness overcomes him, a feeling of safety and security, a feeling he had experienced as a young child when going to his now deceased grandparents' house. He looks down at the rock and glides his hands over its peak, over the slit.

'No Excalibur? It's like the rock from the myth, but without the sword …' Arthur remarks curiously, his pupils heavily dilated.

'Your father believed there are points where myth and the material world synchronise harmoniously; do you think it is mere coincidence that your name is Arthur?' Arthur walks out from the table's centre and looks around in awe at all the chairs.

'All these chairs, there's so many, these are like King Arthur's knights of the round table,' Arthur says somewhat innocently.

Suzy smiles.

'I always thought that Phillip, and your mum for that matter, were a little crazy if I am to be completely honest. Ever since university, I was always the most "grounded" one of the group, and I always kept trying to bring them back down to earth. Obviously, I failed in that regard, and instead they brought me up to their crazy level.' She chuckles. 'But now I must be at least a little crazy myself if I'm involved in such a project as this. At least I can admit it, and although this is all rather weird, I'm not delusional. Honestly, though, I wouldn't have it any other way; I feel since being involved here I have felt meaning like never before. I feel part of something, part of something special …

'Regarding the 24 seats, you are right, it is a lot and a very specific number, and it brings me on nicely to who I want you to meet before I show you the main area where we conduct our ceremonies and various other holistic practices. John's in there now.'

Suzy goes on to describe the Bodleian Library caretaker, Julius, and the prophetic fallen books, including the Grey 24, and how these books inspired Phillip to begin his journey of fulfilling the prophecies.

'During this time after the Bagley Mysteries, our lives all changed. We all became much closer, like a family, and everyone else other than myself were regularly doing this special "research" with Adam. It gave them a unique bond like I have never seen; yet I did worry it was bordering on being cultish, so for that reason I stayed out of it all. It was just too much for me to handle. As I may have mentioned to you before, I had a weird trip and it put me off, not that I was really interested in doing psychedelics in the first place; but I felt my place was keeping the rest of the group grounded in reality. At the end of the day, we all must have stability in our lives, as much as dreams and spiritual experiences are important; how can we achieve our dreams of the future if we can't even feed ourselves *today*? Adam himself always mentioned the importance of keeping a healthy and strong conscious ego, and that's why you see such a large focus on martial arts here; it keeps the initiates grounded, focused, disciplined, humbled, and makes them realise we are still humans with flesh bodies and not some floaty spiritual orbs free to go anywhere in the universe we please; not yet, anyway. In some ways the academy here is a cross between Christianity and Buddhism. We focus on introspection and observe *the way*, yet we do not ignore the struggle and suffering of life. Instead, we accept life's responsibilities, carry our cross and accept we must live like this life is worth living. The people connected to our academy are people of all walks of life, from rich to poor; and everybody here offers wisdom and advice to one another, helping them thrive and lead meaningful lives.'

'And I will continue to keep emphasising the importance of grounding until everyone listens,' Adam says as he enters the room from the double doors, overhearing Suzy. 'As you can imagine, I've seen many of my students "lose it" during psychedelic exploration, and of course this is where the stigma comes from. It's a great shame because, if treated with respect and understanding, they will also treat you with respect and understanding.' Adam turns towards Suzy. 'Suzy, dear, it is highly important you attend to John; we have just got him to drink from a brew, and he is now entering an altered state. He is in desperate need of your love. I will carry on the tour for Arthur myself and introduce him to Julius.'

'I think you are right,' she replies. 'Arthur had a seizure upstairs in the tree garden, did you see?'

'Yes, to some degree. Are you okay?'

'Yes, I'm fine, thank you,' Arthur replies.

Suzy scurries over to the double doors, joining John in the ritual.

'However, Adam, whether I'm fine or not is usually dependent on what I see during them … And what I saw today added suspicion to what I have been worrying about recently.' Adam approaches Arthur and holds his hand out towards one of the seats of the round table, and they both sit down.

'I'm not sure how much you know, but this black cube that has possessed John; well, I think it may have also trapped my father's soul after he died. What I saw upstairs has further confirmed my suspicions. I saw my mother emerge from the tree, in a ghostly form, and she came up to me and said, "Save him", and that was when I awoke.'

Adam squints with curiosity and strokes the stubble on his chin.

'Black cube, you say … Hmm. Well, Arthur, I will not speak directly of the meaning of your vision, nor this cube; however, I will always be here when you need me, and I will try my best to help you. You clearly have a natural gift, similar to that of the shamans in early human civilisations; but, as you may know, this gift can come at a cost. Ultimately, we still need to survive, and for that we must be strong and resilient. Visions of sorts, and partaking in rituals using conscious-altering substances, or even visions that are not induced by substances, like the ones you experience through seizure, these can be great tools for growth but can also be destructive to growth too. The psychologist Carl Jung once said, "Be careful of unearned wisdom." Wisdom you have attained not through work or general life experience can be destabilising, as you may not know what to do with it or how to apply it to your own life. This can lead to great confusion, and it can actually be detrimental. You see, Arthur, it may be a cliché, but it is all about the balance. You may know this logically, but practising what you preach is a different matter altogether. You see, your father believed in the return of a wise, spiritual king, a king who had spiritual foresight, but also a king who could relate to the common man; a man of the high but also the low. A mystical figurehead that is the heart and spirit of a civilisation, and a leader who doesn't burden himself with the day-to-day logistics and gossips of running a country; no. He believed there would be a return of an intuitive king who sits and pays attention, and calmly sees the tension of opposing views from a higher perspective. A king who is connected to the roots of his civilisation, but also one who has eyes to branch into the future. He believed that if civilisation is without such a magical figure, there is nobody to represent all the things that matter and give us meaning in life, and, ultimately, there is no truth to build upon and *grow*.'

'I already feel people around me are disconnected to the land of spirit and meaning,' Arthur adds with an understanding look. 'I have never really known any different because of my condition; but even before the incident, I have always had powerful dreams that gave meaning to my life and spurred me on with energy. The only people who I felt really understood me were my mum and dad. Now I have no choice but to be connected to the dream world, even when I'm awake ... But to be honest, I've always felt like an alien in a world of machines. Do you think this spiritual disconnect is a modern phenomenon?'

'Ultimately, it all comes down to the individual's relationship to their unconscious. The Tree of Life began as a place for people to explore their underworld, their unconscious, a place to learn how to integrate the various instincts and demons that lurk there. The various churches of the past previously did this for us, but times have changed, and these old institutions are quickly dying or becoming deformed. However, we cannot forget the gold they possessed and taught us.'

A moment of silence between them arises.

'So, this academy was my father's way of planting something, an institution to connect us all back to our roots? This is unbelievable ... I mean, how did you guys even manage to build this place?'

Adam chuckles again at Arthurs excitable enthusiasm.

'Oh, Arthur, you haven't even seen all of it yet! Let's just say that we have many ... "members in high places" who believe in our purpose and sponsor what we do here. People who believe in what we represent, but for various reasons, sometimes political, understand that what we do must be kept a secret, for now, at least. Currently we have just over a hundred members, with only half of those trusted to come underground, and only 14 members a part of the Grey 24 table. These 24 of the round table are to be the most trusted, and most initiated members. According to the prophecy of the fallen books, once assembled, they will have a special task to complete. To become a member of the round table, there are various tests and initiations one must go through before one proves oneself worthy. And for this reason, we have never been able to fill all the seats. It is awfully hard to recruit people who possess the spirit for the round table. It requires a certain balance of traits that include high intuitive abilities, strength of spirit, purity of heart and soul, and high psychological development. But to be clear here, I am not referring to just high intellect or intelligence − we have rejected many geniuses from being accepted into the Grey 24; in fact, it is sometimes the smartest ones who are most susceptible to losing purity of heart.'

'What special task, exactly?' Arthur asks with his head tilted and eyes squinting.

'It's a good question, and it's still all very vague … Follow me, Arthur, I want you to meet the gatekeeper of our library, and the caretaker of the books we hold to be dearest and most valuable. His name is Julius.'

4. ON WHAT IS TO COME

Adam leads Arthur through double wooden doors to the right side of the round table.

A grand, two-storey library.

The style of the library itself is quite classic, with the roof structure looking somewhat gothic. The ceiling has many colourful patterns that would not look out of place in many European churches, and the roof has a blue tinge that gives the illusion from afar of looking like the sky. The two floors are filled with many sturdy mahogany bookcases. There are also two black doors on either side of the library, which attract Arthur's attention immediately.

The pair walk towards a mahogany desk in the middle, behind which sits a rather fragile looking old man. He is still, with warm, gentle eyes and a soft, subtle smile which conceals an underlying excitement.

'Arthur, meet Julius, the academy librarian and gatekeeper of wisdom,' Adam says, suppressing a laugh as he clearly notices Julius's unbounded excitement.

Julius stands up off his seat and looks deeply at Arthur whilst his hands begin to shake.

'Come here,' he says softly.

Arthur walks towards Julius.

'Nice to meet you, my name is Arthur,' Arthur says as he holds out his hand.

'I know who you are. And I don't *just* know that either,' Julius replies softly and calmly, yet still with a serious tone.

'What else *do* you know then?'

'Your *destiny*,' Julius says after a pause. 'Adam, do you mind if I have a moment in private with Arthur?'

'Of course, just please try not to be too long as I want him to be in in the ceremonial room as soon as possible.' Julius nods, and Adam walks back through the doors they came through.

'You do not know how long I've waited to meet you, Arthur. In many ways, I feel as if I have already met you. And maybe I already have but in different forms … Please, follow me, allow me to show you our library here.'

Julius begins to walk Arthur around the library.

'Most of the books you will find here are classics of sorts. Most books from the world's religions and mythologies can be found here, as well as some of our culture's most loved mythopoetic works,' Julius says as they approach a 'modern classics' section.

'*Lord of the Rings?*' Arthur asks as he points to a series of books, giving a slight laugh.

'Oh, yes, a classic indeed! You know, *Lord of the Rings* has such a depth; it captures such a wide range of humanity and our instincts, not to mention how its integrated much of the mythology from religions, all wrapped up in a beautiful and unique dream format. It captured the heart of multiple generations; how could we not include it in our sacred collection! We even have the Harry Potter series.'

'Well, what about these fallen books I've been told about?'

'Ah, yes, well isn't that the question indeed! Suzy has told you about them then … Well, we don't keep those books casually on *these* shelves because, believe it or not, they have a habit of randomly falling off onto the floor. Instead, we have a pod system: we disperse the 44 books between those four doors you see.' He points to the four doors on either side of the library. 'Let me show you.'

Julius leads Arthur to the closest of the four doors.

Inside is a very cosy space, looking quite like a bedroom. There is a bed in the centre and an iron cladded wooden chest in front. There is also a sofa, a desk and an armchair in front of a fireplace.

'So, firstly, when you become initiated, which won't be much longer now, you're welcome to come in to any of these rooms to relax, read, reflect, pray, meditate, as often as you wish.'

Julius holds out his hand to bring Arthur's attention to the chest on the floor at the front of the bed.

'This is where we keep the books. In each chest, there are 11. This is chest number one, so inside this chest there are additions one to 11. Go on, open it up.'

Arthur opens the chest and sees the books placed in ascending order.

He picks up book number seven.

'Ah, seven. "And by the seventh day God had finished the work he had been doing; so, on that day he rested from all his work." A number of wholeness and completeness, the beginning of new, and the end of old; a fantastic choice,' Julius says, quoting Genesis 2:2.

'*And the Sword That Set Them Free,*' Arthur reads the title of the book.

'Yes, number seven is an amazing one, and in fact my favourite of all the fallen books. Number seven tells the tale of the return of Excalibur to the tree, and how it is finally used to bring back truth and beauty to a land filled with lies and darkness. The book prophesises the sword returning to the rock in the middle of our round table in the midst of the roots of the great oak. When Excalibur is returned to that rock, that will mark the beginning of the chosen one's journey, eventually bringing forth, and becoming, the holy grail; which will grant great powers indeed, including the ability to travel up and down the Tree of Life. Book seven goes on to say that the grail has many powers, including ones of great healing, but will only produce its healing powers when wielded by the one who has proven his ability to be worthy of the sword by partaking in a holy, sacramental journey into the abyss. If the trial is completed successfully, he will have proved himself worthy to God, and therefore tasked the responsibility to heal the great sickness throughout the earthly kingdom. The king will be gifted the ability to heal through his sword and will release the world from the shackles of the six, gifting them the ability to rejuvenate their souls through the phoenix, through the Christ energy, giving all in the land access to the seventh crown chakra, completing the circuit of the true self and hence restoring truth and beauty to the land.

'Arthur, I believe you are this chosen one and are destined to be this king. I believe it is your destiny to return this holy sword to the stone. And I believe you will be able to both remove it and wield it.'

Arthur takes a deep breath and exhales. He walks over to the armchair in front of the fireplace and begins to look down at his hands whilst rubbing his thumbs.

'Julius, I'm feeling overwhelmed. All of this, my father, this sword in the stone, how you believe I will be a king? John … It's all too much to handle … In all honesty, I do not possess the same confidence in myself as you do. I am a broken child, and I know this. I struggle to be normal, I struggle to fit in, and honestly, I don't even have any real skills. All I have is a big heart for the world and an unquenchable curiosity for what is going on in this journey we are given at birth. But still, I know I must go deeper and keep learning of these things, I know I must. But one thing in particular has been bothering me recently …'

Arthur pauses. Julius tilts his head and raises his eyebrows.

'What is the black cube?'

Julius stays silent for a few moments in contemplation, then walks over to the green leather sofa and sits down.

'Please turn the armchair to face me.'

Arthur does as Julius requests, facing him with an intense stare.

'The black cube is a recurring artefact in many of the fallen books and is most notably mentioned in book six. In the books, it is commonly associated with Satan, and known as *his box,* with Satan himself calling it "my box" and others saying "Satan's box".

'The cube was not always evil; it was once bright and sacred. It originally belonged to God's archangel of spiritual war, Saint Michael, and was a gift from God himself. The cube requires constant movement for it to remain light, and so it was originally inside the hilt of Saint Michael's sword, of where it spun perpetually. It was this very sword, with the cube inside it, that eventually became known through the ages as Excalibur; and it is this sword that was passed down to the various heroes and legends of the generations at times when it was needed the most. Unfortunately, Arthur, the sword alone without its cube is not particularly useful. It is a lifeless, blunt instrument; the cube is its beating heart, which gives it life and spirit.

'When the cube is inside the hilt of the sword, it spins, yet the sword requires a sort of spiritual focus and energy for it to become powerful. It is only through alignment with totality, with pureness, embodying the entirety of the instincts and energy centres, that the sword activates. The cube, when in the sword in an idle state, emits only the first six colours of the rainbow, one for each side of the cube: red, orange, yellow, green, blue, indigo; each representing one of the six universal spirits. For six is the first perfect number, and all things in the universe and beyond are made from sixes. You can even see sixes on earth in nature; just look at beehives!'

'Very interesting, Julius … It reminds me of the chakras in Buddhism – each chakra is a colour of the rainbow. But what about the seventh colour, violet?' Arthur asks with a frown.

'A great question indeed! And one I was hoping you'd ask! As, of course, six without the seven is not complete. As God needed to rest on the seventh day to see where he could improve! Even the strongest of us need rest to reflect on where we are not perfect! And it is the work of evil to trap a spirit to a point of no reflection, and it is pride and attachment that prevents us from seeing flaws. For the final and highest frequency of the rainbow colours to shine, the cube needs to spin very fast. For this to happen, the frequency of the six spirits must align in harmony, and this will happen when the wielder is aligned with truth and beauty, or close to God, one may say. When the colours are in perfect harmony and flow, violet will then glow. This seventh colour completes the symbiosis of the six, and makes them one. The violet is the crown and acts as commander to use the power of the six. The sword was originally given to Saint Michael by God to *defeat* evil but also to prevent him from ever using it *for* evil. Michael is the angel who battles the darkness more than any other archangel, and for that reason the sword is a sort of countermeasure to the darkness of the ones he is fighting; as a way to constantly guide his spirit, and to make sure that when he was at his most powerful, it was always coming from a place of love and not corruption. As old Nietzsche use to say: "Be careful when fighting monsters that you don't turn in to one yourself!"'

Julius sneezes quite loudly and then continues.

'Okay, sorry, where was I? Ah, yes. So, in book five, we learn that the cube was originally inside the hilt of Saint Michael's sword and went on to be known as "Excalibur" in English folklore. The sword in the original King Arthur myth was given to him by an angel of a lake. And then, one day, whilst in battle using Excalibur, a mighty strike from King Arthur's arch nemesis, Mordred, forced Excalibur to the ground. It hit a rock, causing the cube to dislodge. And, by consequence, the cube stopped spinning too. Arthur managed to retrieve the sword, but Mordred took the cube. When Mordred looked at the cube, he no longer saw a bright and colourful glow, but instead saw all six colours of each side looking rather dim. Days, weeks, months went by, and the cube still remained in Mordred's possession. The longer he held it without it spinning, the darker the colours became. The cube eventually became mostly a dark and deep red, and then the shade became even darker until in the end it was just black. It has been speculated that in a certain light, one may still see a slither of the red within it. Regarding the effects of the cube when without the sword … Well, it has the power to prevent inner rebirth, trapping souls within their own inner box. The cube lures with tempting thoughts and spirits, presenting them with seductive concepts that on the surface look good and helpful but in reality are demons burrowing their way deeper inside their souls. The cube's power never allows the possessed to let go or reflect, preventing them from being their whole self. It's tragic, really. It is, however, possible to cure possessed individuals. The first, and easiest, way is to be radiated by the violet glow of Excalibur. But for that, it must be wielded by the chosen one. This light gifted by the grail will overpower the evil, forcing a confrontation with the Holy Spirit, and therefore the spirit of God. The possessed can try and resist, and they will scream like a dying beast trying to cling on, yet they will be cleansed and humbled beyond any doubt. However, seeing as we do not yet have access to the sword, this isn't much help. The other way, and this is what we will be attempting to do with John, is to completely destroy the infected ego and bring the awareness back down to the baseline root level, so they can then be coerced by trained guides to consciously let go of the possession by means of humble self-confession. For the more severe and deep-rooted cases, such as those caused by the black cube, it will be necessary to use ritualistic medicines to loosen up resistance. As you will soon find out, we regularly use various remedies and medicines at this academy, for both healing purposes and for general psychological and spiritual growth. A classic for this country is the liberty cap mushroom, which I believe you are familiar with?' Julius smiles at Arthur, and Arthur smiles back, knowing Suzy or John must have told him at some point about his mushroom habit. 'The mushroom was a ritualistic staple for Britain's early Celtic and pagan druid-based culture. In a way I suppose we at the Tree of Life are like modern druids. And it was those very pagan druids who worshipped the tree. Arthur, imagine we are like trees. And like a tree's branches, we can become infected with disease. If the cycle of letting our leaves go is blocked, our branches become bitter and die, and this will reflect in the infected one's personality, making it bitter too, like a withered tree ... The black cube captures one's branches and traps them, preventing them from completing the cycle to grow taller; in other words, from letting go of their old leaves and growing new ones. Once again, it traps the tree by forcing it to just work on the six days and not allowing it to appreciate the seventh day of rest, which is essential for rebirth and for it to gain its crown of individualism.'

'I have seen the effects of the black cube on my brother. He's become obsessed with it, and he's channelling its power in some way with his friend. If I'm being honest, I'm terrified to what's going to come of it ...' Arthur says as he looks into the fire. 'But for some reason I did not feel the same pull to corruption when I held it myself. I felt ideas and shifts within me, yet it wasn't necessarily or obviously evil at first …'

'For the strong-minded, or ones with a spark of the divine, it will take much longer to possess; and you are indeed one with a spark. Unconscious forces are no stranger to you, am I correct?'

Arthur stays silent in recognition of the fact.

'For it is your familiarity with the underworld and its tendrils that give you a resilience to dark objects and their powers. But even for one as aware as you, given enough time with the cube you could also become possessed like any other.'

'Well, as I said, I fear that my brother is using the cube for no good. And I fear he is in some way accelerating or enhancing the cube's power. Surely we must destroy it, no? What do the prophecies say?'

'No. The black cube can never be destroyed. Instead, it is essential we gain possession of it, merging it with Excalibur and gaining the power of the grail. It must be integrated and safeguarded by ones destined by prophecy, which would be up to us, or more specifically, *by you, the guardian of the grail.* Over history this responsibility has changed hands from group to group; but for this current age, I believe we, the Tree of Life, hold this responsibility. Like I mentioned before, the black cube in its idle form is not black, but has various colours, and then, in its activated form, emits a mighty and bright violet. I don't mean to be repeating myself on such matters, but it really is very important you understand all this. Unfortunately though, Arthur, I can only guide you so much. And whilst I am wise, I am bound by the knowledge of the fallen books. But one thing is certain, you must obtain both the cube and Excalibur. Then you must return them both to the sacred stone within the round table. How exactly you obtain these is for your personal myth only, and only you will find the way. I have seen many Arthurs in my books, but every Arthur has their own journey, and whilst there are commonalities, the precise details do indeed differ based on the individual.'

'Julius … This is …' Arthur shakes his head and takes a few moments to regain his composure. 'So, I must acquire both the sword and the cube, and return them as one to the stone. Well, my brother has possession of the cube, so with help from others this will be difficult yet not impossible, especially if we can get John back to normal because he could help with that, couldn't he? Yet for the sword, how the hell am I meant to get that? You mentioned a lady of a lake?'

'As I said, Arthur, it is different for all the different Arthurs of the ages, yet the patterns remain similar. An angelic spirit of some sort, commonly represented as a lady of the lake, will give the sword to the chosen one. But this will happen at a time outside of your control, when the spirit deems it appropriate. You could possess the sword today, or many years from now.

'And I must tell you one more thing … Like I said, there have been many Arthurs in history, and these Arthurs have had the same task of re-joining the opposites of the sword, bringing the light and dark together into harmony, restoring balance to the kingdom. This task always begins by a disconnect of cube and sword. I'm afraid your brother is just our generation's version of Mordred. And the story always goes the same way …' Julius finishes speaking in a sombre tone and with a concerned expression, pursing his lips. Arthur himself begins to feel rather angry, struggling to accept such a thing to be true.

'No, my brother is not Mordred. He is not evil; he is still good deep down, I know this. You don't know he's the Mordred of this story for a fact, you can't know it. As you said before, the patterns are similar, but the details change.'

Julius listens intently and with respect, nodding his head with a sceptical yet soft expression.

'You are correct, I don't know this for sure. It was a mere assumption. I didn't mean to offend you. Regardless, Arthur., the Mordreds of the past who capture the cube fall in love with it hard and fast. I must stress that all the time whilst our Mordred works with the cube, they have no conscious awareness of the demonic influence. The demon will never show its true face to the victim of the possession and will instead come in the form of ideas, emotions or even attach its spirit to actions and rituals, compelling the victim to do such and such in the name of what he or she believes is actually for the good. This demon, lurking in the underworld, will manipulate the behaviour of the possessed one, guiding their actions and emotions, constantly tempting them to dark paths. And like any successful virus, it will encourage the host to spread the dark spirit to others as much as possible. The spirit of the black cube is the inversion of the Holy Spirit; it is, in fact, the *dark spirit*.

'I have seen the demon in his pure form. He did not pretend to show a false face to me. I saw him for the evil he was. His name was Moloch, and he was the one who originally gave me the cube.'

'Moloch, you say? Hmm … That is one of the higher demons of hell. This may be worse than I first thought. But I must hold back on such negative thoughts. I must warn you, Arthur, it is a certainty that at some point you will have to confront the dark one himself, and I'm not just referring to Moloch; I am referring to Satan himself. In preparation for whenever this happens, I would urge you to learn of his devilish ways beforehand. You must gain at least some understanding of his evil ways and trickery. The details of such are in book six. It is called *The Devil's Diary*. It is a reprehensible work and quite a struggle to read without feeling rather sick and disgusted; but I think it is a very necessary read for you still.'

'Okay, Julius, I'll read it.'

'Now go. Before I get in trouble with Suzy. Join everyone in the ritual room for John's healing; the time has come for you to witness the ceremonial process.'

'Thank you, Julius. This has all been a lot for me as you can probably tell. You've told me so much about so many things, and I need time to process it all. Yet still, for the first time in my life I feel I have a purpose; albeit one that terrifies me …'

Arthur begins to walk out of the library.

'Oh, and Arthur, don't wait too long until you read book six. It's very important.' Arthur nods, and continues to walk out of the library in search of the ceremonial room.

5. NEUROGENESIS

Arthur walks back into the room of the round table. Straight ahead of him, on the other side of the room, he sees what clearly is the entrance to the ceremonial room. There are three large double doors that give access, and above them in the centre is a silver metallic icon of a tree. He walks through the doors and enters a purplish bluey middle chamber with another set of double doors in front. In the short time Arthur had been legally allowed to go out clubbing, he had only been to a couple, but within him he couldn't help but feel that all this was awfully similar. As he stands in the chamber, he hears deep musical vibrations, waves, beats, all coming from the other side, that are both subtle yet pronounced.

On either side of the chamber are two crevices within the stone walls, along which are two pleasantly smooth stone slab surfaces covered in crumpled mushroom particles. Within both the crevices are jugs filled with black liquid and next to them three wooden cups of differing sizes. Arthur picks up some of the crumpled mushroom particles to inspect them.

'Well, if it isn't my familiar friend the liberty cap,' he mutters to himself. And then he thinks, *Well, I suppose they have been put here for a reason* ... He glances over at the doors, pauses for a few moments in contemplation, then swiftly pours himself a large cup of mushroom juice ...

Arthur walks through and sees a truly magnificent sight. An electronically lit, large glass dome structure is all around him, like a glowing church of light. In the centre of this glowing white dome is a vibrantly red Japanese maple tree, which seems to be the main focal point for all the initiates. The entirety of the dome glows a deep white, and this light surrounds whoever stands inside. The light shifts and flows like liquid into different shades, becoming either darker or lighter according to the rhythm and tone of the music that plays.

The music here is directed by Ishmael, who stands in a small booth at the far end of the dome. At this point, he is playing a deep, wavy and somewhat calming type of melodic deep house music. The volume isn't blaringly loud and conversation can still easily take place, yet the music is still penetrating and deeply felt. Beside him stand both Suzy and Adam, who occasionally whisper into his ears. Suzy points at Arthur, and he looks over at her, yet his attention returns to his immediate surroundings. He feels the deep bass within him, which seems to be coming from directly underneath the floor; so much so that he can feel the vibrations deep within his body. On the ground there is a translucent jelly-based mat surface, underneath which the light of the dome radiates. The light is so seamless that it is hard to see where the sides of the dome connect to the floor. It is as if this dome is a sort of womb, providing nourishment for all those who step inside.

The immediate effect Arthur feels is one of deep hypnotism (which he feels before the magic mushrooms kick in). He also starts to feel himself fall into a trance and images flicker through his mind, which often happens whenever he feels his mind beginning to relax.

John is in the centre of the dome, underneath the tree's branches and majestic red leaves, rocking back and forth on his knees like someone suffering great stress and confliction. He moves forwards and backwards like a man who is battling with the inside duality of push and pull, and his soul is the singularity caught between these two forces. He holds his hands together, as if praying in a state of intense mania. The fingers of his clasped hands press up against the centre of his forehead, and he holds his thumbs inside his lip, sucking their tips. It is quite obvious he is battling inner turmoil, a man on a tether it could be said, undergoing a punishing yet fruitful journey. John is battling between holding on tight and simply *letting go*. It is clear that he has been hooked by a deep shadow, but the man underneath is still so mighty and strong that even under darkness his soul continues to shine, battling for liberation.

Around John are many of the other initiates, most of whom dance in a relaxed and flowy way, glancing down occasionally at him with worried expressions. Some couples embrace each other while others lie down on the floor in yoga positions or in trance-like states, staring up towards the top of the electronic dome in their meditations. At this point, Arthur looks up to the ceiling and notices that the natural reds and oranges of the sunset are somehow making their way inside the dome from the sky above; subtly, yet still clearly. It is as if he were looking up at the sky from underwater.

It is clear from the occasional subtle compassionate glances from the initiates that they are concerned for John. Yet they give him the space he needs, thinking it best to not interrupt his struggling state. Other initiates use the space to focus on and practise their jiujitsu, clearly benefitting from this magical room and its atmosphere.

Arthur walks towards the centre of the dome, where John is rocking, and sits in front of him. For many moments he remains still and does not attempt to make any connection; he simply observes whilst not being too invasive. After a minute or so of waiting, he calmly, and subtly, tries to make eye contact. John catches Arthur's eye for a moment but immediately shakes his head left and right skittishly, closing his eyes tight like a child trying to escape a nightmare.

'I can see you,' Arthur says softly.

John slows his rocking to a gentle swaying, then tilts his head towards Arthur. For a brief moment, he again makes eye contact. But once again, he turns his head away with a shake.

'You are the strongest man I have ever known. I think in many ways you are stronger than my own father. I watch you now, in battle, and I see a man who is winning,' Arthur says in a composed, firm yet still soft manner.

John once again closes his eyes tight, this time with more anger and rage. His head shakes and his teeth grind. He unleashes a blood-curdling groan, like a wild animal fighting for survival. And then, with haste and power, he leaps up to his feet with his arms wide at his side, as if ready for animalistic combat. This state of frenzy is not directed at Arthur, but instead seems to be a challenge to the forces waging the psychic battle within him. Ishmael, Suzy and Adam notice this shift in behaviour and start pointing from the control booth.

The light radiating from the dome smoothly and rapidly turns to various fluctuations and shades of red; the music becomes much darker and louder, the vibrations and tempo becoming thicker, more layered and more intense.

John flutters around with great pace in a confused, angry frenzy. He staggers around the dome like a zombie. At this point, many of the other members who are practicing their jiujitsu stop what they are doing and switch their focus to John, clearly knowing it may be dangerous to not be aware of this possessed man's chaos. The other members make sure not to stare at John too much, clearly not wanting to make him feel any more disturbed than he already is. Many other of the initiates even carry on their dancing meditations unaltered. However, as Arthur looks around, he senses a certain apprehension among everybody, noticing cautious sideways glances, as if they were all keeping one eye on John at all times.

As John moves around the dome, he grunts and whimpers; what sounds like aggressive groaning gradually becomes softer, more depressive moaning.

After approximately 10 minutes of this chaotic movement, John staggers back to the centre of the dome and collapses his head into his hands, crying. The conducting trio of Suzy, Adam and Ishmael communicate and the vibe of the dome changes once again. This time the dome is various shades of blue and the music becomes more melancholic, yet still euphoric; it's lower in frequency and slower in tempo, yet still with an element of grandness and importance. John continues to calm until he ceases to cry at all, falling silent.

John regains his composure, sitting cross-legged with a straight back.

'Okay, I think he's reached the first baseline plateau,' Adam says to Suzy. 'Now is a good time for you to intervene with your presence; maybe try and involve Arthur too.' Suzy nods in response and walks over to John, glances over at Arthur who is still sitting and gives him a nod.

'John?' Suzy says as she sits in front of him, putting her hand on his.

John does not respond but instead stays completely immobile, his eyes fixed shut. Suzy's hand remains on his, and she keeps it there for 20 minutes. During this period, Arthur began to feel the effects of the liberty caps, and around him his surroundings start to look more saturated and vivid, his emotional sensitivity heightening. He feels energy rise within him, pulsing within his stomach. He takes many deep breaths and closes his eyes.

'Drop it,' Adam says to Ishmael, keeping his eyes fixed forward vehemently.

Ishmael looks back at Adam, raises his eyebrows, takes a deep breath and faces towards his mixing decks and controls. The name on the screen of his mixer displays: '790 Thz – Crown Violet'.

All sound calms to silence.

Darkness falls.

A sound like classical strings, yet electronic, begins to rise.

The tone begins low but then begins to rise and rise, as does the light in the dome simultaneously. A deep and rumbling bass begins, and the light in the dome slowly, along with the rising chord, becomes more vivid and bright. The colour gradually becomes a very distinctive and powerful violet. As Arthur looks around, he suddenly feels consumed by this dome as if it were a womb from the heavens. An intense euphoria rises within him, and this energy manifests itself through the movements of all, as if the general vibration of everyone has been increased. Multiple other layers add to the tone and it all becomes very intense, like a bomb waiting to explode.

John opens his eyes and looks at his wife.

As soon as Suzy sees his eyes, she knew he was back. Behind his eyes was a man reunited with his soul; they glisten and water, containing an enlightened seriousness, radiating focus and depth; a depth caused by seeing horror but also accepting it. In his heart is a sort of divine love caused from seeing pure evil, and therefore he could now appreciate goodness more than he ever could before. His eyes showed a man *reborn*.

Both of them, still with their hands connected and their eyes locked, say not one word but stand up together simultaneously, embracing in a bittersweet ecstasy.

The music finally releases after the building pressure and a deep, powerful thumping bass begins. Everyone in the dome starts smiling, all previous tension now released, and move ecstatically to the heartbeat rhythm.

Water is released from above, as if it started raining. The cool, refreshing water makes everyone around move with an intensifying frenzy. Yet Suzy and John stay connected and calm, still and in deep embrace.

Arthur can't help but begin to move his body to the rhythm, losing himself to the music and energy around him, eyes wide in awe. His body is feeling extremely loose, and everything around him is beginning to twist and wiggle. He is starting to feel overwhelmed, but his feelings of building anxiety are counterbalanced by an extremely powerful sense of belonging, of family, of unity.

A deep sense of love for everything.

A door opens from the side of the dome and a young and pretty blonde lady appears, holding a microphone in her hand.

'Can we all give a warm welcome to our beloved John! A man returning from the abyss!' she says.

Applause and cheers from initiates all around.

'Take your time, John, we are all here for you,' she says.

The blonde girl closes her eyes and the music stops. She starts to hum gently and sweetly.

As the atmosphere calms, Ishmael plays a slow, relaxing piece of music, which matches the girls angelic hymn. The sounds she hums are light and friendly; they seem to restore a sense of order and balance, calming the chaos of the energy from before. Yet still, her sounds resonate deeply with everyone, provoking tears to run down the cheeks of many.

As everyone around John and Suzy becomes more and more enthralled by the tune, John brings his eyes up to his wife's and gives a rather serious look.

'I am back, my love; but I have much I need to tell you. Let's go to the Hypo,' John says as he clasps her shoulders and then her cheeks.

He looks around to see Arthur wobbling and bumbling in an overwhelmed, spaced-out state.

'Welcome to our secret world, Arthur. I hope it's not all too much…'

Arthur laughs childishly, lost for words.

'I have witnessed something words will struggle to give justice, so for that reason I must talk of it quickly before my mind loses grip of it. I am sorry to interrupt your initiating ceremony, but I need to talk with you. Please, come with me and Suzy to our calming dome.'

Arthur stares at him whilst taking another big breath, and John immediately realises he is indeed overwhelmed.

'I know you are likely feeling very intense right now, but please, come to our secondary dome that is designed for a calmer level of introspection. The dome you are in now is our "hyper-dome" and is for highly energetic pursuits. Our dome next door is our "hypo-dome" and instead provides a calmer and more low-key atmosphere.'

'I'm just happy you're back with us,' Arthur replies with a large smile.

John gives a warm one back.

The trio walk through the same door the female vocalist entered from, which is well concealed as it blends into the side of the main dome.

They enter a smaller dome and close the door behind them, blocking the sound from the larger hyper-dome behind them. Inside this hypo-dome is a smaller Japanese maple tree in the centre, the branches of which lean over a small, spring-like body of water, warm steam diffusing around it. On the opposite side of the water, a clay ornamental flower fountain gently trickles, its calming sound gently echoing around the dome. A light, melodic blend of deep house and electronic classical music plays quietly in the background. The light around refracts into a variety of colours, mostly dark and moody reds, blues, greens and purples. Around this rather cosy dome are many cushions, blankets, chairs, tables and even a few beds.

Arthur notices one initiate stand up from his seated meditations and enter a large tank that is among three others in one area of the dome.

'Sensory deprivation tanks?' Arthur asks with a sudden excitement.

'They are fantastic, and you will have plenty of time to use them,' John says, as he leads both Suzy and Arthur over to an area with multiple leather beanbags.

'Now, I'm going to get straight to this,' he says, sitting down on one of them. 'Firstly, I currently have extreme clarity, and I must make the most of this time before I enter a more grounded, surface-level state and lose the ability to describe what I have seen.

'What has felt to me like years has likely only been a day or two for you both. For my soul was captured by demons and was sent down to a realm of nightmarish suffering. It was within this realm that I experienced something I have no idea how to put into words … A place of horror, where I was periodically shown my body on earth as a means to torment me, yet my soul was still trapped in this plane of torment and futility.

'As my soul was sucked into this hell, caused by the demonic technology created by Jack and his accomplice, I learnt that much of the underpinnings of our reality are directly connected to this underworld, and many who are not aware of it are being secretly controlled by these demons of the abyss, like puppets on dark strings. During my descent, I still felt a part of me that I could hold on to, a part of me that held on to a belief in goodness. It is hard for me to explain, but I felt a part of my soul was protected by a shield, as if I had been blessed by an overseeing power … And this is why, I assume, I was not lost forever …

'It started in what I can only describe as a dimension of pure chaos. Colours and entities all around me, a place of no up or down. It was as if I was floating in an abyss of coloured plasma, and around me there were the endless shrieks and howls of both the tormented and the tormentors. These sounds were like nothing on earth, but still, *I kept my light aflame* amidst it. This chaos would fluctuate between this pure sort and a more solid state, occasionally coagulating into more material realms, which would always be nightmarish and otherworldly yet still similar to earth nonetheless. I remember for a disturbing and long period being trapped in this sort of orange maze, like an empty office block, a never-ending catacomb, tormenting me by blocking anything of light or normality, everything so twisted and uncanny, similar, yet different. Throughout this whole time, I moved helplessly through the torments. I could feel on my back a dark shadow, an ominous pull; a demonic leech of sorts, sucking my spirit out little by little, feeding off the torments that I was given. I had no choice but to accept this state, and no matter how much rationality or logic I tried to implement, there was no hope of any of it working here. But still, I was aware of the wisdoms from my life, and no wisdom stood out —more than, "The only way out is through." So deeper and deeper I went, never giving in to the leech on my back. I kept my soul aligned with the almighty, and never accepted my soul as lost. As I floated through this abyss of chaos and torment, the demons kept adding more and more to torment me, wishing to feed off it like it was fuel. They showed me my robotic form on earth, saying things like, "Your wife only has a shell for a husband now." And they said this over and over again … I must say, it was a thick and punishing suffering; yet still I persisted, asking for them to give me more, never backing down in submission.

'You see, I felt within me a burning light, and this light when wielded caused devastation to the dark around me; so powerful it was. With this light, I knew the demons couldn't suck my spirit away. So I persisted with this burning light shining within me. Eventually, I left this endless sea of chaos, these endless and shifting forms, and as if sent through a wormhole, I fell through a stream of darkness and was sucked into another, deeper layer … I fell, and I fell, and I landed in what I can only remember and describe as an arena of demons. Around me there were six towers, each with a ledge, and each sat a demon on a throne. All had horns and faces of various dark creatures. Arthur, I'm afraid your previous suspicions were correct. One particular demon, with the head of a bull, held a chain and leash. On this leash was a lion-like figure, who was on his hands and knees. He looked shattered, tormented and weak. But the face … The face was your father's.' John holds eye contact with Arthur for a few moments, and Arthur's heart begins to race, dread building within him, feeling lost for words.

'It was at this point, in this slightly more material realm of what can only be hell, that I noticed that I actually had a physical form; but my form was not the form of a human. I observed my hands, and the skin looked thick and tough, like an elephant, and on my face I felt a long trunk. But this bizarre shift was not my concern, for when I looked up into the seemingly infinite blackness, I saw something that was …' John shakes his head and sighs, almost scared to even recall the memory. 'It was a spirit … But it shifted, morphing from one thing to another. It flew around the dark void, circling and flashing. For a moment it looked like a dragon, then a ram, then a snake and then a fish. It weaved and left a trail of light over the blackness, and then it traced itself into a shape of a massive square, as if opening a window, exposing something from far above and outside the void.

'This window revealed a gigantic black cube that spun slowly and ominously. I could see a dark energy radiating from it, flashing like black lightning …

'The dark spirit from the void morphed once again, this time looking like a gigantic armoured solider with a spear.'

John shakes his head, and raises his eyebrows in distress.

'It pointed its spear at me, and I was shot with a gushing beam of darkness from high above. I was filled with a suffering I can't explain, evil filling my form beyond measure. But I held onto my light with all my spirit that remained. And then … The darkness plateaued, as if something was fighting this force. I opened my eyes from their pain and looked back up to see great bright lights entering from the open window. The light came from four floating orbs, one much larger and more magnificent than the others, yet they all descended lightly, like feathers falling with graceful haste. They fell to the ground, and I saw that they were entities of pure light and beauty. They cast a blinding light all around, and I could no longer see any figure of the dark. One of the beings of light approached me, and I saw her face … It was the face of your mother, Áine. She grabbed my wrist, and we flew upwards, out of the abyss …

'As we soared, I was blinded by pure light, yet the feeling was of only comfort and warmth. My vision started to return, and I felt soft earth on my back and palms, as if I had just woken up from a nightmare, and was now soothed by comfort. I was on my back and in a garden. Around me such bright greens and many flowers. I sat up, and Áine was there next to me. I did not speak to her, and did not feel the need to. All she said to me was this, "Tell Arthur to meet me at the lake," and then suddenly she disappeared. I began to feel deep vibrations within my body; and then felt an earthly touch on my face. And that was when I came back down to earth with you, my love.' John puts his hands back on Suzy's, and she looks down, welling up with bittersweet ecstasy.

Arthur looks down at his hands, which he holds together in his lap. His eyes fleet around childishly as he licks his lips in a lizard-like manner, clearly captivated by John's story yet also trying to remain composed.

'Arthur, listen to me: do not lose hope,' John says. 'This tale that is unravelling is distressing and extreme, but we must believe we can rescue Phillip's soul. What we are observing is no stranger to human consciousness;

this tale has happened time and time again, and the myths of the ancients prove it. Whilst we must be honest with ourselves and accept failure is possible, it is up to us to show spirit and fight, and it is only by this that we succeed. We must sacrifice and struggle, otherwise we are sure to get no reward at all. It is only up to us to *choose*. And we must choose to display strength to evil!'

Arthur is inspired by John's words, but suddenly feels a strong urge to get away from everyone and go inwards to contemplate. He stands up from his beanbag and walks over to pool of water. He leans down to glide his hands through the water and stares at the pool as if he were hypnotised by it. As he stares, the water moves and contorts as if it were alive; he looks even more intently, frowning in apprehension.

A ghostly image forms …

His mother's face.

He stares back at the image, mouth gaping; but the face quickly dissolves into nothingness.

'Time for an isolation tank?' John says to Arthur whilst he still sits with Suzy on the bench. 'You said you've always wanted to try one, and right now you need to focus your energy. Maybe in there you will see what you need to see.'

Arthur looks back at John with childish innocence. Suzy is still sitting on the beanbag calmly and smiles at him warmly and with pride, as if he were her own son.

'That massive black cube you saw, do you think that it is connected to the smaller cube here on earth?' Arthur asks.

'As I said before, the lower and upper worlds are connected in mysterious ways. What exists in this world, also exists down there; as if down there were a shadow of what we live up here. In all honesty, I believe they must be connected. Yet I've no idea of the full extent of this connection and its influence up here,' John replies.

Arthur heads to one of the tanks and pulls up a large lid to reveal a pod filled with a rather viscous liquid. He steps inside carefully and pulls the lid shut as he lies down. After a few moments of lying motionless, he lets out a sigh of relief. The stress and stimulations of everything prior ebb away. Within him, all the chaos could now become compartmentalised and ordered, his mind can now finally let go and be free. His mind's eye is now showing clear and vivid imagery of various spiralling geometric shapes, mandalas, fractals; all of which he submitted to, as if they were themselves the tendrils of the great mother.

Around 10 minutes go by. Feelings of dissociation are becoming very strong and Arthur is now feeling detached from his body, as if he cannot feel it at all. He feels a series of intense energy waves wash into him, one after another. The patterns and interconnected imagery become more and more complicated, forming objects and artefacts of infinite complication. Eventually, these shapes, spirals and fractals combine into a clear, tangible reality.

They form a vision.

6. TO BE A SPIRIT WIDOW?

Arthur appears in a forest, with the sun shining brightly, penetrating the green canopy with a golden glow. The surrounding environment is wet, as if it had just stopped raining. Water drips from the leaves and branches above, and from plants all around. To the right of Arthur, the ground rises to what looks like a ridge. He feels compelled to walk up it; and as he reaches its apex, he looks out to see a snow-capped mountain on the distant horizon, with a deep blue lake in front of it.

He continues to walk along the ridge, through the trees and out towards where the lake begins. On his way down, various monkeys gather around him; hopping, bouncing and squeaking. They make various cheeky sounds, expressing their feelings about this lone wanderer; they seem happy and pose no obvious threat. Arthur walks towards one, however the monkey moves away.

He reaches the lakeside and stands on a small patch of grass. He looks up to see the gorgeous mountain, with its peak looking as if it were touching the sun. As he stares more intensely, hypnotised by the perfect alignment, he sees a white dot approaching, becoming larger and larger. He squints to try and get a better look, and sees this dot hurtling towards him at great speed.

The flying figure stops high above the lake. Arthur stares and faintly sees a woman, dressed all in white, soft translucent wings glistening on her back. Her head tilts down and her hands are inside their sleeves at her side. The woman brings up her hands, and faces them palm down towards the lake; a great whooshing and stirring begins from the depths below… Arthur jolts in apprehension when noticing the water beginning to rise. It's not long until he becomes immersed by the water and forced to swim to stay afloat. The water continues to rise until the entire surrounding forest is fully submerged. Arthur paddles hard to not go under; it is certainly not easy for him to remain buoyant, yet he feels a sense of confidence as if this was all necessary; as if a higher being has this all under control. He swims for many minutes, and at this point sees that only the tallest peak of a mountain rises above the surface.

Arthur looks above him and sees the lady much more clearly; it is indeed his mother, and she smiles lovingly towards him. She holds out her hand, and Arthur is pulled out of the water in slow motion. He floats towards his spirit mother, water dripping off him. Arthur stares at his mother in awe, and she floats through the air towards him. She places her hand on his cheek and smiles.

'I will always be looking over you, I hope you know that?' Áine says softly.

'I know. I always feel your presence, and if I did not, I don't know how I would have coped after you left us.' A faint smile plays on his lips.

'In the upperworld I have such great vision; I can see all things that happen on Earth. I can see the past, the present and the future. I see so much, my son. So much that my heart bursts with an endless understanding that no earthly being could ever comprehend. Yet still, I am not complete. Half my essence remains trapped, as you have been told already.' Arthur detects a hint of sadness in the voice of his mother's spirit.

'Dad ...'

'Yes.' Áine looks down, her face full of emotion. 'As you know, Phillip is under the control of Moloch, one of the foulest demons in all of hell; and in the form I am, I have no power to rescue him. I begged the great holy father to unite him with me, and as compassionate as he was, he told me, "That duty is not for me, but for your son, instead." So now I must help you, my beautiful son, as a task lays itself out for you.. You must descend into the very depths and rescue your father.'

'I must go to hell?' Arthur questions, his voice shaking with each word.

'You must, my son. The great heavenly father has set you this task himself. You are the chosen one, you are chosen to lead against the great coming flood of inverted truth.'

'But ... Why me?'

'Because you have the foundations required to be the just and fair king the world needs, a medium between God and man. You may not be ready yet, but with time, training and sacrifice, you will be. You must believe, Arthur, you must have *faith*.'

'I feel such anxiety at the thought, though. The tasks ahead are so important, so essential, but I fear I lack the strength to fulfil what you ask of me. I am also scared because I see that I have no choice, and I'm also scared because all this makes so much sense ... It's almost as if within me, I've always known this would be my destiny. It scares me because I have no choice but to live alongside my conscience. I could never live with myself if I went against it and did not take up this quest and fight for what I love.'

'And that is normal, Arthur. And it is only up to *you* to decide to choose courage, to listen to yourself, your conscience, and choose to face the fear with strength. The pain you will suffer within your soul if you choose not to will be too much for you to bare; and my son, I wish you to live without such a terrible load.'

Áine, with a strange abruptness, closes her eyes, interlocks her fingers and flares her elbows to her side. She faces down towards the waters.

A deep rumbling can be heard coming from deep within the water. It lasts for about five seconds. Silence follows.

A glistening sword appears between Áine's hands, shooting up like an arrow from the sea below.

She turns her head up to face Arthur and lets the sword go. The sword propels towards him with tremendous velocity, and Arthur's eyes open wide as he holds out his hands to grasp it. He realises with alarm that the sword doesn't appear to slow down as it nears him, gliding straight through his hands and body with ghostly ease. He feels no pain, no sensation at all.

Arthur looks around in confusion, then takes a deep breath in response to a feeling of energy entering his system.

'I have given you the blessed sword of Saint Michael. The sword that will return truth and beauty to a land of lies and confusion. Do not expect any fantastic powers straight away though, for this sword will only animate when combined with its soul, just like your father and me. But when this sword is brought together with its opposite, and when your intentions are true, and your spirit pure, flowing with love and intensity, it will be in these moments that the sword will shine and its power will be unrelenting. For one day you will speak to the nation, and the glow of this sword will remind you time and time again, *of what it means to be true.* Allow the glow to be a reminder, a reminder of an all too familiar place, a reminder that will free the lost people from their shackles. The folk of the nations will *feel it* and will have no choice but to face the holy like humble little children. Oh, and the poorly ones, the ones who have sold fragments of their soul to the black box of Satan. For those ones who have their souls hijacked, and attached to false idols, lower than the great awe that comes from aligning with the highest of mysteries. For them, it may take time, *but all is not lost.* Because through your unrelenting spirit, you will help others connect to their *sword within,* and they too can radiate *unrelenting* truth and beauty, as is the way of the Holy Spirit. Let this sword protect you from evil and lead you away from temptation. Always, and forever. Goodbye, my son.'

Áine turns and shoots off back towards the sun where she came from. Arthur is released from the forces holding him in the air and falls directly into the water below. As soon as he hits the surface, he jolts forward in the isolation tank, almost hitting his head, as he awakes violently from his vision and feels a desperate need to get out.

7. 'AND THE SWORD THAT WILL SET THEM FREE'

Arthur slides open the door of the isolation tank and slithers out like a baby exiting a womb into daylight. He flops onto the floor, with water dripping off him. He presses his face against the tiled floor, which up close looks as if the patterns are still slightly waving and colliding, morphing and seizing; the effects of the psilocybin mushroom still clearly lingering, albeit now starting to fade.

He looks around the calming dome and notices everyone is gone, including John and Suzy. In his current state, everything in this dome, with its lights and calming water features, make him feel grounded, relaxed and back down to earth. He takes in a few deep breaths to prepare himself to go back inside the main dome, now desperate to tell others about what he saw.

He enters the main dome and immediately feels the higher energy from the more intensely deep, booming music. The ceremony has now progressed to its later stages, and so has its vibe. Everyone in the dome is fully immersed in trances; they wobble, wave and bob, all in deep dancing meditations. Arthur is deeply connected to the music too, feeling a need to let go and lose himself in meditation.

He looks up at the mixing booth and sees Ishmael still in his groove, mixing, with Adam standing next to him with crossed arms, looking rather serious and analytical. Arthur looks across the dome and sees John and Suzy dancing together hand in hand, looking happy and childishly playful, with bright and joyful faces. As Suzy lets go of her husband's hand momentarily to do a majestic spin, John locks gazes with Arthur from afar and waves his hand over the dance floor as if to say, 'Go on, enjoy yourself.'

Part of Arthur was desperate to tell them all about what he saw in his vision, yet it could wait as he thought it better to stay in the moment. He wanted to experience his first Tree of Life mysteries properly!

And so Arthur goes right to the centre, dancing and getting into the music, losing himself with large swings of his arms. He looks around at the other members, and they smile back as they dance along and with him. Arthur smiles radiantly, more energy adding to his movements, feeling in this moment ever so connected to everyone, as if he was part of a family.

A blonde-haired girl approaches him from the side.

She dances casually and coolly, her movements light and feminine, full of flow and glide; at this point she is only making occasional eye contact with a natural smile.

Arthur locks eyes with her, looking her up and down, keeping his movements in rhythm to the beat.

After a few moments of this dancing, Arthur realises that this girl is in fact the same girl who was humming on the microphone earlier. His facial expressions light up at this.

'You been humming here long then?' he says, with a cheeky smile.

The girl giggles and leans into Arthur's ear, saying, 'I can actually sing words too, but John and Adam think it's best to stick to sounds.'

'I did think it was a bit odd; beautiful, but odd ...'

'They say words direct people's focus outside, whilst sounds send the focus inside.'

Arthur tilts his head in contemplation, looking away to the side.

'That's fascinating and makes a lot of sense. I've always preferred instrumental music to lyrical; and I'm definitely the sort who directs my attention mostly to the inside.'

'Oh really?' she says, increasing the intensity of her stare.

Arthur smirks, which quickly forms into a full-blown grin.

'My name is Arthur, it's lovely to meet you.'

The girl laughs, and for a moment disconnects from him to dance, making Arthur frown in confusion, although he quickly realises the playfulness of it.

'I know who you are, silly. Everyone here knows who you are; you're the chosen one!'

'Really?' Arthur says, smiling playfully, not taking the statement particularly seriously. 'How are you so sure about that?'

'Of course you are! You know you are ... Well, at least I think you are; it just makes so much sense for you to be. Although, some people here aren't so sure ...'

Arthur takes in a deep breath.

'People have told me a lot of things recently that I find hard to believe. Yet, then again, I am standing in an electronic dome that I never knew existed until only earlier today, so right now I'm ready to believe anything.'

'One step at a time, darling, you've got an entire academy ready to support you, no matter what happens.'

Arthur looks down at the floor, squinting in museful excitement, suddenly realising how much he is enjoying this girl's company.

He looks up sharply into her eyes , holding out his hand. She smiles and bites her lip, placing her hand into his.

They dance together playfully, continuing to exchange tender looks.

'My name's Eva,' she says into his ear, softly placing her hand behind his neck.

'You're beautiful,' Arthur replies, placing his arm around her waist.

She giggles.

'Aww, thank you. I've been a member here for about three years and been humming for the last year. Ever since my first ceremony, I realised this place was something special. Whenever I'm having a bad day at work, I come here and I feel my soul is cleansed by the amazing energy. It's like one big family. Nowhere in the world is like this place.'

'John and Suzy kept this all so secret. They are my godparents now, you see; I was adopted by them when my parents died.'

Eva laughs, as if to suggest she already knows his story, as if it were common knowledge to everyone at the academy.

'They have been desperate to tell you and your brother for a long time, but they were waiting for the right moment. We know about you, Arthur, and I know about Phillip. I'm sorry, may he rest in peace. None of this would be here without him.'

'It's fine. But unfortunately, I don't believe he is resting in peace …'

Eva gives a confused look, and Arthur shakes his head with frustration.

'Sorry, it's just … It's too much to talk about right now. I'm still processing it all … Please …'

Eva gives a worried yet tender look, which also betrayed her deep curiosity and intrigue.

'I understand. As I said, everyone here can support you in ways you wouldn't believe. Julius is always someone I've found good to talk to; he is very wise and knows the fallen books inside out. He gave me some really good advice on an ex-boyfriend I had …' She looks away to the side, as if suddenly struck by a memory. 'So, yeah, Julius believes in you and will do anything he can to help.'

'I met him for the first time today, actually. I really like him; he seems very genuine and wise.'

'He's also a complete lunatic!'

Both Eva and Arthur laugh in agreement.

'Well, honestly, I'm a complete weirdo too, I can't lie,' Arthur replies, a grin appearing on his face.

'Oh yes, I would be surprised if you weren't! And also a bit disappointed! All of us here are a bit weird, I suppose. During my last three years, my time here has taught me how to separate who I *think* I am, from who I *actually* am. And I don't think we ever stop learning that.'

'That's so true. I doubt I'll be the same person today as I will be in another five years; especially considering the direction my life seems to be going ...'

'Of course you won't, and that's the beauty of *growth*. However, I believe that no matter how much you grow and change, there is a part of you that always stays the same, stays constant; a beautiful, timeless child, you could say, a core inside that holds everything all together.'

'The soul ...'

'The beginning and the end ...'

The two lock eyes for a few moments, their pupils dilated. During this moment, Arthur couldn't help but think to himself how well he connected with this girl, and how he felt he knew her well only after this brief inter-action. He also sensed that she was feeling the same way.

Arthur gently pulls her towards him and whispers in her ear, 'Let's go to the round table room. I want to look at the roots.'

'Okay,' Eva replies.

They both walk towards the double doors. Just before Arthur reaches out his hand to open them, they burst open, making him pull his hand back to prevent it from being hit. An academy member rushes in, almost bumping into them both. The excitable member's face is a deathly white, as if he'd seen a ghost, and his eyes were wide open with energy and shock.

'It's returned,' the member whispers, looking into Arthur's eyes, as if he was a deer caught in headlights. Arthur gives a confused glance in return, squinting his eyes and tilting his head. The member stumbles awkwardly past the pair and screams at the top of his lungs, 'It's returned! The sword has returned! The sword is in the rock! I've just seen it! It's there!'

The entire academy within the dome turn to look at the shouting mem-ber, and the music stops abruptly. A moment of silence follows, then a wave of general chatter and apprehension fills the room. John and Suzy walk with flurried haste towards the double doors, their mouths ajar and their eyebrows frowning, faces red from excited disbelief. Ishmael and Adam also rush over, with the rest of the members gravitating behind them, exchanging glances with one another, many breathing out dramatically to release the massive amounts of energy they felt inside. Others rubbed their hands together with excitement, pursing their lips whilst making 'ooh' sounds. It was as if the academy had all been waiting for a day like this for a long time, and now it had finally come.

John is the first to reach the door, walking past Arthur and Eva without even looking at them. He pushes the door open aggressively and walks through, with Adam, Ishmael and Suzy following quickly and closely behind. Eva and Arthur exchange glances momentarily; Arthur raises his eyebrows and turns his eyes towards the rest of the members walking through the doors, as if to say, 'Well, I guess everyone's joining us in there now.'

So they go through the double doors and merge with the crowd filling the round table room. Arthur and Eva cram into the crowded room, humbly watching amongst the crowd from one of the corners. The four awe-struck academy leaders stand around the sword in the stone and stare in silence.

'Let's take a closer look,' Arthur says as he grabs Eva's hand, leading her to the other side of the room so they can see the sword in the stone.

And that's when Arthur sees it: the very same sword his mother gave him during his trip to the underworld.

The sword sits inside the rock, with a perfect golden square in the middle of its hilt.

The crowd stares at the leaders in silence, and the silence is deafening; clearly everyone is waiting to see if they are the chosen one.

John approaches the sword first, rather nonchalantly, knowing within his heart his attempt will be futile, but feeling as if he needs to confirm it anyway. He grabs the sword's handle with one hand and gives it a casual tug. The sword doesn't move at all.

'No surprise there,' he says, smiling to himself.

He looks up to see Arthur watching him keenly, and he sends a subtle but knowing wink back in return. Adam approaches next, walking more confidently than John, and attempts to pull the sword out with a much more considered and grounded pose, using two hands to try and pull out the sword. Adam tries and tries with all his energy and might to release the blade from its rocky sheath. But the sword stays firmly planted and does not budge at all.

'Ishmael, you have a go,' Adam says, turning around and holding his hands up. 'I have a feeling I know where this is going. It has been said that God is a DJ, so maybe he has your back here.'

Ishmael and the crowd laugh at Adam's joke, with Ishmael walking towards the sword whilst miming the movements of a DJ, pretending to clasp headphones over his head and scratching imaginary air decks, all whilst bobbing as if there were still a beat. The crowd laughs hysterically at Ishmael's playful banter, further inspiring him to approach the sword as if it too were a part of a DJ deck. He rubs the pommel of the sword in jest and lightly puts his fingers around it, turning and pulling on it as if it were one of the knobs. He stops his playfulness and wraps both his hands round the handle of the sword properly, giving it a good pull.

Once again, the sword doesn't move.

'Unlucky, mate!' a member shouts from the crowd, with others giving casual claps and subtle laughs and smiles.

From the double doors to the library, behind the crowd, Julius enters.

'Is everyone here finished wasting time? I think we know full well who is the one to pull the sword from the rock. Arthur, where are you?'

Arthur emerges from the crowd and walks through the gap in the table. He turns to face Julius.

'Hello, Julius.'

'The time has come for you to prove yourself.' Julius bows his head a little and holds out his hand as if to say, 'Go on.'

Arthur turns to face the sword and looks in to see it glistening; it contains a sort of energetic gravity that pulls him towards it. He walks towards it and turns to his left and right to see a sea of faces looking at him with great interest; some are apprehensive, others excited and a few somewhat sceptical. He places both his hands around the sword's handle. Before he pulls on the sword, he takes a moment to take in what he is experiencing; he closes his eyes and takes some deep breaths. With his eyes closed, he realises how he is still in a highly tranced state; he had become so lost in his journey that he had almost forgotten he is still under the influence of the mushroom. He felt in this moment that he was exactly where he needed to be, and everything was playing out as if he were in a dream. With his eyes closed, he could see many patterns within his mind, which whooshed and merged, twisted and spiralled. They formed a familiar image, a face of his mother once again. His mother lay there in his mind, smiling at him; her lips move, and she says, 'Now.'

Arthur opens his eyes and pulls the sword's hilt above his head, its hilt looking rather like a crown to those in front of him.

There's a collective gasp from the crowd, which then begins to chatter excitedly.

Arthur immediately feels within him a transformation that is hard to describe; a feeling of heaviness, like a load on his shoulders, a huge burden of responsibility. But he also feels something from within him *awaken*. An instinct, an energetic libido, a *primitive code* that has been activated. He feels he has no time to waste. This is the time of his life that many believed would come; and now he knows he has no choice but to *work*. This is now not about himself; it is about *duty*.

He sheaths the sword back inside the rock and walks out to look at the faces around him, none of which any longer express any doubt about his worthiness.

'I feel obliged to introduce myself properly. My name is Arthur. I know I haven't spoken to many of you yet, but please allow me to speak to you all for a few moments.

'There are many things I cannot see, nor understand completely; yet there are times when things feel so overwhelmingly right, and come together, that we know we are on the right path. Today is the day where everything I have felt in the past, all those subtle feelings, the ones so small they are easy to doubt, I realise should be trusted.

'I come to join my father's academy as an ignorant rookie, and I claim to be of no higher experience than any of you merely because I am the son of my father. I promise to work here like any other – not put myself on a pedestal because I pulled some magical sword from a stone.'

Faint laughter from amongst the crowd.

'I understand I have a lot to learn, and I have yet to read the fallen books, so I do not claim to understand the full extent of the prophecies nor the full extent of my duty. But one thing I believe with confidence is that there is a great flood on its way. My father said so himself before he passed away; and whilst I do not know the details of this flood, or how it will be delivered, we must prepare ourselves for it regardless. My father believed that it would be up to us, the Tree of Life Academy, to rescue the soul of human kind and to prevent its spirit from being lost forever …

'Whilst it's true that I don't know how exactly how we will do this, I believe we *can* do this. For we may only be small now, but I believe with time, our tree *will* grow. Only from my brief experience here today, I understand that what happens here captures the essence of what being human is all about. I believe it is here that we can explore ourselves and practise *being human,* keeping that light *alive.*

'Since I was young, I have sensed something missing from our culture, but I've never been able to put a finger on what it is … I believe what was once light has now been inverted and forced into darkness and secrecy. For many on earth deny who we really are and instead blame others for showing true colours. But if we do not show our true colours, what is left but darkness? For I fear many wish our world to darkness, and these forces of evil are building. Many of you here may have heard of the black cube, the essence of evil. Devoid of colour and light. Devoid of truth and beauty. By guidance of the prophecies, I believe our first task now lies in acquiring it. Not so we can use its darkness for evil, but so we can complete Excalibur, bringing light to its form.

'Look, this isn't me trying to be overly prophetic; this is personal. Earlier in today's ceremony, before the sword appeared in the stone, I had a vision. I saw my mother, and she told me what I already suspected. She told me that my father's soul, Phillip's soul, is trapped … *In hell.'*

Gasps and whispers among the crowd.

'So now the urgency to complete the grail intensifies. I was made aware by Julius that when the sword and the cube are united, and under the tree, we may be able to move between higher and lower realms. Julius, am I correct in assuming that if we did acquire the cube, and complete the grail, we may be able to travel down to hell?'

Julius stares back at him with a rather serious expression. The other members around stir, apprehensively muttering to one another.

'First of all, let us please take a seat,' Julius says as he sits down on one of the chairs. 'We can fit 24 of us round this table, and it makes sense we finally bloody well use it. And no, the first to sit aren't magically accepted into the knighthood; this isn't musical chairs, it's just making me rather anxious that everyone is standing up.'

The academy shuffle around and, after some light disputes and exchanges regarding who gets to sit, the seats are finally filled.

The room becomes a lot more relaxed and spacious. At this point some members are clearly struggling to deal with the intense and cramped environment on their varying doses of psilocybin, with some rocking back and forth anxiously and others even having to leave the room to go upstairs or outside. Arthur sits down on the opposite side of the table to Julius, with John and Suzy sitting to his right and Ishmael and Adam to his left.

'Okay,' Julius says after relieving himself with a cough. 'Now that some of us are sitting comfortably, I feel better disposed to answer your question, Arthur. Simply put, yes, absolutely, it is us, the guardians of the "grail to be", that are the mediators of the overworld and the underworld, and the grail is our medium for that. The test of those in the past has always been to fluctuate between higher and lower; to risk their souls going into the depths to bring back lost spirit and wisdom in times of need. Now is no different, for it may be your own father that is trapped, but I don't doubt that what in fact may be down there is of a more ... universal nature. Your father represents an image of symbolism. It is a message for us all.'

'Julius, are you insinuating that Phillip may have become—' Adam begins before being cut off by Julius.

'Yes, Adam. A myth, a symbol of what we may be lacking today in our culture. A synchronicity, perhaps, sent by transcendent powers. We must look at the task we have been set and assess what it means on a greater level. Indeed, it is of great importance we rescue Phillip, if merely for only personal and sentimental reasons. But on a broader level, we must ask ourselves, what is this journey trying to say? What is its underlying *message*?'

'It is a classic,' Adam replies.

'Indeed,' says Julius. 'The journey begins with rescuing Arthur's father, but our work will not be done until we rescue the soul of *the great father* within our culture's soul, as it is only then that our earthly realm will be free of the grips of Satan's box.'

'I am only young, and you both know more than me,' Arthur says with a tone of innocence, 'but is it not ultimately the balance of the masculine and the feminine that we should be aiming for?'

'That is correct, Arthur,' Julius responds. 'However, is it not your father who is the one that needs rescuing? And is the energy we see around us not caused by an angry mother who is in desperate need for her husband to return? Is it not true that a culture based only on the feminine spirit, lacking its opposite, will compensate for this lack by trying to make the masculine energy herself? A mother can never be a father as well as a father, and a father can never be a mother as well as a mother.'

'Enantiodromia,' Adam says, with a focused and intense look. 'If one side is prohibited from existing, in this case the masculine, then the pendulum will swing inwards to the feminine shadow, summoning its inferior masculine animus. A natural effect of not being balanced by its natural masculine counterpart. We can observe this phenomenon quite like a possession. If by fact of large-scale ego attachment to such and such ideas, the collective will inhibit the expression of the natural self-Christ. If this is done by means of force and threat, the energy will be forced to compensate by means of shadow projection. This is, by definition, Antichrist, and therefore anti-truth, and will always end in horror.'

'Okay, okay, please; for now let's keep things simple and practical,' John says shaking his head, albeit with a smirk. He respected the academic and abstract talk, but also wished to focus on the task at hand. 'Julius, you talk as if our world is already corrupted by the black cube, but the black cube has only recently been placed on earth,' John says, lowering his eyebrows.

'You think the devil is stupid? You must think more symbolically, John,' Julius says in an unexpectedly fiery manner. 'The devil is the lord of the intellect; he would only place his dark fruit on earth if he was confident of its readiness to seed. He knows it won't be long until humans will be tempted to use it. It will be the spark to ignite the bomb that has long been growing on earth. Earth has been in a fragile state for many years now, and Satan has been waiting for the perfect opportunity to drop his box on us.'

'Okay, well I can tell you now,' John replies confidently, 'his box will be dropped in the form of some, frankly, fucked-up technology. Excuse my language, but I saw how it is already being used with my own eyes; and, of course, my spirit. My memory of it is still somewhat a blur, but the night I became possessed, the cube was connected with wires to a piece of software: spiral something ...'

'Spiral Siphon?' Arthur asks inquisitively.

'Yes, that was it ... How did you know?'

'One night, a few weeks back, Jack invited me to his room to show me a piece of software he had designed; he told me that he had designed a type of database where he could store information differently. He told me he had learned to store a new type of information, a more complicated kind. He told me that with this program, he could make a much more accurate analysis of the user's input by going into more detail about the "psychological profile" of the user. He told me he was calling it "Spiral Technology" and that it would help companies target their products far more accurately at their consumers. He didn't tell me it was called Spiral Siphon, but I saw it at the top of the screen. Obviously, he didn't say he was using the cube to power it but looking back now it was obvious. I was immediately sceptical and intrigued; I knew he was up to something … But still, my brother is always surprising me. I didn't think too much of it after that.'

'Could it be that Jack and his accomplice have figured out, using the cube, how to upload and map human consciousness through this software?' Adam says.

'Perhaps,' Julius replies. 'However, the real question is how exactly will they deliver the entrapment? We know entrapment is the theme, by way of Satan and his box, but what is the method of its delivery? That is the question,' Julius adds.

'I think he will soon grow the business. That is, if he hasn't already,' John responds. 'He is not working alone; I was attacked by at least three others that night. Jack is a smart man, but the real devil behind this is a man named Harry. Unfortunately, I think he's got Jack under his little finger. From my encounter with him, I could tell he was a manipulative and vile chap. When I was investigating Jack, he was on a regular basis going to this Harry's house. I broke in, went into the attic, and that's where I saw them both hooked up to the cube, wires all of over the place. I have no idea exactly what was happening to them during that process, but this Harry guy told me his fantasy of the "product".' John uses his fingers for the quotation marks. 'He was convinced that this software could eventually allow humans to completely control their emotions, or others, at any time.'

'Harry, you say …' Adam replies with a curious look, with low, frowning eyebrows. 'Do you know his surname?' John looks up in contemplation for a few moments.

'Sickle, I think … I remember reading it on the computer program.'

'Dear God …' Adam says, as his face fills with horror.

'What?'

'Sickle was the man from Phillip and Áine's vision, the one at the Bagley Mysteries.'

John's mouth drops as he hears this, now remembering why he found that name familiar. He shakes his head, closes his eyes and wipes his forehead in disbelief, looking down towards the ground.

Mutters and stirs ripple throughout the room, and Arthur breathes out to try and calm himself.

'Astonishing, I know … But we can't allow this connection to overwhelm us. This technology sounds like a fantastic way to ignore your conscience, so it is indeed extremely worrying,' Adam says ominously.

'Or an amazing way for humans to be toyed with, and controlled by others,' Ishmael says, breaking his silence. 'I'm just imagining masters behind decks playing with society like they are puppets, turning knobs to punish, or give pleasure if they've been "good". A devilish sentiment. It doesn't take a genius to figure out that this could ultimately lead to some nightmarish potential futures …'

'A tyrant's wet dream,' John adds.

'It's definitely a slippery slope,' Arthur says. 'Clearly most people will choose to experience positive emotion most of the time, therefore diluting and reducing the negative ones. But the positive emotion, if given inorganically, will be fake: not coming from a place of nature, but a place of ego. I can only imagine it will make the people with unaddressed problems slip *deeper* into them, as it will make it easier for them to not address their demons head on. And, as I'm sure we all know, if you do not address your demons, they will only continue to grow.' The other initiates around the table, along with the ones still standing, stir and mutter in agreement. The academy leaders also look at Arthur with respect, clearly impressed with such insights from someone so young.

'I agree,' Adam says. 'It will also make unconscious projection far more likely. I would expect to see, if this technology did indeed make it to the public at large, something akin to a "great repression". A great divide would occur between those who use the technology and those who do not. I believe, eventually, the users would end up ignoring much of their true nature, technologically repressing much of it into their unconscious, and demanding that non-users should use the same technology in order to tame themselves. Those "bad emotions and instincts" will always find a way to be expressed without the user's conscious awareness. Think of it like a ticking timebomb, pressure building. I expect to see this energy from those who have failed to address the truth inside by doing the necessary work of the individual, by *accepting who they really are,* eventually forming a great behemoth, a great dragon of chaos. This may be the real weapon of Satan, and his endgame.

'Most would be completely unconscious to what is forming, fully believing they are on the side of good. They would feel no shame or remorse in demonising the ones who refuse to use the self-taming technology because they have a rationalisation that overrides their heart. By the time the dragon has fully formed, it will be too late ...'

The room falls silent as feelings of fear and tension sweeps over it.

'As Keyser Soze once said, "The greatest trick the devil ever pulled was convincing the world he didn't exist,"' Ishmael says, finally breaking the tension of the room. John smirks and shakes his head, trying to remain serious, while the rest of the room feel even more disturbed.

'Well, now that we are all ever too aware of the dangers of the cube, let's get the fucking thing,' John says loudly and with commanding presence, standing up from his seat. 'I know many of you are still heavily incompetent from the ceremonial brew, but for those who are stabilised, and confident, I would ask you to come with me. We are going on a raid. It's time we showed these demonic cretins that we aren't just a bunch of drug-taking hippies ...'

8. TOO HOT TO HANDLE

After gathering a team of nine initiates, whom John picked based on a balance of combat skills, trust and sobriety, they set off in three cars. John was determined to do the raid the morning after the ceremony, with most of the team only picking up an hour or so of sleep. Suzy tried to convince him against this, but John, emotionally charged, felt a deep need for revenge after what was done to him. But there was also some logic behind his actions; he saw some value in utilising the heightened awareness that comes with a low dose of psychedelics. Many of the Tree of Life's jiujitsu team micro-dosed before competitions, and with high levels of success. Seeing how the raid was to be done in the early morning, the dose would only be a lingering one and not enough to lower inhibitions or rationality.

The team was split into two squads, with the first led by John and the second by Ishmael. After some pushing and debate, Arthur was to come along too. Arthur had persuaded a sceptical John that it was a good idea for him to be there, based on the fact that, firstly, he was Jack's brother and, secondly, that he had now been officially *chosen* and had a vital and continual role to play in the unfolding prophecies.

The Tree of Life had also, for occasions like this involving combat or physical exertion, a uniform. In the spirit of jiujitsu, it was pure grey with a tight-fitting spandex rash guard (with a Tree of Life insignia in its centre), shorts, spats and, as an overgarment, a lightweight yet tough leather trench coat. For this operation, they had also acquired sets of in-ear radios for ease of communication.

From the moment they approached the house, an unusual tension washed over them. The feeling was ominous and hard to ignore; as if there were certain cues in the environment that only the primal, unconscious mind could pick up on. This feeling was intuitively noticed by Arthur, who brought it light with the team; it was recognised by some, yet ultimately not pondered upon.

The street was eerily quiet and dark. It was coming up to 3am, and there were no streetlights on. The plan that had been discussed was to split into two small squads of six, with the first team (led by John) to loudly break in through the front door, purposefully alerting whoever may be inside to their presence. This would serve as a distraction while the squad led by Ishmael approached stealthily from the rear. Ishmael would scale the walls that led to the attic room, whilst his squad entered the first floor of the house. The idea of this shock-and-awe strategy was to retrieve the cube behind the backs of whoever may be inside. It was decided that Arthur, given his new-found importance, would join Ishmael's squad seeing as this was lower risk.

The stealth squad move quietly, scaling the fence of the neighbouring garden, entering the rear garden of number 33. The team lingers among some trees, all squatting in low combat positions. Ishmael looks around with a piercing stare, his eyes squinting whilst scouring the walls of the house, analysing the easiest way to scale them.

'Looks like the cube may be home,' Ishmael says softly, as he points to the faint red glow coming from the window of the attic extension.

'I think the cube is home,' Ishmael says whilst pressing his ear piece. 'The attic is glowing red like you described.'

'Roger that, make your way towards the house when you're ready,' John replies from within one of the cars.

Arthur's smartphone pings. Ishmael turns to give Arthur a disapproving raising of the eyebrows, albeit in a very sweet way characteristic of him. Arthur nods subserviently but still can't resist the temptation to check his phone. He notices it is a text that reads:

'Good luck, stay safe. Eva. P.S. Suzy gave me your number.' Arthur can't help but smile as he reads the message but realises he must, for now, focus his energy on the task at hand.

The squad move up the garden and towards the house. Ishmael leads the way, and gives a signal to his squad to hang back behind some hedges until he can scout the lower floor and windows and mark them as clear. Ishmael scurries to the rear of the house.

The rear kitchen door begins to open.

Ishmael quietly, and efficiently, goes behind the door and waits for the person to emerge.

A bearded, well-built man, of middle age, emerges. He walks out and looks up at the moon, fidgeting in his pockets for his cigarettes. As he is about to light one, Ishmael goes up behind him and grips both hands around his waist. He kicks the back of the man's knees, causing them to buckle, and the man fall backwards. Ishmael gains a seatbelt control around the man's upper body and hooks his legs inside the man's legs. Ishmael swiftly applies a rear naked choke before the man even has a chance to defend with his hands.

The man struggles violently, flailing and writhing.

But the thrashing soon stops as he loses consciousness. Ishmael, with haste, pulls out a syringe from a pouch in an inner pocket of his trench coat. He injects it into the man's neck.

Ishmael swirls his index finger up in the air to signal a regroup behind the house. The squad stack up and follow Ishmael's lead, scaling the kitchen extension and gathering on its flat roof. Two members of Ishmael's squad align themselves beside a window that leads into one of the first-floor bedrooms. The member to the left of the window shines his torch inside through the open blinds.

An empty and rather disorganised room.

'Okay, lads, when you enter, I want you to keep your eyes out for anything you consider important or eye-catching. Notes or paperwork, discs or data devices; anything you think can help us understand exactly what's going on here,' Ishmael says quietly.

Both members nod, and the one on the right begins lining up his crowbar to feel out the hinges in preparation to break them.

'Arthur, stay on look out. Looks like I'll be able to enter quietly through that open window,' Ishmael says as he points up at the attic. Arthur nods and gives a little purse of his lips and a glance down, suggesting he understands yet feels a little sad that he is missing out on the action.

Ishmael walks over to a drainpipe that leads all the way up to the right of the open window. He gives the drainpipe a few tugs, checking its stability. He gets a good hold on it and then silently and fairly effortlessly climbs his way up it like a monkey climbing a tree. Once at the top, he glances into the room to take a closer look. The room glows red and Ishmael can clearly see its source coming from the centre. However, his line of sight is blocked by various carboard boxes that are sporadically placed around the room. Ishmael frowns and stays very still. He can hear voices coming from the bathroom.

'Harry was fucking on one the other day,' says a man following a snort.

'Yeah, Bobby was telling me. That guy cracks me up, scares the shit out of me when he does that silent stare out the window.'

'Not being funny, he literally just stood there for three hours without moving yesterday morning.'

'No surprise though, look what he's done.'

The two men begin laughing deeply from the belly, sounding like wild animals.

'Two tangos in the attic extension bathroom,' Ishmael whispers into his earpiece.

'Wait for the diversion and then proceed with caution,' John replies. '10 seconds.'

The seconds tick by.

Smash!

John and four others burst through the front door armed with laser-guided, semi-automatic tranquiliser rifles. Two men emerge from the front room, faces full of panic, eyes lighting up in terror, the rifle-mounted lights blinding and disorientating them.

They freeze like deer in headlights.

Tss–Tss, Tss–Tss, Tss–Tss.

The men drop to the floor, falling unconscious.

Two of the members swiftly cable tie the hands and feet of the sleeping men before continuing to the ground floor.

'Be advised, the two men from the attic bathroom are heading down now,' Ishmael tells John.

'Thanks, we'll be ready for them,' he replies.

Ishmael gets a grip on the window ledge and climbs his way into the room. He walks straight to the centre and looks down.

There is no cube.

Instead, red LED strips are placed around an empty metal cage, giving the illusion of the cube's dark red glow.

Ishmael's pelvic area erupts in an explosive pain.

He collapses to the floor, completely unable to move from the waist down.

A man dressed in a black suit and tie walks out from behind a stack of boxes. In his right hand he holds a suppressed pistol; in his left, a thin-bladed, needle-shaped, black stiletto dagger. With Ishmael now paralysed, and still in shock, the man goes up behind him and carefully inserts his stiletto into the centre of the cervical spine of the neck.

'The sacral region has always been my favourite place to shoot. It's just the cocktail of symptoms you get. I find, all things considered, they are overall the most destabilising long term. A lot of people, even if they survive spinal injuries, can still be pleasured sexually, and at least that gives them release in life to some degree. At least they can still connect with another human. That's not the case with severe sacral damage. As for the wound I put in your neck, that just seals the deal.'

The man kneels beside Ishmael and looks him up and down as if he were a vet inspecting a wounded animal. Ishmael can't even scream or express the immense pain; all of it instead is internalised.

'Yep, here it comes.'

Ishmael starts to urinate.

'I'm going to have to leave now, but it was lovely meeting you.' The man walks behind the boxes he originally emerged from and enters a small wardrobe.

The sound of creaks and squeaks follow.

It wasn't long after Arthur had heard the popping of the suppressor from the attic that he had started climbing the drain up towards the attic. He by no means was as efficient as Ishmael, and it was causing him a lot of stress as he wasn't the biggest fan of heights either.

He makes it to the top, and looks into the window to see the rear of an escaping Harry Sickle, with Ishmael completely paralysed on the floor, blood pouring rapidly out of him. Arthur climbs through the window and rushes over to Ishmael. He holds his hand behind his head, and then sees the wound at the back of the neck, which covers his hand in blood. At this point the other two members of Ishmael's stealth squad were already at the door and beginning to break it off from the hinges with their crowbar, not knowing Arthur was also inside.

Arthur stares into the eyes of Ishmael, immediately knowing he's fully conscious by the look of anguish. Arthur is immediately hit by a wave of Ishmael's pain due to his highly sensitive empathy.

Crack!

The door to the attic room is broken open and the entirety of both teams enter.

John walks over to Ishmael and shines his torch into his eyes. He inspects the wounds and quickly establishes the severity and type of injuries.

'Sickle ...' Arthur says.

'We need to get him to Lord Bell's Manor. Now!' John announces with great urgency, losing his calm momentarily. 'We need to slide a piece of cardboard underneath him to transport him to the car. Quick, quick.'

John picks up one of the many cardboard boxes in the room. He sees what they were covering.

Wired-up oil barrels.

There's much cursing and swearing.

'Forget about them for now. Help me shift Ishmael onto this cardboard,' John says as he starts dismantling the cardboard box that was around the barrel. 'Now, very carefully edge him on. We need to support his spine as much as possible.'

The entirety of the team kneel down beside Ishmael at different points of his body, shifting him onto the cardboard with care and precision. They all hold a bit of the makeshift stretcher, then transport him downstairs and out the front of the house.

'What about them?!' Arthur asks with a worried expression, pointing to the four unconscious cable-tied guards on the ground floor.

'What about them?' John replies gruffly, focusing instead on carrying Ishmael out the door.

'They will burn! Sickle is clearly going to blow the place!'

John tuts and shakes his head.

'If you care that much about a couple of scumbags, drag them out to the front.'

Arthur frantically tries to drag the still unconscious guards outside the house; yet he struggles, only barely managing to get one body out the house.

'Fuck's sake. Darren, go and help him will you,' John says.

A member rushes over to Arthur and helps him drag the sleeping guards.

The team carefully places Ishmael in the back of one of the cars and they begin to drive off. As they do so, they all look back and see the roof of the house explode into a bright ball of fire.

9. LORD BELL'S MANOR

A very tense and quiet car journey took place on the way to Lord Bell's Manor, during which John made a brief phone call to Lord Bell, informing him of Ishmael's condition. Lord Bell didn't ask any questions, quickly realising the severity of the situation and realising only speed and efficiency was of any help.

It was just the one car on its way, with John at the wheel and Arthur sitting in the passenger seat. John drove rapidly where he could, yet still was careful to not get pulled over by police; that was the last thing they needed given they had a paralyzed man bleeding all over the back seats. It wasn't a good look by any means. John's face was deadly serious, and he was focused like a hawk. Arthur was at this point feeling a deep anxiety within him, occasionally looking back at Ishmael, trying not to sob.

'Can Lord Bell help him?' Arthur asks eventually, breaking the silence.

'He will do what he can,' John replies.

After driving for more than 20 minutes on twisting country roads, they pull up to the gates of a house called 'The Phoenix'. They wait just shy of 10 seconds, and the gates open electronically. They drive in.

The house is large, secluded and among many trees. The style from the outside is that of a classic English mansion, with well-maintained grounds and walls. As they pull up in front of it, a statue of the ancient Indian surgeon, Sushruta, catches Arthur's eyes. The figure depicted is sitting with crossed legs in front a circular pond, as if staring into the water meditatively.

A rather well-built man, bald, wearing a white shirt with sleeves rolled up, exits from the large metal-clad front door. Following behind is his team of four assistants, all wearing purple surgical gloves. The assistants carry out a red stretcher containing many straps. John opens the rear door, revealing the sight of Ishmael to Lord Bell.

'Fucking hell …' Lord Bell says in a light Czech accent, sounding rather disturbed, even for a seasoned surgeon, as he analyses the state of Ishmael.

'Hello, Lukas. Okay, Gunshot wound to sacral spinal cord and a stab wound to the cervical,' John says as if in the military.

'Who the hell inflicted these wounds? They are extremely precise. Surgically so, in fact,' Lord Bell replies whilst he and his assistants begin manoeuvring and strapping Ishmael to the stretcher.

'A man called Harry Sickle. I won't go in to the details, but this is someone you may be hearing more of in the coming months.'

'I did receive some word of the breakthroughs at the tree. I've been informed about the return of the sword as well. I must admit, I was beginning to doubt the prophecies …' Lord Bell looks over at Arthur, analysing his face. Arthur gives a somewhat forced smile in return. 'Now is not the time to waste or to ponder on these things. Let's move it,' Lukas says whilst looking back at Ishmael.

They begin moving Ishmael, now securely fastened to the stretcher, inside the house and make their way to Lord Bell's underground private surgery.

'I hope you understand that these injuries are severe enough to cause permanent quadriplegia,' Lord Bell says as he looks back to John.

John gives a serious look in return.

'I did two tours of Iraq, Lukas, I am fully aware of the gravity of these injuries.'

'Look, I'll do my bloody best to treat Ishmael in whatever ways I can. I will treat him with the same focus I would my own family; but I can only do so much. Most of the treatments will revolve around his rehabilitation and psychological adaptations. For now, my focus is on stabilising and realigning the spinal cord and removing the bullet fragments from his pelvic area. From just my brief inspection, the stab wound to his cervical spine is actually quite shallow, done by a very thin blade from the looks of it; the way it's done looks as if it was purely for the purpose of inflicting paralysis; as I said, it was as if done surgically. We need to get him cleaned up as well; I'm sure you've noticed the state of the pelvic area … That's no easy task, I'll have you know. The sacral damage will cause Ishmael much stress even as he begins to recover. For at least a while, he won't be able to send signals to his bladder to control when he urinates. As well as …' Lukas pauses. 'However, there are some modern techniques involving electro nerve stimulation that have been used with some success.'

After walking through the halls of the manor, and heading down a set of stairs, they come to a hidden passage behind a bookcase door. They move down another set of stairs and enter a rather cosy room with many books in bookcases, a pool table, and in the middle two large green leather sofas that face each other, with a square glass table in between. On the table is water, glasses and two decanters of scotch.

Ishmael is carried by the assistants into the operating theatre.

'Okay, so I'm going to be in there for many hours,' Lord Bell says as he points to the double doors that lead into the operating theatre. 'Arthur, sorry I couldn't have met you in more fortunate circumstances,' Lukas holds out his hand, and Arthur shakes it, 'but I think it's clear, from what I hear, that we will have plenty of time to get to know each other. My house is now your house; my daughter, Eva, will take care of you both; she's already prepared you both bedrooms for the night. Please, stay as long as you like.'

'Don't worry about that, I'm going to stay *right here* for the entirety of the surgery,' John says as he takes a seat on one of the sofas, then fills up a glass to the brim with scotch. Arthur sits down on the sofa opposite.

'You are Eva's father?' Arthur says, trying not to sound too surprised.

'He is,' a voice says from the stairwell.

All the men look over to see a girl dressed in a silken white gown.

'Oh, Eva, I did not expect to see you here …' Arthur says, stammering slightly on his words and standing up immediately.

'Likewise. It would even be pleasant if it wasn't for Ishmael …' she says sombrely and with meekness.

'Eva, darling, I'm sorry to keep you up, but I'm sure you won't mind hosting our guests.'

'Are you joking, Dad? Of course I don't mind.'

Lord Bell checks his smart watch.

'Okay, pre-op preparation is complete, it's time for me to get to work. Speak tomorrow. Hopefully …' Lord Bell heads through the double doors with an urgent yet confident swagger. Eva walks over to Arthur and looks him in his eyes.

'Today has been a lot,' Arthur says whilst they hold eye contact.

'I know,' she replies.

They embrace each other tightly, and John's eyes scoot down to his scotch, trying not to stare. Eva scurries straight to John on the sofa and gives him a hug, clinging on to him like a baby chimp would its mother, causing him to almost spill his scotch.

'Careful, darling,' he says.

'I love you, John.'

'Aw, I love you too, Eva,' he replies whilst rubbing her back.

'Is Ishmael going to be okay?' she says.

'We will make his life happy. I will make sure of that, don't you worry. This Sickle bastard doesn't understand that love is stronger than evil; he underestimates its power, you see.'

Eva pulls her head away from nuzzling John's neck and looks at him in the eyes for a few moments. Her eyes glimmer with distress; she immediately knows by his response that, in reality, Ishmael would never be the same. She puts her face back into his shoulder and sobs quietly. Her sobbing has a surprisingly emotional impact on Arthur, clearly triggering his empathy more than usual. It was in this moment that Arthur realised he cared for her rather deeply; above what he usually had for other girls he spent time with. Part of him was sceptical of this emotion, as he had only just met her this same day; yet still, he could not deny his feelings.

A thought then occurred to him: *Maybe some people just have chemistry, and this chemistry is devoid of action but is more a product of DNA. Maybe love at first sight really does exist.* These thoughts he quickly calmed.

Eva stops her sobbing and sits up on the sofa, her hair and face looking rather dishevelled, the moisture from tears covering her cheeks. She wipes them away and organises her hair. She, too, pours herself a glass of scotch and looks over at Arthur.

He sighs slightly whilst glancing right, battling his stubborn conscience, yet eventually decides to pour himself a drink too. Being a bartender for around two years now, he had become sceptical of drinking alcohol. He had witnessed first-hand the effects on people and the dramas and damages it caused. He would still drink on occasion, if there were good reason for it, such as a special occasion with his college friends or gatherings of sorts. But he generally stayed away from casual drinking. Among his sixth-form friends, he had the nickname of 'Father Arthur', as he commonly was the sober one taking care of his intoxicated friends at parties and the like. He also had the realisation that he much preferred being more consciously *aware* rather than in the sedate, numbing state caused by drinking alcohol.

'I'm going to find a book to read,' John says as he stands up, scotch still in hand. 'From the sounds of it, I may even be able to finish one.' John walks to one of the bookcases and begins scouring the books to find something he likes.

Arthur and Eva face each other on the opposing sofas. A tension forms between them. Arthur doesn't really know what to say, and so says nothing.

He thinks, *I flowed so well with this girl earlier. Why now does it feel like I can barely speak …*

They both continue to sip their scotch.

'Fancy a game of pool?' Eva then asks.

'Sure,' Arthur replies.

They both head over to the pool table as John sits back down on the sofa with a book. Eva begins setting up the balls.

'This house is pretty amazing,' Arthur says.

'Yeah, it's not bad. I'll give you a tour after I thrash you.'

Arthur laughs and replies, 'No chance!'

Eva breaks, pots one yellow.

'So, is this some sort of panic room down here?' Arthur asks after missing his shot on the red.

Eva stares at the table like a hunter would their prey.

'My father is a very interesting man,' she states. 'My mother, Vivian, his wife, died 10 years ago due to a feud with a powerful crime family. It's a long story, but you may have deciphered by now he's a surgeon, and a great one too. But even the best make mistakes. Earlier in his career, he did a private heart bypass on this crime syndicate leader Jonathon Gordeno. The surgery went very badly wrong, leading to Gordeno's death. This wasn't the first high-profile operation my dad had done; he was already well known in the medical community for being extremely efficient and was the go-to man for private heart, spinal and even brain surgeries. Very few people were as versatile a surgeon as my father. The syndicate, however, blamed him, and even went as far to say that he botched the surgery intentionally to kill Jonathon. It was true that my father knew Jonathon had done many evil things in his time, but he would never go against his medical duty as a surgeon; it's just never been his style.' Eva takes her shot and pots another yellow with great power. Arthur winces in annoyance.

'And it seems like pool is yours …' he says, nodding his head with an impressed expression. 'Wouldn't your father just choose to decline doing the surgery in the first place? It just seems like it wasn't worth the risk.'

'The gang had already heard about my father's abilities, and they wanted *him* to do it. It's not so easy to simply say no to these people; however, you are right, maybe he should of just put his foot down.'

'I don't mean to be rude, but do you think your father would ever intentionally botch a surgery? As in, it's 100 per cent out of the question?'

Eva looks down at the ground in contemplation for a few moments, and then looks back at Arthur.

'Honestly, I have thought about it … But I haven't seriously asked Dad about it. It's a sensitive subject … All I know is that if my father knew what would eventually happen to my mum, then …' Arthur stares back at her compassionately.

'I'm sorry,' Arthur says.

'It's okay … Anyway, I'm done with pool, let's just do that house tour I mentioned; call it a draw?'

'Ha, no, you definitely would have won this one; I'm actually horrific at pool.'

'Deal. Well, what *are* you good at, Arthur?' she asks playfully, with a devilish smirk and a wink. Arthur smiles, and takes in a breath of air.

'I don't really know. I think I'm good at something, but I can't really put what it is into words …'

'Weirdly enough, I know what you mean, and I agree. However, you really should get good at something more tangible. I think it's a good idea you do more jiujitsu training at the academy. John said you've actually got great potential, but you just don't train enough. A space cadet such as yourself will definitely benefit from a bit more structure and discipline.' They both laugh in agreement and Eva leads Arthur back upstairs.

They return to the main hall by the entrance. Arthur didn't take much notice of this large room as he came in as his attention was on Ishmael instead; but, on second inspection, he finds the hall quite beautiful.

Directly above them, in the centre of the ceiling, is a large glass dome with blue-stained glass, looking like something from an ornate church window. Arthur looks up in bedazzlement, mouth ajar as he sees the moonlight shining through it.

'One second,' Eva says as she walks to a set of light switches. She flicks one switch and the icons of the glass light up in full glory. The dome's colour is in fact only half blue; the other side is red, with the colours merging into purple in the middle. It's clearly Christian symbolism; with the left, blue side showing a group of angels and the right, red side showing a group of tailed demons. In the purple centre, a human-looking Archangel Michael stands with his foot on the face of Satan, ready to plunge his violet-glowing sword into him.

'That is pretty epic,' Arthur says as he stares up with wide eyes, fixated on the imagery. Eva nods and purses her lips together. 'The angel even has the sword with the cube, like in the prophecies ...'

'Yep. It was only after my mother was killed that my father became religious. Before that, he didn't care much for anything spiritual in the slightest. The dome was just clear glass, in fact. It was only after Mum died that he fell into a such a bad place. A military surgeon friend of his reached out to him, recommending he contact John, telling him about the Tree of Life being a specialist academy dealing with complex traumas. Colin, I think his name was ... But yeah, the rest is history. The academy completely changed my dad, made him more focused and calm, gave him something to live by. He's a firm believer in the prophecies, so much so he put the fallen book variation of Saint Michael's sword up into the art work.'

'That seems to happen a lot from my observations.'

'What does?'

'People becoming religious or spiritual after they go through hell.' There's a moment of silence after Arthur says this and Eva looks at him with a curious expression, tilting her head slightly. 'It's as if pain wakes people up. Pain can humanise people, I really believe that,' Arthur adds.

'Are you in pain, Arthur?'

'Well. I feel very human, so I very well might be.'

'Pain can also destroy people too though, no?'

'It can ... And that's why I worry about my brother a lot. He's always dealt with pain differently to me. If pain humanises me, it makes him more mechanical; as if he deals with the pain by detachment, cutting himself completely off from that sweet child within him. Whilst I accept the pain, allow my soul to take it and struggle with it, he ignores it. For me, it was only through that struggle that my soul learnt to cope. I believe it is my experiences, my pains, that have all built me and given me the love I have for everyone.'

'For everyone?' Eva asks, looking down at the ground, then back up at Arthur's eyes. Arthur remains silent for a few seconds.

'Well, I suppose there are different types of love ... Some more broad, such as a general love for humanity, a love for wisdom and truth, and then there are others more ...'

'Sensual?' Eva says as she takes a step towards Arthur, holding eye contact.

'Yes, sensual …' Their hands then touch simultaneously, both rising up at the exact moment, seemingly connected by a natural chemistry.

'I want to show you my favourite place here,' Eva says with a soft smile, leading Arthur by the hand through a door on the left side of the hall.

The door leads to a corridor with many paintings and sculptures along its side.

'*Wanderer Above the Sea Fog*, I've always loved that one,' Arthur says as he looks at the classic painting by Caspar David Fredrich, hung on the wall to his left. Eva chuckles softly in return.

'Why am I not surprised at that?' she says as she turns to meet his eyes. Arthur smirks warmly.

'No way. Is that a Stanislaw Szukalski sculpture? I saw a documentary about that guy,' Arthur asks as he spots a bronze-coloured sculpture of a man with his hand on the side of his head, wearing a thick, blocky crown; the face looks extremely chiselled and exaggerated.

'Boleslaw the Generous, I believe, though it's not an original. So extra, right?' Eva replies.

'Yes, very exaggerated,' Arthur says. 'Szukalski really wanted to capture your attention. I suppose he has a point: why make things mundane when you're trying to capture people's hearts?'

Eva turns to Arthur, grabs his hand and puts it in the centre of her chest, just above her breasts. She puts her hands on top of his, as if to seal his hand to her body, forcing him to feel her heartbeat.

'Isn't that the case for anything romantic? Only the bold can capture the heart,' she says.

Arthur feels Eva's heartbeat pounding into his hand, and he could not deny that this feeling heightened his senses intensely. He felt within him a fire ignite on a primal level. And then, he places his free hand behind the back of Eva's head and rubs her hair gently with his fingertips. Her eyes glance down to the ground and back up to meet Arthur's eyes.

'Show me that favourite place of yours then,' Arthur says with a sudden confidence, no hesitation in his voice at all.

Eva smiles and leads him further down the corridor.

They enter a large Victorian greenhouse that connects directly to the rear of the mansion. Eva flicks on the light switch to reveal much beautiful greenery. The greenhouse has many pillars, with vines and hedges spiralling and sprouting out from them. There are many beds of soil containing various plants. In the centre lies a body of water surrounded by a small, decorative concrete wall.

Arthur looks up and around in awe. A feeling of cosiness warms his stomach. Eva walks up to the wall of the pond and sits on it, looking down to see fish swimming around. Arthur does the same. The pair stare in silence, both with a warm feeling of excitement building in their stomachs, energy radiating between them and their desire building. After a while of riding the tension, Arthur puts his hand on the thin silk fabric covering Eva's leg. Her hand instantly goes on top of his. He spirals his hand to grab it. Arthur turns his body to face her, straddling the concrete wall, all whilst still holding her hand. She too does the same. The pair lock eyes momentarily, staring with burning intensity. Arthur places his free hand behind Eva's head, stroking and caressing her hair intimately.

He pulls her head to his.

They begin kissing.

Their kisses start slow as they feel each other's energy, getting to know one another's body.

The tempo builds.

Their hands work their way underneath each other's clothes. Arthur's cold hand touches Eva's bare side, making her flinch and groan and causing her to become increasingly excited. Eva is at this point blushing and looking unstable, wobbling in a disorientated mess; she's feeling very dizzy from her intense arousal.

Arthur finds a nearby empty flower bed and wraps his hand around Eva's waist, lowering her on to the soil gently. He leans up and takes off his spandex rash guard uniform, spats and shorts. Eva places her finger in her mouth as she stares at his naturally athletic body. Arthur lowers his now bare body to align with her silk gown, the lower part of her body now fully exposed. Arthur teases her neck with his tongue, holding both her hands out wide to the side, pinning her against the soil. He moves his body close to hers, wrapping both his arms around her body. She too wraps hers around his, her moans of pleasure begin echoing all around the greenhouse.

And on it went.

The energy carried on building. Arthur began feeling a peculiar light-headedness, a disconnection from his body. An overwhelming need to close his eyes came to him, and so he did.

An image begins to form: Eva, but older than she is now. She is lying on a bed, covered in a bright, violet light; in fact, the whole room is illuminated. The light reveals her eyes; they are puffy and tired, drained, and lifeless. But the light, it was energising her, like an IV drip would to a person devoid of fluids.

The sexual energy began nearing its climax, and Arthur began feeling a buzzing throughout his body. The image inside his mind's eye becomes clearer and clearer as the energy builds between them. It becomes so clear that he can see an older version of himself next to Eva. He is next to her on the bed, his fist lightly clenched and resting on the centre of her forehead. Inside his fist is a violet-glowing blade.

The light continues to increase in brightness, and Eva's mouth opens slowly; her face is showing massive signs of life and rejuvenation. The light builds and builds, so much so he starts to become blinded by it.

He opens his eyes.

And the couple come together.

Not just in body.

But in spirit.

PART FOUR: REVELATION

1. THE STATE OF THE CULTURE

The year is 2024. And like the century, Arthur is 24 too. Much has happened since the night of Lord Bell's manor; for Arthur personally but also for the culture at large, which is a matter of great complexity involving and affecting *everything*. But first Arthur, the ones close to him and the academy.

Ever since the night Arthur lost his virginity in Lord Bell's manor, a change within his character was noticed by all. Our previously mysterious and fairly quiet young man had now become significantly more confident and extroverted. And not just in times of inspiration either. His seizures had become much less common and were much more manageable when they did come about. He was still often dreamy and detached, but there had arisen a certain sharpness in him; a speed, a focus, a sense of grounding to the material world that allowed him to operate normally with people much more than he previously could. Before he would become stuck in his head at the slightest of distractions and would not be particularly responsive to the physical world unless he was really interested in what was going on. Now, he was far more *on it* than he had ever been, and he was perceived by many as -generally an all-round competent person in many aspects of his life. One person specifically who noticed this shift was his boss at the bar he worked at, Collin. Whilst it is true that much of Arthur's time was now spent training and studying at the Tree of Life, he was still working as a bartender for income to pay off his overheads and rent (as he was now living in a flat with Eva). The relationship he had with Collin was a peculiar one; Collin understood that Arthur was far from a normal young man, and whilst Collin did not know the extent of the phenomenon at the Tree of Life, he knew that what Arthur was involved in was something of importance to be respected in these increasingly dystopian times. It was because of this that Collin gave Arthur extra leeway and even let him off the hook when he missed a shift here and there. It was also true that Arthur had much respect for Collin and would generally give him notice when he couldn't work. Collin was a wise man and, just from the conversations they had regarding the state of modern culture, they shared similar views in regards to what was happening and were both worried about the direction in which things were going. Arthur had on many occasions invited Collin to join the academy, insinuating that there were was much more to it than just martial arts, which piqued Collin's interest; but, for whatever reason, Collin decided to not get involved. He thought it best to leave "that world" to Arthur and keep his focus purely on running The Rabbit.

Arthur's change in personality was due to multiple factors, the first being his lifestyle. Physical training had become a much larger part of his life; he would train in Brazilian jiujitsu grappling at the Tree of Life up to seven days a week, sometimes even multiple times a day. He was beginning to make a name for himself at the Tree of Life as a naturally talented grappler, and a very hard working one too. He stood out from others due to his unorthodox yet methodical, calm and composed style. Over the last six years, he had earnt the respect of the academy, and not just from him pulling the sword. Arthur had now very much proven himself on a personal level to his peers at the academy and was highly respected by all. This level of brotherhood was something that gave Arthur an incredible zest for life and meaning and a sense of belonging like he had never experienced. The ability to talk to people who were on a similar wavelength, with similar outlooks and interests, and to be able to ask questions of other curious people, was something that filled a hole in Arthur's soul like he couldn't describe. Since becoming a concrete and established member, he felt better than he had ever felt.

One thing common to members of the Tree of Life was an interest in the mysteries of consciousness and of reality. It was encouraged among members to read not just the fallen books but also the major (and non-major) religious texts, ancient mythologies and fairy tales. It was generally accepted at the academy that all mythological and religious texts contained at least some degree of useful advice and were an important part of the members' grounding to the fundamental archetypes that provide the bedrock to reality, and to one's individual quest for meaning. Adam was regularly telling the students: 'If you want to engage in plant medicines and psychedelics, it is absolutely vital that you ground yourselves by knowing "the way". If you do not have a solid relationship to the symbols that help you understand the collective unconscious, your ego will crumble. You will become confused, chaotic and end up being possessed by a potentially damaging ideology that will replace your intuitive sensory structure. I don't care if you want to pursue a Christian, Islamic, Hindu, Buddhist or Sikh path, or even just a good understanding of mythology; the most important thing is that you have a good relationship to the ancestral texts that articulate and represent the collective unconscious.'

No one took Adam's advice more seriously than Arthur, mostly because he had been told time and time again how important it was for someone as sensitive as him to find a 'good footing'. Adam had for the last six years noticed that Arthur was at particular risk of ego inflation due to him not having a guiding symbolic system. Whilst it was true that Arthur did read a fair amount about mythologies and religions, the relationship he had with them was very casual and not particularly integrated. Arthur's natural creativity, combined with his visionary, open-minded temperament, had allowed him to connect to the forces of the collective unconscious on a profound level. Adam had never seen anyone with a such a natural relationship to the transcendent. However, this was not sufficient for Arthur because he did not understand consciously what he was experiencing much of the time. Arthur felt in his soul the magic but had poor understanding of how what he was experiencing fitted into the bigger picture, and he was instead just left confused and overwhelmed.

After studying and talking to other members of the Tree of Life, he decided to pursue an orthodox Christian path, feeling it best suited his temperament, and because he already had some knowledge of the gospels due to his own reading. He also felt that Christianity was already somewhat in his spirit by mere means of being brought up in England, and he felt that he had always felt and related with spirit of Christ. He'd always known it as good, but never really understood the depth and meaning to it, that is, to Christ's energy. With that said, he couldn't help feel a natural pull to forms of Buddhism and Taoism, believing that forms of deep meditation were necessary alongside Christian prayer.

Whilst all members of the tree life had their own individual beliefs and relationships to symbolic systems, the dominant one was Christianity. However, the different religious systems all at times came together, pointing to the same things but in different ways. Whilst one man may use one symbol to describe an archetype, another man would use another to relate to the same energy. The system was more a matter of heritage or preference. Regardless, all were connected, and all were connected under the Tree of Life. Many also started to believe that God would return in the form of a spirit, and potentially when the cube and sword combined to make the holy grail; and that this spirit would enter *all* men and women directly, making the common man and woman like gods themselves, rather than the return of a singular, physical man-god to lead as example, as was the case with Christ. This was by no means agreed and accepted unanimously; when Julius was questioned on it, he would simply answer, 'There will be many stages to the evolution of consciousness.'

Eva had such a profound impact on Arthur. And much of Arthur's development was either partly, or largely, supported by Eva every step of the way. They would train a lot with each other, and whilst Eva did not train anywhere near as much jiujitsu as he did, they did have a habit of doing lots of plant medicine rituals with each other, commonly spending time in the academy's domes doing inward work, praying and meditating on their lives and purposes as well as engaging in academic study. It would be common to see them in Julius's library reading and studying together. An inside joke around the academy even emerged, with many members calling them 'Ethur' as if they were one.

The initial word of Ishmael's condition caused a great stir around the academy; everybody wanted to do anything they could to help him. Members would commonly visit Lord Bell's manor to oversee and support his recovery and provide him with emotional support. They would bring him books, for example, and turn the pages for him; along with playing him his favourite music. Thankfully, Ishmael had not lost the ability to communicate through his voice and could turn his head and use his mouth. Unfortunately, he had zero use of any part of his body below the neck.

However, Lord Bell had a highly sophisticated wheelchair made that was operated through either his voice or tongue against the side of his left cheek. A sensor was placed against the cheek, and Ishmael would slide his tongue along the side of it to control the movement of the wheelchair. This was surprisingly effective, and it didn't take long for Ishmael to master it.

Arthur would come down to see Ishmael at least once a week, and this became the highlight of Ishmael's week. Every Sunday afternoon, Arthur and Eva would go with him to the Victorian greenhouse and take a micro-dose of psilocybin. Lord Bell had suggested there was evidence of neurogenesis being stimulated by their use. Lord Bell suggested there could be a chance that, over time with regular use in a loving environment, it could help stimulate new neural pathways and ultimately bring back some muscle function to his body. This fact gave much of the academy hope, and both Arthur and Eva made it their mission to oversee this 'therapy' of his. During these sessions, they would talk about all sorts of things and commonly Ishmael would read his favourite books and stories to them, including some of the fallen books. In regards to replacing Ishmael's DJing for the ceremonies, at first John had stepped in; but this was more like going through a playlist rather than using any sort of skill to read the crowd in terms of its energy and vibe and create atmosphere. Ishmael (and the academy at large) quickly realised that he had no natural knack for it. Instead, Eva volunteered to learn directly from Ishmael in his room, where he had his decks and speakers (Lord Bell had provided him with his own room at this point, along with a group of nurses that provided 24-hour care). She would be on his DJ decks, and he would give her directions and instructions. She learnt the art surprisingly quickly, and it didn't take long (about three sessions in fact) before she began DJing at the ceremonies, and at a level that far surpassed John. It was an added bonus that she would sometimes even add her own vocals live too (after some persuading, she managed to convince John to allow her to some sing words rather than just hum sounds like before).

And now onto Jack. As John and Ishmael were preparing the raid on Harry Sickle's house, Suzy went back home to check on him. As she drove back, she knew intuitively that he would not be there, and she was indeed correct. But what did come as a shock to the entire family was the fact that, to this day, he had not returned and was still nowhere to be seen. Not only this, but he had not made any contact with any of them, including his own brother. However, it did become apparent very quickly after his disappearance what he was up to. About a year after his departure from the family, a company called Snake Box Industries rose up; the name itself immediately captured the attention of the Tree of Life. This company initially provided services and software to help firms understand consumer preferences and personality choices so their marketing departments could more accurately target customers by using data captured by internet browsers. Arthur immediately knew that Jack was helping run this business along with Harry Sickle, which was confirmed after they brought out a product called the 'Snake Box oNe'. This technology was an S-shaped strip, with a small dot in the centre of the S. The strip connected to the cervical area of the spine and sent electrical signals through the spinal cord, allowing the user to control their own emotions through an app provided by the company. The technology came out in 2020, and before the end of that year it had become absolutely massive. It was quickly speculated by the Tree of Life that Snake Box utilised information on human consciousness gathered from using the black cube. Snake Box surprisingly made this data available to other companies, which led to many creating and implementing similar technology. The technology in general became known as 'emotional control technology' (or ECT for short).

As this technology continued to become more widespread, it widened cultural divides. There were those who believed the technology was necessary to control violent and dangerous human behaviour; and there were those who believed the technology was unnatural and unneeded and that it repressed the natural human spirit and self, the normal human instincts which come from natural interaction with the world; and that instead the individual should choose to learn discipline and self-control from their own will and practice rather than relying on the technology. There were also worries that this technology would tiptoe into the hands of those who wish to use it to control people and eventually all humans would be at the mercy of those in control of the ECTs. The ECT supporters argued that the control is still in the hands of the user, as it is they who choose what emotions to dial up or down, with various different smartphone apps and programs becoming available to control every aspect of the human condition. These included, but were not limited to, sexual pleasure, happiness, fear, anger, aggression, depression, anxiety and even mental clarity and sharpness to a certain degree. It quickly became clear that the people who used ECTs began to show certain behavioural patterns and symptoms that could be easily spotted by those who knew what to look for. Firstly, an ECT user would walk more mechanically, and this was the first thing you'd notice from a distance. As you got closer to the user, you would generally see on their face a slight smirk (as most people had happiness dialled up as a standard baseline). But it was clear to anyone with a degree of intuition that this 'happiness' was only skin-deep and behind the eyes, would be a passive-aggressive ferocity reserved for those they didn't like (usually the anti-users). Arguing through smiles, passive aggression and general snideness, quickly became the norm on the streets. The users would express 'happy disgust' at non-users displaying emotion they deemed to be vile; non-users, meanwhile, would convey the natural range of human emotions, including aggression and anger, which the users would look down on with smug superiority, believing it to be primitive. The users of ECTs became colloquially known as 'boxed' and non-users as 'unboxed'.

By 2022, cultural tensions had intensified further. Some companies made it mandatory for staff to use ECTs. This caused much outrage, but also was also supported by many. Companies justified the decision by saying, 'It is ultimately a *choice* to work at our company, and we gave lots of prior warning to current employees before we introduced the compulsory ECTs.' The companies would see a rise in productivity in their workers, at least short-term, as they could dial down their stress levels and increase levels of positive emotion. This led to many seeking to work for the companies with compulsory ECT mandates. Their new levels of higher productivity also meant they could pay more. Naturally, many were sceptical of the long-term stability of the tech and questioned if it was by any means healthy for humans to use. Regardless, it got to the point very shortly after the introduction of ECTs that about half of the UK (and much of the western world, and some of the eastern world too) were using them.

The Tree of Life was never simply *sceptical* of this technology, and by 2023 they had cause for even greater concern. The academy had been experiencing an increase of ECT users hoping to train with them, and with a wide range of symptoms too. One user called Annabel described her symptoms, 'It begun with my family, who don't use ECTs, telling me I was not the daughter they knew anymore. They would ask me, "Where is the Annabel I knew? That sweet girl who was a bit clumsy and would come to us when she had worries about things." And it was true I never had worries anymore, but I still had problems … I just didn't know they were problems at the time. But over time, even with my anxiety levels dialled down, I felt at the back of my mind a bizarre pressure building, a pressure I struggle to explain. I felt as if something was inside me, a lurking shadow or demon that clung to my back, pushing me to do this or that; yet I couldn't truly explain this feeling to my other friends. They just told me to check the settings on my app and find a better algorithmic combination for my baseline E levels.

'But then the nightmares began. And it was really horrible. I would wake in the night sweating, filled with the worst terror I had ever experienced, and it would dissolve into a weird chunky sensation. It was as if I could actively feel my ECT take away the terror from my nightmare as I woke up in chunks, like *bob-bob-bob*. A mechanical feeling, it was really disturbing actually. What disturbed me the most was that I *wanted* to feel the terror, as if my body craved it and was trying to tell me something ... But the ECT in me just took the emotion away. I felt like my soul was being robbed, and I couldn't even cry.'

It was true that the ECT could be removed, and many people did so; but as soon as they did, they would experience such a massive load of negative emotion that most would beg their private surgeon to put it back in them only days after it was removed. The negative emotion that would flood inside them drove many to suicide; and was described by some ex-drug users as 'the worst withdrawal you could ever imagine, times by a hundred'. It didn't help that it was in most powerful companies' interest to avoid negative information spreading regarding the ECTs. Naturally, business owners had relations with big media companies, and they would work together to prevent any negative press, labelling any ECT-sceptic sentiment as 'misinformation' and 'irrational'. A typical line trotted out was, 'There is no scientific evidence to suggest ECTs cause any negative side effects.' But this was, of course, biased use of the statistics available.

Annabel knew otherwise. She was one of those who had her ECT removed and was the first to be treated by the Tree of Life's own surgeon, Lord Bell. This pioneering procedure ultimately gave the Tree of Life a platform from which it could treat those with 'ECT withdrawal'. She initially came to the Tree of Life to train in just jiujitsu, at this point still with her ECT planted. But she was told that the academy does not allow ECT users because it gives an unfair advantage in training and causes a severe cultural divide within the club. She was glad they said this, as she was looking for an excuse to take off her ECT, and this was the final straw. As John spoke to her, he decided (and this had never previously happened) to tell her upfront about the 'other activities' of the academy, and that they would attempt to help her in any way they could once she removed her ECT. She agreed, and the academy began treating her with a disciplined fitness training schedule, to keep her focused and fit, and regular plant medicine rituals involving 'beat meditation', which attempted to train her to meditate and keep her focus on the bass beats and away from the agonising withdrawal feelings.

The Tree of Life knew that at the heart of the ECT origins was the black cube. And whilst they doubted the removal of the cube from the hands of Snake Box would end the technology, they knew that if they didn't acquire the cube, it was highly likely that they would continue to bring out other technologies in the future. This is where the academy had a secret card up its sleeve, and one that had not yet been played.

The raid on Harry Sickle's house led to an interesting discovery. That night, Ishmael had sent two of his squad to the back of the house to search for 'anything of interest'. And whilst the focus was, of course, on Ishmael that night, they did indeed find something …

Whilst they searched Harry Sickle's bedroom, they rummaged through a box in his wardrobe. The box was full of sex toys and BDSM equipment: leashes, whips, gags, homosexual pornography and other paraphernalia. They found a DVD case labelled 'A night to remember'. At first the investigating member thought it was just some porn he made. But he turned over the DVD to find some more writing: 'Dead Ben.' He frowned and decided to take the DVD.

After bringing the DVD back to the academy and watching it, they discovered something very disturbing. The DVD was a video of two people in a car: one was a teenager, about 15 or so, and the other in his 20s.

The camera was placed on the dashboard and faced inwards towards the two sitting in the front seats. The conversation between the two went like this:

'Alright, we have decided to make this video to pay our respects to the loss of a legend,' the older man says. The teenager stares blankly out the window, seemingly disinterested. 'Didn't think it would be some crazy bitch to finish him off … Guess I'm your daddy now then, ain't that right Harry?' the man says as he turns to face the teenager with a rather large grin on his face.

The young Harry Sickle doesn't respond at first but just carries on staring out the window as if he were day dreaming.

'I only have one dad. And you're not him,' Sickle says, after an extended period of silence.

'Yeah, and Charlie killed him,' the man says, then laughs.

'That man was never my father. Charlie always knew who the *real dad* is. And so do I. Our real dad never dies. And you, Ben, have never understood …'

'What?' the older man asks with an awkward smile and laugh, not really understanding the teenage Sickle.

'You've never understood. And you never will. You were always just a pawn to me and Charlie. He knew he would die, and he knew when his time came, it would be me to carry on his spirit.'

'So you're saying I can't be the leader because you and him made a deal?'

Harry slants his eyes to the side with a cold expression.

'You can't be the leader because our leader is not of the flesh. Our leader is ever present and there for those willing to engage with him. Our leader is only for the rare few, the chosen ones of the inversion, the ones to bring his shadowy kingdom to earth. We are the inverted ones, and *we will breed a world of horn and twist.* And you, you have never understood. You are just a fool, Ben.'

Sickle's accomplice, Ben, bursts out laughing.

'What the fuck are you on about?' Ben says in a confused and hysterical state, face bright red.

Harry puts on a fake smile.

But he quickly snaps into a serious, ominous expression.

Ben frowns, and the two stare at one another in silence.

Harry pulls out a knife from the side of the car and begins wildly stabbing his accomplice in the throat,

then chest, murdering his accomplice right then and there.

Harry cuts the video and reappears outside the car, which has been covered in petrol. Harry lights a match and the car goes up in flames. The video cuts.

The video was watched by the majority of the Tree of Life members. Shivers and unsettling waves of anxiety are sent through all who watch this disturbing footage. The video, however, gave the Tree of Life much useful information. Firstly, it provided insight into a young Harry Sickle, a boy who already at this age had been exposed to atrocity and meaningless violence. It was now clearer than ever that what they were dealing with was a monster to the core. For many, this extreme, absent-minded violence was hard to understand. John was not fazed by the brutality, yet he shook his head in disgust, knowing the depths of Sickle's evil all too well …

But things became weirder when Arthur watched it. Arthur was immediately jolted into a hyper-focused, hypnotic state as soon as the clip began. His eyes were glued to this young Harry Sickle: to the way he sat, the way he moved, the way he looked around. Arthur's eyes squinted, and his mouth held ajar. And that's when Arthur realised it. *This was the very teenager that was present at his childhood home invasion.* John didn't notice the connection at first, but as soon as Arthur told him, John felt like an idiot for not realising it. Flashbacks of that haunting night came to John: the Ford Focus speeding away from the house. He muttered 'fuck' under his breath. As disturbed and shocked as they were, finding it hard to believe this link could be pure coincidence, a thought came to Arthur after some time reflecting. Arthur believed that this footage could be used to their advantage. It had been six years since he had last seen his brother, and he and others had made many attempts to re-establish a connection, all failing miserably. This could be the footage to convince Jack that the person he is working with is *evil to the core*, and one that was at least partly responsible for the death of his parents; and therefore, obviously, could not be trusted in the slightest. This presented an opportunity to convince Jack to potentially cut ties with Harry Sickle and join Arthur side by side once again. Arthur thought to himself, *If I can make contact with my brother, I could show him this footage and surely he would realise Harry Sickle is not someone worth trusting and, therefore, not someone he should be working with. My brother means well, he is just misled. I just have to convince him that if we gain possession of the cube, we can gain access to its magic by combining it with the sword. Julius said that when the sword and cube are combined, we would be able to travel between realms, and if we can travel between realms, we may be able to travel down to hell and rescue our father's trapped soul. Surely if I can make Jack understand this he will be willing to help ...*

Then again, my brother isn't one to believe in magic or anything mystical ... but how can he deny what we experienced together? Seeing our father in the dream world? I suppose I'll only know when I speak to him in person. As much as I think I know my brother, he never ceases to surprise me. He thinks I am the trickster, but really, I think he is. But he would never know to admit it ...

And so the task was set for Arthur and the Tree of Life. He had to figure out how to make contact with his brother. But many attempts via Snake Box employees at various levels of the company had led to dead ends. Jack clearly was a man that didn't want to be contacted, no matter how much they tried ...

That is, until Lord Bell received a certain invitation ...

2. JUST ANOTHER SUNDAY

It was just another Sunday afternoon. As per Arthur's routine, he would visit Eva at her father's house, and they would both spend time with Ishmael in the Victorian greenhouse.

Arthur drives his Volkswagen Golf up the exuberant driveway of Lord Bell's manor and parks in front of the house. He opens the rear door of his car and picks up a large tray of orange-flavoured chocolate; this too had become a routine over the years, as they were Ishmael's favourite, and still to this Sunday he was not bored of them. He knocks on the large doors and Lord Bell opens them.

'How's it going, Arthur?' Lord Bell says as he shakes Arthur's hand firmly.

'I'm good, thank you. I could only get the large chocolate tray today, the standard size was sold out.'

Lord Bell lightly chuckles to himself.

'Well, I'm sure Ishmael won't mind. Just don't make it a habit, we don't want him getting fat, do we?' he says with a smile still on his face. 'They are already in the greenhouse by the way; Ishmael says he wants to read to you both from a "peculiar yet important book"; I can only assume he's picked up one of the fallen ones from Julius. No idea which one he's got though.'

'Oh, exciting, I really should start to read them more myself. But I just love Ishmael reading them out loud; he just makes them come alive …'

'Perks of owning a bookshop, I suppose; you get rather good at reading!'

Arthur gives a warm smile and a chuckling sniff in return, and then begins to walk towards the corridor that leads to the greenhouse.

'Oh, Arthur, before you go, I have some news for you.'

'Oh yeah?'

'One second.' Lord Bell walks over to a wooden cabinet next to the entrance. He opens a drawer and pulls out a letter.

'Read this,' he says.

'*Dear Lord Bell, respected member of high society,*' Arthur reads out loud, then looks up at Lord Bell with a puzzled look. '*The Sexennial Hex summit is once again upon us, a gathering of the most wonderful leaders of varying sorts. We would like to invite you to this summit of great importance; and, of course, one that we will take much pleasure in hosting, as we always do. Since our last summit in 2018, much in this world has changed and progressed. Much of this change is down to world leaders of our kind making impacts with their machines, their inventions, their progressions, their technology; but most of all, their much-loved idealism. For it is us, the ones at the apex, that have the responsibility to invoke change in this world; to break the orthodoxy of old and continue to move things forward towards an ever-brightening future.*

'However, new problems have now arisen, which means new challenges; and new challenges mean new solutions are required. But due to our collective brilliance, we should fear not, because new solutions are being brought out in full flow, and at an ever-increasing pace. So it is with our utmost confidence that the challenges of today, such as our climate, our overpopulation, the inequality of those below us, the poor, unrefined behaviour of many a citizen, all these can now be controlled and tackled in new and ingenious ways. So we, the International Hex Society, invite those who we believe appreciate the potential of transformative and progressive concepts to join us. To join us in the unveiling of various new technologies that we believe will move us forward as a species, to take us to that next level of human development.

'As usual, the summit will be over a six-day period, with each day being hosted as follows:

Day 1: Exo-Frank Ltd – Exploring the development of Hydroponic Robotics. How modern robotics can be grown through a semi-organic process, and how it is best evolved through a simplification of the process. What can we learn from the organic and non-organic growth of plant hydroponics, and how this relates to modern robotics.

Day 2: Dwenger & Dermer – Understanding how pigs DNA relates to humans, and how our research and our new understanding provides a bedrock to modern gene therapy, with the potential to evolve and level up humans for the generations to come.

Day 3: Zebra & Johnson – Addressing the crisis of meat fetishism. An unveiling of new protein replication technology that allows a seamless transition from an omnivorous society to a strictly plant-based one.

Day 4: Push Key and Co – An unveiling of their new ECT that addresses the previous algorithmic imbalance from many other ECT companies, and exploring the reasons behind some users experiencing night terrors, and how their new algorithm and spinal alignment addresses this issue.

Day 5: Oedipal Rivers – An unveiling of a new rhythmic conditioning application that can be used via ECTs by teachers and others to help children learn at a faster pace by forcing imagery into the brain stem, as well as giving simultaneous pleasure and other emotional spikes.

Final day: Snake Box — For the finale of the summit, we are proud to present the company that founded the revolutionary emotional control technology. Snake Box will be unveiling their new product, 'Snake Oil', details of which are yet to be announced.'

'My god …' Arthur replies whilst looking at Lukas.

'My thoughts exactly,' Lukas says.

'So you know these people? I mean, they have invited you after all.'

'You tend to get to know a lot of people doing what I do. And after saving the lives of some of these people and their loved ones, even the most twisted and evil can feel in some way indebted to you. Even if that means inviting you to their little gatherings. Regardless, if they think I'm their friend, they are greatly mistaken. However, it is still in our best interest for them to think I'm one of them; it just means more information for us.'

'How many of these summits have you been to, then?' Arthur asks.

'The last five. To be honest, most of the people are well-intentioned types who think their companies are going to bring some sort of great benefit to mankind; and whilst I'm sceptical of these sorts of things, I can respect it to some degree. However, with that said, and as the years have gone by, even the well-intentioned ones still blindly go along with those … what can I say, *less well-intentioned ones*. Over the years, and especially since reading the line-up of new products, I've realised that there are some seriously dark undertones to these conventions. The technology is becoming more and more invasive and is beginning to cross some serious boundaries on human values. There's a growing disgust in humans among these people, seeing us as dirty animals who need to be "cleaned" with their technology. I try to keep myself to myself when I go; I don't want them to ask me too many questions and realise my non-alignment with their "values". John also agrees it's beneficial for us to learn as much as we can about these people and their activities.'

'Didn't know Eva's Dad was 007…' Arthur says. Lukas responds by laughing and pretending to shoot Arthur with his fingers. Lukas keeps staring at him with one raised eyebrow, however.

'The answer is yes, Lukas,' Arthur says with a knowing smirk and nod. 'Of course I'm going to come with you. Can you imagine if Jack himself is presenting Snake Box's new product? It's a no brainer for me. This could very well be the opportunity we've all been waiting for.'

'Well, that's exactly what I was thinking. It's next month in Cologny, Switzerland. I own a chalet in Geneva that is nearby and was thinking the dream scenario would be to get Jack back to the chalet so you two could have a nice catch up and talk things over; and, obviously, show him the video … And … you never know, you may even be able to retrieve the black cube.'

'Jesus, no pressure then.'

'You have become such a confident young man, Arthur, even since I first met you. I have no doubt you'll be able to make some sort of contact.'

'Well, I appreciate your confidence in me, Lukas. And whilst I know my brother is deeply entrenched in this world, I know he still has a heart; even if it may somewhat be blocked, it is still there, and I am still his brother.'

'Let's do it,' Lukas says confidently, whilst he and Arthur lock gazes and shake hands. 'We have the rest of this month to make further preparations and plans. In the meantime, you better go off to Ishmael and Eva. He is gagging to read this book to you.'

'Alright, speak soon,' Arthur says whilst giving a casual thumbs up as he walks away.

Arthur walks into the greenhouse and sees Eva and Ishmael inspecting a certain plant whilst talking to each other. He walks in quietly to try and catch what they are saying without them noticing him.

'This one looks so exotic, what is it?' Eva asks Ishmael as she slides her hands across a particularly vibrant and colourful-looking plant.

'Ah, the bird of paradise; this one is native to South Africa, I believe,' Ishmael replies.

'It looks so alive, doesn't it? Like it could just set itself free from its stem and fly away …'

'Maybe one day I'll be able to set myself free from my stem,' Ishmael says solemnly as he stares deeply into the plant's colourful leaves. Eva turns to face him, purses her lips together and looks at him compassionately; drawing her eyes down and back up, not really knowing in that moment how to reply. But then she notices Arthur standing at the entrance.

'Oh, for goodness' sake, how long have you been standing there?' she says, as Arthur laughs cheekily.

'Not long, don't worry. Sorry I took so long, I was talking to Lukas. Ishmael, I got you a large chocolate orange tray today, didn't think you'd mind.' Arthur puts the chocolates on a wooden table in front of the pond. 'He's invited me to come with him to this weird technocratic summit in Switzerland next month. Snake Box is unveiling a new product, and with any luck my brother may even be there. This could be our chance to finally connect with him.'

'He's been spying on them for years, actually,' Eva says, 'but the things they are discussing these days are just evil to the core. Did you see the one with the "rhythmic conditioning device" for kids? It's disgusting.'

'Yes, I did, and I agree, it's all very unsettling. However, in this day and age, nothing really shocks me anymore. I have accepted the state of the world and realised dwelling on it too much will do nothing outside of providing motivation. All that matters now is our actions that bring the world closer to harmony, to embody the Holy Spirit, to show the world our values by embodying them in ourselves, to lead by example and to keep shining our light in a world full of darkness. This light will eventually be impossible to ignore and will only become brighter the darker the days become.'

'Beautiful, Arthur,' Ishmael says. 'I can feel your light and passion radiating from you as you speak. And that speaks much about your alignment. It is not just your words that matter but the spirit that propels them up. That is power.'

'Well, thank you, Ishmael. Before I began engaging with the Tree of Life, I felt this spirit was uncontained, unfocused, chaotic,' Arthur says, 'but now, I feel I have managed to contain it, to give that spirit form; I feel sturdy and balanced. And I thank you both greatly for your roles in my journey.' Eva smiles gently whilst giving a sort of 'stop it' look with her eyes, as if she was flattered.

Ishmael nods whilst his eyes squint warmly.

'Today I must provide some dark energy to you both, however,' Ishmael says with a tightening of his cheeks. 'Eva, do you mind removing the red book from the bag on my wheelchair?' Eva walks behind Ishmael and rummages through a drawstring bag that hangs behind the back of his chair.

'*The Devil's Diary*,' Eva reads out loud as she looks at the title on the front cover.

'Yes. Number six of the fallen books,' Ishmael says as he stares at a plant, as if in deep contemplation. 'Julius told me to read this one to you, Arthur; he said he told you to read it years ago but you never got round to it.'

'Yes, it's true, I remember him telling me to read it. However, I've always put it off, for a reason I don't fully understand. Part of me knows I should read it, and part of me knows it contains information that will be transformative;

but maybe that's why I'm scared of reading it? Because I know of its potential to transform … And transformations can't happen without pain.'

'Very true, Arthur, and at least you are consciously aware of that. Well, look, I won't read all of it, as it is a large book that will take even the fastest of readers many days to read. But I will recite a few passages that talk about "his box" as, given the circumstances, they are what I, Julius, and others at the academy deem to be of the most importance for you currently. If we do gain access to the cube, and I believe we will, it will not be long after this that you will make your descent into the realm of hell; you must come to terms with this, Arthur. And with this inevitability, we need you to understand the ways of Satan too; the more you understand his tricks, his energy, the less you will be at his mercy.'

'I understand,' Arthur says confidently nodding his head. 'Alright, let's hear it then, I'm ready. Eva, are you ready?'

'Yep, let's do it.'

Eva places the book on Ishmael's lap.

'Turn to page 808, Part 4, Chapter 1: 'My box'',' Ishmael says. Eva flicks through the book to find the page, then turns the book back to face him after she does.

'I'm assuming we aren't taking a micro-dose today then?' Arthur asks just before Ishmael is about to start reading. Ishmael gives a slight chuckle to himself.

'I think today we better not. These words I'm about to read are heavy on the soul, even without the use of soul-sensitising substances; it would be unnecessary, and potentially even a bit dangerous …'

'Oh, and do you mind putting a chocolate orange in my mouth before I begin, Eva? I just fancy a little palette cleanser.'

'Of course, darling; you do make me laugh sometimes …' Eva says whilst warmly giggling. She opens the box of chocolates on the table and Arthur takes a seat.

'Choo-choo,' Eva says jokingly as she moves the chocolate towards his mouth as if it were a train entering a tunnel. They all chuckle, and Ishmael tries his hardest to not spit it out from laughter.

'Love a chocolate orange,' Ishmael says whilst he sucks on it.

'Yes, we know,' Eva says as she grins at Arthur, sharing the in-joke together.

'Okay, *The Devil's Diary* …' Ishmael says, still with his mouth partly full of chocolate.

3. THE DEVIL'S DIARY

'To trap someone in my box, I must restrict them at all costs from knowing their fundamental source. I must distract them from recognising within themselves the operating mechanisms that make them and put barriers in the way of their relationship with them. For if they recognise and know these fundamentals, these arch spirits, and hence know thy selves, they are likely to recognise the way of life and be closer to the father that *I hate*.

'Most of my ways are based on deception and illusion, and nothing gives me more pleasure than seeing someone filled with such passions for things that will ultimately bring them, and others, suffering. It is best instead to smother them with pleasure and distractions, overwhelm them, confuse them and lead them to believe that what they are doing is for the good. The ideal trap is to align their values with a paradox loop. Such is the way for starting with a reason for doing something, containing validity to a certain extent, only to further down the path discover that that reason was of course milked far past its merit. But at that point it is hopefully too late, as they have already had a taste of the dark passions that they were too pathetic to previously entertain. The idea here is to keep their eyes blindly on the target, without ever moving to others. This is the very nature of *my box*. *Everything I say you need to know is all you need to know.*

'Usually, it is the weak ones I target; the weak ones are too pathetic to engage in my passions, so I trick them into entertaining them by making them think they are being "moral". They go off with big heads and perform their busy-bodied duties, and may even think they are aligned *with* him; whilst secretly they are aligned with *me*; gaining great pleasure in their feelings of moral superiority. This is the start of their journey to my corruption and their eventual falling into my realm. The further they are from *him* and his spirit, the closer they are to *me* and to *mine*.

'I usually try and persuade them to idealise rationality, and that's usually where it begins. The good thing about rational thinking is that they quickly love the fruits of it, and those fruits produce positive feedback, encouraging its use again and again. They may think they worship science, but it's really me they are worshipping. Of course, I am not science, as science is still a providence of the father, but it is a great entry point to find me.

The more they love rationality, the less they celebrate the other spirit mechanisms. Eventually, and if all goes to plan, they forget those mechanisms entirely, completely ignorant and oblivious to them. The real pleasure then comes in the pushing downwards of the other spirits, making them still active but in the dark, and hence *inverted*. Nothing gives me more pleasure than to see the heart and empathy neglected and reversed; so instead of empathy being used to hold up a neighbour, it is instead used to inflict *more pain,* eventually leading to a *love of torture.* I call this anti-love, love used to hurt rather than to hold.

'At the beginning, I generally try to blind their eyes to this process, and it is only in such and such moments this fetish of giving pain raises its head. However, in the final stages of my corruption, they will recognise it consciously and will just accept it, at least partly. This is the first stage of *pure evil.* The final stage is to make them *crave* giving pain and make it the sole purpose of their existence.

'Focus their attention only on the *object*, because this will make them blind to the *subject*. If they gain eyes for the subject behind and around the object, they are likely to become enlightened to the spirit forms that bind all things, and once again will be closer to the father *that I hate.* I show people, and glamourise, the object, attempting to make them forget *the point* and their beloved *story.* Once this method becomes reinforced, through the feeling of pleasure from the fruits of the process, it will be ever so hard for them not to also see the earthly ones of their worth; that is, the meaningless flesh sacks that they are. *And nothing more than that.* Once I make one forget the essence of the human, and instead label them with my box, my kind will no longer see any reason to love their neighbour but just see them as *another object in the way of achieving within my box.*

'They say I am the left-handed path, and for good reason too. For it is the lefthanded ones who are the minority, and hence make up the edge, the extremes. And I like extremes and detest conventional orthodoxy. When a culture has my spirit, you will see the freaks become the gods, and they will be *worshipped* and protected. The left-handed ones of the father are the ones *I truly hate* and pose the biggest risk to my spirit. The ones of Saint Michael, these are the ones I have the issue with. The ones who summon the powers of my spirit, yet somehow still align themselves to the entirety of the seven. I have no greater delight than to capture Saint Michael's kind, to squeeze their soul over time, slowly dimming their bright light. This is the greatest pleasure. *Just more juice for me to take pleasure in during torture.*

'Sensitivity to the father's (*that I hate*) beauty function is something better kept suppressed. Beauty is a product of the father that *I hate*. The more my box can smother, the more they are numbed to beauty. The trick is to take their values and turn them on their head. If someone is compassionate, make them believe torture is the compassionate thing and a necessary evil. If someone is dutiful, make their duty the work of the box. If someone is of the left-handed path, make their chaos great but ultimately still aligned to the rules of the box, attacking and destroying all structures outside it. Eventually, they will be so blinded that when things become ugly, they will be so absorbed within my box that they forget what beauty of old looks like, and, in the end, ugly will become beautiful for them. To me, that is beauty.

'Any restriction of the expression of genuine emotion is encouraged by my kind; emotion instead is better filtered through the lens of my box. Passion in its best form is always inverted; the goal is always to focus the passion against what it actually, and truly, wants, leading the person to think that what they are doing is helping their cause whilst actually it is doing the opposite. Ultimately, it comes down to tricking them into sacrificing *everything* for something they believe will bring them fruits but in fact will only bring themselves, and others, *torture.*

'My mark is always there for those who have eyes to see. Ultimately, it is there for the torment of the children of the father that *I hate.* The naïve ones will take my mark ever so willingly, believing it will bring them good, and in some it may even bring good; and this only makes my mark ever more compelling. But that is not the point of my mark. It is the act of *choosing* the mark itself that is ultimately what brings the submission to my spirit. For one to choose my mark, they must submit a bit of their soul to *me.* At all costs, I wish to train souls to doubt the father that *I hate,* to doubt his voice, to doubt his spirit, to doubt he even exists. I wish for souls to instead listen to the *loud* voice and not to the *quiet one.* It is this quiet voice *that I hate the most.*

'It is actually easier to follow *me* than it is *him.* Oh, how liberating it feels to just let go and be free from responsibility, to live a life of glorious chaos, a life of no orthodoxy or rules, to just be free to express all those pent-up instincts ... Oh, how I tempt you? The path of my spirit is full of secret pleasures; how could one not indulge in my path? It is very simple: you either walk my path or be walked over by others *on my path*. Submit to me, submit my *horned and horny children*. My dark lords will always give milk to the faithful.

'The foul creature that is the Christ, the embodiment of the father I hate on earth ... How he and others of that path claim moral superiority. To integrate my spirit without being corrupted disgusts me to the core. Why have a bit of me, when you can have me *completely* ...

'Tease the souls and hang dangling fruits, keeping them constantly on the *edge*, constantly working, but never resting and resetting. For it is my spirit that traps them in the six days of work without ever having the *seventh for rest and rebirth*. My box is that of the six, and how beautiful this endless torture of the soul is. Keep them within my box focused on objects only within the six, and that is the entrapment. *My box exists to prevent rejuvenation of the spirit.*

'Oh, how you will see my flags of the six will wave true, yet they will hide in mysterious ways. Only the ones of Saint Michael will come close to my stench and will have eyes to see my work. *But those are the ones that my kind will hate the most ...*'

4. ARRIVING IN GENEVA

After a relatively painless flight, Arthur and Lukas land at Geneva airport. The International Hex Society (IHA) had, of course, paid for their flights, first class, and supplied them with their own individual private suites. In the private suites, both had been given a bottle of champagne (which neither Arthur or Lukas had drunk), underneath which was a welcoming letter informing them that at this summit, all invited would be provided with a private assistant/chaperone. Their assistant was called Toby. He would pick them up from the airport, drive them to their accommodation and provide supporting services throughout, such as taking notes, fetching drink and food, carrying coats and luggage and any other personal requests. The letter then went into more detail regarding the 'emotional configuration' of the assistant's ECT device, which could be edited by a provided smart tablet during the flight. The response from both Arthur and Lukas was comically similar: rolling their eyes, shaking their heads and tightening their upper cheeks in disgust. The letter went on to say: 'If no customised emotional configuration is chosen, the default algorithm will be applied to Toby, which is as of now: generalized highly positive emotion, reduction in generalized negative emotion; high pleasure response to obedience, low aggression and disagreeableness; and elevated anxiety and negative emotion towards making mistakes that result in a lack of efficiency in tending to members' orders and desires.

Arthur walks through the airport on his way to arrivals. He curiously looks around at the people walking and tries to differentiate between those with and without ECT devices, as he often did in public places these days. One particular woman catches his eye. She is middle-aged and sophisticatedly dressed, wearing a pink fur coat and glossy black heels. She smells strongly of perfume, which can be smelt from more than two metres away. She walks with a gentlemen in a black suit and yellow tie, and beside them is a young girl approximately 10 years old in plain clothes, wearing a black, medical face mask across her mouth. The rear of their necks are all clearly exposed too, as if they had consciously done so to show off the latest version of the classic black Snake Box oNe, looking rather sleek in matte black with the centre dot in the middle of the snake formation now being golden.

Arthur and Lukas step onto the moving walkway beside her, and Arthur discretely looks back to catch the face of the woman. He always liked to see the facial expressions and eyes of the people with ECT devices. He looks at her face and sees her staring directly forward. Her eyes have a certain peculiar squint to them:, feline, and predatorial in many ways. Her mouth is gently smiling, yet more so smirking. Her eyes scream maliciousness, contradicting the smile.

Arthur thinks to himself, *All that pent-up aggression being electronically suppressed … She's a walking bomb, waiting to explode. I can only imagine the sneaky and devious ways that energy will find form in the world. And the scary thing is, she won't even realise it …*

The lady suddenly turns her head mechanically, , locking eyes with Arthur. Instead of immediately turning away like most would, Arthur holds the gaze with her, like two animals had just seen each other in the wild.

'Hello,' Arthur says with a warm smile and a slight wave of his hand, slowly gaining distance on her on the moving walkway.

'Run along now, little doggy, time to play with your other savage friends, that's a good boy,' the woman says passive aggressively in an English accent, smiling like a Cheshire cat throughout.

'I'm assuming you prefer cats?' Arthur replies calmly and politely, not reacting defensively to the snarky comment. He slows down his pace on the walkway to move alongside the lady. Lukas looks back with one raised eyebrow from further up the walkway to try and figure out what is going on. It had become quite easy to detect whether someone had been equipped with an ECT device or not. Other than the device itself, or seeing the facial expressions and the body language, one common trait was a lack of spontaneous action, displays of quirk and individuality, and a general deviation from the trendy 'accepted norms'. It is hard to tell if this is due to the device itself or a personality trait of those more willing to get the device in the first place. For reasons that were still quite mysterious, those who chose to equip themselves with ECT devices tended to despise individuality and preferred people to act within certain boundaries, such as believing everyone should, as a matter of 'moral necessity', equip themselves with an ECT device to control their base instincts. The lady in pink quickly realised that Arthur had not been boxed due to his unorthodox behaviour of making strong eye contact and saying hello to her, a stranger. At this time in Europe, and most of the western world for that matter, to approach a stranger for no logically objective reason was extremely rare and commonly received poorly. She clearly deemed him as too much of an individual, and hence a threat to her collective way of thinking and how people should be in general.

'Does anybody have any pest control spray I can use to get this rabid beast away from me?' the lady says as she looks around at the man and young girl who walk alongside her, still with a large grin like a Cheshire cat. 'Have a good day,' Arthur says, with a subtle nod and bow, not wanting to aggravate the situation any more than needed. He then continues to walk briskly up the moving walkway, away from the lady, and towards a frowning Lukas waiting at the end with an accepting yet exhausted expression that said something along the lines of, 'This trips going to be interesting …'

Arthur and Lukas reach arrivals at the airport and begin looking around for Toby.

'Lukas Bell and Arthur Stanton, there he is,' Arthur says as he spots a short, young blond man holding a rather expensive-looking metallic plaque with their 'names' engraved on it. In accepting the invitation to the Hex summit, Lord Bell had written back stating he would be attending with a 'business associate for medical project development' and had changed Arthur's surname to Stanton in the documentation to avoid suspicion or any unwanted questions related to his brother.

'It's Toby, right?' Lukas says as he holds his hand out for their chaperone to shake.

'Yes, it's a pleasure to meet you,' he replies with an American accent as he shakes Lukas's hand, giving a wide yet rather weird smile. It was at this moment that both Lukas and Arthur glanced at each other, giving knowing looks that communicated something along the lines of. 'How are we going to deal with this, then?'

As was the way with ECT-induced emotions and facial expressions, it was obvious to unboxed people that something was *off*. Interactions were generally awkward and didn't flow naturally, as the standard emotional cues were slanted and twisted, making it harder to relate to one another within a conversation. The naturally-evolved instincts were triggered immediately and made unboxed people to feel rather uncomfortable. Both Lukas and Arthur were used to dealing with people putting a mask on, and both were used to breaking those masks down to access the self beneath so the conversation could become honest and genuine. But with the introduction of ECT devices, accessing the true self beneath the surface was far harder than it had been in the past, as another electronic layer had now been added.

'Likewise. This is my friend and colleague, Arthur,' Lukas replies as he holds his palm up in front Arthur.

'Nice to meet you, Toby; the letter on the plane said you would be our assistant for the week?'

'Oh, yes, that's true, sir. I've been electronically adjusted to be as useful to you both as possible. I sincerely hope I deliver on any of your requests.'

'Yeah … It said about that in the letter,' Arthur replies, 'how do you feel about that?'

'Err … Well, good. I feel good to help you both,' Toby replies. Lukas curses under his breath.

'Come on, let's get moving. Show us to the car please, Toby,' Lukas says, trying hard to not sound frustrated.

He and Arthur follow their servant. Lukas turns to Arthur and gives him a wary tilt of his head and a raise of the eyebrow, as if to say, 'Careful! We can't break our cover!'

After a quiet and rather awkward car journey, with an obvious tension in the air throughout, Toby pulls up to a pleasant and quaint-looking chalet beside Lake Geneva.

'Would you like me to help you get unpacked inside? I can also cook for you if you'd like?' Toby says as he looks back at Arthur and Lukas sitting in the back seat of his electric car.

'I'm going to make it clear to you now, Toby,' Lukas says with a sudden seriousness, leaning forward from his seat, 'My colleague and I will not be needing your services much, if at all, for this summit. Whilst we appreciate your willingness, and we appreciate the IHA's hospitality, we both prefer to work in private.'

'Oh, well, that is no problem at all, sir. Allow me to give you my personal contact number anyway, in case you do need me for *anything*. In the meantime, I will be residing in supplied accommodation with the other helpers. It was a pleasure to meet you both anyway.' Toby gives Lukas a card with his details on, and Lukas and Arthur leave the car. Toby opens the boot and begins to walk out to fetch their luggage for them both, but both Lukas and Arthur quickly leap to it before he gets the chance. Just as Toby is about to get back in the car, Arthur feels a sudden urge to ask a final question; he just couldn't help himself.

'Toby. How long have you been working for the IHA? Just out of pure curiosity.'

As Arthur asks this, Lukas looks at him with barely suppressed fury, his teeth clenching together yet just about managing to avoid giving an overt reaction. Toby stares back at Arthur at first with the same weird smile he gave earlier. It seems apparent that Toby is somewhat shocked and didn't expect to be asked any questions of a personal nature. And then, and just for a moment, the smile drops; and he gives a much more natural expression of curiosity, of intrigue, and Arthur even spotted a glimpse of sadness and desperation within the eyes. But these expressions, these tells, lasted only momentarily and would be missed by most normal people; Lukas didn't see them. Yet this small drop of the mask gave Arthur what he wanted, a glimpse into the true Toby.

'Not long, I must admit, sir. This is the first job I have done since signing up to work for them. I have only recently finished my three-month paid training period with them.'

'Oh, interesting,' Arthur replies. 'And I'm assuming you came over from America for the job?'

'That's correct, sir,' Toby replies hesitantly.

'You sound like an interesting person. Is it against your job's rules to get to know your clients on a more … informal basis?' By this stage, Lukas had gone past the point of being angry and just accepted that Arthur was clearly up to something. He raised his left eyebrow once again and was now more intrigued by Arthur's inquisitive behaviour than anything else.

'They haven't laid out any guidelines specifying I can't. My ECT device is mostly algorithmized to increase dopamine sensitivity for obedient be-haviour shown to my clients. If your wish is to get to know me on a more casual level, and that is your desire, then I suppose that is what will give me emotional reward. Any deviation from my clients' demands results in me receiving a massive load of anxiety and depressive emotion.'

'From now on, Toby, it is my desire for you to be as relaxed and as much yourself as possible. We will not be requiring any assistance with mundane tasks, and in fact it will only bring discomfort to both me and Lukas if you were to act as a servant in any way … Instead, we desire a more friendly and equal relationship where you are not a servant but a friend; at least for the six days of the summit. How does this all sound to you?'

'Honestly, sir, I feel guilty and worried in saying this, but I feel massively grateful. I was becoming very anxious that I would get some very nasty clients for my first summit ...'

'For now, let's leave it at this. But keep an eye on your mobile phone, you very well may be receiving a call from us later.'

'Okay, Mr Stanton, thank you,' Toby says as he rushes to Arthur from around the car, shaking his hand with a deep subservient bow.

Toby gets in his electric car and drives off.

At this point, Lukas had gone awfully quiet and had already walked off briskly towards the chalet, clearly aggravated in his body language and movements.

'Lukas?' Arthur says, following him inside the house.

'What the fuck are you on, Arthur?!' Lukas screams loudly once he closes the chalet door behind him. 'You know that he's probably going straight back to the Hex people and telling them of your bizarre behaviour? It wouldn't surprise me either if they track the conversations he has through the ECT device.'

'He won't. I've got a read on him. I wouldn't have spoken to him the way I did if I didn't feel confident in his position and alignment.'

'Position and alignment?! I know you are meant to be the chosen one, Arthur, but you can't get reads on people with ECT devices; the device blocks the real self from surfacing.'

'Not completely, Lukas, not completely. I know this for a fact. The devices are powerful, it is true; but they are not more powerful than the soul. The soul still finds its way to the surface, but you have to watch the face like a hawk. The self energy appears momentarily before the ECT device sucks away the emotions.'

Lukas sighs and shakes his head whilst looking down to the ground. He then takes a deep breath and looks back up at Arthur.

'Okay, Arthur, but you are being very ballsy with this one. I hope you know the risks. These people are not stupid. What's your plan with this guy, then?'

'Okay, well, firstly he's only young, and from what I've got on him, he seems innocent; I'm getting a somewhat childish vibe from him.'

'Okay, and ..?'

'And, Lukas, I think he is somewhat unwilling to do this job. It's my feeling that he's doing it more so for money, as a means of necessity; I highly doubt he has any sort of emotional investment in the organisation. I also got a glimpse of something in his face … It was like he wanted to tell me something, was almost desperate to, but was also terrified at the same time.'

'You honestly think he would come all the way from America to work for this organisation purely for the money?'

'I don't claim to know everything about this guy, but I know he is innocent and does not have bad intentions. If he isn't doing this job purely for the money, it is for some other similar reason … I think he knows a lot of things that could be useful to us. But for reasons that we can only assume, he is terrified to talk about them. You can't blame him, the amount of power these people have is on a cataclysmic scale.'

'Okay, okay, I get it; and I do respect the angle you are playing here, Arthur. Come downstairs and let's have a beer and talk about it further.'

They both walk downstairs, and Arthur looks around at the beautiful wooden beams of the chalet. The inside is relatively basic compared to Lukas's house back in England, and it is quite obvious he doesn't spend much time here. The ground floor has two large glass double doors that open to a balcony overlooking Lake Geneva. At this point in the late afternoon, the sun shines brightly onto the lake, and the view is eye-catching and picturesque. In the same room, there are two large beige sofas facing each other with a glass table between them.

'Take a seat, I'll be one second,' Lukas says as he heads down to the basement floor to retrieve some bottles of beer.

As Lukas returns from the basement holding a crate of beer, he sees Arthur sitting on the sofa with his head bowed down, eyes closed and hands clasped together. As he approaches, Arthur opens his eyes and tilts his head back up.

'Sorry, I didn't mean to interrupt you there,' Lukas says as he hands Arthur a bottle of beer.

'No, not at all, I only needed a moment to bring myself back together.'

'And I'm also sorry for shouting at you upstairs. I didn't see what you were getting at, but looking at it now, I think this Toby could actually be quite useful.'

'No, you were right to be concerned. I can be quite impulsive with my actions, and I understand this. Whilst I trust my intuition, it's good I have you to reel it in because otherwise I'm sure to get in trouble ...'

Lukas nods.

'Cheers anyway, to a successful trip,' Arthur says as he holds his beer in the air to make a toast.

'To a successful trip without getting murdered,' Lukas jokes as they chink their bottles together and both take a sip.

'We should have just invited him in for a beer there and then, shouldn't we?' Lukas says frowning whilst the side of his lip tightens.

'No, no, it was a heated and tense moment; we needed time to think and make sure it was definitely the right thing to do. I did say we might call him tonight, though, didn't I?'

Lukas takes another few large gulps of his beer.

'Fuck it, let's call him round now,' he says as he stares nervously at Arthur. Arthur smirks and chuckles lightly.

'He's only just driven back to his accommodation though, hasn't he,' Arthur says. 'Let's call him now before he gets there. I have a feeling he will be more than keen to still join us ...'

Lukas pulls out Toby's contact card from his wallet and dials the number.

5. AN UNFORTUNATE STRANGER

'Do you like Corona, Toby?' Lukas asks as he pops open a bottle he'd earlier retrieved from the cellar.

'Yeah, sure,' Toby responds as he sits opposite Arthur on the sofa. Lukas gives him the bottle.

'Cheers!' Arthur toasts, putting his bottle in the air, and they all chink their bottles and take a few sips. After the toast, there's an awkward silence. The tension is certainly not due to a lack of things to talk about because Arthur had many things he wished to say; yet he was still somewhat apprehensive to not overstep any lines. Arthur looks over at Lukas, who at this point was looking quite stressed. Lukas leant forward and gripped his bottle rather anxiously between his hands.

'I'm going to be completely honest with you right now, Toby,' Arthur says with a sincere and confident expression, 'because I believe I can trust you.'

'You can trust me,' Toby says as he looks at Arthur intensely, with a degree of desperation for him to keep talking as if craving genuine and truthful conversation.

'It doesn't take a messiah to work out that this organisation is linked to some very questionable people and organisations. I want firstly to put both mine and Lukas's neck on the line and let you know that we aren't friends with these people. We are undercover; we are pretending.'

'You guys are cops?' Toby asks as his face lights up, looking even more relaxed and relieved. Lukas is also put at ease by this question, somehow finding it encouraging and helping him trust Toby more as it was a rather innocent thing to ask.

'Not quite,' Lukas replies. 'I am a private surgeon, and many of these people feel indebted to me because I either saved their lives or the life of a family member in the past. I've been coming to these events for about 20 years now, purely out of curiosity. Whilst it's true I remain civil with these people, that's about as far as it goes.'

'We are here to establish contact with a family member of mine, my brother in fact, Jack Stanley, the co-founder of Snake Box,' Arthur adds.

As soon as Toby heard this from Arthur, his face immediately and quickly flushed red, and for a split second an intense worry flashed in his eyes. Arthur caught it before it was soaked up and taken away by his Snake Box.

'I saw that. And please don't worry, Toby, I know he's up to no good, and I am in no way working with him; quite the opposite, in fact. I am here to establish contact with him; however, it's been six years since I've seen him.' Toby continues to stare at Arthur, looking rather apathetic. He then breaks his stare, looks over at Lukas, takes a few large gulps of his beer, then leans back on the sofa and exhales deeply.

'Okay, well, allow me to be honest with both of you,' Toby says with a stutter, pinching his fingers together tightly in front of him. 'I regret signing up for this job, and I regret allowing them to have me boxed. I feel so controlled by this organisation; they have penetrated every aspect of my life, and I'm stuck in this contract with them for at least another two years.'

'Just to clarify, Toby, what else does the IHA have you do? I'm assuming it's more than to just be an assistant for elites every six years?' Lukas asks.

'You have no idea … You understand that I am hesitant talking about this with you? I know you saw fear in me earlier, Arthur. I know you saw it in me. I wanted you to … Anyway, I do feel like I trust you both, so let me tell you this. When I originally applied for the job, I didn't fully realise that "legal and above board" doesn't really apply to these people. These people can make you disappear, and they have complete influence over all the media as well. Even if they had me killed, and my parents started causing a fuss, you wouldn't hear a peep about it from the media.'

'Toby, you sound like such a good man, why on earth did you let them box you in like this? And I mean that in both senses of the word …' Arthur says as he looks down and shakes his head, feeling rather upset.

'Because my family and I needed the money! Do you know how much they pay?!' Toby screams loudly as he jolts himself up from the sofa, bursting with emotion. This quickly gets sucked away, like dust up a hoover, but this causes another wave of emotion to be shot through him, and with it a growing frustration with his Snake Box.

'Damn thing!' Toby begins smacking the back of his neck with the palm of his hand, and then all his actions and emotion stop immediately as the ECT kicks in again.

'Toby, Toby! Chill, chill, we got you mate,' Lukas says as he pats him on the back. 'Trust me, we can help you. But please, sit down again. You have to tell us everything you know about what this organisation are doing behind closed doors, and specifically, everything you know about Snake Box.'

Toby sits back down and puts his face into his hands but then quickly sits back up with a blank, apathetic expression.

'This job was originally advertised as a technology testing role for companies that work within the International Hex association. This servant role for the summit, I didn't even have any idea I would have to do this originally. I thought this job would be relatively easy work for high pay. I knew there would be risks, but I kind of saw it like drug testing, you know? Anyway, I quickly found out that during my "three-month paid training period", I would have absolutely zero human rights and essentially give them full legal authority to torture me in ways that have caused me the most horrible, horrible, trauma. I can't even begin to describe to you what I have been through; they have done things to me that I don't even fully understand.'

'I'm so sorry, Toby,' Arthur says softly, 'I know it's hard, but is there any way you could even begin to tell us what they have done to you?'

'Well, you mentioned your brother Jack, the co-founder of Snake Box. I had already read about him online and recognised him immediately when he was standing there with his colleague.

'Harry Sickle. Yep, we know him,' Arthur says as he gives a concerning glance over to Lukas.

'They were both there watching me and three others in a big underground hall from behind a desk, among many other people from their company too. They strapped us to these chairs, and they said they were going to run a new program through the Snake Box to test on us. This was literally the same day they had it installed on me, so I was only just getting used to it. They didn't tell me much else, but then it begun …' Toby looks down to his side and begins grinding his teeth in gloomy reminiscence. 'Have either of you ever taken psychedelic drugs before?'

Arthur immediately coughs in surprise at this question.

'Yes,' he says whilst frowning curiously, not liking where this is going.

'Yes, we both have. Why?' Lukas adds.

'Well, imagine the worst trip you have ever had, and the absolute terror and anxiety you feel, like you are losing your mind, even your soul. Then imagine being put in a dimly-lit underground hall and strapped to a chair. Then imagine not being able to move whilst an intense pain begins all round your body but focused in the centre of your head; it feels like your actual energy is being sucked out of you slowly, a drawn-out feeling, where you can't even scream or shout because your mind is so twisted you don't know how to. All the while you are being stared at by multiple people. It felt like a waking nightmare with no escape. This went on for 12 hours, I was told.'

Arthur and Lukas both look disgusted and are left speechless.

'But you know the bit that stays ingrained in my memory the most? The bit that drew my attention the entire time? The large glass box with a black cube inside it.'

Arthur and Lukas begin stirring at mention of the black cube, and Arthur begins touching his forehead anxiously.

'As the experiment kept going, and I continued to suffer unbearably, the black cube inside the glass box would occasionally squirt a clear fluid … It would squirt a bit here, a bit there, gradually filling up the glass box until the cube inside was floating in the very fluid it was secreting. The whole process was so alien, so disgusting, so horrific. The image of that squirting cube … That is an image I will never forget.' Arthur and Lukas are once again shocked into silence at this harrowing image.

'Snake oil …' Arthur says softly, almost under his breath, finally breaking the silence, leaning forward on his arm that rests on his leg. 'Do you remember, Lukas? That's the name of the new product they are unveiling on day six of the summit?'

'Yes. Unfortunately, I do remember. Your brother has certainly come a long way over the last six years, hasn't he?'

Arthur contorts his face and scratches the back of his head. He then leans back and takes a few gulps of his beer.

'I'm still confident I can get my brother to see the evil in this.' He nods to himself whilst staring down at his beer. 'I can see it. My brother has always been rebellious, it's true, and he's even always been a bit resentful since our parents were killed. But still, to this day, I don't think he's evil. It's this Harry Sickle who is really the dark force behind it all. With Jack, he just needs a "good" reason to do something, a rationalisation, if you like.'

'And what on earth would the rationalisation be for this one then?' Lukas asks.

'I have no idea what this snake oil is, or what it does, but I guess we will find that out later this week. However, I can guarantee you, Jack believes that the ends justify the means here. He will see poor Toby's experience as a mere sacrifice for the greater good, and that rationalisation will override his heart. Harry, on the other hand, I think he may know that no good will come from this, and that ultimately any good that is said to come from it is a mere illusion, a distraction; and he knows it, but he enjoys the evil of it. That man is a completely twisted bastard. My gut tells me that there is something very sinister at play beneath all this.'

'A demonic sort of play?' Toby asks abruptly, causing Arthur and Lukas to turn towards him.

'I was thinking along those lines actually, yes …' Arthur says. 'But what makes you say that?'

'Rumours among some of the other Hex assistants. Apparently, the IHA organises a weird ritual once in a while, open to active associates. Apparently, they all meet up on this island and burn a massive effigy of a pagan god. For a while over the three-month training camp, when things were actually quite fun, and before they turned sinister, we joked about being taken to the island and strapped to the burning effigy. But after what happened with some of us being tortured on the chairs and seeing that squirting cube; well, we didn't really "joke" about it anymore after that. We felt we really had been sacrificed … At least, a part of me feels like it has …'

'Do you feel physically different?' Lukas asks with his usual raised left eyebrow. 'I understand it was a very traumatic experience, and of course you mentioned your psychological trauma, but do you have any peculiar or unusual physical changes since they put you through that experiment?'

'Very much so, yes. I feel significantly weaker as a person, I can't think as easily and I lack the same enthusiasm as before. The weirdest thing, however, is I feel sort of like I'm going through a withdrawal, and part of me wants to go through the whole process again; twisted, I know … But … Well …'

'Go on,' Arthur says.

'Well, the whole process was actually … a bit sexual. I had no control, and all I could do was submit myself to it. I didn't feel any pleasure, or what you would traditionally think of as pleasure, but there was an element to it that was almost forcing me to give up, urging me to realise I had no control, and to give myself to the cube. I felt like my very essence was being squeezed out of me, through the cube, into the glass box. I hate to admit it, and I am ashamed to admit it, but the thought does arouse me a bit. I think this is what is playing on my mind the most, how I'm actually craving something that I hated beyond anything I've ever experienced.'

'Shit, that's dark,' Arthur says raising his cheeks and showing his upper teeth. 'Look, Toby, there's a lot you don't know about me and my friend Lukas here. We are from a secret academy called the Tree of Life, back in England. I mean, it's advertised to normal people as a martial arts academy, but in reality we are more like modern mystics, or maybe you can view us as a group of philosophers. Regardless of our label, our view is that the world has sold its soul, and our purpose is to protect the human soul from being completely destroyed. We offer services to people who feel they have lost connection to their humanity, and we provide rehabilitation for people who have had their ECT boxes removed.'

'And just to clarify here, I can actually remove the devices myself, and have done so many times now,' Lukas says.

'Yes, Lukas is one of the top surgeons in the country, and was the reason for his peerage, in fact. Look, it's still an underground organisation; however, to ones we feel we can trust, we offer our services. And I trust you, Toby, and I think we can help you. I feel a large amount of compassion towards you, in fact.'

'But we have a task we need to do first,' Lukas adds in a more serious tone . 'As Arthur stated earlier, we are here to make contact with Jack Stanley. Our plan is to try and get him back to the chalet, where Arthur can show him some evidence that will hopefully have a profound effect on him.'

'Okay, well, I will help you in any way I can if you can help me like you said. I will appreciate that beyond anything.'

The trio nod and smile at one another sincerely.

'So, you've come all this way to show Jack Stanley this "evidence"?'

'Hmm, partly so. That black cube you saw,' Arthur says with his eyebrows raised, 'it is an extremely powerful magical object. On its own, it is incredibly dangerous and full of dark and corrupting magic. It was originally meant to be inside a powerful sword called Excalibur, and only when it is inside the hilt of the sword, and wielded by a chosen one, can it be used as it was intended; for the good, and for love. Our task is to convince Jack to hand over the cube so we can reunite it with the sword and finally rescue my father's trapped soul in the underworld of hell.'

'Right …' Toby says, looking quite overwhelmed and confused. 'Well. I feel there is much to this I don't understand, but you have definitely got my attention, and as I said, if you can help me connect back to my former self, you have my help.'

'I thought we had your undying obedience before any of this anyway?' Lukas asks with a cheeky smile, and then sticks his tongue out a bit. Toby laughs.

'That was when I was a slave. Now I feel like a free man, and I talk to you instead as friends. And as friends, now, you have my full support and love not from a professional duty, but from both my heart and my soul.'

The trio make a final toast and continue to work their way through the rest of the beer.

6. THE SIXTH DAY

Neither Lukas nor Arthur bothered going to any of the other days leading up to the finale of the summit. Toby said he could retrieve a digital version of each day instead. So instead of dressing up fancy and having to be around many of the other snobby elites at the actual Hex summit in person, they all simply watched the presentations of the new products at the chalet over some beers (which Lukas had no shortage of down in the cellar). During this period, both Arthur and Lukas became quite close to Toby, and the mood between them became even more friendly and relaxed. Not to say this relationship was by any means natural or organic, as of course the ECT box was altering the way Toby responded to certain things – he failed to register certain jokes that an unboxed person would, for example – but all this considered, Toby was able to be himself to a surprising degree.

As the days went on, Toby was becoming more and more committed to finishing this conference and coming back to England with them, not caring whether he was still technically and legally in a contract with the IHA.

Arthur told him, 'The worst-case scenario is we have you sleep underground at the Tree of Life until the heat settles down. But frankly, I can't imagine these people will cause that much of a fuss over a mere "assistant". You can at least rest knowing we have your back.'

The days leading up to the sixth day also provided a time of reflection for the trio. Specifically Arthur, whose morning routine involved walking around Lake Geneva, pondering his thoughts for what was to come. Within his heart, he did indeed feel apprehension; but mostly, he felt confident, he felt on track, and he felt that he would indeed be able to save his father's soul. It was only in moments of intense realism and rationality that he begun to doubt himself and lose faith. But every time he felt himself leaning this way, he would stare out at the lake and remember his vision with his mother, who not too long ago above another lake gave him the sacred blessing of Excalibur.

Arthur sits at one of the many hexagon-shaped tables inside the International Hex Association's auditorium, with Toby sitting down to his right with a smart tablet organiser on the table's surface, currently checking the time of when the talk will begin. Lukas is three tables away and wears a classic black suit and tie, as Arthur is too. Lukas is standing up in conversation with a rather strange-looking man wearing an eccentric white suit, with fluffy black inlays, and a red bow tie. The man, who looks in his mid-60s, also has a large beard and moustache and wears small, circular black glasses.

The theatre itself is rather large and prestigious and piano music plays in the background. The room has two large windows on either side of the main stage, allowing large amounts of natural light to enter. However, a large crystal chandelier also hangs from the centre of the ceiling and various other smaller ones are beside and around it. Arthur had already noticed a few odd looks from people at other tables around him, which he mainly put down to the fact that Toby, clearly identified as a Hex employee by his white, branded Hex shirt uniform, was sitting down with him at the table instead of standing up like all the others. Another fact that makes his and Lukas's table stand out, was the fact that it was literally just three of them, with other tables sitting up to 18.

They stand out like sore thumbs.

'Are you noticing it too, then?' Toby asks.

'What's that?' Arthur replies.

'Most people here don't actually have a Snake Box or other sort of ECT device.'

Arthur nods with a slight squint of his eyes.

'I can't say I'm surprised. These elites probably know better. But I bet that won't stop many of them from forcing them upon their employees.'

Toby nods in response and then points to a man in a black Hex uniform who just walked past their table.

'You see the ones dressed in black,' he whispers, 'they are the ones who we take orders from. They are Hex black operatives, with most just calling them "the Hex black". They are very cold-hearted and quite terrifying, if I'm honest … I'm pretty sure they dial down their empathy levels.'

Artur nods and frowns, takes in a deep breath, and says, 'Let's not make it too obvious that we are on a more friendly basis, Toby. It's just going to make these people more suspicious than they need to be.' Toby nods and purses his lips. 'Sorry, I didn't mean to be rude there; it's just right here with all these people looking over, we've got to be careful.'

'No, no, you are right, I get it.'

'Looks like Lukas is finished anyway,' Arthur says as he points towards Lukas, who has now finished his conversation and is walking back to the table.

'That chap looked like quite the character,' Arthur says as Lukas sits back down. Lukas smiles knowingly.

'Yes. I have to say, out of all the people I have a connection with here, Jeffrey is someone who I actually think is quite normal.' Lukas pauses for a second and tilts his head as if contemplating what he just said. 'Okay, well, I wouldn't say normal, but he has a certain charm, I must admit.'

'Who is he?' Arthur asks.

'Jeffrey Lux. He owns a surgical light company called Optake. He's an ex-surgeon himself, actually; he used to have his own private practice too.'

'Well, if he's as normal as you say, maybe he's here for similar reasons as you are.'

'You know what, I wouldn't be surprised. I felt on a similar wavelength to him. I even found myself smiling whilst talking to him, and he too was giving a similar smile. It was like we both felt like friends in an ocean of aliens.'

Both Arthur and Toby start laughing.

'Well, having someone we can trust here can only be a good thing,' Arthur says.

'Well, he did have a bit of reputation of botching surgeries back in the day. And I don't just mean a one off like I did. He botched about five.'

'No wonder he's not a surgeon anymore! Jesus Christ …' Toby adds with light-hearted shock in his voice. Arthur can't help but laugh again.

Arthur feels his smartphone buzz. He opens his phone and reads the text: 'Dad said today is the day. Good luck. You've got this, babe. Good is more powerful than evil. Xx'

After reading this text, a sudden feeling of déjà vu makes Arthur shiver a little, but overall he is happy to hear from Eva.

'Your daughter just texted me. She says good luck.'

'Bless her,' Lukas replies with a warm smile. 'Toby, how long have we got?' His face quickly turns serious.

'Any minute now.'

'Oh, I think this is it, actually,' Arthur says as he notices a shift in the room's atmosphere.

The light from the chandeliers dims and the large windows beside the main stage fade to black using an embedded filter technology inside the glass, blocking all natural light from entering. The piano music stops and tense and excited chattering can be heard from all around the room. Shuffling and shifting, whispers and rumbles. Even Arthur and Lukas can't help but feel rather anxious from the anticipation.

A spotlight focuses on the main stage. An old bald man, with a highly wrinkled face and slightly hunched back, walks out from the right side of it. He wears a black suit and has small, silver spectacles.

The audience begins to loudly and enthusiastically clap.

'Who is this guy?' Arthur asks.

'Nicholas Scarr, founder of the IHA,' Lukas replies.

'Thank you, thank you,' the man says, and the audience begins to settle down. 'Welcome to the final day of the summit. This is the day we have been waiting for.' The man begins to look very smug. Arthur glances quickly to his left and sees a man's face so red from excitement that it looks like his head is going to explode. 'I won't hold you here for long, but I will say, *thank you*. Thank you for the visionaries, thank you for the optimism, and thank you, above all, for your dedication to the International Hex project. We would be nothing without collaboration, for on our own we are weak, but together, we are strong. And that is the power of shared values.'

The audience begins clapping again.

'It has been 36 years since our first summit. And look how far we have come. Back then, they called me "delusional", "a crazy utopist", "a dangerous psychopath".' The crowd begins laughing. 'And yes, now we laugh, but it wasn't easy. Now, no one would dare call me or my association such names.' The man laughs to himself, and other laughs can be heard scattered among the crowd. 'I said we would change the world, and before it was just me and a handful of companies who actually believed me. Now, not only do we have the support of more than 50 of the world's largest corporations, but we have the support from many members of governments as well. But most importantly, through the collaboration of the Hex group's media network, we have managed to align much of the public to our vision as well. And I'm going to be honest with you all here; it is this that is our most powerful achievement. Because if you can control the people, you can control the world. And this means a great responsibility for us, because it is up to us, the experts, to lead the world towards a bright new age. And we can do this, and we will do this. Just speak to someone, anyone here, and they understand that for the greater good of all of us, we must sometimes do things that many once considered wrong. And it is true, there are certain things that people said, and still say, should never be done. But we, together, have proven, time and time again, that these boundaries are merely illusions; constructs that society of old has forced upon us. But if we can stay strong, and keep that vision of that great future in mind, nothing will stop us.' The crowd claps and cheers at the loudest volume yet. 'And on that note, ladies and gentlemen, I present to you a man who is not scared to make these great changes. It is indeed, the co-founder of Snake Box, *Jack Stanley!*"

Jack enters from the same side of the stage as Nicholas Scarr and the crowd goes ballistic; they cheer and give a standing ovation. Arthur, Lukas and Toby look at each other rather surprised at how wild everyone is becoming merely from Jack walking on stage. Worried about standing out more than they already were, they too reluctantly join in with the ovation.

Jack puts his hands up in the air and waves them down towards the floor to quieten the crowd.

'Thank you so much everybody, this is a great honour for me.' Jack begins laughing to himself, looking genuinely overwhelmed at the crowd's response. 'So, um, where to begin … Well, let me start with this.' Jack clicks his presentation remote controller, and on the left of the large screen behind him, a picture of the original Snake Box oNe pops up. 'Four years ago, we brought out the Snake Box oNe.'

Much of the crowd cheers.

'And I think we can all agree, it changed the world. Then, two years later …' Jack clicks the controller again, '… we brought out the Snake Box tWo. A faster, more efficient device that delivered everything the first Snake Box did, but without as much "emotional lag" as it has come be known. So most of what we have been working on with the new Snake Box devices is a reduction of this emotional lag and making them as efficient as possible in heightening or dampening the inputted emotion. This is all well and good, and is something that you can all expect, along with much more, with our upcoming Snake Box devices in the future. And, of course, this includes the much-awaited Snake Box thrEE. But today is a day when we are introducing something completely different. Something, I dare say, even more revolutionary than the introduction of the original Snake Box emotional control technology. Today, we introduce …' Jack clicks his controller, '… snake oil.' Jack says to the words as the text appears on screen.

The crowd gasps and stirs, with many whispering to each other in antici-pation and curiosity.

'What is snake oil, you ask. Well, rather than introducing an entirely new physical device, we have instead introduced an entirely new concept, a new system, to the existing Snake Box technology. Please, allow me to demonstrate.'

From the left side of the stage, a few IHA employees bring on a wheel-chair, a small wooden table, a glass box and a pint glass. One of the Hex fe-male employees then sits down on the wheelchair, which has been placed in front of Jack. The girl is in her 20s and looks rather apathetic.

'Fucking hell,' Arthur says under his breath as he glances to his left at Toby; who at this point is completely transfixed by what's happening on stage. The glass box is placed on the table on stage, with the pint glass be-side it. Jack then places the black cube, that he pulls from his suit pocket, inside the glass box.

'Okay. So what would usually happen now is the user would activate the snake oil sequence themselves, from the Snake Box application. When, of course, they are in a comfortable and safe location to do so. But for the sake of the demonstration today, I will be breaking down the steps of the process.' Jack pulls out his mobile device and activates the first stage.

The girl in the chair falls asleep immediately.

Gasps from among the crowd.

'So, as deep and thorough interactions are about to take place within the user's consciousness, for their safety and well-being, the program puts them to sleep at the beginning before the main process begins. Other than some enhanced dreams, the user won't feel anything unpleasant in the slightest.

'So, now I'm about to begin the second stage, which we at Snake Box call the "libidic siphoning stage". This stage can last anywhere from four to 24 hours, depending on the user's chosen input on the application.'

Jack enters an input on his mobile device, and the head of the girl jolts to the other side of the chair. She lets out a subtle moan that sounds rather sexual in nature, causing murmurings in the crowd.

'During the process, the user may have some intense dreams, as I have already said. I can assure you they are for the most part in a nice, deep REM sleep. But yes, they may stir a bit during this process, and at points enter a lighter, more hypnagogic type of sleep. But now, everybody, I want to focus your attention on the cube here, inside this glass box.'

On the screen in the centre of the stage, a feed of the glass box and black cube can be seen. There's a deathly quiet, and a bizarre tension fills the room. Everyone is fixated on the screen, yet they have no idea at all what they are meant to be waiting for.

'Keep watching; it takes a few moments for it to really begin.'

After a short, tense pause, the cube secretes a small squirt of fluid.

The crowd gasps with bewilderment and confusion.

'We all saw that, yeah? Give it a few more seconds, it will begin to happen more rapidly as time goes on.'

Squirt, squirt, squirt. The cube goes on to secrete more fluid in three quick bursts.

'What am I looking at right now?' Lukas says in shocked bewilderment, with a shake of his head.

'I think this is what they used to call "black magic" back in the day ...' Arthur replies. 'You okay, mate?' he asks as he turns to Toby.

'Yes,' Toby says after a slight delay, and with a heavy sigh; he is still fixated, if not hypnotised, by the screen.

'Okay, we can wheel the lovely lady off to a nice private space now, where she will continue to be siphoned. Can I get a round of applause for our volunteer!' Jack says. The crowd starts clapping, and the unconscious girl is wheeled off stage. 'So what exactly is happening here? What is this mysterious liquid being secreted from our "snake core" here, as we like to call it? Well, ladies and gentlemen, it is *liquid consciousness*.'

The audience, clearly bewildered, begins talking among themselves.

'We have figured out a way to convert human essence into pure, clean, energy. And my god, ladies and gentlemen, is it powerful ...'

Jack pulls out a handkerchief from his suit's front pocket and wraps it around the black cube in the glass box. He quickly transfers the dripping cube to the pint glass.

'Got to try and not waste any!' Jack says. The crowd laughs.

At this point, the cube is consistently leaking fluid into the glass. Jack holds the pint glass high in the air, as if he was about to make a toast to the crowd, and says, 'One of these glasses holds enough to power a family home for four people, for two, whole, days!' Gasps followed by a thunderous round of applause from the audience. 'But more than that, this fluid doesn't combust like normal crude oil, no. It operates more like steam and is completely harmless to the environment. Ladies and gentlemen, if you don't yet see what we are doing, we are giving the people the power to convert their very own life force into an energy that can be used for everybody. Imagine a world where people can, from their own homes, donate their own essence for the greater good of mankind. Those who feel like their life lacks meaning or purpose can now be fulfilled, knowing they are giving themselves to a worthy cause that will benefit everyone. Through the Snake Box series, we can now allow anyone, anywhere, anytime, to siphon their energy to us at the Snake Box headquarters. Through the wireless Snake Box connection, we will stockpile the snake oil and then distribute it around the world for a fair price. Far cheaper than any fossil fuel could be. And, of course, there are millions of humans willing to donate their essence to us, making this a completely renewable source. So please allow me to demonstrate. Can we please bring out the snake oil generator?'

Two men dressed in black Hex uniforms emerge from side of the stage, carrying with them a peculiar-looking generator using a handle on each side. The generator is black and looks very similar in style to the black cube itself, but instead has many electrical ports, connections and a central capped entrance point for snake oil fuel insertion. They put the generator down on stage and Jack uncaps the snake oil receptor. He pours in the contents of the pint glass, which at this point is approximately half full. Once poured in, Jack presses a button on the top of the generator, which lets out a strong gust of steam from the rear in a big, sudden release, making a loud pshh sound.

'And just like that, the entirety of the snake oil has been potently converted into useable electricity. This generator, off only half a glass, contains a mighty 26 kilowatt hours of energy. Meaning a pint will equate to an incredible 52 kilowatt hours of energy.

'Can I please borrow someone's mobile phone from the audience, anyone's will do.'

A smiling bald man sat at a table at the front holds his phone up in the air for taking.

'Ah, thank you sir. Don't worry, I won't be long.'

Jack pulls out a charging USB cable from his pocket and plugs the mobile phone into the generator. He holds the phone up in the air for the camera to capture it.

'70% charged' pops up on the phone. Jack holds his hands out to the side and purses his lips together smugly. The crowd begins to clap. He leans down and gives the mobile phone back to its owner.

'Thank you, kind sir. So, this is all very well, but how will we encourage people to commit to the "libidic siphoning process"? What is the incentive? Well, every nation will be wanting this clean renewable source. Given the inevitable future demand for snake oil, we will be in a perfect economic position to give back to the people. Allow me to introduce to you our snake oil reward scheme. Based on every user's snake oil profile, the more a person donates, the more we reward them. For example, and this is of course subject to change, eight hours of siphoning will equate to a net average of £96. But, if a person commits to donating every day consistently, we will start to be able to apply "snake oil multipliers" to the equation. If loyal enough to the scheme, people will be able to make as much as £1,000 per day from the safety of their own home. All while knowing they are helping a great cause. Ladies and gentlemen, this is the energy revolution we have been waiting for; we have finally got there.' Jack, once again, holds the glass with the squirting cube high up in the air to toast the crowd. 'And I, ladies and gentlemen, raise my glass to that.'

The crowd goes wild. They clap, cheer and many hold their own glasses up in the air to join in with Jack's toast. Like a Mexican wave, people begin to stand up one table at a time until the entire room is giving a tremendous standing ovation of thunderous intensity. Lukas and Toby reluctantly stand up from their table to try and blend in with everyone else. Arthur, however, remains firmly planted on his seat, unwilling to join in. Lukas looks down at him subtly and gives him a slight nudge, but Arthur nods his head in disagreement, focusing straight ahead like a laser beam. Lukas looks around anxiously to see if they have attracted any attention from the Hex staff or the other technocrats. He notices a small lady in her 60s glancing over at his table in disgust, and then sees a couple of other people taking notice too, still clapping and cheering but looking rather suspicious. From the corner of his eye, to his right, he sees a few of the Hex black congregating, talking to each other and casting suspicious glances towards the trio's table.

'Just so you know, Arthur, they are on to us,' he says as he leans down, trying not to panic, feeling rather annoyed yet still hoping that Arthur had this under control. Whilst he had no reason to believe this was the case, he really did believe it.

'I know. Just relax, Lukas, we've got this.'

'I hope you're bloody right …'

The three men in black Hex uniforms begin to walk towards the table. As soon as they do, Toby immediately stands up to confront them.

'Hey guys, is everything okay?' he says, showing loyalty to his new friends. The men, without any hesitation, push Toby to the side with a considerable force, making him fall to the ground. People from other tables are now beginning to look at what is going on.

'Oh, there's always someone who ruins it for everybody, isn't there?' Jack says from the stage, noticing the change in atmosphere and the Hex black people over by the table. 'Don't worry, we will get him escorted out, and then I'll carry on.'

An intense awkwardness and tension fills the room; the ovation has died down and what is left are a smattering of confused conversations among a general silence. The men, without a word, grab Arthur underneath both his arms and pull him to his feet aggressively. Arthur doesn't resist at all and is dragged on his feet towards one of the doors at the front right of the room. Arthur is trying his best to keep his composure and walk normally. Clearly, these men want to make a fool out of him and make it look like he's resisting. Many of the elites at the tables stare at Arthur like he is some sort of abomination; they snarl and shake their heads.

As Arthur is moved closer to the stage, there's a clear line of sight between him and his brother. Arthur makes sure to stare his brother right in the eyes. Jack's face suddenly fixes in position as he clocks Arthur; he is clearly shocked but is trying to remain composed for the crowd and keep a neutral poker face. Arthur smirks cheekily and flicks his eyebrows. as if to say, 'I may look in a weak position, but don't let that fool you.'

Arthur is led out of the room. Jack is caught completely off guard and left feeling perplexed and stunned on stage. The audience has now redirected their attention back to him, but he is struggling to find words. After a rather awkward pause, he finally says, 'Unfortunately, ladies and gentlemen, there will always be snakes that exist outside of Snake Box.' The audience laugh. 'Let us have a brief 30-minute interval. I have much more to tell you all. I hope you have all been enjoying the presentation so far, thank you very much.'

As the crowd give a final ovation before scattering to go about their business during the interval, Lukas and Toby remain seated at their table with three Hex employees standing behind them, keeping a watchful eye. Lukas leans forward on the table and rubs his temples whilst taking a deep inhale. He looks up and notices a familiar man looking at him. The man and the rest of his table (five others) also remain seated. The man looks over with a gentle warm smile that exudes a friendly confidence. And this made Lukas feel strangely more relaxed. It was the very same eccentrically-dressed man he was speaking to earlier: Jeffrey Lux.

7. THE HOSTILE BROTHERS

Arthur sits in a rather small room, yellow-beige in colour with no windows. The room feels as if it was purposely designed for interrogation. The light hanging above is cold, white and sharp. The solid steel, matte black table in front of him is fixed permanently to the ground.

Arthur sits and looks calm, his hands together in his lap and his shoulders slightly rounded. His head tilts downwards too, as if he could be in a state of prayer, yet his eyes remain open. Behind him stands a Hex black operative, who stares straight forward coldly and mechanically. The operative stands strangely close behind him, so close that Arthur feels the warmth radiating from him. Arthur intuitively sensed this was intentional to try and make him feel as uncomfortable as possible, but he did not let this affect him and maintained his cool. On the other side of the table stand the other two Hex black operatives who dragged him here earlier; they stare at Arthur like hawks, with expressions of mild disgust, just looking for any excuse to inflict pain of any means.

The door then opens. Arthur brings his head up carefully and sees his brother. Jack sits down at the table, and the brothers make eye contact. For a good few moments, they say nothing to each other.

'You have 15 minutes,' Jack says, breaking the silence.

'I love you,' Arthur says with a deep sincerity, being the deepest truth he could muster in that moment.

After a few moments' pause, Jack rolls his eyes as if Arthur's sincerity is a manipulative ploy rather than from the heart.

'What do you want, Arthur? Why have you come here?'

'I haven't seen you in six years, Jack. Above all, I miss you. Have you forgotten that I am still your brother?'

'Arthur, I know you were always one for childish sentimentalities and fantasies, but when adults grow up and enter the real world, sometimes other things take priority; and if you haven't noticed, I've been kind of busy over the last six years.'

'I know you have been busy. As have I, with my life.'

'Oh yeah, what have you been doing, Arthur? Let me guess, spending your days with a bunch of drugged-up fanatics, fantasising about some sort of new age I don't doubt ...'

Arthur looks down and squints, wondering how much Jack knows about the Tree of Life.

'Oh, yes, I know about John's little cult, by the way,' he says with his eyebrows raised, whilst nodding belittlingly. 'I've known about it since we were kids, Arthur. You think I would tell *you*, someone who was always essentially on the brink of losing it, about a secret society full of delusional man-children who partake in rituals and take drugs? Arthur ...' Jack shakes his head, looking at Arthur like he is a child.

'You have no idea what the Tree of Life can do to help people,' Arthur says emphatically, eyes wide and innocent.

Jack begins to laugh sarcastically, leans back on his chair and looks up towards the ceiling.

'It's a cult, Arthur! My goodness, how can you not see it? Ever since the dawn of humanity we have created nonsense to make us feel a little better about the tragedy of life. Naturally, smart men saw its power and continued to fuel it to control the weak and stupid. Look, I'm sure it does help some people; delusion, faith in things that have no evidence or science, these things are a mere reaction to suffering, a comfort blanket. Do you not understand that we are finally at a stage in human understanding and development that we can actually, truly, rid ourselves of these things? Yes, in times of old they may have needed delusion to comfort them, to provide them with a sort of religious morphine; but now we have actually solved the problem with science and rational understanding. You are a smart man, Arthur, surely you can see this?'

'Out of interest, Jack, do you have a Snake Box on the back of *your* neck?' Arthur asks, knowing for a while that Jack does not.

'Here we go ...' Jack says as he rolls his eyes. 'You do understand I am not exactly in a position where I need to wear one. I keep busy and have a position of responsibility; I am in a stable financial position, and I don't need one by job mandate. As a matter of generalisation though, their use should be encouraged for the *majority* of people. Collectively speaking, surely you understand that if we can get as many people wearing them as possible, we can actually bring down people's aggression levels and therefore reduce crimes of all kinds? You do know every Snake Box reduces aggressive behaviour by more than 60%? And that number will increase with each generation? If this product was around when we were kids, Arthur, maybe our parents wouldn't have been brutally murdered and incapacitated. Yes, there are people with certain roles in society who don't need them, but they are the exception that proves the rule. For the average Joe, it's most likely rather selfish that they would choose to not wear one. And if I'm completely honest with you, Arthur, it's usually down to some personal delusion, such as an attachment to a religion or some other sort of dangerous dogma.'

'Or maybe it is an alignment with conscience?' Arthur says as he stares with great intensity into his brother's eyes, clearly not startled or put off by his brother's passionate arguments.

'Conscience? You mean the social conditioning we have been taught to believe and act out over generations, with people thinking they were doing the right thing? Arthur ...' He shakes his head belittlingly once again. 'Surely you are aware of Pavlov's dogs? Yeah? Okay, well, over the generations, we have been programmed into thinking certain things, and then these things become social norms. These things may have worked in the past but now linger unwanted like rotting food; they are dated and best forgotten. Surely you wouldn't want to be held back by such old-fashioned ideas would you, Arthur? More people are realising that now; we can free ourselves from these limiting beliefs. The possibilities are endless, Arthur! We just have to set ourselves free from these limits. *Anything can now be permitted!* There are no limits to our progression.'

'You are a fool. And even more so, you are a cliché. Many men have said similar things to you. Men who think there are no true limits, no fundamental rights and wrongs, no universally true conscience to tame the actions of man. Men like you who break all boundaries with their endless and spiralling rationalisations. You distract yourselves with grand narratives and tell yourselves what you are doing is for the greater good. What you forget is that good is not something found or created in the outside world; good is something found *within*.'

'Good is relative, Arthur. It is time we went beyond these childish notions of good and evil. For too long they have held us back. We must rise above.'

'And how can we rise above if we first do not look low? You think you have the right to decide what is best for everybody? What makes you so much smarter? What makes you think you know what is best for the individual? Jack, my brother. My brother who I love with all my heart. Do you not see that it is only the individual's connection with his self, his conscience, his Jesus Christ within him, it is only through this that he can find peace and radiate balance and love? You have no right to think you know otherwise. You speak of relativity, but inside is something constant, something tangible, *something some are close to and others far.* One may call it Christ, another conscience, another the narrow path; but the fact still stands that within us is a guiding light. And it is this light that ever pulls us towards the good. Everything else is a temptation, a distraction. I believe, with all my heart, that inside us is something that unites all life together, something that resembles purity, wholeness and balance. I believe this is God's image, and it can be seen in *everything,* high and low, for those who have eyes to see it. And I see it. And it is beautiful.'

Jack shakes his head whilst leaning back in his chair.

'You are well and truly possessed, aren't you? A true, deluded nutter. Well, Arthur. I have said everything I need or want to say to you, and I'm afraid I have business to attend to. Now, I'm sure you will understand that, for obvious reasons, I can't have someone like you parading around with such dangerous ideas. You have got too close to this project, and I'm sure you understand that whilst you are my brother, some things are bigger than both of us. And for that reason, these men will painlessly end things for you downstairs. Look, I really did hope I could have got you to see things a little more rationally, but, in all honesty, what did I expect? You've always been a loser. Goodbye, Arthur.' Jack stands up from the table and begins to make his way out. Arthur then says, 'Jack … What about the time we went inside dad's soul? We saw him as a lion, and he said magical things to us? How can you say that wasn't special, that that wasn't divine, magical or otherworldly?'

'A mere fantasy. The black cube affects consciousness in ways we don't fully understand yet, but we will.'

'Oh, and you think this black cube just mysteriously came into your possession from nowhere? I think you are forgetting who originally had the cube …'

'I admit that has been the one thing that has always boggled my mind. But something I have accepted as an anomaly nonetheless. Anyway, I leave the workings of the cube up to my business partner, who I understand your cult is already acquainted with … He has a far greater understanding of its science than I do.' Jack is now quite anxious to leave his brother and get back on stage; he is standing at the door's threshold with one foot in and one foot out. Just before he fully steps outside, Arthur manages to say, 'He was also there the night our parents were killed. You know that, right?'

'What did you say?' Jack says as he walks back through the door, with it closing behind him. His face is now scrunched up, full of annoyance and frustration.

'I said, your accomplice, Harry Sickle, was there the night our family were murdered.'

'Bullshit. It clearly just took the threat of me ending your life for you to finally lie about something. You've always been honest, I'll give you that.'

'I have proof.'

'Enough of these games. Enjoy heaven, or whatever it is you believe in.'

Jack attempts to walk back out through the door, but as he tries, he finds the door is locked shut.

'What the fuck?' he says under his breath.

'The guiding light inside us. Well. It has a tendency to pull more light towards it.'

Jack frowns at Arthur, looking very angry and frustrated, his eyes full of fire and his face red from a rising pressure. The Hex operatives begin to investigate the door, trying to open it with their key cards, but to no avail. The operative closest to the door then looks through the misted glass to try and see if anyone is out there.

There's a blindingly bright white flash. All three operatives in the room drop to the floor, falling unconscious.

Jack looks at Arthur completely stunned but still conscious. He moves backwards cautiously, away from the door.

The door opens slowly.

Jeffrey Lux enters …

'Good night,' Jeffrey says to Jack. He then raises his arm to neck height, with his fist clenched. Inside his fist he holds a circular black tube. He points the tube at Jack, which emits a solid beam of colder, blue light. Jeffrey points and shakes the light directly into and over his eyes, causing Jack to lose consciousness and crumple to the floor.

'A pleasure to meet you,' Jeffrey says as he looks to Arthur.

'Likewise. It's Jeffrey, right?' Arthur replies as he stands up from the table.

'Yes,' Jeffrey says as he smiles. 'I can get us out of here. But we must move quickly.'

'I believe you.' Arthur raises his eyebrows and gives a smirk, amazed yet not surprised by his dramatic rescue. It was as if he simply *expected* he would be saved.

Lukas and Toby then rush in to the room. Toby immediately catches Arthur's eye as he is wearing peculiar orange goggles; however, given the nature of the situation, he doesn't ask about them.

'You've got bollocks, I'll give you that,' Lukas says with a smile on his face, shaking his head in disbelief.

'It's called faith, Lukas,' Arthur says light-heartedly. The two then smash their hands together informally, clearly happy to see each other again.

'More like stupidity … But it worked out well, I'll give you that.' Lukas then has a moment of revelation. 'The cube!' He rushes over to Jack, who is on the floor.

'No, no, no. Lukas!' Arthur says sharply, his eyes lighting up suddenly. 'Don't touch it; it alters consciousness in bizarre ways. I have dealt with it before, I know what to expect. Let me carry it.'

'Let's make this quick, guys,' Jeffrey says as he looks out into the corridor anxiously, where five of his men (who were the five with him at his table) are currently standing on lookout.

Arthur rushes to Jack and rummages through the pockets of his suit. He finds the cube and stares into it. As he does so, he feels distracted and uneasy; a feeling of stress, a loss of comfort, of agitation. He quickly regains his focus, however, and puts it into his inside suit pocket.

Jeffrey calls for his men to enter the room, and one of the larger ones picks up Jack via a fireman's lift.

'Okay, let's move,' Jeffrey announces to everyone confidently, waving Arthur, Lukas and Toby to move into the corridor and begin their escape from the Hex compound.

'Oh, and please,' he says as he stops abruptly, as if suddenly remembering something, 'take one of these each.' Jeffrey signals to one of his men to give Arthur, Lukas and Toby one of the circular light-emitting tubes.

'We call these Tez-Lights. Three settings: twist the top here to select either the blue ray, which sedates organic unboxed ones, or the white flash setting for boxed ones. Leave it on flash for now, as it is likely we are going to be facing some boxed Hex black operatives.'

'What about the third setting?' Arthur asks. Jeffrey smiles, looks to the floor and then back up to Arthur.

'Curious fellow, aren't you? A red beam for electrical hacking. Don't worry about that right now though.'

8. THE ESCAPE

The group of nine (or 10 with the unconscious Jack) rush down the corridor outside the interrogation room, following this mysterious Dr Lux with apparently blind faith. It was true, Arthur did not have any idea who he was, or what his intentions were; but he knew within himself that this man genuinely wanted to help him. He was thinking, *Is this man a friend of the academy? A friend of John, perhaps? Sent here to keep an eye on us?* But ultimately, he was at peace with the fact that he was being helped in this extreme scenario. And it was also true that he felt a good spirit radiate from Jeffrey Lux.

Jeffrey leads the team to an emergency staircase. Arthur follows closely behind him, then Lukas, then Toby. Jeffrey's men tag along at the back, with the largest of the men still carrying Jack.

'These stairs go all the way down to the underground car park,' Jeffrey says as he rushes down them, setting a surprisingly fast pace considering his age.

'They *will* follow us though, I know what they are like,' Toby says from the middle of the pack, holding the banister as he tries to not fall over

'Oh I don't doubt it,' Jeffrey replies, 'that's why I suggest you let *us* do the driving; leave your car here. You may have to say goodbye to it for good, however.'

'It's fine, it wasn't mine anyway.'

'Toby's coming back to England with us, Jeffrey,' Lukas adds.

'To the Tree of Life, I presume?' Jeffrey says as he turns and gives both Lukas and Arthur a confident look.

'You know about us?' Arthur adds with curiosity.

'Of course. And whilst I am not officially connected to your academy, I support what you stand for in these dark times. Rumours of these things spread in certain circles. Just know that you have my support. However, I do not wish to get too involved; instead I will be viewing you and your activities from a distance. I may help you in ways that you least expect. But please, do not attempt to contact me. I wish to stay off the radar as much as possible.'

'That's very kind, Jeffrey, and of course that's fine,' Arthur says. 'I feel we may need all the support we can get in the months and years to come. I won't ask any more questions. However, I trust you to keep quiet about what you do know. Deal?' Jeffrey gives Arthur a sincere nod.

'Deal. I don't know everything about what you do, don't mistake me here. But I know you help people who are recovering from ECT box withdrawals. And for reasons close and personal to me, I feel very passionate about this.'

The door through which they entered the staircase can be heard slamming open, followed by a rush of footsteps and shouting men.

'Quickly! We are almost there,' Jeffrey says soon after the group is jolted by the sound.

After going down three more flights of stairs, they reach a door with meshed glass in the middle of it, clearly showing the underground car park on the other side. Jeffrey tries opening it, but it's locked.

Arthur shines his Tez-Light on the key-card module before Jeffrey even had a chance to bring his out.

'I got you,' Arthur says with a cheeky wink. Jeffrey smiles in return.

'Half on this side, half on that side,' Jeffrey says as he steps into a long car park containing two levels, dimly lit with a yellowish hue. He points to the team to split and hide on either side of the staircase exit. 'Get your Tez-Lights ready. Prepare for a pincer attack. Wait for my mark.'

The team wait, holding their Tez-Lights ready.

'Roman, walk out as a decoy,' Jeffrey says to one of his men. The man walks out, facing away from the staircase, and pretends to tie his shoes.

A squad of six Hex black burst through the door. They stack up in tactical formation, aiming down the barrels of their P90 submachine guns.

'Hands out to your side! Now!' one Hex black operative shouts, as the squad moves up slowly towards him. Jeffrey's man slowly puts his hands out to his side.

'On your belly!' another Hex operative shouts.

Once the entire squad has moved out of the staircase and into the car park, Jeffrey clicks his fingers. The Hex squad turn around.

An almighty cascade of seven Tez-Light flashes pop off. The Hex squad flop to the ground like a sack of potatoes.

'Bet you're glad I gave you those goggles now, aren't you, Toby?' Jeffrey says.

'Not to mention he looks like a sexy beast,' Arthur says with a slight chuckle. Toby looks awkwardly down at the ground, a little overwhelmed yet still smiling nonetheless, and then says, 'My flash didn't even go off ...'

'That's because you've got it on the beam setting for the unboxed, you doughnut,' Lukas says as he points to the end of Toby's Tez-Light. Toby, rather restless, exhales in annoyance, shakes his head then looks up at the ceiling.

'Let's move. The cars are over at the other end,' Jeffrey says as he begins to move up the car park, turning round to address the team.

As the team follow him with a light jog, half moving to the left side and half to the right, Jack begins stirring on the shoulder of the team member who carries him.

'He's waking up, I need a re-beam,' he says.

Jeffrey rushes to Jack and shines the blue Tez beam in his eyes, instantly putting any signs of movement or life at bay and reinducing a state of unconsciousness.

'Usually only lasts anywhere from five to 10 minutes, just so we all know, yeah? But there are only minimal side effects,' he says, 'so don't be shy in using them.'

Just after Jeffrey finished his sentence, another Hex squad emerges from a door at the far end of the car park which they were walking towards. The squad is moving quickly and shouting something in French whilst pointing at the team.

They start laying down fire with their submachine guns, bullets whizzing around everywhere, hitting the concrete and the cars and some even ricocheting towards the ceiling. A bullet hits one of Jeffrey's men, Roman, directly in the head. He falls to the ground and starts bleeding over the concrete. The rest of the team dives for cover behind various other cars.

'You bastards!! Shit ...' Jeffrey says, looking at the floor in a disgusted rage, shaking his head. He hides behind a Rolls Royce.

Arthur, Toby and Lukas are taking cover behind a black Range Rover on the left side of the car park. Arthur leans out carefully from the front of the car and points his Tez-Light at the squad, trying not to reveal too much of his body. He flashes his Tez-Light towards them, narrowly avoiding being shot in the process.

'Too far, Arthur! Here, take these!' Jeffrey pulls out two small metallic silver orbs from the inside of his suit and rolls them across the car park floor towards Lukas and Arthur. 'Press the button in the centre and throw!' Jeffrey pulls out another one of these metallic spheres for himself.

'Now!' he says.

Lukas and Arthur cock the metallic grenades and hurl them over towards the squad. The grenades explode on impact with the ground and immediately burst with a similar flash as the white Tez-Light. The flash once again drops the squad to the floor.

'We got more incoming from above!' Arthur shouts as he notices another squad coming in from the upper car park level.

'Come on, let's get to the cars!' Jeffrey says he begins running towards his silver Range Rovers.

'But Roman!' Arthur replies.

'He's dead! Let's move!'

The team quickly move up to the cars and Jack is bundled into the boot of one of them. Jeffrey then cocks his light grenade and hurls it to the other end of the car park before getting into the front of the car which has Jack in the boot.

'You got two of them!' Arthur says as he sees two Hex squad members being caught by the flash.

Arthur and Toby then get into the back of the car, and Lukas rides shotgun.

'I'll meet you guys at the airport,' Jeffrey says through the window to the rest of his team who are getting into the other car. 'Try and keep them off our tail. I have faith in you, my brothers. For Roman.' He nods at his team member, and the team member nods back.

'For Roman,' the team member replies.

Jeffrey pulls out of his parking space with haste, spinning the wheels as he does so. He bombs it down the car park with the other Range Rover following closely behind him. The Hex squad begins shooting at the car.

'Don't worry, it's bullet-proof glass. We are safe in here.'

The Hex squad are forced to dive out of the way of the oncoming vehicles. Jeffrey then enters a drift and negotiates the ramp leading to the second level whilst still skidding, using the utmost precision and skill.

'I didn't know you were a rally driver before you were a surgeon,' Lukas says with his mouth held ajar in shock.

'This isn't my first rodeo, let's just say that.'

'The shutters are closing!' Arthur says, pointing at the exit.

'Get out your Tez-Light, aim for the module when we get close.'

Arthur leans out the window keenly before the car has even stopped. When it screeches to a halt, Arthur shines the red hacking light over the module.

'No?' Jeffrey asks, frowning.

'It's not doing anything,' Arthur replies with a worried voice.

'Fuck! Sorry, excuse my language. We are going to have to use the laser.'

'The laser?' Arthur asks as he pulls himself back into the car.

'Yes. The laser,' Jeffrey replies nonchalantly. He then waves his hand out the window to signal to the car behind to reverse.

Jeffrey leaves about 10 metres between his car and the shutters and selects the 'front cutting beam' from a touchscreen display on the dashboard.

'This is pretty amazing, I can't lie,' Arthur says.

'Madness,' Lukas adds.

'I feel numb,' Toby says, leaning his hand on his knee. 'This is the most exciting thing I've ever done, and I still feel my emotions are being restricted. I can't believe I let them do this to me … I don't feel human.'

'Toby, it's fine, we will get your box removed and get you into a good mental place, don't worry, alright?' Arthur says as he leans over and looks him intensely in the eye.

'I know, I know, thank you, Arthur,' Toby replies with a more confident expression, nodding back.

'Okay, we are all good to go. Watch this …' Jeffrey says after finishing with the laser settings. Jeffrey presses a circular icon on the screen.

A powerful purple beam shoots out from the centre of the front grill.

'I can control the direction of the beam through here,' Jeffrey says as he moves his finger across the touchscreen in the shape of a cross, causing a big black cross to appear on the shutters.

'Wouldn't a square have been better?' Arthur asks.

'That would have taken longer. Plus …' Jeffrey revs the engine and then launches his car forward, accelerating with speed and ramming into the shutters. The car smashes through them, leaving a large hole for the car behind to use. '… I wouldn't have been able to do that.'

Arthur and Lukas begin giggling rather childishly, yet Toby looks rather distant at this point and out of sync with the other two. Both cars drive rapidly out of the compound and onto the main road.

'I think we've done it,' Lukas says.

Arthur looks behind and around to see if any cars are on their tail.

'For some reason, I'm not so sure about that. What's the plan though, Jeff?'

'Ha, I like it when people call me that. Well, the plan is we get to the airport and get you back to England using my private jet. I just pray to the Lord we won't have any trouble at the airport …'

'You're a very interesting guy, Jeffrey,' Arthur says. Jeffrey laughs.

'Oh, thank you. I like to think I'm a passionate person; and how I see it is if I start acting old, I'll become old too. I want to be part of the good fight you see, Arthur. I am fully aware of the shadowy forces that lurk in the undergrowth of our civilisation. In fact, I've known about them for a long time. So, naturally, I have made some investments and preparations accordingly.'

'I can see that,' Lukas says with a smirk and a nod. 'It's funny though, I was telling Arthur and Toby after I spoke to you that I felt that we were somewhat on the same page, as if we were at this convention for the same reasons; that is, out of curiosity to learn about something which is clearly evil.'

'Oh they are evil alright,' Jeffrey replies. 'Some may say a symptom of the Antichrist spirit prevalent in our culture. They worship utopia; they believe they will be the ones to bring in some great heaven on earth; a great united tower of Babel, and they believe themselves to be the gods.'

'I agree, it's arrogance isn't it …' Arthur chips in.

'Absolutely,' Jeffrey replies.

'I tried to convey my thoughts to my brother, but he thinks I am the one who's crazy. He won't listen to me right now … And I understand, he's in deep with this project of his, it's a lot to let go of. I still believe I can wake him up; I still believe I can bring him back to the source of good within him.'

'Oh, yes? Do you have a plan as to how exactly you're going to do that?' Jeffrey asks with raised eyebrows.

Arthur stares forward for a few moments out the front window, in a trance, stroking his chin.

'I have a few ideas, actually …' Arthur squints his eyes, as if distracted by a revelatory thought. 'Yes … But yes, we have a particular piece of evidence that will hopefully cause a dramatic shift in his perspective. Actually, how is he back there? Do you think he'll be awake yet?' Arthur turns and pulls down the arm rest to see if he can see into the boot.

'There's a good chance, yes,' Jeffrey replies.

'We should have cable-tied his hands together, really,' Lukas says. Arthur laughs.

'Sorry. It's just bizarre for me to even consider tying up my brother and having him in the boot.'

A thud comes from behind the back seats.

'Jack, mate, are you okay back there?' Arthur asks rather softly, feeling sympathy for his brother.

A muffled 'fuck you' comes from the boot.

'Yep, he's awake ...' Lukas says, as he looks at the others in the car warily.

'Don't worry,' Jeffrey says as he turns back to face them. 'I can guarantee he's quite secure in there.'

'We are taking you to the airport,' Arthur says as he puts his mouth close to the centre of the seats to try and communicate more easily. 'You are coming back to see the people you left without saying goodbye. You at least owe them that.'

Jack does not reply.

'Oh shit, Arthur, we left the footage at the chalet, didn't we?' Lukas says, suddenly remembering they didn't collect their things.

Arthur laughs.

'It's not the '90s, Lukas, we've got plenty of back-ups at the Tree of Life. And I'm sure we can pick up our clothes another day.'

'True,' Lukas says as he chuckles lightly.

Surprisingly, neither of the cars encountered any trouble on their way to the airport. However, all in the car felt rather anxious during the short journey and constantly looked out the windows, checked the mirrors and inspected other cars that drove beside them. Except Jack, of course, who remained inside the boot in complete darkness. Once they got to the airport, they passed freely without trouble to Jeffrey's private jet. The car with Jeffrey's men took Jack off to be 'packed' into the private jet separately; Arthur, Lukas and Toby were rather mystified as to how exactly they managed this, especially considering Jack had no passport to hand. Whilst they were puzzled, they were also not particularly surprised; this Jeffrey Lux had not stopped surprising them since he came into the equation earlier that day.

The flight itself was short yet intense. For the majority of it, Jack did not say a word. Despite many attempts by Arthur to make contact with him, he just sat there, handcuffed to the seat, in silence. Arthur did manage to get a subtle shake of Jack's head after saying, 'I know in your heart you mean well. I know that you believe what you are doing is helping our society, and I respect you for working this hard towards a goal. However, I would be lying if I didn't say I think you've been deceived. And dare I say deceived by the force of Satan himself. You may laugh at this, but this is what I believe. At least understand that evil forces exist on a psychological level, regardless of whether they do on a theological one.

'Many of our generation think like you: they think they can change human nature; they think they can mould us into something better. And the truth is we might be able to mould people, to a certain extent, as you have proved with your technology. However, what makes you think that what you have created is in any way better? The truth is you are pissing into the wind, telling yourself you are saving humanity; but in reality, you are just chasing the pride of being a hero, regardless of the consequences. This technology of yours is clearly being used to control rather than help, regardless of the original intentions. The fact that you are forcing people to use it against their will, and they cannot properly function in society without it, is not giving people the freedom to choose for themselves. You are instead telling people what is best for them, through force rather than choice. You don't know someone's exact thoughts, experiences and perspectives, so ultimately it is wrong for you to be this forceful in telling them what's best for them. You are so connected to your ego, to the world of intellect and statistics, that you have disconnected yourself from the whole of yourself; you have left behind that Jack I knew as a boy. But I know he's still in there, I know this without doubt. I know that you have single-mindedly obsessed over this technology for a long, long time, believing with all your heart that you will be the one to save all the world's problems; but this has come at the cost of your own soul. As your brother, I will do everything in my power to bring you back to it, and I will make sure you are reminded of what it means to be good. As good is to be found *within*.'

9. A HEAVY-HEARTED REUNION

After landing back in England, our group parted ways from the mysterious Jeffrey Lux. The last thing Jeffrey told Arthur was, 'It has been an honour to meet you, and I am sure we will meet again. But for now, I say goodbye. Remember what I told you; I will be hanging back for times when you need me most. As I said, important information spreads fast in certain circles, and nothing is more important than the return of a redeeming man, a man that can restore balance to our kingdom on earth. I know of the prophecies that are safeguarded at your academy; and I know about the prophecies of the chosen one. I have no doubt from those who gravitate around you, and the spirit that does too, that you are indeed this one. I have faith in you, as I have faith in the magic of the Lord above. This magic I see swimming all around you, and that is something quite obvious to me. God bless you, Arthur, although you already clearly are. Goodbye.'

Jeffrey's men had once again clinically transferred Jack into the boot of Arthur's Volkswagen Golf parked in the Gatwick long-stay car park. Arthur, still loving his brother deeply, made sure Jack had a water bottle in the boot with him, and in the two-hour drive back up to the Tree of Life near Oxford made two stops at service stations to check on him; albeit surreptitiously and with great caution, having Lukas stand by the boot with him every time he opened it so Jack wasn't tempted to make a sudden dash for it. However, Arthur intuitively felt that Jack would not run away. He felt like a part of Jack actually wanted to submit to this capture. Arthur thought about this deeply on the drive back. He thought to himself: *Could this be Jack's conscience? His conscience guiding him to retribution? A need to repent his wrongdoings? A godly whisper, perhaps, a part of him that feels he has made mistakes and that he in fact owes a debt. Even if he could run away, and even if he had an urge to, I feel a part of him would make it very difficult … like a mysterious force, it would pull him back in the opposite direction.*

Regardless, Jack was securely transported to the Tree of Life.

'Take my car back to yours,' Arthur says to Lukas, leaning through the window after he stepped outside the car, which had just pulled up outside the academy. 'And Toby, I'm sure I'll see you back here soon for your rehabilitation. You're in safe hands with Lukas, I can assure you. He's one of the world's best.'

Lukas looks back to the rear seats where Toby is sitting and nods his head with faux smugness. He gives Toby a thumbs up, saying, 'You're going to be fine, Toby. It's not the surgery that's the hard part, it's the psychological rebab. But just be thankful you've got these guys to help you.'

'I don't care what I have to go through,' Toby says. 'I just want to feel normal again. I'm done with feeling manipulated. I know it's going to be hard, but I'm just thankful I met you both.'

'You haven't even seen the half of it yet,' Arthur adds. 'But when you do, I know for a fact you will fit right in with us here. Anyway, I better bring Jack inside. John and Suzy are waiting underground. I've already let them know about the situation.'

'Yeah … Arthur, I just want to say, before you go …' Lukas says, with an almost guilty expression, '… This trip, it's been bizarre; but I feel I have got to know you on a different level, and I respect you in a way I didn't before. Not to say I didn't respect you previously, but clearly, as the protective father of Eva, my natural instinct is to be wary of people she decides to spend her time with. And whilst we always got along as friends, and of course as training partners, I never saw the side of you that gets things done; the part that means business, you could say. I can't lie, mate, at the beginning of the trip I felt like I didn't have much faith in you, and I'm sure you noticed this yourself. I wasn't sure if you were competent, if I'm being honest. However, I know now that you are guided by something that is beyond my rational understanding. Now I know you have such an unshakeable faith in your intuition, I can't help but have respect for you. I consider myself a man of humble faith too, but for most of my life I have been a man of pragmatism and scepticism, and that core will always remain within me. You are very different to me, though; your belief and spirit are on another level, and it will always be hard for me to fully understand that, so much so that I cannot put it into words. But just know I cannot help but respect you because of it. Clearly, the success of this trip has shown that your faith really has paid off. I never should have doubted you.'

Arthur smiles and holds his hand out for a casual handshake.

'I'm not normal, Lukas, I understand that. And don't worry; as I said before, I feel we needed each other for this trip. My unshakeable faith in my intuition also needed your pragmatism and experience. We made a good team. And I respect you too.'

'You will succeed in your mission, Arthur. It is clear to me now that you have what it takes. I have no doubt that you will pass this test set by God, and I have no doubt you will stay strong and save your father's soul.'

Arthur stares at Lukas for a few moments, and then looks to his side at the ground.

'Speak soon, Lukas,' he says as he looks back up. They nod to each other with sincerity.

Arthur goes round to the back of the car and opens the boot, and Lukas walks around to jump into the driver's seat. Jack looks up at his brother with tired, squinting eyes which are trying to adjust from the darkness of the boot.

'I am sorry I have to treat you like this, Jack. But you are not the brother I knew as a child. But I know this child still exists inside you. And I will find him.'

Arthur shines the Tez-Light over Jack's eyes, putting him back to sleep. He then picks him up using a fireman's lift. Lukas drives off and Arthur enters the Tree of Life.

As soon as Arthur enters the central dojo, the members who are casually rolling and training immediately stop what they are doing, and a tense silence falls over the room. Everyone begins looking over at Arthur, and how could they not? For word had spread about Arthur's escapade, and the inner circle knew about the successful acquirement of the cube. And whilst not everyone knew all the details, everyone knew that Arthur had come back from an important mission; and *everyone* knew that the man over his shoulder was his brother, Jack, the founder of Snake Box. No matter how long someone had been at the Tree of Life, one thing that bonded all together was a general scepticism of the invasive technologies of this age; and whilst this belief was held more strongly by some, all knew and agreed on the dangers of ECTs, and all knew that it was Jack who had been pivotal in their development. But if there was one arch, spiritual value that bonded the academy together, it was the importance of *redemption*. And this was the value that was celebrated commonly during ritual. So whilst many looked at the slumped Jack with mild anger or even disgust, it was of a very different type to how those at the Hex summit looked upon Arthur. For the ones at the Tree of Life saw the potential in Jack but also felt pity and had mercy. So this anger and disgust was tempered, held back, tamed; this raw emotion was balanced with a knowing of future potential.

At the far end of the dojo, on a rather basic black plastic chair, sat John. He watches the approaching brothers quietly. As they get closer, he stands up. At this point, those in the room, about 40 academy members, were also standing up out of respect to the situation.

'Well done, Arthur. I have no words to show how proud I am,' he says, with warm eyes and a smile.

'No words are needed right now, John, only action. Let's get to it.'

John nods and begins to walk towards the back door leading to the rear garden. Arthur follows.

'Suzy and the others are downstairs in the hyper-dome. She's made chilli beef ramen for us, Jack's favourite. However, his has been made more *special,* as you requested,' John says as he walks, turning to face Arthur.

'So, it's all set up and ready then?' Arthur asks.

'Yes. Ishmael and Eva have got it all sorted. Let's just pray that this works …'

'It will. I know it. And Julius?'

John opens the door to the rear and both walk through. Julius can be clearly seen on his knees in front of the tree, clasping his hands together, rocking back and forth in a state of intense prayer.

'He's been intensely studying the books, awaiting your arrival. And as you can see, he's now preparing his spirit.'

'Okay, well, let's not interrupt him; let's just head down.'

They head down through the secret passage and enter the room of the sacred sword. Arthur can't help but briefly pause to stare at Excalibur. The sword looks brighter than it did before and glimmers more strongly. He feels a great energy pull him towards it; as if the sword is craving the cube.

'I better not put the cube inside the sword yet,' he says whilst still staring.

'One thing at a time, Arthur; wait for Julius to be ready first.'

They walk through to the main hyper-dome and see Suzy, Adam, Eva and Ishmael sitting in the middle, forming a small circle. The dome's lights project the surroundings of a virtual forest: the floor is green like grass and trees can be seen on the side of the dome. At the top is an artificial sky. Forest sounds are also playing, with birdsong, rustles and other subtle animal noises being played, alongside the sound of a gentle breeze.

Suzy and Eva stand up as soon as they see them enter.

'Is he okay?!' Suzy asks frantically, as she briskly walks towards them from the circle.

'Yes, he's fine.' Arthur replies. 'He's going to wake soon. I've put him to sleep using this light technology that a friend has given me. I'll tell you about it another time, but he's fine; let's just get started.'

Suzy purses her lips together and then beckons them to the centre where the rest are sitting cross-legged upon woollen blankets, a feast laid out. Arthur follows Suzy to where the others are already situated.

'That soup is his,' Suzy says as she points to a bowl of ramen on the ground, which sits on top of a red blanket. Everyone else also has a bowl, and in the middle is a basket of bread, a jug of water and a collection of wooden cups.

Arthur takes Jack off his shoulders and gently places him on the floor so that he is lying down face up, next to his soup.

'And are you okay?' Suzy asks. Arthur smiles at her warmly in return and gives her a hug.

'Yes, I'm fine. It's all been quite crazy, but it's all coming together.'

'Yes, welcome back, Arthur,' Adam adds from the floor, as he sits quietly and composed with crossed legs.

'Thank you, Adam,' Arthur replies. 'Ishmael.' Arthur gives Ishmael a nod and a smile. Ishmael just stares back with a focused, enlightened look that conveys more than any words could; it conveyed a seriousness for what he knew was about to happen … Yet still, his eyes look warm and proud as they swell with tears.

Arthur and Eva then lock gazes and move towards each other magnetically to embrace.

'I missed you so much,' Eva sobs softly into his shoulder. 'I was so worried, Arthur …'

'I'm here now. It's okay.'

'It's not over yet though, is it?'

'No, it's not. But it will be soon.'

They pull slightly apart and look into each other's eyes.

'I love you,' Eva says with a tear in her eye.

'I love you too.'

Eva sits down to the left of Ishmael, who has been propped up against the side of his wheelchair. His legs are out straight and cushions have been placed to support his back comfortably. Arthur sits next to Eva. John sits down by his bowl, sandwiching Jack's sleeping head between himself and

Arthur (this was pre-planned so John and Arthur could intervene if Jack tried to do anything erratic).

'He's going to wake up very soon. Let's just start eating now,' Arthur announces to circle. They all begin eating, with Eva feeding Ishmael the ramen with a spoon and chopsticks.

After another minute or so, Jack's eyes slowly open, and he begins to writhe and stir. He sits up, facing away from the group. He rubs his eyes and looks up and around at the dome, curious as to what is going on and where exactly he has awoken. He looks behind him and sees the familiar faces of the people he left behind six years ago. He has no words at this point; however, Arthur notices signs of shock in his face, and even a slither of shame.

'At least join in with us and eat,' Arthur says, signalling with his hand.

'Beef ramen …' he mumbles, looking at the bowls laid out on the blanket.

'Yes. Your favourite, so you have no excuse to not eat,' Suzy says with passive aggression, sounding as if she is trying to hold herself back from saying more.

Jack shakes his head but reluctantly sits down in front of his bowl between John and Arthur. Jack puts his face over the bowl and inhales the spicy aroma of the ramen. His eyes are puffy, and he gives off the vibe of someone a little hungover.

'Here, have some water,' Arthur says as he pours his brother a cup. Jack takes the cup and has a few sips.

For a short period of time, everyone eats in awkward silence. Jack takes small, slow slurps of his soup whilst looking at the others around him, who are not looking back but instead continue to focus on their eating. By the time the silence is broken, Jack has consumed about a third of his soup yet none of the beef.

'So this is it. The famous Tree of Life …' he says, finally breaking the silence.

'Hopefully not too famous,' John adds, glancing up from his soup suspiciously, meeting Jack's eye.

'I haven't seen it as relevant to make you lot famous, but I easily could if I wanted to. Honestly, I don't even see you as enough of a threat. As I said to Arthur, ever since finding out about this academy's bizarre antics as a child, I knew that it's just a bunch of man-children engaging in classic cult fanaticism.'

'Oh, and you and your conscious-altering devices that are now required by half the world to simply participate isn't a cult?!' Suzy explodes with pent-up anger, clearly no longer able to hold herself back. 'How can you be such a hypocrite?! At least people can choose to come to this place; if they don't like what we do here, it is their choice to stay or not!'

'Calm down, you hysterical woman,' Jack replies after rolling his eyes. 'I've got to hand it to you, Suzy, I know you never really involved yourself that much with the cult here; so for that, I actually have a lot of respect for you. That guy there, however ...' He points to Adam. 'I don't know exactly who you are, but from my research I blame it on you; you were the main reason for this place. I know you were the one behind its beginnings when my parents were at Oxford. Have you ever thought about getting a real job instead? And actually growing up?'

Adam has one last mouthful of his ramen and takes a large inhale of air before looking deeply into Jack's eyes.

'You have a very narrow idea of what this place is. But let me start by saying where I agree with you, for argument's sake. Firstly, I can understand why you think this is place is a cult; I may even agree with you to some extent. However, what you don't understand is that I have been studying ritual and the effects of psychedelics on people all my life. Secondly, I do not claim for them to be a catch-all solution, and I don't recommend them to everyone, or even most people. Thirdly, we have built this place around an understanding of the unconscious mind, and intertwined the rituals with an understanding of mythology, to have the most possible amount of love and understanding for the souls of the members; ultimately leading to the safest possible place to engage in the ritualistic use of consciousness-altering substances. We are not merely a hippy group for martial arts and psychedelic drugs. Everyone at this academy is a family: we look out for each other and guide each other in our lives outside, as well as giving people structure and discipline through the martial arts training. We see the rituals here as relating to the life of the individual; what people partake in here isn't for mere pleasure or recreation; everything we do here is for the long-term benefit of its members, and I am always advocating for good grounding with a solid life structure. If I ever see an individual who is in chaos, and lacking discipline and responsibility, I will only on rare occasions allow them to engage in ritual; and if I do, I will make sure to give specific attention and guidance to them before and after, to help them make connections with their current situation. I respect these substances, you see; I understand their dangers and accept people can become destabilised by them. I am also aware that certain fantasies may surface that could be confusing and possessive, but thankfully I, along with others here, can help guide people through this and decipher their meaning. And for that reason, I will not allow people to engage in ritual until they have a good understanding of mythos and religion, to ground them in the way of all things. Up until that point, I advocate for prayer and meditational types of practices alone, long before I would psychedelic ones. You must understand, Jack, we have systems and processes here; we are not just winging it. You have to respect this.'

Jack grimaces disrespectfully.

'Nope, I don't respect it. You keep telling yourself all that, I'm sure it makes you feel far better to think you have some objective process; but I think we all know that's just an excuse to rationalise what you do here. But who kidnapped me and brought me here against my will? Hmm, and you have the audacity to take the moral high ground? And claim that what you do here is *good*? Pathetic …' Jack's cheeks tighten in disgust, and he turns to look away.

'I don't think he's taking the moral high ground,' John interjects. 'He's just rationally stating the justification behind the academy. You could argue that it's a cult, but you have to admit it's easy to simply write the whole place off as evil without understanding what we have done to help people or judge us before really observing the effects the academy has on people.'

'Okay, John, but that same logic applies to what I'm doing at Snake Box. All of you have clearly written off ECT technology and simply labelled it as bad and evil without taking into account the potential to help people.'

'But we can, and we have, physically observed the negative effects of ECTs!' Suzy adds. 'People have killed themselves after removing them! I have dealt first-hand with screaming men and women who are begging for me to kill them, to put an end to the withdrawal effects.'

'I'm not saying they are perfect, am I?' Jack says, beginning to sound rather frustrated. 'With each generation we continue to improve their efficiency. And yes, I agree, the withdrawal symptoms can be nasty; but as I'm sure you can understand, people shouldn't have the need to remove them in the first place, as the product should only be a positive thing for them. It's still the individual's choice to become boxed or not.'

'Is it though, Jack?' Arthur chips in, finally speaking after listening intensely to the back and forth. 'From what I have seen, many people do not want the ECTs to be a choice. They'd prefer them to be mandated by law, as a means of moral responsibility. Some people even believe that these devices should be installed at birth as a means to regulate emotions and instincts they deem to be "inappropriate" or "problematic". Can't you see the arrogance in all this, Jack? Can you not see that we still have these instincts for a reason? And it should be individual choice and responsibility which regulates behaviour, through our own understanding and integration. Techniques such as prayer, spiritual practice, training and discipline; not through artificial technology.'

'Well, that is just your opinion, Arthur,' Jack replies with a patronising shake of his head. 'Many people haven't got the time, nor the belief, to engage in these "spiritual practices" that you describe. And actually, Arthur, I think you are forgetting that people still have control over their emotions using the algorithm through the app.'

'Unless they are at the many places of work where they are forced to transfer their control to an ECT box coordinator,' Ishmael says, looking at Jack with squinting, suspicious eyes.

'Okay, Ishmael, but work is work. Work somewhere which doesn't mandate an ECT if you're that bothered …' Jack responds sarcastically, turning to Ishmael and widening his eyelids.

'Jack, the bottom line here is that many people's gut feeling tells them that these devices will lead to an evil ending,' Arthur says with a certain strength and clarity. 'And you are right, I suppose it comes down to whether you believe in this gut feeling or not. Yes, this "feeling" has no easy rational or scientific grounding, but frankly, to ignore what many call listening to God as mere rubbish is arrogant beyond belief. I'll be honest with you, Jack. You've always been smarter than me, I don't deny that. However, I've always recognised that within you, you've always ignored something; something that I have always felt so heavily. Call it intuition, call it gut feeling, call it a sixth sense, call it the unconscious, call it God. The fact is, many can sense that some things are just bad and will lead us to nowhere but hell. When I communicate with this spirit, I passionately believe that what you are playing with is nothing short of demonic. What you think of as "the greater good" is merely, as you said before, something you tell yourself to rationalise evil.

I don't hate you for it; I have mercy. But you, like many others, have been deceived. You, are one of those who our dad warned us about, the ones led astray by the temptation of great changes and advancements that will do nothing but pave the way to hell. And today, I'm going to try and give you back this connection, Jack. Today, I'm going to connect you back to God.'

Jack smirks slyly and bobs his head up and down.

'Oh yeah? And how exactly do you intend on doing that?'

'Look around, Jack ...' Arthur says as turns his head to look around the dome.

Jack frowns but reluctantly looks around at the dome. He realises that something is definitely different, but he cannot figure out what exactly has changed yet. He takes a deep breath and his jaw loosens and hangs a little lower.

'What have you done?' he says, starting to feel a tingling within his stomach.

'My name is Eva,' Eva says as she stands up suddenly, looking down at Jack who is now leaning back on his hands. 'I've always wanted to meet Arthur's brother. You know, he always described you in such a positive light. And whilst he said you made mistakes, he never stopped believing in your ability to be reborn. He has never stopped loving you.'

Jack struggles to find words and is caught off guard by Eva, who up until this point he had barely noticed.

'You've met Ishmael before, haven't you?' she says as she points to him. 'Are you not wondering why he has a wheelchair now? I've got to know him quite well, actually. For six years, I've helped care for him. He is one of the most beautiful souls I've ever met. Do you know why he has a wheelchair, Jack?'

Jack is now breathing heavily and struggles to think of anything clever to say; the fact is, he actually had no idea what happened to Ishmael. Eva noticed this in his dumbfounded face, and so she says, 'No? I didn't think you did. Well, let me tell you. He was stabbed, and shot, with surgical precision in his upper and lower spine. Do you know who did it?'

Jack now looks rather anxious. Everything around him is becoming far more vivid and sensitive; he is beginning to feel completely overwhelmed, every word spoken by Eva sticking in him like daggers.

'Your business partner, Harry Sickle,' she says.

'He destroyed my life, Jack,' Ishmael says softly.

'There's also something else …' Arthur says, standing up and looking down at Jack who is clearly, by his posture, slowly becoming more and more detached from reality. 'Do you remember in the integration room, when I said Harry was there the night our parents were killed? Well, he was more than just there. We found a DVD in his house, and we have all decided that it's rather important you watch it. So, we are now going to leave you here for a bit. I'll be back to check on you later.'

The group quickly pick up the blankets, bowls and cups, and John and Adam help Ishmael back into his chair. Apart from Arthur, they all begin to make their way towards the exit.

'What?! Tell me?! What?!' Jack suddenly screams, feeling a large wave of panic flood into him as he crawls towards Arthur, grabbing his ankles.

'You must find out for yourself, Jack. You must go down before you can come back up. You *can* do this.'

Arthur kicks Jack's hands away.

'Arthur! Please!' Jack screams.

After giving a final sombre look to his brother, Arthur leaves the dome.

The environment of the dome then shifts. The lights turn off completely and voices are heard, saying, 'Alright, we have decided to make this video to pay our respects to the loss of a legend. Didn't think it would be some crazy bitch to finish him off … Guess I'm your daddy now then, ain't that right, Harry?'

'I only have one dad. And you're not him.'

'Yeah, and Charlie killed him …'

'That man was never my father. Charlie always knew who the *real dad* is. And so do I. Our real dad never dies. And you, Ben, have never under-stood …'

'What?'

'You've never understood. And you never will. You were always just a pawn to me and Charlie. He knew he would die, and he knew when his time came, it would be *me* to carry on his spirit.'

'So you're saying I can't be the leader because you and him made a deal?'

'You can't be the leader because our leader is not of the flesh. Our leader is ever present and there for those willing to engage with him. Our leader is only for the rare few, the chosen ones of the inversion, the ones to bring his shadowy kingdom to earth. We are the inverted ones, and *we will breed a world of horn and twist.* And you, you have never understood. You are just a fool, Ben. A fool we have used like cattle.'

'What the fuck are you on about?'

Sounds of violent stabbing and screaming.

Sounds of burning.

The dome lights up again. However, this time, the light is coming from the video footage. The footage is played 360 degrees all around Jack, covering all the screens of the dome: high, low and all around. Jack stumbles to his feet and looks around him, his face full of shock and horror. He puts both his hands to his cheeks and begins panting and choking, sobbing pressure building in his throat. He drops to his knees and bows his head to the ground. The footage finishes but then instantaneously starts again.

'That's him ...' Jack says softly, under his breath. 'That's him ...' he repeats a little louder. 'That's him!!' he shouts, his voice full of wild panic and confusion.

He unleashes a bloodcurdling howl.

Arthur listens in from just outside the doors.

Then locks them, and walks away.

10. LIGHT AND DARK

Arthur walks through the second set of double doors and once again enters the room of Excalibur; leaving, with a heavy heart, the sound of his screaming brother behind.

Arthur sees the group who just left him sitting around the table, all looking up with curiosity.

'Keep a close eye on him please, Ishmael,' Arthur says. Ishmael nods and looks down at his wheelchair computer screen, which shows footage of Jack, who is rocking back and forth on his knees in the centre of the dome. 'I don't want him to experience any unnecessary suffering; modulate the environment to something brighter when you see fit.'

'I can assure you, he will be *beyond* fine very soon,' says a voice from the staircase around the corner.

'Julius, it is lovely to see you,' Arthur says with a warm smile as Julius's hunched form appears from the shadows.

'And you. But we must not waste time,' Julius replies. Soon after, many other academy members flood into the room.

'Okay, can everyone please sit down where you can. We need space and calm,' John announces quite loudly as he sees the members crowding inside.

As the rest of the initiates continue to fill the room, Julius walks through the gap in the table and into the centre, placing himself beside the rock and sword.

'It is time. This is the beginning of the great mystery. Just as the fallen books have prophesised. The mystery some have been faithful to and others sceptical. Arthur, please bring the cube.' Julius nods at Arthur, and Arthur enters the inner circle of the table.

Arthur walks up to the sword and looks around at all the apprehensive stares. He stands directly over the sword and looks down at it. For a moment, he puts his hands together, bows his head and prays. After this short prayer, he gets on both his knees and once again bows his head, clasps his hands and prays. He takes one final deep breath and puts his hand into his suit pocket. He had not touched the cube since he placed it there in Switzerland, and lo and behold, it had not moved. For this entire time it had rested against his ribs, causing an uneasy sensation within him that he had been secretly fighting.

It was time for this cube to be cleansed and returned to its pure form.

He pulls the cube from his pocket. For a brief moment, he holds it up in front of the sword's hilt, intending to look at it; but as he does, and as the initiates look too, the cube becomes harder to hold. He naturally lets go of it, and the cube floats towards the space inside the sword's hilt. The room doesn't utter a peep; everyone is awestruck. The cube finds its place nestled inside the perfectly-formed square. It is not touching anything, yet holds still and steady, floating as if kept buoyant by a force. The cube does not yet spin, its colour still deeply black.

'Remove the sword from the stone,' Julius says calmly, yet with conviction.

Arthur wraps his left hand around the handle and rips out the sword into the air.

The room erupts into a multi-coloured light.

He holds the blade up steady and watches the cube inside, now no longer black but bright and multi-coloured.

The cube spins slowly and shines like a glittery disco ball.

The cube spins clockwise and twists upwards at the same time, as if it were spinning on two invisible axes. The light glows in the first six colours of the rainbow, just as Julius said. The room is still silent, but all the faces are hypnotised by this light and beauty. They stare in awe. Ishmael sits in his chair and his eyes widen with childlike purity, a smile cracking on his face. Suzy holds her hands loosely to her mouth, breathing through them deeply whilst a tear runs down her cheek. John stares at the lights with a degree of stoicism, yet his mouth gapes and his tongue presses against his front two teeth. As Adam stares, he leans forward onto an elbow, holding his chin with his hand, squinting in deep ponder. And Eva. Well, she is less fixated by the light than the others, with her attention instead focusing on Arthur. Within her, she feels great pride for him. She watches his face carefully and sees a man now with true purpose, true status and true responsibility. An overwhelming feeling comes over her; a need, a need to support this man, a need to prevent him from being led astray by temptation from his duty. She feels love bubble up inside her, desperate to find form and do anything she can for him. She feels so much love in this moment; a love that is almost is too much to bear. It almost hurts her.

'Arthur, you must now learn how to wield and activate the sword's power,' Julius says, finally breaking the room's stunned silence. 'We must manoeuvre to where we have space. Oh, and where is Douglas?'

'Here! Here I am! Take it! Please, please, take it!' a small, sturdily-built man says as he appears from a corner of the room, almost wrestling his way through the crowd. The man hands Julius a leather sheath with a Tree of Life insignia.

'I made sure you had a scabbard,' Julius says. 'You'll need it for the journey soon to come.'

'I eyed up the sword as soon as I saw it, after you proved you were the one,' Douglas adds.

Arthur looks at this scabbard rather sceptically at first, but his face quickly shifts to a more accepting expression.

'Thank you,' he says.

Arthur puts the sword inside the leather sheath and nods smugly to himself before giving Douglas an appreciative thumbs up. The light from the cube still glows rather brightly but is significantly dimmed. He slings it over his back.

'Let's not waste time. As you said, we don't want Jack to suffer any more unnecessary penance than he needs to. Once you master the sword, we can shed the violet light upon him,' Julius says.

'And what will happen when I do?' Arthur asks.

'He will be able to see clearly once again ...'

Arthur looks away to the side for a moment in contemplation, finishing with a confident nod to himself and an urgent look back up.

'Okay, let's go then,' he says, leading the way up the stairs with Julius and the others following closely behind. As the rest of the academy makes their way up, the last to leave is John. He hangs back for a moment and stares over at the double door to the dome. He puts his hand on his heart, closes his eyes and takes a deep breath. His eyes are wide as he stares at the doors in silence for around 10 seconds. He then turns away and walks up the stairs to join everybody else.

Burning. Pain. Screaming. Crying. Being torn apart. Pulling. Just some of the words to describe the torment Jack experiences in the dome. Ishmael has only just switched off the loop of the footage and returned the dome's atmosphere back to a forest as before; yet this time, the forest is not sunny but it's raining and dark. Ishmael releases cool water from the dome's ceiling to imitate rain, cleansing Jack. Jack curls into the foetal position on the floor as the water drenches him. His body moves backwards and forwards rhythmically.

His hands are clasped together and tears run down his cheeks. His moans grow louder and words begin forming.

'Jerr ... Jerr ... Jerr ...' He shakes, his body contracting like a muscle spasm. 'Jesus. Jesus. Jesus. Jesus. Please Jesus. Please Jesus. Please Jesus. Please Jesus, forgive me. Please Jesus, forgive me. Please Jesus, forgive me.'

His body continues to shake and he continues to beg for Jesus.

Above ground is very different. Night-time has now fallen, and Arthur and Julius stand together in front of the tree, looking at one another. Everybody else crowds around in front of the tree, giving Julius and Arthur space, watching in anticipation for what is to come ...

Julius nods to Arthur. Arthur rips the sword from its sheath and grips it tightly with both hands. Once again, the colours shine brightly. In the darkness of night, the lights look even more powerful. Each of the six colours shoot out, appearing now like beams: up into the sky, onto the tree, onto the ground and into the crowd. The colours spin and catch the faces of the onlookers, who now all stare like children seeing light for the first time.

'Arthur, to unify the sword's colours as violet, I can only guide you so much,' Julius says as he stares up at the rotating beams. 'You must first focus and enter a state of deep purity. This act of inner alignment will cause the cube to spin faster and become a singularity. You must think of the sword as an extension of your inner state.'

Arthur closes his eyes to try and focus himself. He takes a deep breath ...

The cube does not change.

'Relax, relax. You must stay loose. You must forget about fear or expectation ...'

Once again, Arthur tries; this time planting the sword's blade into the ground, gripping the handle and trying to become more relaxed.

Arthur shakes his head and begins to look rather frustrated.

'I don't understand ... What must I feel within me for violet to shine?' he says.

'You must remember the sword's origin,' Julius replies. 'It was originally for Saint Michael. Given to him as a defence and to make him stay close to God and not fall like Lucifer. The blade only works when you channel the love of God. If you are not aligned with God, with wholeness, with purity, with soft heart, then the blade will not emit the beam *of wholeness*. As I said, the sword is a reflection of your inner state. If you wish to make the colours whole, you must become whole yourself.'

Arthur nods his head, and suddenly his face shifts … His expression is one of detachment, yet also peace. He opens his eyes and, with his left hand, pulls the sword from the ground. He holds the blade out to his side and begins walking around. He walks past the onlooking crowd of initiates and looks at their faces; he purses his lips, occasionally smiling at them. Within him he feels a great purpose; he feels these people have faith in him, believing he is bringing something much needed back to earth. But as he thinks this, he also recognises the fact that it is not him that they should ultimately look up to. Within Arthur, he realises that this notion of pride, this arrogance, is the downfall of many leaders; they become addicted to the feeling when others looking at them like gods. Arthur has a sudden vision of himself, in a distant future, sitting on a throne being worshipped like a god, enjoying these feelings. The thought terrifies him. He knows that his power doesn't come from ego or the flesh but, ultimately, from above, from a higher source. And he is a mere conduit to channel this energy as a servant.

'Members, brothers, sisters. Look at me not as special but as a mere man, a child. A man on the earth, with a humility to subordinate himself to the spirit above. This is what we should all try and do. Let us not serve our fellow man as God, as we are not. It is our purpose to be servants to the tasks set for us, and that is all I am doing, living my purpose faithfully. We all have purpose in our hearts, a guiding light; and it is all of our duty to live according to that light. To be close to that light is to be holy, and to be tempted to move away is not; yet it is clear we all fail, and this too is to be expected, as we are all human, and therefore not perfect nor sinless. I tell all of you: do not worship any man who claims to be a king, claims to be a messiah. The messiah will not claim these things. I do not claim to be these things. I am a mere servant, and you are all my family. All I know is I have work to do, as you all do too. What is the nature of this work, I am not sure. Today, I know I must learn to use this blade; and for that, I must believe. My family, I ask you, do you believe?'

Yesses can be heard from all the crowd. Arthur nods and takes a deep breath.

'So then, it is clear. We all believe together. For a single believer is powerful, but a family of them can move mountains and more … Allow me, then, to make this blade shine violet. Allow me to do it for all of those who watch me now. Allow me to activate this blade for the rescue of my father.

Allow me to activate this blade for the salvation of mankind from evil. Allow me to activate this blade's divine light, for the glory of all on earth, and for the kingdom of the great father above!'

Arthur starts swinging the sword through the air with one hand. It flows, thrusts and spins in circles. He begins a sort of dance with it, a smile cracking on his face as he feels the handle start to vibrate and gain in energy. His swings then slows and holds the sword with two hands in front of his face, the blade now pointing down towards the grassy ground, facing towards the onlooking crowd. Arthur holds the glowing cube in alignment with his forehead, the flickering, spinning lights covering his whole face and illuminating it like an angel.

He holds the sword steady and closes his eyes. He begins to hear murmurs and gasps from the crowd. Through his eyelids he can see the lights flashing faster and faster. He can feel the sword vibrating with an increasing intensity in his hands, a deep humming which begins to rise in volume. Within him, he feels a divine warmth radiate, a clarity of thought, vision and purpose. His mind's eye becomes more active with visions of light: patterns and divine geometry, all of which are beautifully symmetrical and glowing. Whooshing and swirling, spinning and rocking; there's an ever-increasing energy focused inside his head.

His eyes open.

He sees the entire crowd covered in a deep, bright glow of violet. He holds the sword higher than he did before, the cube now aligned above his head, like a sort of violet crown. Not only does the cube give off a bright violet glow but the blade too illuminates, radiating physical warmth that feels healing, regenerative and *good*. The faces of the crowd are in lucid ecstasy: relaxed, awestruck and even in tearful bliss. Some of the crowd hold their hands out in front of them like the glow is a warming fire, feeling comfort from this holy radiation. Many of the crowd drop to their knees and clasp their hands together, focusing on the feelings continuing to wash over them.

Arthur feels overwhelmed with a sort of love he had felt before fleetingly: a familiar love of cosmic proportions, a love so powerful and overwhelming that he feels weightless. A compulsion to put the blade down comes to him. He turns around to face the tree, still holding the hilt and cube above his head. He walks closer to the tree, and in front of him he plants the sword's blade deeply into the grassy soil. He removes his hands from the handle and takes a step back. He drops to his knees, stares into the light and clasps his hands together. Everybody else then follows suit, moving up towards the blade in the ground and dropping to their knees in front of it. The cube now spins so quicky that only a violet orb of light can be seen. The light radiates all around, covering everything within half a mile in its glow.

Everyone touched by this light had clear and focused minds, so pure and holy. Any weight or tension, any demons or complexes the person felt within them, any stress or worries were vanquished; and a clear path set itself within their mind, a vision of how to approach issues personal to them. A light was shone on the way to success, to victory, to redemption, to *salvation*. Everything was made clear in a way that they could handle and digest. The energy that presented itself was like the divine and loving dichotomic harmony of both mother and father. Together. As one …

And so, when they had finished, Arthur knew what he needed to do. He had taken in enough light to see things more clearly than ever before. Now, he realised, was time for his brother's healing. A sudden urgency arose in him, but one that seemed well placed and well timed. He felt his brother had been left in the dome for long enough; a fair and necessary amount of time, combining both mercy and *justice*.

Many initiates wanted to witness the healing of Jack. But, instead, Arthur and John, decided it was best that only those close to him would enter the dome to witness his rebirth. And so, Arthur entered the dome, and behind him came John and Suzy.

What they saw was a destroyed man lying on his back. A lifeless body looking drained. The water had stopped dripping on him, but his clothes were completely soaked through, making him look like a starved, drowned rat.

Arthur approached his brother. The sword's violet had faded and resumed its default multi-coloured spin. But within Arthur, a strong afterglow from the light lingered. He had felt the warmth of its glow and now felt he *knew* it, and therefore could activate it again more easily than before. Suzy and John wait at the side of the dome. They nod to Ishmael, who is on the other side of the double doors with Eva and Adam observing the unfolding events through Ishmael's chair screen. Ishmael changes the atmosphere once again within the dome to that of a calm and gentle woodland. The dome is dimly and moodily lit, with the rising sun gently shining through the screens.

Arthur unsheathes the blade, and throws the sheath to the floor. The cube's multi-coloured light shines bright again, spinning the colours around the dome. Ishmael lowers the intensity of the artificial rising sun so the cube's light is more pronounced against the darkness.

Arthur drops to his knees beside Jack and rests the blade across his brother's chest, holding it gently at the end of the blade. He closes his eyes and tries to focus and channel the energy within him as he did before. This time he does not need to struggle to activate the violet; the cube spools up seamlessly, with no resistance. The blade glows hot with violet, like a blacksmith's metal in the furnace. But instead of burning, the glow is energetic and rejuvenating to the touch. Those close by feel a calming sensation, one of gentle warmth and budding energy, an illumination of body and spirit.

Jack begins to make sounds once again.

Life enters him. He takes a small breath at first, and then another, this time longer in duration. And then his third breath is an almighty inhale. Arthur grabs his brother's hand and holds it tightly, and lovingly. The glow seemed to make everything within its proximity seem more real.

'Breathe, Jack. It's okay. It's your brother,' Arthur says softly. Jack responds by gently squeezing Arthur's hand.

Jack starts moaning quietly, but his moans are light and painless, the sort one would make after finally drinking water after a long period of thirst.

Jack's eyes slowly open and he looks at Arthur.

'Arthur ...' he says weakly, yet with notes of purity and positivity.

'Shh, allow the sword to give you strength.'

'Arthur, I'm so sorry ...'

Arthur takes his other hand off the sword and places it on his brother's cheek.

'You are with me now. That's all that matters.'

Arthur glances back at John and Suzy, and they make their way over to their born-again godson.

Jack looks up at them, with eyes that are now fully open.

'Hello,' Jack says, briefly making eye contact with them both but then quickly glancing away, feeling shame come over him.

'Don't feel shame,' John says, noticing this emotion in his eyes. 'Who you were before is not who you are now. You were tricked by dark forces.'

'I was ...' Jack says as he pulls on his brother's hand, sitting up.

'Come here,' Suzy says, as she goes to her knees, trying to hold back tears. She, too, goes in for a deep embrace with her godson.

'I'm so sorry,' he says, a tear now running down his cheek.

'Your mother is guiding you. I know it,' she adds, and they embrace a little longer.

'Now look into the cube's light,' Arthur says after they finish, holding the sword vertically and penetrating the blade into the gel mat floor.

Jack stares into the light.

'Relax. Allow the light to enter your mind. Tell me what you see.'

Jack stares into the cube's light, his head now only inches from it. A need to close his eyes washes over him, so he does and enters a deep state of focus.

His face flinches, but ultimately shows no fear. Instead, it shows courage and composure; yet clearly what he sees is powerful and moving. Half a minute goes by, and his face continues to animate as if a whole story is being told to him. Just before he opens his eyes again, he opens his mouth slightly then slowly closes it. When his eyes finally open, he looks away from the light and down at the ground. He looks humble, showing signs of a man who has just accepted something tremendous, but has accepted it so fully that it proves to be no burden to his soul.

Arthur sheathes the blade and the light dims to the six colours. John turns to look at a peeping Ishmael, staring next to two other heads through the cracks of the double doors. Ishmael once again changes the atmosphere, illuminating the room with a clean and bright white.

'What did you see?' Arthur asks.

'What we must do.'

'So you know of the task?'

Jack pauses for a few moments whilst looking his brother intensely in the eye.

'Yes.'

Arthur helps his brother to his feet. Jack now looks strong: his eyes are wide and awake and his face glows with calmness, composure and purity.

The brothers embrace each other.

'Oh, Arthur ... How could I not have seen it before?'

'Because you are human.'

'How long has he been down there?'

'Since the night he passed.'

Jack pulls away from the embrace and shakes his head.

'I saw him down there, Arthur. He was in a horrible tower. He was suffering greatly. He was strapped to a cross ...'

Arthur pauses. His cheeks tighten momentarily in disgust. He then nods in acceptance and takes a deep breath.

'Was there a demon with him too?'

Jack pauses and looks down to the floor.

'A horrific beast guarded him. His head was horned and bullish, and his body black and powerful ...'

'This was the demon I told you of all those years ago. This was the demon who first gave me the cube. We were both tricked, Jack! Not just you. I too, was tricked.'

'Well, all that matters is we rescue him. But how?'

'I am so sorry to interrupt you both,' Julius says, appearing through dome's entrance. 'A pleasure to meet you, Jack, my name is Julius, guardian of the books of wisdom and knowledge. Welcome to the Tree of Life. Yet, and I am afraid to say, you may not have much time to get acquainted with everything here. Our window is small ...'

The brothers look at each other rather confused.

'The cube, you see,' Julius continues, 'is no longer in the hands of dark forces. And this is good; we have made it light once again. But as brilliant and integral as this is, it is not without consequence. Allow me to explain ...' Julius beckons with his head for the brothers, and John and Suzy, to follow him.

Julius leads them all to the round table, where Ishmael, Eva and Adam are already waiting. Arthur puts the sheathed sword on the table, not thinking at first how it will not sit flush because of the cube that bulges at the hilt. He panics momentarily that it might fall, but as he inspects it he is relieved that the cube simply moves slightly out of its central position, like a magnet pushed off course. The cube still spins gracefully, hovering slightly above the table with a glow. His brother sits next to him.

'We must keep our flow going,' Julius says, as he stands inside the ring of the table. 'I know recent events have been very tiring and intense for everybody; but the end of the beginning has now come, and we must act. It is now or never.

'As you may know from the prophecies, the naked cube is a perversion of goodness. And when in the hands of Satan's kind, it can bring much danger and darkness to mankind. Hypnotic spells, possessions, trickery, torture … Moloch, you see, the demon lord of the orange spirit, has been chosen to spearhead the enslavement process for this generation. Each lord has his turn, and the styles of dark meddling change throughout history. Oh yes, this isn't the first time Satan has tried it. It is this Moloch who demands sacrifice from those on earth. And it is ultimately this Moloch who provides his "milk" in return for it.'

'Snake oil …' Jack says, bowing his head in shame.

'Yes, Jack. Snake oil,' Julius replies, trying his best to be gentle with his tone. 'And whilst it seems the snake oil project was an attempt to force the sacrifice of souls on a massive scale, the abduction of your father's soul in particular seems likely to be a sort of test for you both.'

'A test?' Jack asks. 'I don't understand why this demon out of all people chose our father …'

'A soul stuck in limbo in an animal form is always needed for milk to be sent from hell to earth. The "conduit soul", as it's referred to, is both a symbol and a conductor; it is, in a way, a pact between the two realms, allowing interdimensional travel of the milk to occur. The milk in its pure form is black, but through a shadow enantiodromia, it appears as white when arriving on earth. Regarding the origin of the milk itself, this is something I will not get into; you will find out for yourself as you descend. Regardless, the reason why Moloch picked your father does indeed strikes me as a test, but exactly why I do not fully understand. I say this simply because of the roles you both are playing in the prophecy. Arthur has adopted the role of divine hero, and you, Jack, of the fool. The fool can be both good and bad. It very well could have been the case that, in another timeline, you could have discovered the nature of your father's soul under demonic possession, and as a result would have simply accepted your father's entrapment as a necessary sacrifice for the pursuits of both you and Sickle. This is what the demons hoped for. But, thankfully, the course of this destiny was changed by both your spirits. And for that, we should breathe a sigh of relief.'

Those around the table take deep breaths and give one another uneasy looks.

'Arthur …' Jack says with a trembling voice, shaking his head.

'We're going to get him. Okay?' Arthur smiles and puts his hand on his brother's shoulder. 'Okay?'

'Okay,' Jack replies, looking into his brother's eyes. They are both on the edge of tears.

'I can't lie to you boys,' Julius continues, 'your father's spirit would have already suffered greatly. Now that we have acquired the cube, the Snake Box project has been halted and Moloch may become impatient. He may very well decide to destroy your father's soul completely, turning it to milk form. But these demons are always resentful. They will indulge themselves in evil pleasures whilst he is still in animal limbo form. Inflicting pain and suffering is for them a compensation for their moral failures as angels.'

'But Julius …' Arthur says, with a frown of confusion. 'How could God allow this? Hell is meant to be for those who live lives of great sin and evil. Even if my father was not entirely sinless, how could this punishment be justified?'

'None of us on earth are sinless, Arthur. God does not expect us to be perfect; he just expects us to be honest about our mistakes and failures and to not deceive ourselves through arrogance and pride. Your father, however, was a very good man. And more so, he was a strong man, a courageous man. And as he got older, he too, like you, became closer to God. And like Job in the Old Testament, God chose to test him for these reasons. God makes examples of his kind, you see. He makes examples of good people, to show to the demons that some spirits will never break. But the ways of God are only within our understanding fleetingly, for his plans are great and complex. And I am sure you too are involved in his plan; and he now has a test for your spirit. For both of your spirits. But the question is, will you accept his test? Are you both willing to go into hell to try and rescue him?'

The brothers both look at each other, and then back to Julius. They both reply with 'yes' in unison.

'Good. Then have one final rest tonight, and then at dawn, you must both join hands on the sword. For whoever touches the activated sword whilst it lays in the rock will be transported to wherever the powers above wish to take them.'

'So we have no control or say to where we are teleported to?' Arthur asks.

'And how do we get back?' Jack adds.

'It is my understanding, through my readings, that you never will know exactly where the tree will send you. Heroes of the past have used the stone in times of great need, whenever they had a problem that could not be solved by orthodox means; the stone provided a portal that sent them to a place that provided the answer. The answer is always in the journey you are given, and it may not become clear until long after the journey is completed. In your case, the journey is to save your father's soul, so I cannot imagine you would be sent anywhere else but hell. But this is simply my own logical deduction and assumption. It is also quite possible that you may have to go through various stages before finally reaching him. But once again, I must emphasise, I only have general and broad understandings of these things; the details are always personal to the hero of the age. And regarding getting back to earth ... Well, I believe the old saying "the only way out is through" applies here.'

'If you're going through hell, keep going,' John adds, looking up whilst holding his hands in his lap.

'Churchill,' Ishmael adds. And the table all around nod.

The brothers are directed to two separate rooms in the library to rest before they make their descent at dawn. Laid out on both their beds are neatly-folded uniforms, similar in fashion to those worn by the members who raided Sickle's house when Ishmael was paralysed. The difference with these uniforms was that they were dark black instead of grey, and the spandex rash guard has a white Tree of Life insignia in the centre of the chest.

Arthur sits on his bed, hands clasped in prayer, before he goes to sleep. Eva lies in the bed next to him, half asleep. The cube, sheathed within the sword, lightly glistens at the side of the bed, the six spinning colours shining dimly. A knock on the door causes Eva to stir, and Arthur to stop praying to look up.

'Come in,' he says.

Jack enters, holding the uniform folded over his arm.

'We actually wearing this? I look like a member of a ballerina death cult.'

Arthur laughs.

'I think they are quite cool. And since when do ballerinas wear black leather trench coats?'

'I thought it's meant to be hot in hell?'

They both laugh.

'Well, you can always take it off, can't you? But I don't think hell will be quite the place that's depicted in popular culture. I have a feeling most of that is metaphorical. Just see the uniforms as a representation of the academy;

we have to wear something, don't we? T-shirts and jeans would be a bit too casual for where we are going, don't you think?'

'Fair comment. Anyway, it wasn't the uniforms that I wanted to talk to you about …'

'Go on.'

'Well, I just wanted to say … that …' Jacks turns his head to the side, lost for words.

'I think it's better we just sleep, Jack; you've been through a lot today.'

Jack continues to stare at Arthur deeply, and tenderly, his eyes swelling a little. Arthur then purses his lips and stands up.

'Come here, mate,' he says as he shakes his head, walking towards his brother. Jack drops his uniform abruptly on the floor, and the brothers embrace.

'We got this,' Arthur says softly.

'Yes, I know. Anyway, you're right, we should sleep. Bye, Arthur.'

Arthur nods, and Jack quickly picks up his uniform and scurries off again.

Arthur puts the sword under the bed and then sits down for a few moments in contemplation; a feeling of confusion rises within him, and a frown forms on his face. They clearly both had reason to be apprehensive, but he felt Jack wanted to say something more specific but simply could not summon the spirit, nor the words to do so.

'What was that about?' Eva groans with her eyes still closed.

'I'm not sure …'

Arthur shakes his head, turns off the lights and goes to sleep.

Morning comes and Arthur knocks on Jack's door, the sword neatly sheathed in the scabbard –connected to a custom-made belt. Eva is by his side. They hear no response so they just walk in, and they see him putting on his boots. They wait for Jack to be ready and then walk to the room of the round table together in silence. Around the table sit John, Ishmael and Adam; and in the centre, standing by the rock, Julius. Once again, all present are silent. They stare at the brothers as they enter the ring of the table. Eva takes a seat next to Ishmael.

'Please, can you both just go!' Suzy shouts as she comes in through the double doors abruptly, looking rather distressed and fidgety. 'I can't bear the waiting! We all believe in you both and your mission, but please, just go! Go!' She then scurries through the gap in the table and kisses both her godsons on their cheeks. 'Go rescue him! Go!'

'Come on,' Arthur says as he unsheathes his sword, preparing it for penetration, lighting up the room with a multitude of colour once again.

'Okay, put the sword inside the rock when you're ready,' Julius says as he takes a step back.

Arthur inserts the sword into the rock and slings the leather sheath onto his back.

'And now wrap your hands on the handle,' Julius says.

The brothers both wrap their hands around the handle.

'This brings back memories,' Jack says as he looks up at his brother opposite, the sword in between them.

Arthur smiles lightly and meets his brother's gaze.

'It's been quite the journey since then, hasn't it?'

'Yes. And now, I know what I must do. I have been humbled beyond words, Arthur. Now I see so clearly,' Jack replies with a strange conviction.

Arthur's eyes flicker down to the ground as he feels a faint sadness; however, he has no time to dwell on this feeling.

'Arthur, you must now focus on the cube. Once you activate the spinning violet, you will both be teleported.'

Looking on from the table, Suzy is cuddling up closely to John and sobbing quietly into his shoulder; yet she still looks up at the brothers with a sidewards glance. John strokes the back of her head softly.

Arthur closes his eyes and takes a deep breath.

'Ready?' he says as he opens his eyes.

'Yep.'

'Okay, here we go.'

Arthur closes his eyes again, yet this time he looks more serious and focused. His face then becomes more relaxed and in a trance as the cube begins to gain speed.

The violet glows, engulfing the room.

The brothers fade into nothingness …

PART FIVE: KNIGHTS OF THE INFERNO

1. THE HILL TO HELL

The brothers appear in a field full of daffodils, still clutching the sword's handle. Arthur sheathes it on his waist. The yellow field expands in one direction as far as the eye can see; in another, trees can be seen; in another, mountains; and in another, a wide and grassy hill, extending high up into the clouds. They look around in awe at their surroundings, squinting with curiosity at what they see. However, this is not the same childlike euphoria they experienced the first time they were in an alternate realm together.

'Look!' Arthur points. 'There's some people.'

They begin to move towards a group of people in the distance. The group is sitting down in a circle. As they get closer, they see six individuals who are not quite human in appearance. They have human-shaped bodies but each with different animal heads: a lion, a worm, a horse, an elephant, a wolf and a snake. Their hands, limbs and torsos possess the texture and attributes of the associated animal. As the brothers approach, the humanoid entities do not take much notice, or at least do not appear concerned; they seem strangely calm, in fact.

'Hello?' Arthur says as he gets within earshot.

'Hello. Would you like to sit with us?' the lion-headed humanoid replies, calmly turning to look at them.

Jack and Arthur look at each other, acknowledge the invite and agree to sit down. The horse and the elephant open the circle to allow space between them.

'What brings you here then?' the lion asks.

'Me and my brother Jack have been sent here from earth. We are trying to get to hell to save our father's spirit. It has been trapped by a demon through none of the faults of his earthly life.'

The horse snorts, and the snake hisses.

'Very interesting,' the lion replies. 'It is rare for ones who appear in this plane to ask for hell. Usually those who arrive here seek heaven instead. However, those that seek heaven always end up in hell ... So maybe it is true that those who seek hell will end up in heaven? But if you seek hell, and hell is what you *need*, then you too very well may go there.'

'How do you know this?' Jack asks with a frown.

'Come. Follow me, I will show you.'

The brothers and the humanoids all stand up and follow the lion-headed man as he walks in the direction of the great grassy hill in the distance.

'Our father, the one that is trapped. He has a lion's head like you,' Arthur says.

'Oh, yes? These heads of ours are our spirit. They represent the style of the life we led. I was once a loyal man on earth, but also very violent. However, whilst my violence was limited, it was not always justified. And for this, my salvation is not guaranteed but not completely denied either. My period of judgement has been prolonged.'

The group walk in silence for about a mile, with the lion setting a steady walking pace.

'Stop here,' he says, raising his hand in the air.

The group reach the side of the large, green hill. It is wide and looks very inviting, as if it's just asking to be climbed.

'This is the hill that leads down to hell,' the lion says. 'Before you ask how I know this, I ask you to wait and watch. It is never long before a spirit attempts to climb it.'

'Down to hell?' Jack asks with a confused expression.

'You will see. Look, someone is approaching now.' The lion nods in the direction of an approaching bumble bee-headed spirit in the distance. After some waiting, the bee finally approaches the hill and looks up towards where it meets with the clouds. The bee then turns to face the group and continues to stare at them all for a few moments.

'Do not be tricked by this hill. It will lead you to doom, please reconsider,' the lion spirit says.

The bee spirit does not listen. It turns back towards the hill, and as soon as it takes its first step, its foot goes directly *through* the hill, as if it was merely an illusion. The bee then can be seen sinking lower and lower into the ground, as if the hill was actually going down rather than up. The bee then completely disappears into the hill's mass, swallowed up completely.

'As you can see, this hill deceives its walkers,' the lion says morbidly. 'I am quite sure that even as they walk down, they still believe they are walking up. And before they realise they have been tricked, it is too late … No one ever comes back, you see. But you both are odd. You are conscious that this is a trick, yet you still wish to go down?'

'Yes. As I said, we have a task,' Arthur says.

'Hmm … You both are very brave then, and I wish you both the best in your task.'

'Thank you,' Arthur replies, 'and thank you for leading us here; I hope you are granted salvation; you seem very nice and friendly.'

The lion nods in appreciation.

'I have been here for a very, very long time. And my time here has humbled me greatly. The only way for me to find meaning here now is to try and lead other spirits and prevent them from falling into the same trap as that bumble bee. But I try and do this out of the purity of my heart and not merely for salvation.'

'I believe your intentions are pure, and you are close to salvation. I wish your friends the same.'

The lion nods again and begins to lead his group away. The horse makes a final snort, the worm a wiggle, the wolf a howl, the snake a hiss and the elephant raises its trunk.

Jack then turns to face the hill and bends down to pat the grass at its base.

'Feels solid to touch.'

Arthur touches it with his foot.

'Yes, very weird isn't it …'

'Nothing seems weird to me now.'

'Come on, let's not overthink it and start making our way up … I mean down …'

The brothers both laugh a bit uneasily and take their first steps on the hill.

'Well, it definitely feels like I'm walking up something. Seems like the lion was right,' Jack says as he takes a few steps up the hill.

'It even looks like you're going up from down here.'

Arthur's face suddenly shifts and a childish smile appears. He begins sprinting as fast as he can up the hill.

'Race ya!' he says as he passes his brother. Jack shakes his head, smiles and begins trying to catch up with his brother.

After a short period of playfully racing up the hill, Jack can no longer keep up with Arthur and finds himself quite out of breath. He bends down and puts one hand on his knee, and holds the other up at Arthur to signal him to stop.

'Do you even exercise these days?' Arthur says with a teasing smile, showing little signs of fatigue.

'Not really. I use the gym at Snake Box, but only once in a blue moon.' Arthur laughs.

'Okay, well, let's stop here for a bit then. Look, that view is quite something, isn't it?'

Jack turns round to look back at the view. The yellow fields of daffodils stretch out towards the horizon and the mountains seem to go on infinitely. Strangely, there is no source in the sky for the light that illuminates the landscape.

'It's all too much, Arthur. Yet I have nothing else to do but to just accept it. I have based my entire life on trying to explain everything, to know how things work; but now, I am faced with the reality that I will never understand everything. I don't even know if I understand anything ...'

'Yes. Humbling, isn't it? From a young age I have felt that same vulnerability you describe. But I promise it gets easier. In fact, being vulnerable can be a strength too. A person who is vulnerable is constantly open to new things; and in that state, those new things will keep them growing. A person who feels safe has no need to open themselves to new things as they grow old. But those who stay vulnerable stay young.'

Jack pauses for a few moments, then decides to sit down on the hill and stare out at the landscape. Arthur joins him.

'When you shined the violet glow into my eyes, I saw everything, Arthur.'

'You said to me you felt your task was clear.'

'Yes. My task is clear beyond belief. So much so, I feel sick to the stomach if I was to choose any other path than the one that laid itself before my eyes.'

A moment of silence falls between them.

'Anyway, let's keep moving,' Jack continues. 'As I said, I feel anxious and sick whenever I feel I'm deviating from my task.' Jack's voice quivers as he says this, and he quickly stands up and begins to walk back up the hill.

'Wait. Jack. You keep saying "your task", but we are on this journey together. What is different about what you must do personally? What do you mean by this exactly?'

'It doesn't matter ...' Jack says whilst shaking his head, continuing to storm up the hill, now almost touching the bottom layer of cloud.

'It does matter. We are in this together.'

Jack stops again and looks down at his feet. He sighs deeply.

'I don't make it back to earth, Arthur,' Jack says, his eyes moving erratically then meeting his brother's gaze intensely. Arthur's face turns very serious.

They hold each other's gaze for several moments in silence.

'And you know what? I have never felt calmer about anything else in my entire life,' Jack continues. 'My entire life I have convinced myself that what I was doing was good. I truly believed I would change the world in a good way. But looking back now, it is clear I was living a lie. I never felt completely content with my actions; I was always on edge, always a little anxious something within me wasn't happy. I never truly felt aligned with good. Yet I still convinced myself I was happy. You can say I was deceived by Sickle, and that may be true but only partly. I chose to work with him myself, and I must accept that only I am to blame. He enticed me with his visions of what we could achieve, and I allowed him to entertain my fantasies of creating a better world through technology. I don't doubt that's possible, when done in a certain way, but what happened with this project was clearly a distraction from what you say is my conscience. The deeper I committed myself to this project, the company, the technology, the harder it became to give any thought elsewhere to how it could possibly be wrong or bad.

'That light from your sword, those feelings it gave me weren't new to me. What the sword showed me was something that I have felt my entire life but only subtly in the background. But the light made it so bright, so loud, that for the first time in my life, it was impossible for me to ignore it. Now I look back at my time obsessing over grand fantasies to change the world, and I am ashamed of how I was so distracted from that part inside me that I now feel so clearly. I always labelled it as my "irrational" side, my primitive side, my side not worthy of any thought or consideration. But now I see that everything that springs up in my mind, no matter how daft or silly it may seem, is at the very least worth consideration, even if it doesn't seem like it at the time. But whilst I have accepted all that I did that was wrong, I still feel indebted to give more ...'

'You don't need to give more!' Arthur shouts, shaking his head and putting his hand on his brother's shoulder. 'Accepting you made a mistake, accepting it with all your heart, this is enough! The very nature of accepting you were wrong has already humbled you, it has already changed you. Why do you want to punish yourself further?'

'It isn't the fact I want to punish myself, it is because it is what I must do!' Jack shakes his head again and begins storming further up the hill, into and through the clouds.

'Jack!' Arthur shouts, following him into the mist.

The brothers are now firmly inside the clouds, high up on the hill. Jack has picked up the pace again, and Arthur loses sight of him.

'Jack, slow down! We need to stick together!'

Approximately 10 minutes go by, and Arthur still cannot see his brother. Arthur notices that the light inside the clouds isn't fading just because of the mist, but that it is becoming darker.

This isn't good ... Arthur thinks to himself.

In his desperation, he pulls out Excalibur from its sheath and the six colours of the cube light up the mist as it rotates and shines. He continues to push further into the darkening clouds. The lights from the cube do make things brighter, but they are mostly reflected by the mist and do not actually penetrate particularly deep.

He takes a moment to stop and close his eyes.

He spools up the cube, and reopens his eyes. The clouds around him disappear completely, and he sees nothing but a violet-tinted black abyss. The hill is no longer grassy but rocky. He sees his brother, around 10 or so metres in front. Jack stops and turns to look back, unable to resist the sensations he feels deep in his body, a gentle and warm quivering rumble.

Arthur reduces his focus, and the cube slows its spins, returning to its baseline six colours; yet now the path is cloudless and well-lit, the way clear.

'I thought I lost you!' Arthur says, sounding only the slightest bit irritated.

'Sorry, I Just needed some space. I know you wouldn't approve of what I saw in my vision, but I am content with it, Arthur, I promise.'

'Look, Jack, let's cross that bridge when we get to it. I've had visions all my life and not all of them are literal in their meanings; they contain half-truths, metaphorical truths. They are to be taken seriously, of course, but not always literally.'

'I understand that. But you have no idea how clear the vision I had was. It was beyond any dream or anything I have ever had in terms of clarity. It was as clear as day, Arthur ...'

Arthur pauses for a few moments in contemplation. He then sighs, and says, 'Come on, we can't dwell on this, can we? Let's just keep moving.'

So the brothers keep pushing up the hill. They take a moment to look out over the edge at one point, but neither can bear to stare down for very long; for what they see is a pure black abyss, filling them both with unease.

Arthur has decided that using the sword as a sort of walking stick is the most efficient way to light the path, with the cube's spinning light illuminating the way. Strangely, though, as the blade clunks against the stony ground, there is not the slightest echo, almost as if it were happening in a small room. The patterns of light it makes around them are rather beautiful too; the beams shine into the darkness and off the path, causing staggering brightness. As Arthur shone the light into the black, it gave them both the same uncanny feeling inside; like walking into the dark, unknown depths of a cave.

'Do you think this is hell?' Jack asks finally after a rather long period of walking without talking.

'What? Being forced to walk up a hill in the darkness for all eternity? With no end in sight?' Arthur laughs lightly to himself. 'Yeah, that would be quite hellish, wouldn't it?'

Jack shudders at the mere thought of it.

'Saying that ... Is it me or can you see a faint white glow over the peak?' Arthur says as he squints, looking up to the hill's apex.

Jack squints too as both brothers stop to try and focus on it.

'There's definitely some sort of light. What?!' Jack says looking rather shaken, noticing something has startled Arthur.

Arthur turns his head rather rapidly to look behind him, bringing up his sword with two hands in a defensive position.

'I don't know. I sensed something ...' Arthur says softly with a frown, turning his head left and right to investigate.

'I didn't hear anything.'

Arthur tilts his head sceptically and frowns again.

'Come on, let's just keep moving towards that light; we can't be far from reaching the top now. Just be careful of what's behind us from now on ...'

The brothers continue to make their way up the hill at a faster pace, with a renewed sense of danger and awareness.

2. EYES IN THE DARKNESS

Phillip writhes and shakes; his eyes are tired but never resting. His arms shake against their bonds, and his head throbs from being upside down.

Moloch bathes in his pitch-black spirit pool. It's a large circle of thick, black liquid soul with a metallic, black imposing statue of him in the middle. At the statue's base is an open blowhole, black gunk gushing out of it and filling the pool with a steady stream. On his knees, the liquid rising to his upper chest, is Moloch. He cups the liquid into his mouth, slurping it as if it were the finest of fruits. There's a look of calm on this bull-headed demon, a subtle smirk, as he bathes in the pleasure he's receiving from the sweetness of tortured souls.

Phillip writhes whilst strapped to an upside-down crucifix in the centre of a black and white tiled hall. The hall has no walls, only pillars soaring up to a ceiling of great height. There is nothing but darkness outside. On top of the ceiling is a great spire, dark metallic spikes ominously decorating the circumference.

Phillip's body is limp and tired, his fur dishevelled. Oozing and gaping black gashes are all over his body, as if he has endured a brutal whipping. A disgusting creature enters the hall from the spiral staircase of the tower. This creature has furry legs, hooves and black, spiky antlers. His head is similar to that of a moose, yet is darker and less symmetrical, the nose to the left side of its face. The creature isn't particularly tall and as it walks, it stumbles clumsily. It also makes a vibrating, moist sound with its mouth similar to someone slapping their lips together, along with a bizarre, growling similar to a cat's purr, yet deeper and less harmonious.

The beast approaches Moloch as he bathes.

'My lord, my lord. We have eyes on the sons, the sons have been seen!' the creature says with a pathetic yet growly voice as it approaches.

'Come closer, Deggrog,' Moloch says calmly. Deggrog stumbles over to the edge of the spirit pool and looks down at Moloch. Moloch stands up, oily essence dripping from him as he towers over this lesser demon in a domineering way. 'Where were they sighted?' he says after a period of silent intimidation.

'On the hill! A Draxler is stalking them as we speak! He says the sword they wield is very powerful! It got rid of all the clouds, my lord.'

'They will need to get rid of more than clouds to survive my desire. They are of the earthly flesh, and for that reason they lack resilience to hellish form. Tell the Draxler that he must strike fear into them, for with fear in their hearts they are weak and ready for my forced depravity. Have them not killed, but scarred.'

'Scar them with fear! Yes, my lord!'

The creature scurries off back down the stairs.

Moloch stares ahead at the strung-up Phillip with intrigue, eyes squinting and lips licking. He emerges from the pool and picks up a shadowy, black whip that lays on a marble table nearby. He stands up from his chair and walks towards Phillip's inverted cross. He walks in front him and unfurls the whip tauntingly as he looks him in the eyes.

'Your sons have entered our realm,' Moloch says.

'My sons will destroy you,' Phillip mutters weakly, yet with an underlying bedrock of strength.

Moloch begins hysterically laughing, causing the ground to shake and Phillip's face to flinch.

'The only reason I haven't milked your soul yet is so I can lure in your sons. I will trap their souls in torture, force insanity within their hearts and then feed you their essence. I will then take back the cube, strip its light and make it ready to resume milking your kind on earth.'

'I will be happy when I see them banish you from existence. They will put an end to your meddling.'

Moloch laughs again.

'The damage is already done. Have you not learnt anything from this?' Moloch leans back and prepares to crack his whip. Phillip's face contorts in preparation, and his body begins to strain. 'Slowly but surely, all of your kind will be directly connected to the one true lord: Satan. Our forces spread quickly, like a virus, a parasite infecting everyone. There is no escaping the contagion. The ones you think are aligned with your father, they will break easier than you think. No one is safe from our contagion; your kind are too weak to resist our temptation. They love it, they enjoy it; it makes them feel so good.' Moloch throws his whip to the floor, and Phillip's face contorts with surprise.

Moloch slowly walks back over to the pool of darkness with a cocky swagger. Phillip perceives this as intentionally intimidating, piquing his interest.

The bull-headed dark one leans to pick up a thick, long spouted obsidian jug from the pool's rim. He dunks it in to fill it.

He walks back towards Phillip, holding his gaze as he does; the demon is smiling like a demented clown. He holds the jug with one thick, furred hand and scoops his leathery finger inside it, holding it up in front of the lion spirit, now covered and dripping with black gunk.

The finger moves towards Phillip's lower abdomen.

It makes contact.

The lower stomach of the lion pulses and starts to warm up, glowing orange with energy.

Phillip firstly shakes his head and grits his teeth in resistance, but the glow only builds, covering more of his stomach. Phillip's expression changes to one of dissociated, wide-eyed fear, his eyes darting around as if seeing things that weren't there. His entire head starts wobbling around as he desperately fights against his bonds.

'God, my father! Help me!!' he roars deeply.

'No! He will not! Only the darkness can be your friend now …' Moloch moves closer to the flailing Phillip, thrusting the jug's spout towards Phillip's lips. 'Shh, still now. Let the darkness enter you.'

Phillip mumbles and gargles in resistance, but his attempts are futile. Moloch inserts the jug's spout inside Phillip's mouth and tilts it at a steep angle, forcing the black fluid inside.

Jack and Arthur continue to climb the hill with caution, but still at a brisk pace. The path is now very narrow, so much so that it would be dangerous to run, as they would risk falling into the abyss below.

'Are we even getting any closer? The light looks the same distance away as it did half an hour ago,' Jack says in a rather tired and fed-up tone, his walk now slouched and lacking spirit.

'Things aren't like earth here, Jack. Everything here is more spiritual than material. These demons and dark spirits, they feed off your soul; they enjoy seeing you demoralized. Don't let them have what they want! Stay strong. We must believe and have faith that we are getting closer to the light!'

Jack puffs a little, but then acknowledges Arthur has a point and ultimately realises that he has no other choice but to stay positive in this situation. A few more minutes go by, and then the brothers hear something behind them …

'Okay, I heard that,' Jack says as he turns around at the same time as his brother.

'Shh!' Arthur shines the rotating cube light into the darkness behind.

The sound of footsteps now become clear.

'Do you think it's a soul trying to walk the hill to heaven?' Jack asks.

Arthur does not reply at first but instead continues to shine the light down the hill while moving forward cautiously.

'I'm not sure about this, but I feel we should show strength and confront it anyway,' he says, finally.

The brothers begin to walk towards the oncoming entity, and they see clearly now a rather old-looking man of average height, dressed in white robes almost Ancient Greek in style. The man is clean-shaven and has a very emotionless expression on his face. His movements do not match his age, however, and this gives him an uncanny energy. He moves swiftly and with zest and grace, as if he is many years younger than his wrinkled face suggests.

'Hello,' Arthur says when within earshot.

'Hello. So you are seeking heaven?' says the man in a deep voice, getting straight to the point.

'This hill actually leads to hell, I'm afraid,' Jack says rather abruptly.

The man in white laughs.

'No, no, this path leads to heaven, my friends. I have travelled up and down this hill many times. I am a guide sent to help those needing guidance. Allow me to offer my assistance.' The man gives a shallow and modest bow to the brothers.

'What's your name, then?' Arthur asks.

'They call me Hazlot.'

'Forgive me, but I am confused,' Arthur says. 'We met a lion-headed man down in the field of daffodils, and he told us this hill is a trick, and it actually leads down to hell. To me, he seemed very honest and genuine. But you are now telling me that this path does in fact lead to heaven?'

The man sniffs and nods in a scoffing manner.

'Do not trust everyone you meet in these realms, friend. Many here are deceivers, tricksters.'

'Oh, I don't doubt that at all,' Arthur says, tilting his head down and looking at Hazlot through his eyebrows. 'Tell me, Hazlot, how do you walk the hill with no light? Even with my sword of light here, the path is a struggle to follow.'

A tense silence forms between them.

'Well, that is a beautiful sword,' Hazlot says, suddenly fixing his gaze intensely on the shining cube within it. 'Can I hold it?' He turns his eyes back to Arthur.

'This sword is only to be wielded by me.'

'Oh, yes, of course. I understand possessions and our attachments to them. We all need items to care about, don't we? *Things,* I mean. We all have them, and I can respect a man and his things. And regarding how I walk without light, well, as I said, I have travelled this path many times; I can do it with my eyes closed, in fact. I have no need for light, you see; but yes, you are not far from the entrance now; carry on down this path. The path flattens out soon, you are nearly there. Goodbye.'

The man walks past the brothers and carries on up the hill. The brothers watch him disappear into the darkness.

'Doesn't feel right, does it?' Jack whispers to Arthur.

Arthur smiles with a strange confidence, and then says, 'Of course not. I was preparing to defend us at any moment there. He was very weird, wasn't he?'

'What do you reckon then?'

'Well, there's not much we can do other than keep our eyes open and stay aware. If anything happens, I'll activate the sword.'

'And if you can't?'

'What do you mean?'

'Well, both the times I have seen you switch it on, you look very focused. It would be funny if it wasn't for the light being so captivating. My point is you clearly are trying quite hard to activate the violet light. So what happens if we get attacked and you can't trigger it?'

'I have been told that this sword was originally the Archangel Saint Michael's. The violet only works when you are in a state of holy inner wholeness, aligned with the Holy Spirit of God. So yes, I need to put myself in a very calm and focused frame of mind. I have to have full faith in myself that it will work, and then it will work.'

Jack frowns and purses his lips together, clearly not completely convinced.

'Jack, I have done it quite a few times now. I'm confident in my ability to activate it. Don't worry, it'll be fine. Trust me.' Arthur forces a smile and nods, all whilst staring at Jack dead in the eye.

Jack raises an eyebrow with scepticism and begins to walk forward.

'Okay ... Well, all I'm saying is if we come across some sort of monster or demons or what not, I have some doubts about you maintaining a state of "holy inner wholeness".' Jack says, denoting the air quotes with his fingers.

Arthur does not reply but carries on smiling to himself, initially brushing off Jack's doubt as not deserving any consideration. However, this smile does not stay on his face for long. Doubt creeps into his mind, and he thinks, *I can't allow myself to become scared. Fear is the real killer. Fear and doubt will cause me to lose focus. Stay calm, Arthur. Have faith.*

They continue to carry on pushing up the hill for another 10 minutes. Now they both move with added urgency and pace. Their demeanours become similar. Originally, when Arthur was setting the pace, his assertive body language was radiating positivity. He made sure to stay upbeat, his body language reflected this. As much as Jack wanted to slump, and as close as he was to becoming demoralized, Arthur's vibe previously kept him from this. Now, however, Arthur felt himself begin to slip ... And just as his brother had previously mentioned, fear started to creep its way into his mind ...

'Stop!' Arthur says firmly, stopping in his tracks immediately.

'What?'

'I need to gather myself. Ever since you mentioned fear, I have begun to feel doubt.'

'You are only human, of course you are going to be scared. I didn't mean to knock your self-confidence or anything, but I'm just trying to be realistic; it's at least something you should be aware of.'

'Sorry, just give me a moment, Jack, please,' Arthur says as he leans on his sword's pommel, closing his eyes in focus.

Jack turns away and stares at the hill inquisitively, squinting and tilting his head.

'Sorry to interrupt, but have you not noticed that the hill is becoming ... less of a hill? It's definitely getting flatter.'

Arthur opens his eyes again and looks forward.

'Oh yeah ... And look!' Arthur points to the light in the distance.

'It's definitely getting brighter, isn't it?'

The light flashes twice. And the brothers look at each other simultaneously with open mouths.

'Come on, let's keep moving! The weird man said we don't have long.

I know he wasn't trustworthy, but clearly we are making progress!' Arthur says as he begins to run forward, albeit with caution.

'Please don't move too fast, I don't want to fall off the sides. Who would flash the light at us anyway? Could it be a trap?' Jack asks as he jogs behind Arthur, looking rather uncomfortable at picking up the pace.

'I don't want to make any assumptions, but I have a good feeling about it. Let's just wait and see.'

They move up the hill for a while longer. And the hill was indeed becoming less and less steep. The closer they got to the peak, the brighter this white glow became. They reach the top and look forward towards the glow. However, they see no source of beautiful white light like they were hoping; but instead a cave opening at the end of the path. The opening glows a deep red.

'Arthur ...' Jack says with a worried tone.

'I don't understand ...'

'You still have a good feeling about this?'

Clatters, croaking, scurrying, gargles, groaning: faint but certain sounds coming from behind them down the hill.

'The light! Turn it on! Turn it on!' Jack shouts.

At this point, the path had widened substantially, and the flatness of the path now made running easier. They both run forward rapidly.

'Activate it!' Jack shouts as they both run in tandem.

'I can't!'

'Yes, you can! Believe in yourself!'

The sounds were becoming louder and louder, and now they can hear sounds from in front of them too, coming from inside the glowing red opening. They stopped running abruptly.

'Arthur, please! Please!'

Jack continues to stare at Arthur, and Arthur just stares back at him, as if in a disassociated daze. Arthur then turns his head to look around, listening to the disgusting sounds amplify in volume. He feels fear flood into him, intensifying horror; his heart pumps faster, he feels dazed and confused, detached and out of control. His confidence is sapped, and he feels light-headed.

'We can't die like this,' Jack says on the verge of tears, shaking his head.

'No, we can't,' Arthur replies.

Arthur leans on the sword's handle once again and closes his eyes. His lips begin moving quickly as he recites the words of The Lord's Prayer as fast as he can yet still manages to articulate every word perfectly.

'Our father, who art in heaven, hallowed be thy name; thy kingdom come; thy will be done; on earth as it is on heaven. Give us this day our daily bread, and forgive us our trespasses, as we forgive those who trespass against us. Lead us not into temptation, but deliver us from evil. For the kingdom, the power and the glory are yours, now and forever. Amen.'

The cube begins to spin and the violet light illuminates the darkness all around them. He holds the sword high up in the air with two hands. And then sees an abysmal sight indeed ... The light reveals dozens upon dozens of disgusting, grey, little goblin-like creatures coming from behind and in front. The creatures' eyes reflect the violet light and all have forked tongues that dangle loosely from their mouths, which writhe as if they had a life of their own. The creatures are all covered in a strange, slimy liquid, so a repulsive moist sound is heard whenever they rub up against each other in their tightly-packed hordes. The heads of these creatures are small and their bellies fat and bloated, covered in boils and growths. But what stood out the most about these little demons was the size of their hands: each were the size of their bodies, and sprouting from them were six razor-sharp talons that rattled against each other, causing a similar sound to that of deer locking horns.

The feral demons are at first stunned by the violet glow, slowing down their movements and putting their mammoth hands up over their little pin heads. But the light itself is not enough to stop them, and they continue to push forward, trapping the brothers in a pincer movement from behind and in front. The brothers stand back to back as the demons advance.

'You're going to have to attack them. I'm just waiting to die here,' Jack says, turning his head slightly towards his brother.

Arthur charges forward courageously. He swings the glowing blade in front of the beasts in a show of force. As the violet-glowing blade swooshes through the air, it produces an awesome crackling sound, comparable to a fighter jet. The very sound causes some of the demons to back off; however, one of them decides to attack and leaps at Arthur, claws first, to try and strike his face. Arthur reacts quickly and slices off the demon's hand with one swift cut, like a knife through soft butter. The energy from the violet blade lingers on the demon's flesh and burns it like holy fire. The demon squeals and falls to the floor, writhing in agony as it completely dissolves into a burning slag of molten violet. Meanwhile, this first attack had set off a violent chain reaction in the others. The demons begin circling the brothers and launch themselves at Arthur, who is now finding a rhythm with the sword and slices through them, one by one.

'I think they are about to come for me!' Jack screams as the monsters close in on him.

'I got them!' Arthur replies, as he adopts an attacking stance.

Arthur is now loosening up, looking lighter and more in flow. He feels a great spirit inside him; he feels calm, light and relaxed. The demons now try to attack en masse, pushing harder and harder, but Arthur swings his blade and cuts through them with ease. He had no idea that the blade was this powerful; it was making such light work of these seemingly pathetic demons.

The creatures try to sneak up behind him, but whenever they do, Arthur is so alert and in tune with his feelings that he senses their presence with ease and cuts them down. He is beginning to move around with grace and confidence, and Jack can't help but stare at his brother in awe, unable to believe his brother could be capable of such combat. Arthur notices a demon making its way for Jack. The demon launches from behind, forcing Jack to fall flat on his face. The demon lets out a dramatic squeal and raises its giant clawed hand behind Jack's neck. Out of the centre of its hand, a small hole opens and a little writhing worm-like spike slides out, dripping with a dark yellow fluid. At this moment, Arthur is about five or so metres away from Jack. He sees no other choice but to throw the sword at the demon. He launches the glowing blade. It rips through the air and impales the demon's little pin head, almost dead centre. Arthur rushes over to Jack on the floor and holds out a hand to help him back to his feet, but there are still five demons lurking around them, albeit now less eager to attack. Jack gets back to his feet as Arthur rips the sword from the creature's skull.

'Finish them!' Jack shouts.

But the time the sword had spent out of Arthur's hand had deactivated it; the six colours still shone, but the violet did not. Arthur begins to panic; all this work he had done, killing dozens of these creatures, only to be finished off by the last five! He strikes one of the demons through the claw, albeit with less confidence and conviction as he showed before. The claw is sliced clean off; however, the demon does not melt with the molten violet as the others had done before. The demons' groans and growls become more enthusiastic as they see their chance to subdue the brothers. They begin to close in, tightening their circle around the brothers. The demons all hold their hands out in front, allowing the hole in the centre of their hands to open to once again reveal the yellow, dripping spikes. The brothers, losing confidence, both start showing signs of distress. The demons see this on their faces and feed off this lack of belief. In this moment of tension, the faces of the demons become clear. They are mostly grey and wrinkly crevices, almost like an old human man but scrunched to the size of a clenched fist. They all seem to be smiling in a twisted pleasure.

'Attack them! What are you waiting for?!' Jack shouts again.

Arthur waves his blade chaotically, desperately and carelessly. His movements are low in energy and lacking the same grace he possessed before. One of the creatures seizes this opportunity and launches itself at Excalibur. Arthur is forced to let go of the sword, fearing his hand would be sliced clean off. The creature launches itself off the side, into the abyss, apparently sacrificing itself kamikaze style. The brothers are plunged into near complete darkness, the only light coming from the glowing red cave opening and the six beams of light rapidly falling into the abyss.

Arthur's and Jack's faces fill with dread. But then …

A beam of white light shoots down into the darkness. The beam is as fast as lightning, but it quickly returns to the top of the hill; not as a sharp beam, but as a floating and glistening body of beauty. The source of this white light radiates around a person.

Áine.

She hovers above and Excalibur attaches to her glowing aura with magical force, levitating in front of her. Her radiating light makes much of the black abyss glow white.

The remaining demons are stunned by this glistening angel. She holds out her hand in front of the sword, and the cube itself begins to charge and spin up. The sword activates its violet form and then, with a seamless, flowy transition, Áine shoots the charged sword directly into the hands of Arthur. He instinctively slams the sword into the ground in one motion, in front of the remaining demons. The sword causes a bright violet explosion which completely obliterates all the remaining creatures, turning them all into molten goo.

Áine lands on the path, glowing with angelic beauty. Her white translucent wings spread wide and her eyes glow large and pure. Both brothers are awestruck, their mouths wide; lost for words completely.

3. THE CATACOMBS OF THE POSSESSED

Arthur cannot help but smile to himself as he sheaths his sword to his waist. He feels the muscles around his face tighten with warmth and contentment. Ever since seeing that light up the hill, he had a nagging feeling that it was in his mother. Jack, however, looks shaken, and even quite disturbed.

'Mum?' Jack says softly, with childish disbelief.

Áine holds a calm and radiant smile but does not reply.

By this point, Jack's face has turned white, and he looks almost catatonic. 'I never thought I would see you again,' he says.

Jack walks towards her, and Arthur follows behind him.

'I tried to make contact with you, many times. But your heart was closed, my love. Your soul has been detached for such a long time,' she says.

'I know it has. And I'm so sorry,' Jack says with a quivering voice, close to tears, looking down in shame. 'If I knew I could have connected with you, I doubt I would have gone down the path I did.'

Áine walks towards him until she is standing directly in front of him. She puts her hand on the side of his face. He looks up at her, and they look into each other's eyes. A tear streams down his face.

'What you went through …' Áine says, her tone soft and her eyes piercing, '… what you both went through was enough to push any heart to the extreme. For you, Jack, it hardened it to the point of stone. For you, Arthur, it softened it to putty. Do not feel guilty that you were misled, for that guilt has already hit where it was needed. It has now been cleansed with light. But darling, it is true; I tried so hard to connect with you. I reached out to you in your dreams; but even then, you put barriers in my way. I saw it all happen; I saw your descent from the very beginning, and I tried so hard to keep you afloat, I really did. I did everything in my power to prevent you from falling into the darkness. But this darkness which enveloped you was not normal. I am a mere lower angel, and whilst I have powers to intervene in earthly matters, I am no match for the pull of such great evil. The evil you were involved with, Jack, it is powered by forces that come straight from the lord of darkness himself. I couldn't bear to see you fall, and my heart bled from heaven; I knew you would never pray or connect with the Lord and ask for his help. So in my desperation, I asked the great father himself to have mercy on you;

371

and he agreed that you would be given a chance to redeem yourself. Thankfully, Jack, you have people around you who care and love for you deeply.'

'I have now seen the task set for me. I have no denial left in me,' Jack says with the same quivering voice, full of bitter-sweet sadness. 'I have accepted it willingly. Much to Arthur's grief ...' He turns back to look at Arthur, who takes in a big breath of air.

'Is this true, Mum? What he says about having to sacrifice himself for Dad?' Arthur adds with his head down, looking up through his eyebrows.

'Only Jack himself knows what is true and what he must do. He was given a taste of the Holy Spirit, and that spirit is always there within him as guidance. It is up to him only to choose what he does, or what to believe is right for him. I will not influence his thoughts or actions. All I will say is this. Christ is watching both of you with great contentment. He is within you both, acting as an ever-present guiding light.'

Arthur's shoulders jolt, and he turns to look behind him.

'What's that?' he says, his attention caught by a faint booming drumbeat coming from the red glowing cave.

'Stand close to me,' Áine says calmly.

The brothers stand close to her, and she holds her palms face down to the ground.

The trio begin to hover, rising up into the darkness above.

They keep on rising, yet the drumbeats keep on getting louder and louder from below. A feeling of warmth, contentment and protection arises inside Arthur and Jack; the same cosy feeling when inside a warm house during a lightning storm.

Áine's aura light then fades intentionally to avoid being sighted.

'Pass me the blade, I need to dull it,' Áine says.

Arthur passes Excalibur to her, still sheathed. She holds her hands over the cube, which is still faintly emitting the six colours, and dims the light completely. She passes it back to him.

They all look down to see what emerges from the cave. They see a battalion of darkened troops emerge, led by a familiar character.

'It's the same man as before!' Arthur exclaims in a whisper.

'Are you sure? He's wearing black robes, though,' Jack replies.

'That there is a Draxler,' Áine says softly. 'They are the loyal servants of the six princes of hell, ultimately all subordinate to Satan himself. They are known to shapeshift; to trick and deceive, appearing as friend at first when really they are foe. They are very cunning and command battalions of demons.'

'His movements, I could tell they looked familiar …' Arthur adds.

And Áine was right. Behind this Draxler were many tall, muscular troops. They looked more focused and deadly than any the brothers encountered previously. They moved in a much more human way; that is, in an upright, postured manner. Their skin looked burnt, and they had ripped flesh in varying places, which was peeling off. Many of them were missing some of the skin on their faces, exposing their back teeth and yellowish bone underneath. The hands and feet of these demons were webbed like reptiles, and each of them had a black, barbed tail. They all carried a variety of different tools and weapons: metal spiked drums, maces, swords and nets with lead balls attached to them.

The Draxler commander led the entirety of these troops, around 100, out of the cave to the centre of the path.

'Fear not! I am Hazlot!' the Draxler shouted loudly from below, looking all around for the hiding brothers. 'I am the same guide who spoke to you formerly. I have been sent by the true lord, and so please take my drum-beating arrival only as an honour to him. Follow me, children, I will take you to the true lord, so prepare yourselves to feel great awe!'

The Draxler commander begins walking further down the path, away from his troops.

'You should be excited, for is it not the glory of heaven you seek? Oh, your faces will shine with bliss when you witness the glory of it! Oh, the glory! Come, come out, I will show you the way!'

'What do we do?' Jack asks in a worried whisper.

'I don't feel confident in fighting them, there's too many …' Arthur adds.

'We sneak into the cave from behind,' Áine says. 'I'll put a light field between the path and the cave's entrance; it will block any of them from following us, at least long enough for us to escape.'

'Okay, that sounds like plan. I'm ready,' Arthur says. 'Jack, are you?' Jack warily nods in agreement.

In a flash of light, Áine lowers them to the entrance of the red cave, and they all cross the threshold immediately after landing. The descending flash immediately catches the attention of the Draxler, and he instantly reacts by flying over his troops using black wings that suddenly and violently sprout from his back. He swoops like a hawk down to towards the cave entrance, but Áine holds her hand out, and a sheet of light radiates from it and covers the cave entrance completely. The Draxler hits this field of light head on and bounces straight off it, tumbling and rolling on the ground. The powerful demon does not stay on the floor for long however, getting back to his feet to look at the trio face to face.

The Draxler smiles as he stands, not showing any signs of embarrassment or shame. He begins laughing and walks towards the light field.

'You think you will survive long in this realm?' he says with an exaggerated grin.

Arthur walks out from behind Áine and looks him in the eye.

'Long enough to complete our task,' he says, tightening his jaw in a bold display of courage.

Hazlot starts laughing deeply from the belly.

'So pure, so innocent, so sweet and tender; oozing down to us, drip by drip; oh, great Cubus, take these souls at once!' The Draxler mashes and clatters his teeth, smiling at Arthur as if he was indeed a fine fruit about to be eaten.

The demon commander contorts his eyes inwards towards his nose and opens his mouth. A thin, red forked tongue emerges, sliding further and further outside his mouth. It keeps coming, and the Draxler tilts his head in a taunting way. The tongue keeps descending until it reaches the floor, writhing around like a snake. Still in this odd position, mouth gaping open, the Draxler laughs to himself once again, immediately setting off chains of laughter from his battalion behind him, who do so with unfazed confidence.

'Come on, let's leave the madness,' Áine says as she walks away from the light field and deeper into the cave system.

Jack quickly and closely follows her, yet Arthur moves away from the demons more slowly, holding gazes with Hazlot for a little longer. It is true he is scared, but he is also fascinated. The more he looks into the eyes of this monstrosity of a lifeform, the more he feels pity for him. He sees behind the eyes of Hazlot a tormented soul, an empty soul, a soul that has no real purpose other than gaining meaningless pleasure by inflicting pain and suffering, devoid of any real meaning or purpose. Arthur thinks to himself, *He inflicts pain; he worships this as his highest value, but why is giving pain for the sake of it so important to him? It seems so important to many, but why? Could it be the very fact that these demons have*

never used pain to improve themselves, but instead have time and time again fell in mean-
ingless love with it, to no real end? It's like when Ishmael read The Devil's Diary *to*
me: he spoke of the six days of work and six days of pain; but pain with no meaning or
depth, no end or goal; pain that has no fulfilment or hope in victory or accomplishment.
Is it the number of these beasts, 666, that really means pure pain, but never with hope?
That is the worst pain I can think of; to endure pain with no hope. I suppose crazed
laughter would be the only release ... 'As Arthur thinks this, and carries on staring
into Hazlot's eyes, Hazlot shifts his demeanour and seems to stop laughing as
intensely. He instead looks a little angry and more aggressive. Arthur squints
curiously at this noticeable shift, and continues to back off whilst still locking
gazes until he is completely out of sight behind the first corner of the cave.

Áine leads them deeper and deeper into this glowing red catacomb system. The tunnels glow this dark red from no clear source; it is as if the red
glow is part of the very essence of the tunnels themselves. The tunnels split
off at various crossroads, yet Áine leads with confidence and doesn't even
falter or hesitate as she moves. The path once again slopes upwards, but only
slightly. This goes on for approximately 10 minutes, during which time the
brothers blindly put their confidence in their angel mother.

'You know this place like the back of your hand. I thought you were an
angel living in heaven?' Arthur asks with a light-hearted and playful tone.
Áine looks back and smiles at him softly, and then pretends to claw him like
a demon by swiping a hand through the air.

'I've never been here before, actually. I'm simply allowing the Lord to
guide me through the Holy Spirit. I have no fear of these demons you see;
I encourage you both to have no fear either. They thrive off your lack of
belief; it is this that gives them life and energy.'

'Where are we going, then?' Jack asks, now sounding a little bit demoralized and fed up.

'Somewhere painful, but necessary,' she says.

'Great ...' Jack says sarcastically with a small smile, but also with an undertone of irritability.

'Come on, mate. I know all of this is mad; but see it as an adventure!'

'I know, I know; I'm fine, don't worry. I'm just a bit shaken by it all. I
don't mean to put a negative spin on the situation, I just don't know how to
cope with all this. At least I'm being honest with you about how I'm feeling.' Jack raises his eyebrows as if to say, 'Please, work with me here.'

Arthur nods, and looks his brother up and down, realising that he is actually proud of who Jack has become.

'Oh, definitely; but please, Jack, don't mistake me, I mean this in a light-hearted way. So far, we have done so well together, and I feel we are already close to finishing this. Already I know that Dad would be proud of both the men we have become.'

'Well, I know Dad is going to see you both very soon,' Áine says. 'And the way that you will make him feel when he sees you will give him more energy and spirit than words alone ever could.'

Áine suddenly stops in her tracks after finishing her sentence. She holds her hand up in the air, and then edges around a corner, slowly, and stares down it carefully.

'A demon?' Jack asks with a panicked whisper.

'No. Something even more unfortunate,' she says as she turns her head back. She begins walking forward again, this time a lot slower and more casually, as if something ahead was worth acknowledging. The boys follow behind.

Around the corner, the brothers see a change in surroundings completely. The cave walls are no longer rocky, and the light has shifted to a warm yellow, albeit only dimly. It is coming from electric lamps illuminating paintings and pictures below along a corridor, the sort you would find in an old English manor house. There are black and white tiles on the floor and the walls are patterned wood, with brick painted green above. At the very end of the corridor, hung up on the wall, is a ram's head looking down the corridor as if it were keeping an eye at arriving visitors. Below it is a peculiar little plastic Wendy house, with a red roof, beige walls and a little yellow door.

'This corridor has a horrible energy to it,' Arthur says immediately as he is hit by a feeling of cold dread. He thought he could even smell a subtle hint of burning flesh, but this was only for a moment.

'Very bizarre,' Jack adds.

Áine walks over to the closest painting and inspects it. It is an oil painting, but the oils flow as if they are alive, morphing and contorting; the observer can never capture the exact details due to the movements, but the general spirit of the artwork can still be seen; it clearly shows a man rushing around an English pub, clearing plates and glasses and pouring drinks. She notices a plaque below the painting, and begins reading it out loud:

'My name is Jeffrey Lee. Here I am, always working in my bar; day in, day out. I hate working here, but I have been trapped here, at the mercy of my lord Satan, and at the mercy of his passions and pleasures. I do not know I am trapped, because I still believe I am free to live a normal life on earth, but this is only because I have been tricked by the lord of tricksters. He has convinced me I am free, but all my decisions bring me closer to him. I have no escape. I will never be able to leave this place, even though I may tell myself I can at any time. I will work here until I die; and I will die full of regret and heavy conscience. Like a lead balloon. This heavy conscience will drag me all the way down to hell. Forever my heart will be possessed by the king of the dark angels. My soul is slowly being squeezed, drop by drop, into the hands of my lord below. And there is nothing I can do about it.'

'That's horrible …' Arthur says as he turns to look at his spirit mother and Jack with a face full of disgust. 'Surely there is an angel that can help wake him up from his endless trance?'

'So this guy is still on earth?' Jack asks whilst frowning and turning to his mother.

'I believe this place is a sort of gallery of the possessed. All the paintings and objects we see here represent a soul that is not yet in the real *metaphysical* hell, but is instead in a *metaphorical* hell on earth. The souls here have been tainted, cursed or possessed by demonic spirits. These spirits come to them in psychological ways, posing as emotions, temptations, complexes; and they make it hard for that individual to be free, and to live their life in a way that their soul actually desires. This place seems to be projected and materialised dream energy from earth. This is not hell, but is more like a sort of nether region … A void where unbounded chaos can accumulate like lost radio signals.'

'Like a dreamcatcher?' Arthur asks with a childish smile.

Jack and Áine laugh lightly.

'That's a good way to put it. But yes, this Jeffrey here, I'm sure he does have an angel who is helping him in ways they can. However, like me, personal angels can only do so much. In situations like his, he needs help from something greater. He must connect with the source of all light within him; and only then will he be liberated and able to free enough energy to take responsibility, and follow and live in accordance with his conscience.'

After both the brothers take a few moments to process what Áine said, Arthur turns his head down the corridor to look at the little plastic Wendy house and begins walking towards it.

'But we really should keep moving ...' Áine says, noticing the brothers getting distracted.

Arthur hears Áine say this, but he cannot help but investigate the play house. He stares down at it, and inside him he feels a subtle dread that he can't quite explain. As he stands closely and directly in front, he puts out his hand and touches the roof of the house. He is immediately surprised, and even takes a jolted step back as he hears a sound coming from the ram head above. The ram's mouth opens with a oddly organic sound, a sort of cracking. This immediately catches the attention of Áine and Jack too. Once the mouth fully opens, a disproportionately large tongue drops out.

'Say hello to Ryan Stanford!' says a strangely young-sounding voice coming from the ram's head, the mouth even moving along with the words. The voice is rather robotic, and has the accent of a young American lady. 'Ryan doesn't know it, but his soul has been turned into this inanimate object! Every day, he sits in his home, his home that his mother pays for. He never animates himself; he instead relies on his mother to animate his life for him. So now his soul has in-animated itself, and become this house! He has no real purpose or meaning. He simply sits, as safe as houses! He plays his games, he plays with himself, he plays like the little child he is. All he has is pleasure and fun! The pleasure a child might get from playing in a Wendy house! So now his soul has found this house, forever to be its home!'

'Is it weird that I can tell this house has a male spirit from just looking at it?' Arthur says whilst focusing intently on the house, surprisingly unbothered by the audio description.

'Part of him really does exist in this house,' Áine says. 'He may even spend hours there in dreams. But he is very much unaware of this. Even for someone in a dream. Come on now, boys, we must continue to focus on the task.' Áine turns left round the corner and continues to lead the brothers once again.

The corridor they move into now is the same style yet much longer. In fact, it stretches as far as the eye can see, with only a faint blob of black at the very end. This corridor, too, has many artefacts, paintings, furniture of all sorts, hats, clothes. All sorts of random assortments. As our trio walk down it, they occasionally glance at each other, knowing all too well these objects have some sort of unfortunate story …

'So can I just confirm, Mum,' Jack says from behind, trying to not fall too far back, 'Is this or is this not hell?'

'I am taking you there. You will know when we have crossed over to the other side, I promise you that. We are close, but we are not there. Yet, as you know, evil spirits roam and guard these parts, so we must continue to be careful.' She then stops abruptly and holds her arms to her sides, facing her palms up, and closes her eyes.

'Yes …' she says, as she opens her eyes and looks back at the brothers over her shoulder. 'We are not far at all. At the end of this corridor, in fact.' She carries on leading, now with an even brisker walk.

Arthur continues to follow closely behind Áine, but then notices Jack has been distracted by something, which completely stops him in his tracks.

'Jack?!' Arthur shouts from in front. 'Are you okay? We can't keep getting distracted.'

Jack doesn't respond. He stares at this artefact, completely transfixed, his face empty and apathetic.

'Hold on, Mum, I think this is something,' Arthur says.

Áine looks down to the floor. A sad expression crosses her face: a look of helplessness, but also a look of accepting the inevitable.

'What is it, mate?' Arthur says as he puts his hand on Jack's upper back.

Arthur then looks at what Jack is staring at. He sees a black marble statue of a man wearing a black suit with horns on his head and a devilish smirk on his face. In his left hand, he holds a lead, which connects to a collar on a dog. On closer inspection, the brother's notice the dog has a human face, and one that looks awfully familiar …

Dread runs through Arthur. He has seen this man before: Harry Sickle. It is also clear to Arthur now that the face of the dog is that of Jack.

'Don't let it torment you,' Arthur says softly, after sharing a brief moment of silence. 'His possession over you has been broken; it's done, it's in the past.'

Jack shakes his head and looks down at the floor. He then tilts his head to look up at the ceiling, bites his bottom lip, and breathes out exasperated.

'Come on.' Arthur puts his arm around him and prises his focus away from the dark statue. They both continue to follow Áine further down the corridor.

4. THE CHAMBER OF ROUND CHAOS

The walk to the end of the corridor was quite miserable, and lasted about 15 minutes. Nothing at all was said in this time, but the general tone of negativity among the group was impossible to ignore. At least, this was the case between Arthur and Jack. Áine just kept leading without turning back once. And to the surprise of the brothers, this corridor really did have an end and wasn't merely a devilish illusion.

And at the end was a rather alien-looking door. It was not completely flush with the surrounding walls either: it bulged out crookedly and did not have well-defined corners. The door had various contortions that glimmered in differing colours and a popping texture that looked very crystalline. It was unlike any normal door but instead looked more like an organic opening. It had a rounded yet sharp crystalline chunk to pull on instead of a handle. The door was not completely inanimate but instead possessed a certain kind of living fluidity to it; it was as if it was moving inside itself, contorting and folding subtly.

'I don't understand this door,' Jack says whilst shaking his head.

'Neither do I,' Arthur follows. 'It gives me the feeling that there is literally more to it than meets the eye, but my eyes can only see so much of it. I feel as if my brain is receiving many more signals than my eyes can handle …'

'Well, yes, Arthur,' Áine replies, 'that's because it is. This is the door to the first region of hell. And I'm afraid that hell in its pure form cannot be processed by the human mind.'

The brothers both turn to look at her with deep curiosity.

'Imagine it like this: across this door is the centre of the gas giant Saturn. Human beings can never experience Saturn's inner climate, or appreciate it with the senses, because its chaos is simply far too tremendous. Even just for one second, just one glance inside; that alone would be far too much to handle.'

'Are you saying hell is inside Saturn?' Jack asks with a sly smirk.

'You can both decide that for yourself. However, through this door is the completely unbounded chaos of hell. The chaos is of a dimension that is uninterpretable to you, and your human bodies will be immediately destroyed, starting with your minds. As I am an angelic spirit, I can enter, and I can slow down the chaos, giving you both a chance to enter without being spiritually ripped apart. Inside here should be a safe chamber where you, Arthur, can bring the forces of order into alignment with the chaos.'

'Using the glow?' he asks.

'Yes. But you must act swiftly, as you only have a small window to use it; I will only be able to keep the chaos from spinning for a short while. This period of conversion should give your unconscious minds time to assimilate the hell chaos into consciousness safely, without causing complete interior destruction.'

Áine pauses for a moment and looks at her sons' worried faces. She notices Arthur's face in particular; that, along with the worry, is a curious look that she had seen in him many a time before.

'How are you so focused, Mum?' he asks. 'Never on earth were you like this. It's almost like you have more of Dad in you, more masculinity, yet you are still as gentle and light as when you were a normal human.'

'My love,' she says, as she gently entices him in for an embrace. Arthur wraps his arms around her light body and underneath her lightly glowing wings. 'You forget I am no longer a human like you. I know I look human, but now I am very different,' she says as she pulls away, her face warming while she smiles, her aura even glowing brighter than before. 'It is true, I am still similar. But now, I can see far further and far deeper into things. I see more pathways, more potential. I see all the successes but also the failures and suffering too. My soul has been given more depth, it has been gifted expansion, it has been freed from the shackles of human flesh and allowed to become more harmonised with divine balance. Now, *I can love more than I did before.* But this depth of love comes at a price. I have been gifted this greater love because it has been decided by the great father that my soul can handle it. However, I am not God and cannot see everything. Only God can experience ultimate love without being overwhelmed and destroyed. I cannot see inside your minds, and I don't know exactly what will happen on the other side of this door. However, I see all the potentialities of what *may happen,* and that means I see all the failures too.'

'So, do we have need for worry?' Jack asks slowly.

'There is always need for worry. There is a reason you have that ability in the first place. But more importantly, there is a larger reason to hope.' She pauses, and the brothers continue to stare at her in captivation. 'Now please stand back.

I'm going to open this door, stand in the middle and slow the chaos down. You will then both enter, one after the other. And then, Arthur, you will begin to focus your energy into the cube. Inside, I will be honest with you, it will not be an easy task to focus the cube, as the chaos around will be great. But you must know that *you can do it*; but more importantly, *you must do it.*'

Áine turns away from the brothers and faces the door.

'Stand back a bit; you're not going to want to stare too deeply inside before I slow everything down.' The brothers both walk down the corridor for 10 or so metres.

She pulls the handle. The door opens slowly, and with a certain thickness, as if it was a far larger and heavier door. As soon as it cracks open, a yellow light floods into the corridor. She opens the door fully and a thick, almost molten, substance fills the space completely. To the brothers, it looked as if this light was a sort of plasma. Within this plasma were fragments, contortions, spirals, pulses, mandala-like imagery, artefacts of all differing mathematical proportions; all whizzing and swirling around at great speed within the molten light substance. What lay on the other side of this door was indeed something truly otherworldly and utterly chaotic. Even just glancing from a distance, it did not make sense at all to either Jack or Arthur. But this alien chaos scared them to their core, far more than even the monsters on the hill from earlier, causing them both to freeze in place.

Áine walks towards the plasma and is sucked into it completely, vanishing from the sight of the brothers. The boys' continue to stare forward as a tension grows between them, knowing one of them must do or say something; but even Arthur at this point was feeling more overwhelmed than he ever had in his entire life.

'I can't go in there …' Jack says after the extended period of silence. 'I can't. Mum didn't rule out the fact that we could fail, and there's no guarantee whatever is going on in there won't swallow us up completely. Who knows what will happen to us? It might be the most painful thing imaginable, we might go mad for the rest of eternity, we just don't know! Arthur, I think we should just go back. Surely you can use the sword to go back? This whole journey is complete madness!'

Arthur takes a moment to breathe, and then turns his head slowly to Jack and says, 'Calm down, mate. It's fine.' Although he is trying very hard himself to stay calm, the worry in his voice betrays him.

'It's not fine! You know it's not! You also know full well that Mum is not like she was! She's not a human anymore, she said it herself! Can we even call her Mum anymore?! Can we even trust her? Is she even real? Have I gone mad? You know what? I can't tell! I can't tell! I just can't handle all this anymore!' I can't, Arthur! I can't!' Jack says as he becomes more and more hysterical, finally breaking down completely into tears. He collapses into Arthur's embrace and frantically cries, almost screaming, into his shoulder. He continues to sob 'I can't! I can't!' as Arthur squeezes him back tightly.

As Arthur embraces his frantic brother, a tear runs down his face. He puts his tongue to the side of his cheek in a sign of stress. He is trying with all his spirit to keep calm and not to lose control. He knows he's being tested, but he also knows failure is not an option.

Arthur then pushes Jack off him abruptly.

'Centre yourself, Brother! Focus! See the whole picture here! Have you forgotten? You're going to die! You know you're going to die; you saw it yourself in your vision, and you accepted it. Why now are you suddenly breaking down?!'

Jack's red, teary face looks at his brother in confusion.

'Exactly. I see it in your face,' Arthur continues. 'And I get it, I understand. This is the reality of human nature. We know what we must do, and it is all so clear to us in our moments of peace and clarity. So we make this decision beforehand to accept that it will be hard, and we tell ourselves we must do it; but then the time actually comes and life plays tricks on us, just at the very moment when you don't need to be tricked. It is these tricks that lead us to see things in a distorted way. Don't allow these tricks to control you and distract you from your end goal! Even if that end goal or purpose is the ultimate sacrifice! We know what we must do, we know we have a purpose, so we must have faith that whatever power gave us this purpose actually wants us to achieve it! The power is in our own hands, it's only a matter of belief! It's only the tricks themselves that convince us to choose otherwise! Now, have you been tricked? Or are you coming? Because I want to have some fun! So let's go to the other side, and let's experience what no one else has ever experienced! Life is short, we might as well live it magically! On the other side of fear is a new life! And Jack,' he pauses, 'I choose new life!' He leans his head forward as he says this final phrase, and then runs away from his brother and towards the plasma. Looking from the outside, the spinning motion inside is now slower than before, and the artefacts and patterns are now moving in slow motion. As Arthur runs down the corridor, he rips Excalibur from its sheath and holds it out at his side like a warrior. He enters the plasma without looking back, and he too, like Áine, disappears into the glowing yellow void.

'Fuck!' Jack shouts through gritted teeth.

He shakes his head, and his upper cheeks tighten like a wild beast. He, too, then sprints towards the entrance, screaming at the top of his lungs as he gets close.

Jack enters through the yellow plasma and is blinded by utter chaos: powerful patterns and geometry of unintelligible proportions assault his senses, tormenting him with their bizarreness; he has no words or logic to make sense of it. The moment he steps through, he is taken away by a whirlwind of force; even though Áine had clearly slowed down the chaos, it was still tremendous and oppressive. Every couple of seconds he would see a bit of her refract through the atmosphere, yet during his spins the environment around him seemed to mirror and fold inside itself. He would catch glimpses of a foot up high, an arm down low, and then he would catch Arthur's cheek randomly whizz in front of his eyes. He could not comprehend this at all; it was overwhelming him, and he was in utter horror. He was spinning around and around and could do nothing to control what was happening; fear and panic like he had never felt gripped him. He could not see anything properly, and he could feel the thick plasma all over his body, like a sort of electric jelly: not painful, yet alive, smothering and forceful. He could still breathe, though there was a massive pressure on his chest, making it *so much harder.*

'Arthur!' he tried shouting. But the sound didn't formulate properly, and all that came out was a muffled scream.

After a while of this he didn't even feel like he was spinning anymore; in fact, he couldn't even feel his own body. He tried putting his hands out in front him, but all he could see was his fingers spread all over the place, in places they shouldn't be. At one point his fingers even turned into something akin to jellied pitchforks. This image disgusted him, so he quickly put his hands back down. In his utter dissociation, he remembered that his brother had a task here: to put this chaos into habitable order, to formulate this *dissolved* world into something *solid.* This suddenly relieved his pain, eased his worry and gave him *hope.*

Arthur breathed. He closed his eyes. Yet even now, with his eyes shut and his focus on his breath, he could not escape the sensations and the effects on his thought processes. It quickly became clear to Arthur that this place was not a mere physical shift; whatever this plasma was, it had a real spirit to it. It really did seem to Arthur that wherever he was, there was life all around him; and this life was loud and invasive. He gripped the sword's handle tightly with both his hands in front of him. However, he felt he couldn't grip it well and true. The sword simply didn't feel solid like it usually did; it felt like it could slip out at any moment. The handle pulsed, wiggled and slid inside his palm; it was also becoming hotter and hotter, and then colder and colder, slithering inside his palm like melting butter. Arthur could not even see the blade, nor the cube; he was relying on feel alone.

'But you must know that *you can do it*; but more importantly, *you must do it*.' The words of his mother echoed through his mind, the image of her face flickering through it too.

'I can do it, I can do it, I can do it,' he tried to say. But, like Jack, these words came out his mouth distorted. He tried thinking the words instead, but even then they distorted themselves.

But then he calmed himself, and instead tried to experience the chaos fully. He decided not fight it, but to let go. His reality was beginning to break down, and this reality was making his psyche dissolve along with it. In this realm, it seemed there was no distinction between the interior and exterior worlds. He even realised that inside himself, his thoughts could manifest themselves in the exterior chaos that whizzed around him; although he could not tell if this was a mere illusion or a true physical reality. Nonetheless, he tried to accept what he was feeling and focus this chaos into and through his hands, through the handle and into the cube.

But then he notices something. An artefact floats towards him. Instead of whizzing straight past him like the others, this image holds itself in front of him steadily, as if it were somehow intended for him. The image is an oak tree. And this tree is *alive,* and rushes through its cycle, gaining momentum and speed. This tree would lose its leaves, all to then flourish once again, all in front of his eyes. The cycle of the tree carries on through the seasons, through autumn to spring, continuing to grow higher. Arthur can see in front of his eyes the roots continue to grow down lower, and the branches continue to grow up higher. The tree keeps growing larger and larger until it finally reaches a grand height, and then begins to grow old and wither.

Acorns fall from the branches like rain.

Hundreds of squirrels come rushing in.

From all angles around the tree, these squirrels take the oak's acorns off the ground. The squirrels are rushing around everywhere, being the busybodies they are. Some bury their nuts in the ground for later, and others munch on them. But two squirrels forget about their buried nuts …

And these two nuts sprout into oak saplings. And the cycle begins again, now accelerating in speed. These two trees go through their entire life cycle in a flash: they drop their seeds, the squirrels come again and more saplings sprout. Thousands upon thousands of years of growth flicker in front of Arthur's eyes, and now he can't help but feel euphoric and in awe of this vision.

The oak trees carry on multiplying, and multiplying; stacking upon each other, tessellating into a massive, cohesive pattern everywhere around him. Just as he starts to feel overwhelmed, he notices something: the trees are beginning to join together, connecting into something unified.

They form one massive tree.

This tree fills a massive space in front him, towering over him like a skyscraper, stretching up into a seemingly never-ending void of yellow light. As he looks up, the tree's foliage seems to twist as if it was a man bending down to look at him.

From inside the tree, a ghostly figure emerges and stands parallel with the trunk. The figure towers over Arthur, looking down at him. The figure has a calm, strong and fatherly face. Yet the face also has a certain look of judgement. The spirit slowly raises a hand and holds it close to the ground, palm down to the floor. White light begins to radiate from the ghost, concentrating at the centre of his palm. The white light becomes brighter and brighter until the yellow light of before is completely vanquished.

The white light fades out, extinguished.

Everything around calms.

The whizzing chaos around is no more, and things once again are solid.

He feels the sword between his hands as it should be: strong and true.

Violet radiates from the cube and blade.

But he had only just noticed. He looks around and sees his mother where the tree was, in the middle of a circular room. They are in what looks like an organic hive, with circular grooves all around the edges and on the floor. Jack is at the opposite side of the room his face flushed and jaw slack.

5. TERRA STULTORUM

Áine holds her hands out in front of her and lowers them towards the floor slowly, as if to say 'Calm. You have done it.' Arthur then begins laughing and shaking his head. Jack's slack jaw slowly returns to normal and a smile finds its way onto his face; he walks towards his brother.

'Thank you,' he says as he hugs him tight.

'I got you, Jack.'

As the brothers embrace, Áine walks towards the light shining through into this circular, almost pot-shaped room and pokes her head out to look around outside.

'Terra Stultorum,' she says calmly, yet with a certain level of concern.

'Latin, right? Land of something …' Arthur says.

'Yes. It means the Land of Fools. This is the realm above the Land of Demons.

'What's that in Latin then?' Jack asks.

'Terra Daemonum,' Áine replies.

Arthur and Jack both laugh.

'Why does everything sound so much more dramatic in Latin?' Jack asks whilst still smiling.

'Come on, let's not dwell on it,' Arthur says as he walks out of the cave-like room.

Áine follows behind him, but stops briefly to look Jack in the eye. She puts her hand on his face and smiles. He looks at the floor briefly, and then follows too.

Outside the cave the climate is unlike anything found on earth. The surroundings in Terra Stultorum are like a desert, but there is no light source from a sun or the like, and the atmosphere above, what on earth would be called the sky, is instead a sort of self-illuminating yellow plasma. Not completely dissimilar to the plasma in the conversion chamber, however now it is thoroughly dispersed and nowhere near same concentration. The plasma has the same jelly-like texture to it, and it shoots and vibrates into itself, morphing and colliding up into the air. The ultimate effect is quite a translucent atmosphere, with little visibility of anything that may be above. The ground is yellow like a desert too, yet it is not at all like sand. Instead, the ground is rather sticky, like a gel, making walking extremely awkward.

The group look around at their surroundings, and even Áine seems fascinated at what she sees. Jack looks down at his feet, clearly annoyed at how his boots stick to the ground after every step; however, something interesting catches his eye.

'Have you noticed the floor turns red after you step on it?'

Arthur looks at the ground and also notices the phenomenon.

'Bizarre.'

There is little to see around them in terms of matter or objects, only a yellow abyss. At most they can only see 10 metres ahead of them due to the poor visibility. The trio scatter and walk around seemingly randomly, looking for a clue or signal to indicate where they must go next.

This random wandering carries on for about another 20 minutes before Arthur starts to feel an irrational panic encroach on him. It is as if he is a radio transmitter and has received something of a ghastly frequency.

'I feel very bad,' he says as he turns around quickly with a pounding heart and a face looking desperate.

'Calm, calm yourself, my son. You as my kindred will naturally pick up on the evil here; that sensitivity was of my own flesh on earth. Understand that this evil is simply the nature of lower realms, and something you have no choice but to contend with.'

'Where are we going then? Can't you guide us as you did before?' Jack asks, his voice quivering.

'I'm afraid I cannot,' Áine replies as her face drops with a sort of childish sadness. 'Here there exists such a dark spirit so powerful that it blocks many of the frequencies from heaven reaching us. I was guided by the Holy Spirit before, but now I alone cannot make a firm connection. The only way for us to get to the depths of hell and succeed now is to combine our energies together and *create a trinity*.'

'Well, let's put our energy into the cube,' Arthur follows. 'It is true, I feel I cannot summon enough energy alone. We must work together.'

'Okay, come on then. I think I'm starting to feel that same fear you're feeling ...' Jack adds.

Arthur pulls the sword from its sheath and propels the blade into the jellied floor. He wraps his hands around the blade.

'Come on,' he says.

The other two come over. Jack stands opposite, also wrapping his hand around the handle. Lastly, Áine walks towards them and stops a little further away. She reaches out just one hand, her right, and rests it gently and gracefully on the pommel of the sword.

They stand in silence, all feeling the stillness in the atmosphere, the subtle sounds around them becoming more apparent: a slight slobbering, the sound of semi-liquid matter colliding, causing gentle microcosmic waves through the atmosphere.

They close their eyes one after another.

More silence.

The cube spins and turns violet.

They open their eyes simultaneously. And all look a little shocked at how easy it was. They continue to hold on, intuitively feeling it is necessary. They feel the humming vibration reverberate through the handle, followed by the all-encompassing warmth. As the vibration peaks, a golden beam shoots out from the cube and into the open space next to them. They turn their heads to see where the beam goes, but they see nothing but the beam shooting into the depths of the yellow plasma.

The beam dissipates.

But they continue to stare in silent apprehension.

An outline.

Then another ... And another ...

These shadowy outlines look human in stature, but it soon becomes obvious that their movements are extremely unhuman, awkward and staggered.

'Keep holding on. Let the violet protect us,' Arthur says calmly.

The figures continue to move towards them until the closest one becomes fully visible.

A waddling, zombie-like entity, with arms open wide, approaches. There's a fixed grin on its greyish-white face, which holds a completely spiritless expression. The eyes are tightly shut, almost as if it were wearing a mask. The entity is completely naked, its skin very humanlike. However, the most significant trait to note was that the entity had a large, phallic-shaped mass protruding from its groin, and a vaginal-like hole below it. The sprouting mass is spiked with sharp, bony growths, yet flops around as if it is fleshy. These genital-like areas glimmer as if moist, and are slightly tinged in red and darkened with black dirt.

'Stulti,' Áine says, and the entity sharply turns its head, acutely reacting to her words. 'They cannot see, they can only hear and feel us. They will not harm us right now; they will be completely transfixed by the glow. It will be the only beauty they would have felt for God knows how long.'

'We can't keep up this forever,' Jack says with a fearful face.

'It's fine, I can hold it,' Arthur says whilst staring forward with intense focus.

He then picks up the sword from the ground and holds it in the air, slowly walking towards the closest Stult, which is now almost completely frozen in a trance. As Arthur comes directly in front of it, the Stult drops to its knees as if in awestruck worship, like a vagrant begging for water. Arthur rests the glowing blade on its shoulder and closes his eyes. His lips then begin moving silently and unintelligibly, and the Stult's head begins to rotate, swirl and shake.

Arthur maintains his focus on the Stult and calmly watches as it rises to its feet. The Stult then begins to walk away, and Arthur follows. He turns his head back to the other two and signals for them to follow; he is firmly holding his blade in his left hand, which is acting as a sort of torch. The other Stulti around notice, and they, like moths to light, begin to cling to the group, following them as if being led to some great treasure or fruit.

'What did you do?' Jack whispers as he walks closely behind, looking around at the Stulti anxiously.

'I transmitted an image from my imagination. I pictured the Land of Demons, and he reacted strongly to my signal; let's hope he can lead us there.'

'I never thought I would have actually hoped to be led to the Land of Demons ...'

Arthur turns back to face his brother, winks and says, 'That's the spirit.'

'It is true things are going to get slightly more interesting,' Áine says. 'But just know that you are both ready for this, and remember I am here as your guardian angel; and I will summon all the powers I can to help you.'

The brothers both look at her thankfully.

They carry on following the Stult for about 20 minutes, going deeper and deeper into the yellow abyss. They have now attracted even more Stulti hoverers; in fact, there are around 30 of them, and the group are beginning to feel a little apprehensive, albeit still calmed by the violet glow. The other Stulti that surround them are of differing skin colours and sizes. They also have different builds: some slender and female, others large and bulky. Regardless, all have the same fixed, closed-eyed grinning faces, and all have the same intersex genitalia.

'You hear that?' Jack says softly, as repetitive booming is heard in the distance.

'Those are some very deep drum beats,' Arthur replies.

The visibility had been improving for a while, and now they can see far further ahead than they could before. A large, crudely built, big top-like structure comes into view ahead. The outside is rather beige in colour, likely made from skin, partly smothered in a blotchy red liquid, likely blood. At the very top, the skin contorts unsymmetrically into a kind of tunnelled chimney shape, that faces away from the direction they are coming from.

The booming continues to get louder as they approach.

'The Stulti make up the shallowest and least evil part of hell,' Áine says, noticing Jack becoming increasingly anxious. 'They are low-frequency beings: low in awareness and low in love. They lived foolish lives on earth, living without competence, never thinking about their actions, acting inappropriately, chaotically; allowing their stupidity and foolishness to affect others and to, ultimately, pave the way for true evil to flourish. The demons of hell have not much use for these beings, as they lack spirit, so they are instead banished to the surrounding regions, captivated by never-ending, entrancing beats. As you likely noticed, they live in hermaphroditic bodies, which is a deformed representation of the eternal balanced energies of God. A natural consequence, when a spirit does not recognise the Holy Spirit on earth, it will, by nature of projection, worship hermaphroditism as a sort of shadow compensation for the repression of the God spirit. The Stulti now, quite literally, live in the shadow of the Lord.'

The drum beats continue to become clearer and clearer until the group feels the thumping in their chests. In the distance, surrounding the big top, they begin to see Stulti who had not yet become entranced by the violet light. These entities move far faster than the ones in close proximity, and far more wildly too. To the right of the big top, a group of three Stulti take it in turns to chop off each other's penile chunks with a crudely made bone sword. Strangely, the penile mass would grow back shortly after, and the Stult would offer it to be chopped off once again. This cycle continued mechanically, as if it was a game they played for fun. To the left side of the big top, there are multiple other Stulti engaging in various primitive and savage sexual acts. The sight causes the group, especially Arthur, to feel quite disgusted. What Arthur found particularly unnerving was how no sound was made from the sex at all. Regardless, this rampant fucking didn't last long, because as soon as our group approached the skin-flap opening of the big top, the dirty deeds stopped as the Stulti became perplexed by the glow instead.

The group and their stragglers enter the big top and note the booming beats originate from various Stulti on large, bloodied skin drums that hang around their necks. Other Stulti can be seen 'dancing' (more like chaotic flailing) to the beat. Others are seen engaging in similar sexual acts to the ones outside. Light streams in through the chimney hole in the roof, basking the inside with a soft glow. It becomes clear that this seems to be a sort of everlasting ritual of worship, because lying perfectly within the epicentre of the chimneyed opening in the roof, as if in its crosshairs, is a *gigantic black cube.* This cube floats in the air on the far horizon and is angled on one of its corners, giving the illusion of it being a hexagon. Around this great cube are massive black storm clouds with seemingly endless flashes of lightning.

The Stulti within do not stop completely in their tracks like the others. Instead, they remain continue their flailing movements, captivated by the ongoing beat. However, they turn their expressionless faces towards the sword and its cube, as if acquiring a new object of worship.

Arthur walks to the centre of this cult-like amphitheatre, with Stulti moving out the way instinctively as if respecting his presence. Áine and Jack stay glued to the glow, a circle of Stulti forming around them, shaking and moving frenetically.

Arthur thrusts the sword high up into the air.

The drum beats stop, and so does the dancing.

The Stulti thrash their heads upwards to keep their attention on the humming glow. Arthur then closes his eyes and begins to focus intensely. His lips begin moving silently as before, and the Stulti are captivated, clearly reacting to Arthur's attempts at communication. Their zombie-like bodies begin wobbling and stirring more aggressively, until finally their movements calm. One Stult close to them moves its hand out to its side, as if it were signalling on a bicycle, which at first confused the trio. But then other Stulti start to do the same, all holding their arms out in the same direction. It becomes clear that they are pointing at the great cube in the distance. The trio turn to focus on the cube.

'The cube is the Land of Demons?' Jack asks with frowning features.

Arthur shakes his head whilst his eyes are still closed, a clear vision showing itself to him. He then opens them.

'No, they aren't pointing up, they are pointing down. The cube hovers above Terra Daemonum.'

'Okay, well let's leave then …' Jack pauses, and takes a breath. 'These guys aren't going to leave us, are they?'

'They will stay glued to the light as if their very existence depends on it,' Áine says in a rather detached and monotone voice.

The Stulti one by one drop their arms and begin shuffling closer and closer towards them, like a wild pack of wolves cautiously moving towards their prey.

'We are going to have to run away. Mum, how fast can the Stulti move?' Arthur says, with only the slightest bit of panic.

'Faster than both of you on foot, that is certain. Stand beside me, I can get us out of here.'

The brothers move directly to either side of their spirit mother, the Stulti now almost within touching distance.

'Arthur, you will need to sheathe the sword to keep it safe; but as you do, the Stulti will attack. This is my window.'

'Window for what?' Jack asks with a frown.

Arthur sheathes the blade.

The Stulti launch themselves like beasts to prey.

An explosion of white light.

The trio launch into the air.

6. THE MAGNUS CUBUS

They exit through the hole of the skin tent like a bullet, continuing to cut deeper and deeper into the yellow atmosphere above. The yellow plasma is thin and transparent, making this entire hellish landscape clear to them. They reach an awesome peak and Áine stops her flight, leaving them all hovering high up in the atmosphere beside the great cube.

Around, they see a vast mountainous region of cliffs and canyons. Thick, highly dense plasma, looking like a living jellied organism, moves slowly through the realm, expanding and contracting. Within this area are many other Stulti settlements dotted around, containing basic tents and huts.

But it wasn't the areas occupied by the Stulti that caught the attention of the trio. Instead, it was the great cube. It was a formidable sight indeed, with its dark black aura and stormy atmosphere. Even at the height they were now, they were only just about parallel to the centre of the vast cube, with its upper half reaching high above them. From this angle, it was clear that the cube itself seemed to cause a contortion in the atmospheric gasses and plasmas, like a star distorting gravity. The atmosphere above the cube swirled into a hexagon-shaped, black cloud. This dark cloud caused the area of Stultorum directly below to be almost completely engulfed in darkness. Only the lightning and residual light from the rest of Stultorum provided any illumination.

And below this great cube, a sort of thick steam accumulated and flowed downwards towards a singularity. This steam was dark black and flickered like fire. Arthur stares at the point to where this dark essence was being pulled and bites his cheeks anxiously at the sight.

'That, my sons, is what we must go through. Through that black hole exists the deepest hell,' Áine says in a calm but serious tone.

'So the Land of Demons is through *there*?' Jack struggles to ask, as if being at a loss for breath.

'Yes. It is through the great mass of this essence, released from the suffering souls inside the Magnus Cubus, that a recess is created. A void of darkness, where demons of high and low reside. The demons below suck the essence from the souls trapped inside the cube. The souls are rinsed of any spirit they have, being continually forced into manic and insane states within a simulated hyperdimensional plane of varying chaos. The souls are siphoned until there is nothing corporeal left for them to hold onto. It is this dark matter that gives the demons their strength.'

'They tried to suck John's soul from him; he described a place just like it when Sickle and …' Arthur turns to his brother, but quickly looks down and away in guilt. '… when John was connected to the black cube. He said he was sent to a plane of chaos, and he felt a demon on his back, sucking his light. But he managed to hang on and remained grounded in his faith. But John was sent there through technology, through forced means … How do ordinary souls become trapped inside the cube?' Arthur asks whilst shaking his head a little.

'I believe you have been told about the origins of the cube, have you not?' Áine asks.

'I have been told about the origins of the smaller cube within my sword, yes. Caretaker Julius told me it belonged to the sword of Saint Michael, and it was passed down to various earthly legends such as King Arthur, only to be separated from its rightful place within the sword, becoming corrupted in the process.'

'Yes. And like the small cube, the great cube here beside us was not always an artefact of evil either. This cube once shone the six colours brightly and spun violet whenever the angels in heaven were all in harmony with the Lord. Whenever the heavens aligned perfectly in great chorus, the cube would resonate with this holy vibration; and it would spin so fast that it would blossom into a giant cross, opening up its tesseract form to reveal its true state, that is, the Corpus Hypercubus. It is, in literal essence, the *body of the Holy Spirit*. And its opening symbolised a complete heavenly resonation with pure divinity.'

Arthur frowns curiously with his mouth slightly ajar, and then looks to the side as if recalling something.

'Also known as the Dali cross, right? I think I've seen Salvador's artwork depicting it.'

Áine nods and smiles.

'Regardless, from what I have been told by high angels, there was for a long time in heaven no blossoming of the great cube into the violet Corpus Hypercubus. This non-blossoming caused great stirs within heaven. This was the beginning of Lucifer's fall, as he had for a while begun to feel superior to the others and felt no need to join in singing the tune of the harmonious choir. The other angels kept singing, but he continually refused. He convinced a third of the angels that they need not hum in harmony, and he convinced them that there should be no need to resonate with the vibration of God's spirit; and that instead, they should align themselves with him to create a new kingdom and a new universal order. The great war of the heavens shortly followed, and of course, the holy angels of the Lord were victorious. However, Lucifer and his third of angels were not the only things to fall. Lucifer managed to bring the great cube down with him, in one last foul attempt to curse his father. And so, the Magnus Cubus fell from the heavens, and it too was destined to be spiritless, motionless and lacking light. The cube now is simply a shell. A shell used to store nothing but trapped souls within its complex chaotic form.

'And so begun Satan's quest to corrupt, to tempt, to feed off any soul on earth he could, all in an attempt to trap them within his great box and create slaves for his own means. Over time, many humans have chosen to side with Satan and his demons, and now most don't even realise they're doing it. Satan has been building the density of this box for a long, long time now, starting on earth and carrying over to the afterlife, leading to Daemonum increasing in density. The more souls he can milk in his box, the larger his kingdom becomes, in both hell and earth.'

'But souls can never be truly destroyed can they, only transferred? The energy of the trapped souls, when squeezed and sent below, where do they go?' asked Arthur.

'Yes. He has been building an army, starting on earth, paving the way for his Antichrist son to rise. These slaves are firstly fooled into accepting their slave mentality in human form, when they still have free choice, with this destiny solidifying and becoming permanent after death. Awareness of this process is brutal but is also necessary for you to know … You see, the souls' entrapment in the Magnus Cubus is only the beginning of their suffering. Once they have been completely milked of soul, their soulless body is transported down to Daemonum, where their spirit body will be given a new life working as a slave. They will at this point be desperate for life force and will be fed scrapings of liquid soul at the discretion of the demons that rule, who take the lion's share. These slaves are blinded by a box encasing their head, and the energy they are given spurts out their mouth tubes at the command of the demon princes. Each boxed head is designated one of the six colours to orally spurt, the frequency being dependent on the soul's alignment, and it will be this that designates their demonic overlord.'

At this point Jack was beginning to look very stressed, rubbing his hair and bowing his head into his hands rather manically. The other two say nothing but look at him intrigued.

'Sickle … He's clearly a demon, isn't he? This whole time, it was so obvious. His plans with the cube on earth, his moments of solitude, his cunning ponderings, I should have known! I didn't believe in such things, and even now I can't believe that I believe! But now I see so clearly what he was doing all along, what his real intentions were. He must be connected somehow to these evil spirits, luring people into giving their essence to these creatures. The whole Snake Box project, it promised so much, but the whole thing was a trick! How did *I* not see this, but you, Arthur, saw it for what it was so easily? How were you so wise, and I such a fool? I've always thought of myself as so clever, but now I realise arrogance really does blind people …' He shakes his head to himself.

'Because that's what demons do,' Arthur replies. 'Demons take your wisdom and turn you into a fool. Sickle is clearly more evil than we ever imagined, and I cannot help but agree with you that he is indeed a demon. And dare I even say that he could be … he could be …' He briefly glances at Áine with raised eyebrows, before looking back to Jack whilst shaking his head. 'Jack, I can't help but think that the killing of our parents … I can't help but think this was a part of his plan all along.'

Jack began to frown in horror.

'It is said, if you want to know someone's true intentions,' Arthur continues, 'look at the end result of their actions. Look what happened with you: you ended up being Sickle's apprentice, he had you under his thumb; can you honestly say you weren't at least a little vulnerable because of what happened to our parents? He took advantage of you, he took advantage of your own demons and replaced them with his own.'

Jack shakes his head aggressively and purses his lips tightly.

'But how could it all be a master plan? He was only just a teenager when he killed our parents.'

'Exactly, weird, isn't it? If he were a mere human, that wouldn't make sense, but if he were something more …'

'Something more akin to pure evil?'

'Exactly. Then, it makes sense.'

The brothers stare at each other intensely for a few moments, and then turn away to look back down at the spiralling wormhole.

'You have no idea of the realisations I have felt within me, Arthur. I have experienced things, seen things, had glimpses of the bigger picture. It's hard to explain, yet the shifts that I have felt have allowed me to understand things I never could before. I am a completely different person now, and because of this, I feel more desperate than ever to talk to Dad one last time. Let's just get this over and done with; we've come this far, haven't we?'

'The only way out is through,' Arthur says, turning away from his brother and looking downwards with a deadly, piercing focus.

'I am blessed to be with you both on this journey,' Áine says, which for some reason surprises the brothers. 'I told you this before, Arthur; but it is true, I am not complete without Phillip. In heaven I am treated divinely, and it is a love of unimaginable proportion, one I will not even try to explain with mere words. But still, I know you both sense a coldness within me, and I cannot deny it. But this is because I need Phillip beside me. I, too, miss him greatly.'

Both Arthur and Jack look at their spirit mother tenderly, and their eyes well a little.

Arthur shakes his head and says, 'Nah, you are still our mum. If the mum I knew on earth went to heaven and came back, it would be the lady I'm talking to right now. I understand you have transcended and have witnessed things that humble you beyond belief. I will love you until the end of time, and I feel the same way about you now as the love you can't describe in heaven.'

Áine looks down at the ground, and for the first time looks quite vulnerable. She keeps her head bowed and then gracefully wipes a tear off her face. She puts her hand down by her side. The tear runs off her finger, falling through the sky towards the wormhole below.

7. TERRA DAEMONUM

The tear falls down from where they float. Áine senses enough to look down towards the black hole, but does not exactly know what she is sensing. She carries on staring intently, causing both the brothers to look at her with curiosity. After approximately 10 seconds of this intense staring, a shift occurs inside the centre of the black hole. A white, circular blob appears. This white beacon, looking like a white pupil within an eye, blocks the black steam from entering, and instead it dissipates into the atmosphere.

'This is our chance,' Áine says seriously, looking up at the brothers abruptly. 'We have been gifted this opportunity: we must fall; it is now or never.'

'Okay. Okay, I am ready,' Arthur says.

Jack says nothing, but takes in a deep breath.

Áine holds her hands out in front of her, palms down, and then slowly pushes them towards the ground.

They fall.

The brothers' faces fill with fear, and their stomachs quiver. They feel their fall being guided by a force, like a magnet finding its opposite.

They are being pulled in by the white eye.

Áine pulls in her arms tight to her body to make herself as small as possible. The brothers quickly follow suit.

They fall through …

Black, black, black. Nothing around them but black.

Nothing can be seen; they cannot even see each other. They feel nothing. The force they felt upon falling is immediately vanquished, as if they fell to the ground but did not hit anything solid.

Arthur moves his limbs, and knows he is doing so, by mere muscle memory, but has no other sensory input to indicate his movement.

Panic builds within him.

But before his emotions intensify further, the void quickly brightens into various shades of brown, green and grey; and then everything solidifies into something tangible. This transition happens quickly, but still there's an observable effect of chaotically-stretched matter being compressed and forming into a solid.

Arthur is in a forest.

The way he suddenly went from dark to something real fills Arthur with a deep sense of uneasiness. He now feels little control in this realm; and to top it off, he is no longer beside his brother, nor his spirit mother.

He looks around with a strong, brave and serious face, frowning deeply with scepticism at his surroundings; as if they are a living entity. But then he stops abruptly with his frantic turning and looking because he sees a familiar figure.

He sees his father's lion form in the distance.

'Dad?!' he shouts, his eyes instantly widening with child-like excitement.

He begins running towards him. But as he does, Phillip's form fades, and Arthur immediately freezes. Great anxiety fills him suddenly.

'Do you not understand?' a deep and thick voice whispers in his left ear, making him jump and turn quickly to look behind him.

Nothing is there.

He waits again, frozen, feeling weak and powerless. He begins to go for his sword. He grabs the handle, but as soon as he does, a vine from a tree beside him wraps itself around the blade and holds it tightly. Arthur struggles against the tree's grip and pulls against its power; yet his efforts are futile. The tree pulls the sword away from him and sucks it under the ground, deep into its roots.

Arthur takes a few steps back, and his face flashes red in a fluster.

A vine violently whips around his legs, binding them together. He falls down to the ground, hitting his head. He immediately goes to loosen his bonds, but just as he does, another set of vines whip around his body and arms. He is in complete bondage, like a mummy. He strains and struggles, but it is hopeless.

His environment begins to melt once again.

Arthur turns his head as much as he can to reassess his position.

He is in a dungeon, strapped to a rack.

The dungeon is dark and glows red from an unknown light source. He is bound upright, into the shape of an X, with each of his arms and legs spread wide. Directly in front of him, about five metres away, is a large, flamboyant throne. The throne is golden and has deep red velvet padding. The gold frame meets sharply at the top of it, forming a blade-like apex.

Arthur stares at the throne in anticipation.

'Oh, you were expecting a person?' the chair says, with an uncannily gentle and well-spoken male English accent. The voice projects itself through a small opening within the red velvet; yet the hole did not move at all as it spoke.

'What are you? And where are my brother and mother?' Arthur says whilst shaking his head in disbelief.

'I am anything I wish to be. This is my realm; everything here is fluid, and I am the master that dictates its direction. I am both the void and everything within it.'

'You are the demon from my childhood, aren't you?'

The chair begins laughing.

'It is true Moloch lives within my realm, but no, I am not Moloch. He is but a hand.'

Arthur stares at the throne in silence, his suspicions of who this dark spirit *really* was immediately being confirmed.

'Tell me, what did you expect from coming here?' the throne asks, the voice now sounding a little deeper and more masculine, and even a little rougher.

Arthur does not reply but instead stares fiercely and courageously at the throne's form.

The throne slides quickly towards Arthur, causing a high-pitched screech as it moves along the floor.

'Answer me!' the throne screams in an even deeper and more demonic tone.

'To rescue my father from your lightless void! He deserves better than to be tormented by your demonic followers.'

'Oh, he deserves better?' the throne says, reverting to the previous gentle voice. 'What makes you think any of your earthly ones deserve better than to live alongside me in my planes? They themselves have the power to choose us or not. We merely tempt by hanging fruits in front of their eyes.'

'My father lived a good life; he never chose you. If it is anyone's fault, it is mine. I used the cube to enter his soul, and that was how Moloch captured him. Take me instead; but release him.'

The throne laughs.

'A son would sacrifice himself for his dead father's soul?' The throne begins laughing again. 'You have no idea of my plans, nor my ways, of which you are so ignorant. But allow me to enlighten you. Your father is but a figure, a figure that was chosen. It was mere destiny for your father to be sacrificed. Do not take it personally, for your father's death was merely an offering, a symbol; a symbol that represents the spiritual alignment on earth. For it is the collective father, the father of all your people, that all of you, together, have chosen to kill. But, oh my, your kind still aren't content without one, are they? They scream, they beg, they crave direction throughout the chaos; the chaos they just refuse to accept. But alas, it is in times of carnage, times of desperation, times of light-lessness, this is when I poke my earthly head. For where there exists an absence of light and direction, I inevitably follow. For where you, as little children, cry and scream for a father, I am always there to lend hands. That is, the hands of my demons …'

The throne begins laughing to himself once again, now in the deep and demonic tone.

Arthur drops through the floor and carries on falling. He hears the chair's laughing echo as he falls …

He continues his descent through a spiralling void, around him a massive supernova of colours and fractal patterns.

Yet out of all the matter, the black, flickering essence stands dominant, its mainstream culminating in a focused beam. The essence is all around him and transitions from gas to liquid continuously in different areas. He feels as if he is falling, yet here there is nothing with which to measure or to compare his movement.

'I am the void, I am the darkness, I, am the *unseen!*' This deep voice reverberates all around him and echoes deeply through him. 'Look around you.'

Arthur turns his head to look around. He sees the black, flickering steam moving upwards, like a reverse black waterfall. On closer inspection, he notices dark entities shooting through the various flickering streams, being propelled upwards as if cells through dark veins.

'You have noticed my essence in its physical form, then? This is the transport for my hands.'

'Your hands?' Arthur asks in a rather childish tone.

'Yes, my demons. It is my demons, that glide through my spirit and manifest it on earth. Everything that is not respected in the light is mine. The denser this spirit is on earth, the more demons I can summon to build my spirit further. My demons linger in the shadows, they live in the buried parts of people's souls. Allow me to demonstrate.'

Arthur is pulled against his will and with violent force towards the main stream of black essence.

He is shot upwards.

The nova void bends and shoots past him as he is fired further and further upwards. Light then begins to manifest in front of him, and he is propelled into a more solid realm.

A white flash explodes around him.

And in a blink, he appears inside the body of someone else, seeing and feeling as they would, yet with no control of the body; he simply observes.

'We could change everything: I have the vision, and you, the technical knowledge,' a handsome, black-haired man sitting opposite says. Both the men are sitting down in a booth in a quiet pub.

'No, I'm definitely interested, yet also concerned. Look at it from my perspective; firstly, I don't know you, and secondly, you somehow know I possess this cube,' a younger Jack says. 'You understand this makes me feel a little uneasy?'

'I can understand that, and I apologise for my lack of gentleness in approach. But what me and my team are doing is very serious, and naturally, we have a lots of eyes and ears. I work with a team of very dedicated people, I am sure you will understand. Regardless, we know you have the cube because it has been in my company's best interest to locate it. So no, we are not idiots, and we actually get things done. Even if that means using slightly unorthodox methods.'

'Yeah, no, I see that. And I agree, sometimes more unorthodox methods are justified if the end result is necessary for the greater good.'

'Good, I'm glad we are on the same page. Now, I have seen your work, and it is beyond any doubt that you are a genius; I would guess, 155?'

'Yeah, about that.'

The black-haired man nods and gives an impressed look.

'Great. Now, the company is small but is already very powerful. We have multiple, very wealthy investors; investors who have a particular interest in the cultural and political implications of this project. And for this reason, our work, for now, must stay quiet. As you may have already guessed, I have done my research on you, and this is the reason we are sitting with each other today; you intrigue me, Jack, you do.' The man pauses and looks Jack squarely in the eye to indicate his sincerity. 'Other than your work, I also know of your past, and I know how things like that build character. Because of this, you have my respect; and I would like you to consider us becoming business partners; your financial return would also, of course, reflect this position.'

Jack nods and takes a few moments to contemplate.

'Well, I thank you for the offer, but that's a big decision to make … And I think I need some time to think about this.'

The two men look at each other in silence for a few more moments, the black-haired man looking down and then looking back at up at Jack through his eyebrows.

'Okay, well, firstly tell me how we are going to improve the world?' Jack says, and then laughs to himself a little. The black-haired man gives a subtle smile.

'Imagine if we could destroy evil. Imagine if we could prevent the peo-ple who killed your parents from even wanting to do such a thing. We aren't that far away now, Jack; you honestly must see what we have already accom-plished in this regard. You see, my position, which I indeed hope you share, is that we have outgrown the majority of human instincts; the instincts that were once needed for survival are now merely a toxicity on this planet. They are simply not needed in today's civilised and progressive world. With mod-ern understanding of people's behavioural patterns, along with advances in technology, it is going to become possible to further unite technology with man for the advancement of our species.'

'Go on.'

'Through a technological manipulation of instincts and emotions, we will be able to improve individuals, and it won't be long until crime will be reduced because of our adjustments. We will soon be able to increase posi-tive emotion and decrease negative emotion. All we need to do is establish an efficient and effective product that gives consumers positive feedback and improves quality of life for them and others around them. The aim is to ul-timately make this product as ubiquitous and vital for humans as the smart-phone. Not only that, our aim is to also make buying this product a moral responsibility so that those who don't have it feel shame and are shunned.'

Jack nods and frowns as he looks up to the right.

'Well, that's quite the vision … But it's quite unrealistic from a busi-ness perspective, don't you think? To rely on this product being a moral responsibility; I just don't know what to think about that …'

'You don't understand. As I mentioned before, we are working with some very powerful people. People who can manipulate public opinion. Whilst you may think that is a little radical, it is simply just high-level advertising which at the very least will get the company's foot through the door.'

Jack is taken aback by this final statement. A rush of adrenaline fills his body.

'We live in an age where people no longer know how to take care of themselves,' the black-haired man continues. 'So it's time we took care of the people. We could live in a world where our devices could get a person feeling lazy out of bed and into work without any delay or struggle. Our devices could get rid of any bad habit, and would allow complete collective enhancement and ordering. Over time, a new order will form; an order of harmony, an order of bliss. The device would be like clothing: it would be a necessity. It would be our mark on the world, a mark needed to buy, to sell, to enjoy, to do anything. There would be no war, no crime, no hate, just pure love; everyone working together, like *clockwork*.'

The vision freezes in time.

Arthur looks through Jack's eyes at the black-haired man, the word 'clockwork' repeating in his head over and over again, causing him to feel paralysed in horror.

'This is your first test,' rumbles the dark voice of the void, which Arthur struggles to isolate. 'Be my hand; tempt your brother to his destiny.'

'No, I will not,' Arthur says with a furrowed brow.

The darkness laughs.

'How can you be so stupid? Surely a smart man would realise this is a mere vision, and that it is impossible to turn a man away from something that has already happened?'

'I will never align myself with your temptations, nor your spirit; that will not come from me, no matter its effect.'

The darkness laughs.

'Very well, say what you wish, I will not interfere. The only thing you *must* do, is to say *something*. I will keep you here until you accomplish this task. You see, I wish to get to know you, Arthur. And I am watching you *very, very carefully*.'

Arthur re-enters Jack's body, now having control over him.

'So, what do you think?' the black-haired man says with a smouldering smile, oozing arrogance.

Arthur is lost for words and just carries on staring back.

'Well, surely you have something to say, don't you?' the man says, his expression suddenly shifting to a cunning smirk. He gives a knowing look, and Arthur feels this immediately. Panic hits him like a ton of bricks.

'Or should I say, you *have* to say something … Oh yes, I can take form on earth too.'

The man begins smiling almost manically. Arthur is frozen in place, shocked in disbelief.

'It has been my desire to become man for a long, long time. My hands have paved the way for my arrival, and I, as the Sickle, will destroy all fatherly crop that stands in my path.'

'Destroy crops of goodness, and I will just plant more. Your spirit only destroys, yet the spirit of good builds!' Arthur replies sharply, as if spitting venom. 'You underestimate how many good people still exist. People who embody the totality of their humanity, people who live truthfully and honestly. Your deceptive ways may be fashionable, but they are by no means stable or strong. You underestimate people's ability to bounce back from darkness and to be reborn into the light.'

'The battle for dark is already won. For my mere arrival is only possible because the foundations have already been laid. The age of the fish is dead, and now you rise above the sea with no morning star. A dark night above the ocean, with no light to guide you. So, therefore, my time has come, as Aquarius ignites the power of the morning star's keen eyes. And so, I will rise through your culture and will relish in giving the world everything they want. For I am everything that is missing. I am the burning star waiting to crash. Oh, how beautiful the establishment of my order will be, for I am the opposite of everything that was previously held sacred; I am your kingdom's great shadow, I am the polar, I am the inversion; *I am the Antichrist.*'

As the spirit of darkness, in the form of Harry Sickle, finishes speaking, he, and the environment with him, fade into blackness. Arthur is, once again, plunged into the void.

8. SHOWDOWN

'**Y**ou are a rare breed, I give you that,' the dark spirit says. 'For it is your kind, the kind that possess both gentleness and power, who sicken me the most. I see no potential in making you a hand. And how disappointing, for at first I thought you had the potential for greatness ...'

'I have no wish to be the hand of such an unholy spirit, and I don't care about your power or your temptations. I know about your ways, and I have no time for them. The way of totality, the way of harmonious grace, the way of our heavenly father is the only way to live life. That is truth, and that is the way I follow.'

'How foolish can you be to think you are protected by this *way* of yours. But alas, you talk of offers, so let me make one you cannot refuse ... You understand that you are in my realm, and it is only up to me to choose if you see your father again.'

Arthur suddenly feels a coldness within him, the powerlessness he experienced before. He looks down and to the side, searching within himself for ideas or inspiration; yet he finds nothing.

'And what offer may that be?' Arthur asks reluctantly, his voice sounding frustrated.

'Oh, so now the little dove wishes to do dealings with his dark lord?' The darkness laughs. 'I thought you only choose the way devoid of temptation? Yet look now how I tempt you ... Now, listen to my words carefully. You may have seen my great cube that hovers above my void, am I correct?' Arthur does not reply but just stares with contempt. 'And you are, of course, aware of my hand, who goes by the name of Moloch?'

'Unfortunately, yes.'

The darkness laughs again.

'He is a hand who helps tempt on earth, teasing little ones into submitting themselves to my cube, or getting others to sacrifice them instead. It is he who governs the orange plane of my kingdom; and it is he who had aspirations for you to become his under-lord. He is disappointed ... He had great visions of you working with my Sickle on earth, helping to rise the morning star. But alas, how you failed. Oh, how you failed! So now I am left with little option. You see, Moloch wishes to personally feed on your soul;

in fact, you make his lips moist with excitement. He wants you and your family not through the great Cubus but all to himself. You have offended him, little one; you have made a mockery of him; and he is *very angry*. So hear my offer to you now. I propose a duel. A duel between you and Moloch. If you win, and defeat Moloch, I will allow you, your father's soul and your brother all to leave my void *unharmed*. If you lose, however, then you and the souls of your entire family will be torn apart under the insanity Moloch will force into you. Moloch will feed on your lost essence, drop by drop, every bit of heavenly connection you have; he will milk it, drink it and enjoy it. He will trap you in your own personal box, together, forced to watch each other's souls lose connection to your beloved way.'

'You are pure evil,' Arthur says softly, under his breath.

'Yet, I still am. And for that I am still a product of the father, no? Oh, how naïve you are, for you have no respect nor understanding of the greater matters. But enough of this, you bore me. Do you accept my offer? Or do you submit yourself to Moloch without fight? These are your options.'

Arthur begins breathing heavily, feeling a strange, burning anger within. Even his teeth begin to clench.

'I fight. On one condition: that you grant me access to *my sword*. If you grant me this, I will fight to my last breath. But know that I will never submit myself to you, or any of your kind. I will stay true to my integrity, and this you cannot break. You may laugh at me, torment me, torture me; but I will never let go of my Self; for that is mine, and mine only.'

'Very well. Your sword will be in the battlegrounds waiting for you. But enough talking. Let the games begin!'

Arthur is dropped from the void with pronounced and forceful acceleration, the dark, flickering matter forming and foaming all around him.

He continues to drop, the essence becoming denser and denser, until he is fully merged with it. He cannot escape its smothering nature; it consumes him, and he cannot help but feel its spirit within him. Dark visions swarm his mind: visions of suffering, disgusting insects, pain and torture, demons smiling whilst committing atrocities, alien entities folding and bending, , people making decisions they regret from the past, and finally, f the night his parents were brutalised. All to a soundtrack of horrific screaming.

'No, no, no!' Arthur shakes his head, trying to rid himself of the visions invading his mind.

But then it all stops.

The flickering essence concentrates into a thick, beam-like stream, and Arthur falls beside it.

He now has vision, and audio, of what lies below.

He sees a giant, glowing, hexagonal land mass split into six segments, each one of the first six colours of the rainbow, and together forming a vast, interconnected plane. Within each segment exist animations: bulges and chunks, wobbles and waves, glitches and flashes.

In the atmosphere he feels heavily resonant vibrations, deep, dark and booming. As Arthur falls, he attempts to gauge the scale of this world below. Although he has no real point of reference to judge, he is still filled with awe at the sheer magnitude of what he sees. As he continues to descend, he is pulled towards the centre of these six coloured areas, and he sees that where they meet exists a small, dark area, like a black bullseye. It now becomes clear that these six coloured planes are themselves massive regions, each containing their own realm and their own vibration. Each coloured realm has its own coloured plasma, and each of these fields emits a unique tune, some higher in frequency and others lower, resulting in a sort of eerie orchestra.

Arthur notices that each edge of the hexagon is not a smooth, straight line but instead a spiky, wobbly one, with explosions and protrusions continually expanding the hexagon.

The slaves, Arthur thinks to himself, attributing the hexagon's expansion to the 'box-head slaves' that his mother told him about earlier.

As Arthur continues to be sucked in, he can't help but feel saddened by this horrific music. Not just any sadness, but a supercharged depression, a forced sorrow which someone may feel living under the tune of a god who hated everything; a god who hated existence, hated purpose, hated *light*.

Arthur is sucked towards a cesspit of smothering torment, falling into a world of beating sound that penetrates his form.

But then he feels acceptance.

He allows himself to fall. He falls with his arms stretched out and his body facing upwards. Visions of duty, purpose and hope begin to fill him. He decides to close his eyes and allow whatever is going to happen to happen. But the falling just goes on and on, for longer than he anticipated; yet he keeps on breathing through it, even as his heart quickens with budding panic …

He starts to feel atmospheric pressure like that experienced on earth. He feels as if he has entered a more physical plane. Sensations of cold and wind hit his skin, as does a certain humidity: a sensation of cold, moist steam.

He opens his eyes.

Just before he can acclimatise himself to his surroundings, he feels a heavy …

Splodge.

He lands.

His landing is not painful, yet he is immediately dazed and not completely lucid. He is cold and filled with disgust. A bitter taste of death fills his mouth. A thick, black, mud-like substance encases him like he's in a womb, covering him entirely from head to toe. He sits up from the engulfing mud, takes a large breath of air, and rubs the filth off his face. He quickly realises that the black, muddy substance is the least of his worries. His attention instead shifts to the arena he finds himself in. He realises that he is in the eye of the great hexagon. Around him are six plasma gates, all entrances to the six segments. These gates pulse and reverberate, as if they are musical instruments, each emitting its own tune.

At each point of the hexagon stands a tower, gothic in style and grey in colour. These towers each have sharp spires, and below them the pillared residences of whatever entity has its throne there. Protruding from these residences are balconies overlooking the muddy arena below. Arthur's eyes squint as he faintly sees tall, black figures standing on these platforms. Whilst Arthur cannot make out their features, he can see they are waving their arms in a summoning motion, as if they are conducting an orchestra in slow motion. The demons' movements fill Arthur with dread; they dance and twist, the vibrations all around in symbiosis. As the arms of these demons move, the sound frequency of their coloured kingdoms changes, shifting in pitch and tempo, stretching and elongating. This causes visible shifts in the coloured plasma of each gate too, as it bulges, wobbles, stretches, bounces and contorts.

Arthur's attention shifts once again. Now he looks at the centre of the arena. The stream of liquid soul from above is concentrated into a small, circular, grey-bricked dark hole, which is about the size of a modest well. The muddy moistness of the ground is due to this dark stream penetrating into the depths of the void and permeating the ground, like a plant being watered with liquid evil.

Arthur's jaw goes slack and he frowns in fear. He notices on closer inspection that this dark essence is being carried up to each of the six towers, as if it's a fuel feeding the demons. They are obscured at first, as they are covered in the mud; but as he observes more closely, he can clearly see grey, translucent metallic tubes, connected to the hole in the middle and leading all the way up the sides of the towers, transporting the essence to each tower's summit. At the base of each tower, there are large, metal-barred vents. From these vents, the mud that forms the base of the arena gushes out. It is thicker but less dark than the essence that streams from above; it seems as if this sludge is a sort of waste product, rejected by whatever is processing the black essence.

Arthur stands up and pats down his body to try and rid himself of the mud. He looks around and takes in many breaths, levelling himself out, fully processing the arena he stands in. Arthur then senses a shift in atmosphere, the dreary musical tone around fading just a little, as if a player has stopped playing in the orchestra. He squints his eyes squint, and he sees the orange-field fluctuations slow. He tilts his eyes up to the nearest tower and sees the demon on its ledge no longer moving like the others.

'Moloch …' he says under his breath.

The black demon jumps from his ledge and lands on the sludgy surface with a loud clatter from his sharp, metallic armour.

The demon walks towards Arthur; slowly, yet with conviction and swagger. Arthur now sees clearly the familiar sight of the bull-headed Moloch, looking larger than he remembered as a child. The demon also has a darker face, looking in places rather burnt and disfigured. Moloch wears thick black armour, with spikes rising from each shoulder plate. In Moloch's left hand, he holds Excalibur by the leather sheath covering the blade.

He launches the weapon high into the air with ease.

It lands beside Arthur, and he immediately notices that it is cube-less.

'I was promised my sword. This is just the blade,' Arthur says in a weak, child-like tone, quickly realising how foolish he was by trying to make a deal with the devil. His tone exudes no confidence and has undertones of sadness.

'I am becoming glad you turned your back on me. Your stupidity means you would have never stood up to the works required to bring the morning star,' Moloch says.

Arthur begins to analyse the situation. He quickly realises he is hopeless against this demon without the full power of his sword.

'The darkness told me you wished for a duel. And I agreed to this. But a duel against someone as clearly as weak as me will surely be boring for you, no? Would you not prefer to at least have a little challenge? For that, you must give me the cube, so I can access the power of my sword and give you an exciting duel.'

'Oh, you wish for the cube I once gave you so simply? How I told you of its fruits, and how you now rely on my cube for your power. What is the difference between us, then? Us lords, our power comes from the great cube above our domain, just as yours comes from this one.'

'Whilst this cube gives me power, it is not my only source of it. The power I gain from this cube is based on light. I use the cube in its pure and intended state, its power only working when aligned with the spiritual balance of the Lord. Its willingness to activate comes from alignment with totality. Your power instead comes from disharmonic fragments, fragments that only love themselves and never submit to the whole. No wonder your tune sounds so ugly. It has no grounding in the ultimate.'

Moloch pauses for several moments. He then pulls out a black whip that is holstered to his back and unravels it slowly. The whip is long and slimy, like a black anaconda. It flickers with darkness, in the same way the essence concentrating at the centre does. This whip has many shadowy spikes, and at its end a larger, spiked-ball head.

'You speak in the tongues of the spirit; and you speak to me with such unbounded confidence. It reminds me why I saw your potential, but you chose light over greater darkness. For in the beginning there was only dark-ness, and it is darkness that shall once again reign eternal. For pleasure and pain shall be the only things to exist, and the only things that need to exist. The busybodies who adopt false hope and purpose are foolish. True pur-pose lies in lesser bodies submitting to their masters for pleasure, accepting their pain as necessary to please their overlords. Once one understands that life is about sacrificing oneself for the pleasure of one's masters, then all pain becomes pleasurable. And, in the end, all becomes pleasure.'

'You are the one that speaks in twisted words, but I see through you so easily. I submit to only one, and that is totality itself. That is the father. Lord of lords. And whilst I have obedience, it is not for mere pleasure that I sub-mit; but it is from a place of awe and understanding, a relationship not forced but one I have built over my years of observation. You wish to be feared, but I fear you not. I instead fear only God. You wish to be gods, but you are not. You wish instead to be worshipped, because you lack humility and have only pride. You will never force everyone to worship your kind, no matter how much trickery or deception you use. Yes, you may play in the darkness, in the land that no one sees, but as soon as you poke out your head, you are immediately vanquished by the light, and your lies are deciphered. To me, I only feel sadness and pity for you.'

'You have much ignorance of what is to come. Satan's son now exists for your world to see. He is our spearhead and has penetrated his way into the light; yet none smell his approaching stench. He has risen, and he is bright, his star shining all around him. He is the snake that will become respected by all. For your men on earth have become weakened, and we have struck. Your obsession with light and love has made you pathetic. The real master now comes; the master sent from the depths, the master that will pave the way for a new order of deception. Your kind need not ask questions, or need not understand his way; for it is not truth that you need, but only submission. You need not a relationship with your so-called father; you need submission only to our dark lord's son. He will be the one your kind have been waiting for. He will be the one to release the fetish, the fetish that lurks in the shadow of your kind, the desperate need to *submit* will soon be realised.'

'I will never kneel to your inversed and perverted order! I follow only the way of truth!' Arthur says as he rips the empty blade from its sheath.

Moloch roars with a moist gargle, his head shakes, and he snaps his whip aggressively into the mud, causing it to splatter all around him. Steam erupts from his nostrils, and he begins to roar with brutal anger, both his arms wide at his side.

'Enough! Look, up at my tower! Look!' Moloch screams.

Arthur glances up and sees movement on the tower's ledge. Multiple entities are up there, and they seem to be pushing objects along the ground.

'Your kin are in *my possession*. Oh, look how they hang like meat for the fire.'

Moloch raises his hand.

From his tower, two inverted wooden crosses are lowered down by slimy black vines. Carrying out this task are four box heads under the supervision of two Draxlers.

The box heads each have one large, black box around their head, and another smaller one attached to the top of it via a tube at the rear. At the front of the main box is barrel-like tube protruding from a circular mouthpiece.

Phillip and Jack are bound tightly to the crosses, rendering them immobile. The crosses are lowered further and further until they hang approximately halfway down the tower.

Arthur's face erupts in shock. He rushes towards the tower from where they are being hung.

'Dad! Jack! Can you hear me?'

'Arthur ...' Jack groans with a struggle. 'He's going ...'

'What? Jack? What is it?'

'He's fading ... His soul ... It's draining ...'

Arthur looks to Phillip's furry lion form and sees how lifeless it is. Arthur's face tenses with contempt, and within him a fire begins to build. He stares at Moloch with his face tilted down.

'How you rage at the sight!' Moloch says, smiling smugly. 'Rage, oh beautiful rage! And how I will take pleasure in dousing the fire, until only wet embers remain.'

In this rage, Arthur charges at Moloch as if he were not in control of his body. Moloch smiles with pleasure at this sight. Arthur prepares to pierce the demon's flesh, but Moloch, with a swift flick of his whip, takes out Arthur by his legs, forcing him to land face first in the mud.

Moloch begins laughing and then, in an instant, shifts to screaming with rage.

'So weak! So pathetic!'

Moloch walks up to Arthur on the ground, who is clearly weakened, disorientated and hurt by this fall. With Moloch's free hand, he begins dragging him by his hair through the mud and launches him high into the air. Arthur flies through the air, and hits the orange-coloured field with great force, bouncing off it and landing nearby on the mud once again.

'How easily I could destroy you! For you are mistaken, I wish not for a challenge! But wish only for your torment!' Moloch screams from mid-arena, now standing next to the dark, streaming black matter.

He begins charging towards Arthur like the demonic bull he is, his gargled screaming emitting true and loud.

As he charges, Arthur is barely just getting back to his feet.

The demons on their towers intensify the dark rhythm of their tune.

Arthur is feeling severely drained by the continual droning sounds from the towers around him; they are starting to take their toll on him emotionally, weakening his morale. In his detached disorientation, he thinks to himself, *Centre yourself, Arthur. Pay attention to the task at hand. You have been sent here by the holy. Every problem can be solved with belief. There must be something you can do ... There must be a way ...*

Before Arthur can fully come back to his senses, Moloch has approached and picks him off the ground by his throat. He lets out a deep, shaking Roar into Arthur's face.

Arthur, in a dazed frenzy, wildly begins plunging his sword with both hands into the breastplate of Moloch, taking the suffocating strangle like a warrior. At first his strikes do not penetrate the thick metal, but then he manages to find a gap between two plates covering Moloch's stomach area. He twists and wiggles the blade upon penetration, but Moloch does not react or show any pain. Instead, the demon opens his mouth to reveal his sharp teeth and scrunches his features in twisted pleasure.

The two stare at each other, Moloch's orange, glowing eyes now only centimetres from Arthur's. Arthur can smell the stench so clearly now: the dark mud he tasted earlier, the taste of bitter death – Moloch smells exactly the same. Arthur now reluctantly drops his sword and moves his hands to try and loosen Moloch's grip around his throat, but his attempts are futile. The choke is not cutting off enough blood to put him to sleep, but Arthur feels his windpipe being severely restricted and is extremely vulnerable against this demon, who clearly possesses an unnatural strength like he had never known.

Moloch pushes against Arthur's forehead with the base of his shadowy whip. The back of Arthur's head rubs harder and harder against the orange plasma field until enough force is applied for it to penetrate. Arthur strains against it as he feels an intense pain begin to form.

'Feel it. Feel it. Yesss, that's it, feel it,' Moloch says, voice full of pleasure, near laughter, his face lighting up in twisted happiness.

Moloch continues to plunge Arthur's head further and further into the orange plasma field, until his entire skull is entombed deeply within it. Dark visions and energies begin flooding into Arthur's consciousness. He begins groaning and moaning, overwhelmed by the shift in consciousness triggered by the field.

Arthur is helpless and suffering.

He cannot breathe, yet he does not pass out.

He experiences the suffering, but without the consequence.

Finally, Moloch lets Arthur go. He pulls him from the field and throws him back onto the mud.

Arthur coughs, wheezes and gasps for air.

He looks back up at Moloch from the ground, covered in dirt and on all fours like a lamb for the slaughter. Moloch kicks his sword back towards him.

'Pick it up.'

Arthur picks up the blade and stands back to his feet, still panting heavily. He stares back at Moloch, now looking less energetic and lower in spirit than he did before.

Moloch laughs.

'Did I not say I will douse the embers?'

'Well done, you have weakened me,' Arthur says softly, as he puts a hand up in the air. 'Tell me, does this really give you pleasure? To bully an earthly man? A demon like you surely needs a bigger match than me …'

'You wish for help? Then I will lend you a kin.'

Moloch whips his weapon in the direction of where Arthur's family hang, his mouth widening into a smile. The whip extends beyond its natural length, and its spiky end slashes the vine from which Jack's cross hangs.

Jack, head first, and his cross plunge towards the muddy ground.

'Jack!!' Arthur shouts desperately.

The cross falls and pierces the mud deeply, submerging Jack's head entirely. Arthur sprints awkwardly with all his energy towards him; Moloch continues to watch with enjoyment.

Arthur reaches the buried cross, but it is well and truly wedged into the ground. Jack's body writhes in panicked suffocation, his arms straining against their bonds.

'I got you, Jack, just stay calm.'

Arthur uses his sword to cut the black vine binding Jack to his cross. He starts with the arms, being careful not cut the flesh; he then frees the legs.

Once the bonds are cut, he pulls him out the mud with all his might and lays him on the ground.

Jack gasps violently, almost with a scream.

'It's okay, it's okay, you are fine, Jack. We are back together again.'

Jack begins crying in agony, his body convulsing and shaking; petrified from both pain and fear.

'Arthur …' Jack says through his tears.

'Yes?' Arthur leans in closer, putting his hand on his brother's chest.

'Dad … There's not much time now …'

Arthur sighs deeply and tilts his eyes up to look at Moloch, who is still smiling smugly as he walks towards them.

'Yes, I know, I know! But I have no power, Jack, I don't know what to do …'

'My time is near …'

'What?' Arthur replies with a confused face.

But then he turns and catches sight of his spirit father hanging on his cross. He stares intensely, as if in a trance. His face adopts an even more serious frown.

A shift begins within Arthur as he finds himself captivated by this image of his father. Emotions of bittersweet nostalgia fill him; a sadness, yes, yet also a deep love and respect for the man, the spirit and the image. He is well aware of the approaching Moloch, who he can see in the corner of his eye; yet right now, he did not care. The longer he stares, the more he is filled with spirit and passion and a plethora of emotions stream through him, an energy that only continues to build.

His vision then begins to blur, his lips quiver, his knees buckle.

He falls.

He begins to seizure …

9. IN FILTH, IT WILL BE FOUND

Arthur's consciousness is now no longer present in the dark arena of mud but has instead entered a black, empty realm where the only light comes from a square, standalone room in the distance. This room has walls, a door, yet no ceiling, causing light to spill out above and illuminate its position. Arthur floats closer towards this light until he reaches the door.

As he is about to enter, he hears a bloodcurdling scream coming from inside, and one he immediately recognises.

'Who are you, who are you?!' the voice brutally shouts shortly after the scream.

He freezes, immediately realising that this voice is from his younger self. More matter has appeared around him, and he now stands on the landing of his childhood home. His family from his childhood past gather around him, yet they cannot see his spectral form. Everything is happening on that fateful night just as he remembers, and an intense feeling of déjà vu overwhelms him.

Phillip's human form is now sitting on the bed talking to Arthur, giving him the caring words of wisdom he remembers. The Arthur of the present stares into the fearful face of his younger self, remembering the very nightmare like it were yesterday.

As Phillip talks, the Arthur of the past is becoming more and more wide eyed, and his features become warmer, a smile eventually cracking on his face. And whilst spectral Arthur enjoys this sight, he is struggling to hear Phillip's words, so he moves closer to where Arthur is sitting on the bed. The words are muffled, sounding distorted as if they were underwater.

But then, suddenly, the words became crystal clear, and sound much louder.

'So remember these words, Arthur.'

As this is spoken, Phillip shifts into his lion form and his head turns to face spectral Arthur, who is struck with awe and surprise. 'If you are ever struggling with something, remember that what you most need is where you least want to look. In filth, it will be found …'

'Dad, is that you?'

Phillip nods slowly, keeping firm eye contact.

'The answer is right under your nose,' Phillip says softly.

'Where?'

Phillip puts his paw to his lips, points towards the ceiling and turns his head upwards.

Arthur and his spirit father lock gazes. Phillip gives a gentle smile that causes Arthur to feel calm and content.

But this contentment is short lived. As the gaze is held, Arthur feels his surroundings start to dissolve, his spirit father's fur melt and his family home dissipate. An empty void forms around him once again, and then it all coagulates into the familiar, depressing sight of the arena of mud. Arthur's consciousness fully surfaces and his senses return.

He feels a weight on his chest, an uncomfortable sensation that is restricting his breathing.

A black hoof.

He coughs and wheezes, paralysed by the great pressure upon him.

'Turn and look at your kin,' Moloch says, towering dominantly over him.

Arthur turns his head reluctantly to see a severely brutalised and bloodied Jack lying in the mud.

Moloch cracks his whip.

More of Jack's flesh splits open.

Jack gives a groan low in energy yet deep in spirit, coming from a place of profound agony; it is clear he has taken much punishment during Arthur's seizure.

'This is no ordinary whip,' Moloch says deeply, whilst bending down closer to Arthur's face. 'After every crack, a slice of the soul enters me. Your kin has sated much of my appetite, but I have a hunger for soul that can never be quenched.' Arthur carries on staring at Moloch, lost for words. 'You see, little one, an earthly body without soul is like a machine that can do nothing but observe. Observation without spirit to act is the greatest of tortures. So look again, and observe your kin, as this is all I permit you. For he has very little spirit left. No fight, just surrender. This is the destiny for all your kind on earth. The order of the mechanical observers approaches. Oh, how your kind will be glad at its coming, and how glorious it will be.'

'You will never rid humans of their spirit,' Arthur struggles to project.

'Rid? No. Trap? Yes. Whilst you yourself have much un-trapped soul, you are a rarity in the years present. Most are simply at the mercy of the flow and will do so unquestionably. Once the Sickle sets the way to follow, most will be only too happy to eat the fruits without falter.'

'Most follow, yes … But I will return the spirit and set the path of truth for all to see …'

'No, you will not. Today is the day that your spirit is destroyed. This is without question.' Moloch leans down, picks up a handful of the black sludge and squeezes it so it oozes through his fingers. 'This is what will become of your soul. Your remnant body will be given a cubed head, and your only task will be to slave for Daemonum's expansion. Your purpose now is simply to help pave the way for the new order of Antichrist. That will ultimately be your only destiny.'

'No!'

'Yes.'

At this moment, something happens that takes both Moloch and Arthur by surprise. Jack, covered in bloodied welts and oozing gashes, despite missing parts of his soul and looking like a man with no will left, is dragging himself across the mud by his arms, making struggled groaning sounds, inching closer and closer towards Moloch. Arthur looks over surprised, and even Moloch lets off the pressure on Arthur's stomach.

'Well, what is this?' Moloch says with a slight chuckle. 'It appears the failed kin has a little fight still left to give. I will admit, I am surprised.'

Arthur frowns in confusion, yet within him a slice of hope emerges. As Jack approaches, Moloch doesn't even bother to stop him and lets him crawl uninterrupted. Even when Jack goes for Arthur's blade, Moloch just laughs and rubs his boot across Jack's face, leaving Arthur free to move once again.

'You now realise you are completely helpless?' Moloch says as he looks down at Jack and points. 'Look what I've done to him, he's pathetic beyond words.'

A concerned Arthur rolls over beside Jack and pops up to his knees. He puts a hand on his back.

'Jack?' Arthur says with a quivering voice, sounding sad and desperate.

Jack slowly, and with struggle and shake, turns his head to face his brother.

'This is *my time* … So *allow yours to shine* …' Jack says with a throaty depth, saliva dripping from his mouth only centimetres from his brother's face.

Arthur frowns curiously with his mouth wide open, and then eureka! A sudden, fleeting realisation hits him. Following Jack's words, Arthur starts to back away from him, giving him more space. Jack focuses again on his crawl, dragging the sword along with him by its bare blade, not caring for its sharpness.

'What are you going to do, little one?' Moloch taunts as he moves his boot to the back of Jack's neck, forcing him down into the muddy, black matter. 'Now he is almost fully broken,' he says as he looks up at Arthur backing off. 'It is in these moments of desperation that souls have sudden eccentric outbursts. And whilst I anticipate them, they never cease to entertain me. In fact, I savour them; because it is in these moments where they arouse their last ounces of hope, that they show their true spirit for what it is, giving me a good indication of what they have to offer for my feasting. It is, in a way, a palate teaser. And I think your kin here will taste better than expected ...' Moloch finishes by looking down at Jack and stomping his hoof violently into the back of Jack's head, forcing it inside the mud. Spurting and bubbling sounds erupt as Jack attempts to breathe.

Arthur starts shaking his head and breathing heavily. He closes his eyes. His lips start to move as he whispers and mumbles. The vision he just experienced flashes through his mind's eye, the words, 'What you most need is where you least want to look. In filth, it will be found' repeat over and over.

The vision is quickly followed by the actual memory of him as a child sitting on the bed with his father, and once again the phrase is repeated again and again. Arthur starts repeating it to himself out loud.

'In filth, it will be found.

'In filth, it will be found.

'In filth, it will be found.'

As Arthur continues this trance-like mumbling, the vision of his father putting his paw to his lips re-enters his mind, and he is curious to note the paw pointing *upwards*. Arthur keeps repeating his father's mantra whilst he looks up at the streaming black essence, his eyes slowly following the stream down as it concentrates into the hole.

Jack continues to be taunted by the bullish demon. Moloch is grabbing Jack by his hair and dunking him in and out of the mud in a tortuous style of drowning. Jack's gasps are raw, coarse and violent. He desperately clamours for the sword he just dropped next to him, his hands flailing around looking for it. Moloch pulls him up high by the hair, forcing his spine to bend back harshly. He leans down to his level and says, 'What are you going to do with that? Mere matter can do no harm to me.' Moloch leans in even closer towards Jack's face, so close that the steam from his nostrils moistens Jack's cheeks. 'Go on. Slice me, stab me, anywhere you want. I am not weak like you, it does no harm to me.'

Jack starts slicing and stabbing at Moloch's legs and feet; a thick, black tar-like liquid oozes out from the wounds, yet Moloch simply finds this hilarious and laughs deeply from the belly.

Arthur's eyes open.

It has now come clear to him.

He begins sprinting as fast as he can, until he reaches Jack and Moloch.

Jack stops his stabbing, rolls over on to his back and launches the blade up into the air with one hand.

Arthur catches it by the handle smoothly, without hesitation.

He carries on his sprint until he reaches the hole and the streaming matter at the centre of the arena. He stops abruptly, and his breath is taken away by the force of the whirlwind of streaming black matter that is being sucked deep into this hole. He looks down into the pit, seeing nothing but the streaming black matter and darkness. He gives one last look behind him and notices a shift in Moloch's expression. The smugness is somewhat muted, and the smirk has shifted to more of a frown. Arthur returns his attention to the hole. He holds the sword by its handle, blade down and close to his chest.

He jumps into the pit.

Moloch erupts in anger, screaming and roaring, turning his attention back to Jack. He tilts his bull head down slowly, looking at him with an ominous and disgusted expression …

Arthur falls. The beam of dark matter beside him is thin yet concentrated and powerful. He keeps his body held tightly together like a pencil, but the sensations in the hole keep building in intensity. A whooshing, crackling and bubbling. The deeper Arthur fell, the more intense the dark beam became, the louder the bubbling and crackling and the thicker the atmosphere. Arthur's eyes are closed, and he keeps repeating to himself, *In filth it will be found. In filth it will be found. In filth it will be found.*

He feels an urge to open his eyes, for even through his eyelids he notices a shift in light. He opens them and sees the walls of this pit illuminate more and more with multicoloured light. This light is not solid but flickering and changes in intensity. At some moments the colours are bright, and at others dimmed.

He smashes into a whirlpool of cool, black liquid.

He is swirling around and around the black beam.

The stench is fierce, yet the light beneath the surface provides powerful illumination.

As he spins around and around in this whirlpool, he is not immediately filled with fear; he is held afloat and cradled by the whirling liquid in an almost calming way. The flickering colours that refract on the wells grey walls are actually quite beautiful; and whilst darkened through their refraction, the effect fills him with a deep sense of awe. He notices this whirlpool effect is being created from six outlets on the sides of the well which the black liquid is being sucked into. Arthur assumes these holes connect to the tubes he noticed above. He continues to cling to his blade with both hands and uses his feet to tread and stay afloat. Daunting thoughts that he must descend underneath the surface continue to impede his awareness and cause doubt.

He takes a deep breath and tries to descend. Yet the thick substance is very buoyant, the current is too aggressive and his arms are restricted from carrying the sword, so he immediately bobs right back up again. He then pushes himself off from the sides in a bid to gain enough thrust to descend, yet this is also to no avail; instead, he gets caught inside the streaming black beam, which forces him under the liquid, causing a brutal shift in his consciousness by filling it with disgusting images, fear and anxiety. He frantically resurfaces, gasping and letting out a panic-filled groan that echoes all around him.

And then it hits him.

He thinks to himself, *The only way I'm going to get underneath the surface is by using the power of the beam.*

It was at this moment that it became obvious he would have to endure much pain and suffering on multiple levels. He knew he would be forced to endure fear, anxiety, disgust, panic, not being able to breathe; all whilst knowing there was no other way …

So, he takes some deep breaths and closes his eyes. When he opens them, he pushes his legs against the side and propels himself head first down into the flow of the stream. The beam begins to push him under, and this time he holds the blade in front of him, cutting through the liquid like the bow of a ship, guiding his descent deeper and deeper.

He is submerged and panicked, smothered in darkness and suffering, head shaking in fear and torment, eyes held wide open.

Yet he still dives deeper, firmly focused on the light.

The spinning tidal currents are now calm, but he continues to hurtle downwards. Yes, he is scared; yes, he cannot breathe; but still the approaching light gives him hope and the courage to push deeper and deeper …

'Your kin has chosen to give up; are you shocked at his cowardice?' Moloch says whilst standing over Jack, his hooved feet straddling Jack's torso.

'Lies!'

'Lies?' Moloch laughs. 'No, not lies. The fear he could not handle, and now he will drown down there. I will tell you a secret, little one. The cube he wishes for is down there; yes, it's true, its light is in process of being stripped, and it will soon return to darkened state. Yet have no worry, for it is far too deep for him to reach. He will try, I have no doubt, but this will be futile, and he we will be tormented by false hope. His body will eventually be consumed down there, and his soul turned to liquid for all our devouring. Shame. I wished to feast on it myself … No matter, for I still have yours and your father's for my tender and ready palate.'

'My brother … You underestimate … He has the spirit of a king, and the heart of a lion.'

Moloch gives a sinister grin.

'Look up at your father. You think lion-hearted mortals are of any threat? Their courage is merely foolishness in virtuous disguise.'

At this moment, Jack decides his words are of no use. But inside he knew with certainty that he did not need them, for what he felt was a burning confidence, at which even he was amazed. This confidence was fuelled by the fact he had seen before the events which were unfolding around him …

He begins smiling whilst staring Moloch straight in the eyes.

Moloch frowns, shakes his head and lets out a bull-like bellow. He looks at Jack with furious stubbornness.

'On your knees!'

Jack writhes on the ground but does not get up and kneel. Moloch activates a change in his whip, causing it to glow dark red; he cracks it on Jack's thigh, leaving a red-hot, smouldering gash. Burnt, black flesh seeps through the fabric of his spats.

Jack screams in pain and begins crying and moaning, rocking and spasming his body in agony. After a period of convulsing, he eventually calms down and reluctantly, through sheer willpower, manoeuvres his body into a kneeling position, his head hanging low.

Moloch stands in front of the kneeling Jack and rubs his long, black fingers through his hair, and then strokes Jack's cheeks. Moloch slowly and calmly ties the end of his whip around Jack's neck and holds the shadowy vine taut, as if it were a collar and lead.

'One movement and your head will leave your body, and your soul will be fully absorbed in here.' Moloch holds the handle of his whip in front of Jack's face. Jack looks up and sees a small pane of glass in the middle of the handle, a window to a chamber containing black liquid. 'Inside this chamber is what I have of your and your father's soul. I have, as of now, but only taken a few drops from you; the rest in here is from your father.'

Moloch turns away from Jack and stares at the centre of the arena towards the streaming well.

'Why do you look there?' Jack asks with his head still hanging low, his voice monotone. 'You said he has no hope.'

Moloch looks down at his pet and looks like he's about to speak, but then decides to say nothing. He looks back, frowning, towards the centre of the arena in anticipation …

10. LUX IN TENEBRIS

Moloch laughs to himself, turning his focus away from the hole; he instead looks down to the ground as he shakes his head smugly, in bewilderment at his own fixation, surprised at himself for expecting Arthur to emerge.

'It's been a rather long time, hasn't it?' he says, turning back to face Jack. 'If I was you, I would accept his death and start preparing yourself for yours.' Moloch tugs on the cord of his whip, teasing Jack with the threat of death.

Jack stares up at the demon with a brutalised face, his expression calm, content even, showing now no signs of fear. He breaks Moloch's gaze, turning to face the hole once again.

'Enough!' Moloch screams, tensing his arm in preparation to decapitate. But Moloch is suddenly distracted, flinching his head away.

Arthur erupts from the hole like a violet rocket, cutting through the streaming black matter like a hot knife through butter. Black essence is dripping off him as he lands gracefully, his violet glowing blade penetrating the mud.

A sound of great depth and volume hums throughout the amphitheatre, emitted by the cube, which is spinning faster than it ever had. The sound overpowers the awful demonic tones. The demons of the towers moan, croak and weep. Their sick orchestra is now dulled, hurt and beaten; sickened by the power of the violet glow that radiates across their black flesh. Arthur's shining eyes widen in awe at what is happening to him. He feels an energy of magnificent proportions enter him; he feels holy, and he feels blessed.

Moloch's head bends, and he holds his free hand over his face to shield his eyes from the bright violet light. Jack stares right into the warming light, and at Arthur, a bittersweet smile forming on his face as a tear runs down his bloodied cheek.

'This was it …' Jack says under his breath.

At this moment, Arthur's face is serious, almost stern.

'Release him,' Arthur says calmly, yet confidently, seeing his brother held in a shadowy collar.

'As you wish.'

Moloch rips on the whip with great power.

Jack's head is removed from his body and falls to the ground …

Almost immediately after Jack's decapitation, something ghostly yet still opaque emerges from Jack's earthly body. Like a butterfly leaving its cocoon, the ethereal form floats away. It looks mostly the same as the earthly Jack, yet it is naked and the head is toad-like. Moloch tightly holds his whip, which is dark black again, Moloch clenches harder and harder, pulling Jack's ghostly form closer towards the soul chamber of his whip.

Arthur notices this immediately but shows no signs of shock. By the look of his face, he has already accepted Jack's fate. Yet Arthur does not wish for his brother's soul to fall into the hands of demons, so he moves up towards his brother's ghostly form and holds his sword tightly with two hands, spinning the cube faster and faster in an attempt to attract the soul. Jack's ghostly form is now being pulled back and forth between the dark, shadowy whip of Moloch and Arthur's cubed sword of light. The demon and the hero lock gazes with great intensity, frowning and tensing their features. Jack's toad-headed form is being stretched and pulled apart under the strain of the equally strong opposing forces

'His soul is of the light! You have lost, dark one! Accept your defeat! And yield to truth and beauty!' a focused Arthur shouts.

Moloch does not answer immediately but continues to smile, his nostrils steaming intensely.

'Your strength is of a lesser magnitude, you are mere mortal, not demon nor angel. Accept your loss as destiny!'

Arthur feels a sudden compulsion to close his eyes. Within him he feels a force pulling on his blade, like a fish tugging on a line.

'His soul has desire to come to the side of truth! I can feel it!'

'His desire is of no consequence! *My desire* will conclude his fateful fall to darkness …'

Moloch's expression becomes more aggressive, and he widens his stance. He begins roaring ferociously.

Jack's ghost is pulled closer to darkness …

'No! It is not yours to take!' Arthur shouts desperately, also adopting a more aggressive posture.

'Your spirit is waning!' Moloch spits. 'That sword was made for angels, and you are but a charlatan.'

At this moment, Arthur's senses intuitively pick up on an energy, a vibration, a shift in atmosphere that he can't explain, only feel.

He looks up into the black void.

'Yesss! I can feel him start to enter!' Moloch shouts with enthusiasm as he feels some soul enter the chamber on his whip.

Arthur grits his teeth and looks up at his hanging father's form. Feeling inspired by this sight and his duty to rescue, he begins screaming with all his might and re-focuses his attention on his brother's ghost.

One last push, Arthur! Light is approaching! He thinks to himself, knowing in reality he could not keep up this level of concentration for much longer.

Arthur summons his last ounces of energy, and the cube spins even faster. Jack's ghost once again moves away from Moloch and towards Arthur. However, it doesn't break the deadlock, and Jack's ghostly form remains stretched between them.

Then Arthur senses the approaching force as he did before, but this time more intensely. He feels something coming closer, a force causing warmth to rise within him; a loving force of light.

And then he starts to hear it ...

Sweet notes.

Notes of heavenly proportions.

Notes that cause a man to shed a tear.

A choir of all frequencies, high and low, emitting a sound like no other that captured all and everything.

Arthur looks up into the void.

Bright moving lights, gliding with sublime grace.

A great legion of light drawing ever closer ...

Leading the legion is a violet-cubed angel of brightness. The archangel has broad and mighty white crystal wings 10 times bigger than its own body. They cover the black void in such divine white light, it is as if the sun itself has entered with gliding grace. The archangel's crystal-cube body pulses, spins and hums, casting a powerful violet glow and rhythm all around. The lesser angels look classically human in form, much the same as Áine, and are dressed in white gowns, all with modest translucent wings.

This archangel leads its legion closer until their vibrating hymn is overwhelming. The demons of the towers screech and shout, the noise reverberating through their coloured kingdoms, as they try with all their might to fight the light with their disharmonized music. But these miserable sounds of inferior frequency are drowned out by the truly holy.

Moloch screams and writhes, his face contorting and his burnt bull head shaking and steaming with ferocious aggression. Yet he is gradually pacified by the light and hum of the holy legion until he has not even the strength to keep hold of Jack's spirit form and is forced to let go. Jack's ethereal body glides towards his brother. Moloch's legs buckle and he falls to his knees in weakness.

The demon on the tower of the red-plasma kingdom shifts his ritualistic movements, making fists and pulling them down slowly by his side. He then makes a loud, moose-like call. The movement is reciprocated by the other demons on the tower ledges, who all let out their own unique animal call. The sound from their coloured kingdoms shifts from an eerie humming groan to a constant, steady, low frequency, like a bass note. This tone then quietens until silence falls …

The demonic lords leave their platforms, retreating to their coloured kingdoms.

Within the towers, Draxlers and lesser demons enter a sort of frenzied panic, shouting commands, scurrying and pointing at their cube-head slaves as they attempt to herd them like cattle. The cube heads, who lowered Jack and Phillip on the crosses earlier, are aggressively whipped and commanded to pull Phillip back up the tower to the summit.

The archangel quickly notices this and signals its angels to destroy both the Draxlers and the cube heads aiming to capture Phillip. Ten or so angels thrust down in a flash and send white beams of light towards them. The Draxlers and cube heads instantly evaporate into burning blue flames. The archangel majestically hovers over the centre stage, its wings spanning almost the entire breadth of the arena and eclipsing the light as its legion wait above. It stares down at the collapsed and kneeling Moloch. The archangel has subtle facial features covered in light, making them hard to see; yet an expression of divine calmness and mercy is clear, but it also exudes complete confidence in its ability to convict and execute.

Arthur tilts his head up at the archangel in awe, instinctively holding up his sword in gentle offering. The archangel keeps his gaze locked on Moloch, shedding white and violet light upon everything below. It reaches its right hand towards the sword, causing it gravitate into its grasp. As the angel holds the sword, it increases in size to match the proportions of its form.

The archangel continues to stare intensely at Moloch, making it clear that even the slightest offensive action would lead to his total destruction. Moloch keeps his head bowed, refusing to make eye contact.

The archangel, without breaking its focused stare, holds its free arm out to his side towards where Phillip is hanging, and then to below where Arthur and his spirit brother stand. Many of its angels begin working on freeing Phillip from his inverted cross and bringing him down to be reunited with his sons. He is lowered gracefully under the watchful gaze of their captain of light.

Phillip's body is laid in front of the brothers, and the lesser angels gather round. The archangel slowly puts its hands together on the sword's handle, bows its head once and then reverts to its previous pose, keeping an eye still on Moloch. The circling angels begin praying, each humming in harmony, creating an intensely beautiful frequency. The vibration from their lips forms a golden wave of light, which combined together form a golden spirit ball in the centre of the circle that is then dropped into Phillip's heart. The brothers watch wide-eyed in awe and silence.

Phillip takes in a slow, drawn-out breath.

His eyes open, and he exhales.

Both the brothers lean down to hug their father, who they never thought they would see in this form again.

'My boys ...' Phillip says, sounding fatigued yet happy. His sons bury their faces in his fur. 'I never had doubt that your faith would remain, and your actions would be so bold.'

'We've done it,' Arthur says, breaking his hug to look his father in the eye.

'Yes, Arthur, you have. And I am proud, and so should you both be too,' he says as he turns to look at Jack.

And then all three are distracted by a certain angel who suddenly drops and lands beside them. This angel looks down with gentle, glowing features at the hugging trio.

Áine.

'Knew it ...' Jack says whilst shaking his toadish head, grinning cheekily, his voice sounding the same as before even though it came from the face of a toad.

'You didn't think I would just leave you, did you?' Áine says. 'As soon as you entered Daemonum, I knew light from any but the most powerful angels could escape the void. So I never actually entered, but instead reversed my flight back to the heavens and returned with my heavenly commander, Michael.' Áine looks up at Saint Michael, who still hovers with a gentle stillness, gaze locked on Moloch.

'That is Archangel Michael?' Arthur asks as he looks up with his mouth open wide.

Áine nods, and then turns her attention to Phillip on the floor. Phillip stands to face his other half, and they stare into each other's eyes in silence.

'You need not compensate with excess hardness now,' Phillip says to her with gentle smile, 'allow me to be that side instead, and allow us together to be close to the image of our heavenly father, merging ourselves together as one.'

Áine closes her eyes, and her features immediately soften; she looks down, and a tear runs down her cheek. She looks back up to face Phillip's lion form. Her soft hand strokes the back of his head, and she smiles deeply at him.

She looks down at Jack and says, 'Our spirits now belong to heaven, whilst Arthur's still to earth. Your work has been completed and has not gone unnoticed by the Lord.'

Jack nods.

Áine looks up at Michael, communicating to him telepathically: *Moloch still has much of Phillip's soul within his possession, I feel it in his energy.* Michael does not break his stare, yet Áine feels within her angelic spirit that her message is acknowledged.

Michael holds the sword with two hands high above his head.

A violet beam shoots from the blade, high into the void, covering the blackness with a nebula of violet light.

'From Lord to darkness, I say, rebuke you all!' Michael announces, focusing firstly on Moloch but then at the surroundings. His voice is gentle, yet strong and resonant. 'Lord, Lord, oh, how he curses you all. Your meddling has brought corruption to earth in the most deceptive of ways, and all daemons in this realm shall and should feel shame. It is my duty, as set by the heavenly father, to alter the course of your evil to a measure of divine balance, to a measure where righteousness and grace can find their way back; yes, your mark has been gratuitously overstepped. All six lords of the hexagon are guilty, this is true and without question, as is also the fact that none shall be let off lightly. Yet, there is one who stands out above all, and that is the one who kneels beneath me …' Michael looks down at Moloch, who still faces down in silence. 'Moloch, it was through *your* shadowy orange spirit that an Antichrist inversion has arrived on earth, and it is your spirit of obsessive filth and corruptive fantasies that has plagued earth with distraction from totality in the Lord. For these crimes, your spirit will be ripped apart and spread across your void, until earth can once again find its way and learn to accommodate you gracefully.'

'But brother from above, *his job is already done*. His orange spirit of the second was only needed for the arrival of my son,' speaks a deep and cunning voice from the void.

Michael breaks his gaze on Moloch to focus on the void.

'Your pride and arrogance have never faltered,' Michael says. 'For do you not realise that my son, too, has a place on earth ...'

'Oh, but Michael, my dark box reigns already; *and more walk willingly inside everyday* ...'

'Your house will grow old and withered, yet the house of the holy falls and is continually repaired, for that is the way of loving father and son in unison. You see this not, only because of pride.'

The ground starts to shake, the void wobbles and bends and the violet nebula warps around the darkness.

Moloch uses these moments of disorientation to mutter a deep howl.

A command.

Hundreds upon hundreds of orange projectiles come bursting through Moloch's orange plasma field.

Moloch stands up quickly and runs through the plasma into his kingdom.

Michael had sensed the attack before it came and swiftly created a transparent violet orb shield that covers both himself and his group gathering below. A couple of lingering angels that hover up and around the amphitheatre are hit by the beams and evaporate in a flash into white gaseous matter, their souls shooting upwards and out of Daemonum faster than any eye could see.

'Box-head projectiles ...' Áine says calmly to the others within the shield.

Michael fires himself like a rocket out of the shield, penetrating Moloch's orange plasma in pursuit of him.

The projectiles stop.

The angels and the family look at one another cautiously.

'Is he going to be alright?' Jack asks innocently.

Arthur can't help but let out a smile; Áine and Phillip follow suit.

Áine points and nods at the orange plasma and the black and violet void above it, prompting Jack to focus on it. Jack squints and bows his head a little in anticipation.

Time goes by. Yet still nothing …

The angels remain calm and have their hands placed together in humble prayer.

The rumbling continues, the shaking ever true, the violet-shot void now tearing and becoming more violent and chaotic, like a stomach in desperate need to rid itself of toxins.

'There!' Arthur shouts, seeing Michael's violet-cubed form and bright white wings rise high up into the void above the hexagon kingdom.

The brothers squint to try and see more clearly, all whilst Phillip watches casually from behind them with his paws on his sons' backs, his face struck with warmth and hope. Áine watches calmly with a raised eyebrow amongst her angelic kin, all now facing up to watch the spectacle.

'Moloch's with him too, look! I think he has him impaled on his sword, you know,' Jack says.

And it is true, the archangel has Moloch impaled by the pelvis on his glowing blade, a field of violet wrapping around Moloch's form, securing him with no chance of release. Michael raises him higher and higher up into the void, holding Moloch's form casually out at the side as if he was a candlestick being carried by a reluctant choir boy.

Michael reaches a great height, so much so that his intensely glowing aura is but a speck in the distance. The speck stops moving and glows like a star.

'It's getting brighter!' Arthur says whilst his eyes widen with awe.

'Stay inside the orb shield, he's about to come down very soon,' Áine says.

The brothers look at each other and smile childishly, trying their best to hold in their excitement.

'He's coming back down!' Jack says.

'And fast …' Arthur follows with a surprised chuckle.

'Brace,' Áine says.

Michael is shooting down from the void like a white and violet comet.

He goes faster, faster, faster …

Until …

There's a blinding flash of many colours.

Jack, Arthur and Phillip cover their eyes, yet the angels stare without falter.

The explosion engulfs everything, covering the entirety of the violet shield, blinding all inside to anything outside. Yet the shield remains intact and does not fade. Nothing but a dust-ridden, russet light can now be seen.

The explosion settles.

Shards upon shards of orange rise up and around the void, expanding to colour the void's nebula, looking like molten glass that has erupted high out of a volcano.

Moloch's tower is no more. His orange kingdom has been obliterated into pieces.

And there is no sight of Moloch ...

Yet, within the large empty void where his kingdom previously resided, a figure of light hovers ...

Michael.

He flies back with haste, and grace.

He hovers above the shield orb and relaxes it with a swipe of his sword. The void above is now booming in contortion, the atmosphere bending and making everything look a little wobbly and melty.

Michael looks back down at the group and lays a closed fist above them. He opens his fist wide, and out comes two streams of white light which gravitate to Phillip and Jack, with the larger stream entering Phillip's heart and the smaller stream going into Jack.

Both Jack and Phillip take a deep breath, as if a weight was suddenly taken off their shoulders and replaced with new-found joy and spirit; smiles instantly form on their faces.

Michael sharply and quickly looks down at Arthur below.

'Chosen one, open yourself,' he says. Arthur does not completely understand, yet tries to relax and takes a deep breath.

Michael shoots down at the speed of light, entering Arthur's body.

Arthur is filled with spirit, and the sword in its original size enters his hands once again. Wings of the same shape as Michael's, yet smaller, sprout from his back, and his skin and veins have a subtle violet glow.

I have entered you in spirit, now pay attention and learn my ways, as they will be of use for you on earth, says Michael's voice inside Arthur's mind.

Announce these words to my legion, command as commander: 'Assume launch formation.'

'Assume launch formation!' Arthur says out loud to the angels, his mother Áine moving in front of Jack and Phillip, preparing them for launch.

We haven't much time now; Satan's dragon form will attempt to dull the choir and trap us, Michael says from within. *Hold the sword high, and focus the beam upwards; activate in three, two, one. Execute.*

Arthur shoots the violet beam high into the void, holding it steady.

Launch in three seconds. Prepare yourself.

As Arthur quickly braces in anticipation, he looks up into the void and sees a flying behemoth: a black and red beast, zigzagging in front of the violet-lit void. Its eyes are bright with fire, its forked tongue poking out, its tail sharp like wire and its wings slimy like a snake.

Energy builds within Arthur, and he launches.

The choir of angels and alike thrust upwards too.

Arthur holds his sword out in front, its beam penetrating through the void's atmosphere.

As Arthur's flight upwards continues, he glances back behind him and sees the legion of light following closely. He can't help but smile at how he is leading them. He glances over and sees Áine, with Jack and Phillip gliding by her side.

Arthur notices the behemoth now giving chase, cutting through to the left of them.

'Satan is approaching!' Arthur shouts.

Do not fear, Michael replies within. *He wishes for weakness of spirit, but my spirit strengthens you, and he has already been rebuked, for he in this form poses no threat to those of divine alignment.*

The behemoth catches up with the legion of light and flies beside them. Its face, which has fins and barbels, looks like a cross between a fish and dragon.

'Arthur … I see you, Arthur …' the beast says mockingly.

Ignore him, for he will try trickery and temptation.

'You are so strong! You must surely feel great pride,' Satan says. 'How you rise above your fellow man with such glorious spirit! You are superior, I have no doubt in this.'

Arthur briefly turns his head to focus on Satan, who is now almost within touching distance. However, he shakes his head in response to this attempt to stoke his pride.

'Not everyone is like you. Most on earth are weak and easily tempted. So be careful of those who you think are close, because it is those that I will target. Am I really so evil if I give such warnings? Maybe I am not all I am made out to be …'

The dragon fish changes course and flies off into the void.

'Goodbye,' echoes around as he drifts off into darkness.

Approaching dark matter's edge. Increase intensity of focus for penetration, Michael says from within. Arthur does as he is told.

With the void now illuminated by violet, Arthur notices the black, bendy edge, which curves like a dome, approaching fast.

'I can see the edge,' Arthur says out loud.

Let the beam open space for the legion to follow. Impact in five seconds.

Arthur smashes into the void's edge with a burst of violet light.

He erupts into Terra Stultorum.

Streams of light, like glowing birds exiting at ferocious speed, shoot their way up through Stultorum and into the heavens.

Arthur can't help but laugh to himself at what just happened.

'Well done, Arthur, it's smooth sailing from here. Pull your wings back and we will enter astral speeds.'

Arthur pulls back his wings into a more streamlined position, and the angels behind follow suit.

Their speed reaches epic proportions, everything around morphing into a different state completely and glowing bright and strong with ultraviolet.

And that's when it became clear.

They are flying alongside the universal Tree of Life.

Its form is ghostly, translucent, yet it glows with subtle tints of gold and wobbles and breathes as if it were itself a living entity, puffing and contracting.

Arthur stares at the glistening bark, from which he feels an energy filling him with great warmth and comfort.

He turns his attention upwards.

A towering canopy of white and gold leaves and branches, rising high into blinding light. At its base is a wide platform.

And now for the landing: follow up the side of the tree and slowly curve around the edge of the platform. That is where we land and say our goodbyes …

'Okay, thank you,' an astonished Arthur replies to the voice within.

Arthur carefully curves his way around the great tree and the platform. Michael leaves Arthur's body immediately upon landing and hovers out in front; his legion land in designated positions on the ledge.

Áine lands soon after, and beside her Jack and Phillip stand, all together as a family. Phillip, Jack and Arthur all stare forward awestruck into the distance at the white and golden gates and the tree's golden glow. Behind these gates is a spiral staircase, which curves all the way around the tree, leading into the canopy's blinding light.

Michael stands high above all and stares down, waiting for all to settle and be ready.

'I now speak to the one bounded by flesh, the one who has earned his title of chosen one, the one to pave the way for the return of the holy; yet still, I speak for all to hear.

'It is rare for one of flesh to stand so close to heaven; but see this as re-ward, a reward well due for the spirit and action shown to save his father. Arthur, may the rescue and return of your father be a symbol to you, and represent good news to come. But before this, work must still be done. The image of Christ on earth has become deformed; for his way, which is truth, has been stripped of its totality in past and present culture. It has been split and deformed. For this false image has caused generations past and present to have weakness and cowardice in the face of wickedness and evil; yet the true Christ was neither, presenting the image of his father in human form. The true image is one of courage against lies and perversion; it is the spirit that, even against ones of tainted corruption, will embody truth in a way that is digestible and tender, like a mother gently telling her children truths; for his way is both honest yet sweet. But his image laid down was not simply left and right as harmonious lovers; it was also the compass, the guiding beacon that sparked connection to the familiar conscience within, the singularity within us all, the place with no confusion or lies, only truth and wisdom.

'It is in this relationship that one may begin connecting to all that is holy, and become closer and closer to the true image of God, which is truth incarnate. The kingdom of heaven is within oneself, and is still there for seekers to find. For the son was both there in the beginning and there at the end; and he will continue to live inside all and everything forever; he is there for those who have eyes to see. But you, Arthur, are but a mortal man; not God, not divine and not perfection. Yet this is why you have been tasked to bring the return of the spirit, to return divine grace in the face of the budding Antichrist. The road will be hard, and strife and suffering will be common, but my violet cube and sword are now yours; may they be a beacon and a reminder to you and your kind. May they provide truth and guidance, an image of familiarity, connecting those to their *God within*. May this gift vanquish distortion and perversion, may it shed dead wood and leaves of old to those of corrupted nature; may the holy beam initiate rebirth for those who cease to let go. Blessings to you, Arthur, and may you bring return of a stable and fruitful Tree of Life to those who live on earth, the same as it is for us angels in heaven. Amen.'

Áine, Arthur, Jack and Phillip and the Angels all say amen together.

EPILOGUE

As all settles, and as Michael finishes his speech, he moves towards the gate, and all his angels but Áine follow. He reaches the gate, still glistening brightly, ushering the angels through. The angels float upwards and around the great staircase and back to their heavenly reside.

The newly reunited family stay back, and together on the great tree's side platform exchange warm smiles. Arthur leans on the pommel of his sword, the cube gently spinning whilst it radiates the six colours in its idle state. The sword is now bare of the leather scabbard gifted to him, which was left behind in Terra Daemonum due to the nature of the swift escape.

'This isn't the end, Arthur,' Phillip says as he turns to his son. 'Now that you have returned me to Áine, connecting with us will be easier than it ever was. Your talent to reach out to planes high and low has only grown in power. So if you ever need us, we are here watching and looking down.'

'Don't worry, though,' Jack intercepts with a smirk. 'I won't look when you are having ... private moments.'

'Still got your sense of humour then?' Arthurs says with a cheeky grin. 'Even if you do have the face of a toad.'

'Well, he won't be a toad for much longer,' Áine says, turning to face Jack. 'You will be glad to know that this form is only transitional, and I have received word and confirmation that both my husband and son will be up-graded to sit with me in my ring of choir.'

'We are becoming angels like you?' Jack asks with a curious and ex-cited look.

'Yes, and once you become one, you will learn and see many things; your eyes will be opened and your heart expanded.'

Jack nods and moves his toady lips in a pleased manner. The family then turn around and see Saint Michael walking towards them. The archangel's wings are now neatly folded in. The many crystal cubes that make up his form now glow gently in various colours, rather than in the powerful vi-olet when wings were out wide. Beside him walk two lesser angels, who hold strings of light and weave.

'Your sword is bare of scabbard, and that leather one of earthly craft will not suffice for such a holy relic,' Michael says.

He turns and glances at the angels beside him. They float down towards Arthur and begin weaving and knitting patches of golden light into Arthur's flesh. He doesn't feel much during this process, just subtle warmth and tingles.

One of the angels then pulls her hands apart slowly, and between them a transparent crystal tube forms. This tube gently glows white and glistens ever so subtly with a light blue. The angel who crafted this tube places it on Arthur's right side, and it sticks to his flesh softly, yet solidly, like a powerful magnet. With a finger, Arthur touches the crystal sheath, yet he feels no solid mass at all; it seems this scabbard is weightless.

As Arthur moves his sword towards the crystal scabbard, it immediately becomes absorbed by the tube of crystal light, locking the sword in place. Arthur rubs his finger along the crystal tube; with the sword inside, he can now feel the smoothness of the scabbard. He pulls it off his body with ease.

'This scabbard is now bound to your spirit,' Michael says, 'and will remain unseen in the earthly realm, until your times of need. It will do its best to understand your intentions, but if you wish for the sword to appear you may always pray to me for its emergence if it not be time of emergency. May it help you keep the cube safe from evil hands.'

'Thank you, Saint Michael,' Arthur says as he looks up at the towering angel tenderly and with awe. 'Thank you for everything you have shown and given me. It is beyond words the experiences I have had, and I can't even begin to truly express my thanks for your help and protection down there.'

'Help will always be given and justice administered when the Lord deems it fair. For he gives you the choice to act as you wish, and shows mercy for those who bare their cross responsibly and honestly. You, Arthur, have so far acted nobly, and in close alignment with the spirit. But be aware, still, no man or woman of the earth is ever free from the temptations of evil. A great feat achieved can induce a pride that may lead one to fall. And I say, to fall or not to fall, this is a question that only you can call. But alas, it is on this rhyming note that I send you back down to earth, for much work is still to be done; for *you have now become my earthly son.*'

Arthur bows his head in respect to the archangel, who nods back. Michael sprouts his wings once again, violet igniting, and flies back towards heaven with the two angels.

Arthur turns his focus to his family once again. He approaches his brother until they are very close and looks him in the eye..

'We did it, Jack. Look what we've done and achieved; look where we are now!'

Jack takes in a breath, looks down, and then looks back up to face his brother.

'Thank you,' Jack says intensely, and then pauses for a few moments. 'I am blessed to have had you as my brother on earth, and now from the heavens we will be brothers of the spirit. I will do whatever I can to help you; and although I'm not sure of my duties when I become an angel, I will give you my word that I will do everything in my power to help you fight the order of Antichrist.' The brothers embrace. 'Honestly, Arthur, if it weren't for you, I would have fallen well and truly; I would have been stuck in my own box, never believing in anything magical or transcendent. If it wasn't for you, I would have still been the Jack we both knew from not too long ago ...'

Arthur nods to his brother, and then turns to his father who stands between them.

'Dad ...' They embrace. 'I can't imagine what you were put through down there ...' Arthur says whilst still hugging him.

'The torments were great, it cannot be denied,' Phillip says, pulling away to look at Arthur in the eye, pursing his lips and tilting his head down. 'But what was greater was the faith in my sons to save me; and that was what kept my spirit strong. You demonstrated all the traits I wished for you: the love and wisdom I gave you in your youth. To see this wisdom flourish, in such extreme and defining moments, fulfils me more than any father could possibly wish for. I could not have hoped for a greater son; and, of course, I will always be looking down from above, to give you supporting wisdom in your times of need. Michael is right, though; your task is only just beginning, and you must not become complacent nor overly proud. Whilst I know you know this, it is still important to be aware of the ever lingering snake of trickery and chaos.'

Arthur nods, and purses his lips together contentedly.

'Mum, I knew deep down you were on your way to help us,' Arthur says with a soft smile as he turns to his mother. 'I didn't want to say it to myself or out loud though, but I had an intuitive feeling.'

Áine giggles and smiles softly.

'Oh, you know I would have never left you. But as has been said, do not be too sad in this goodbye, for we aren't really gone. We will continue to be with you. This moment is just a happy one, and not even bittersweet.'

'I know ... But I'm still a man of the earth, aren't I? To not have you all down there with me brings me feelings of loss that I simply can't get rid of. I will always be at least a little bit saddened by this.'

'And do not try to rid yourself of these feelings. For these are given to you for a reason. It is this sadness that opens your heart to much beauty and love for others,' Áine says.

Arthur looks to the side and smiles.

'Well, this is it then I guess ...'

Áine nods and walks closer towards her son, puts her hand against his cheek and gives a loving, gentle smiles.

'Goodbye, my son,' she says.

Áine takes a step back and whispers a prayer. She holds out a palm in front of him, lowering it slowly.

A golden mist forms around Arthur.

Arthur's tenderly smiling family dissolve in front of his eyes, fading away softly until they disappear completely.

Julius stands outside just before midday. He leans on a black and silver cane whilst the sun shines brightly, warming the cool air and illuminating the burnt ruins around him.

He looks down at his watch – 11:59am.

He frowns and purses his lips in anticipation. As he continues to stare forward at the crater within the ruined field, he squints as he notices a shift from the rays of sun that beam through clouds above. A new ray of light emerges, and it focuses directly in the centre of the crater.

'Just in time,' he says to himself as he begins to walk forward.

Arthur finds himself in the crater, and he looks around with frowning curiosity. He is initially surprised that his sword is no longer bound to him visibly, but then he remembers what he was told up in heaven about it being 'bound to his spirit'. In the centre of this blackened mound of soil, he spots the sparkling white rock that once bore the sword, in clean contrast to the dirt around it.

He gasps in fear, shaking his head.

'Yes, it is unfortunate,' Julius says from above, looking down at the battered and filthy Arthur standing in the crater. 'But fear not, young hero, for the ones closest to you still stand and breathe, even if the academy does not.'

'Julius!' Arthur says as his expression immediately brightens, forgetting the fear he felt prior.

Julius nods and smiles.

'You look a right state, don't you? What a warrior you have become! It is no surprise, though, as you have in fact been to hell and back!

Come, come walk with me.' Julius walks away out of view, and Arthur begins climbing up the crater to reach the grassy surface.

As Arthur reaches surface level, he takes a good look around and sees the devastation that surrounds him. Everything has been blown to smithereens: mounds of dirt and piles of metal and glass, the remnants of the equipment and materials that were once underground, are scattered chaotically.

'It's all gone, Julius ...' Arthur says as shakes his head. 'All of it ...'

Julius faces away from Arthur and walks towards the forest next to where the academy once stood. Arthur shakes his head to himself again then catches up to walk alongside him.

After a few moments of silence, the temptation for Arthur to ask a question is too much.

'How long have I been away for, then?'

'Exactly six months and six days. Just as I personally predicted. However, the texts suggesting the time of your arrival are vague and full of riddles; some members perceived the return as being six days, some 66 days and some even thought it would be 666 days; yet I was always confident it would be six months and six days. Regardless, we unanimously agreed it would be at midday on whatever day it came to be.'

Arthur frowns curiously and nods his head, but then he becomes more serious.

'Okay, but everyone is fine? How is Eva? And my godparents?'

'Yes, all fine, Arthur, please don't worry. Whilst we are in dangerous times, of that there is no doubt, all ones closest to you are alive and well. In fact, the inner circle is waiting at Lord Bell's manor for your arrival. Both the inner circle and the academy in general have become accustomed to a great deal of excitement and anxiety; however, today was the day I had always predicted, so I can assure you they are all in very good spirits.'

'Okay, good.' Arthur takes a relieved breath and nods whilst looking at the floor. 'Something tells me that not all the members outside the inner circle were so lucky ... And what about your library? The fallen books? Have they well and truly fallen from existence?'

Julius gives a fleeting glance towards Arthur, and they lock gazes for a few moments before Julius looks up into the sun streaming through the forest's canopy before changing the direction of his walk.

'This way. John has been picking me up on a lane away from the academy in case of spies.'

'Spies?' Arthur asks slowly, only slightly shocked as he had a good idea who might be behind this.

'About three months ago, there was a tragic incident at a virology research lab in Scotland. A young man called Logan Anderson acquired a semi-automatic rifle and shot and killed 39 scientists, and then himself. It sent shockwaves through the community and gained a lot of both national and international media attention. It set off a psychological and political timebomb that has been long waiting to go off. I won't go into the exact details, but in Anderson's pocket was a note with some psychotic ramblings saying how all the world's problems are due to scientists, and how the "cult of science" must be exterminated in favour of the "cult of God". It was, of course, not long before this act of extremism caused a lot of finger pointing and was quickly hijacked by the IHA-funded media. It then went on to be used as a scapegoat to bring in "special emergency powers" that were used to justify the need to investigate, and potentially destroy, all religious associations or organisations that have links to anything mythological in nature, or practise anything that deviates from the currently-accepted technocratic political lines. These so called "investigations" were glamourised and propagandised in the media as a crack special operations group "ridding the country of religious extremism". In reality, they are simply a blunt instrument, a para-policing unit owned by a company with links to the IHA. When they arrived here, there was no investigation; no questions were ever even asked. They just turned up, arrested some of the members who were present at the time and then carried out a controlled demolition. And no, we still haven't heard back from Gary and Charlie since their arrest …'

Arthur stares at Julius with raised eyebrows.

'Okay, well this is clearly very bad news. I think the powers-that-be already had us on their radar, and this tragedy was the excuse that they were waiting for. For now, we need to make sure all the other members are kept safe. Has the academy still been meeting elsewhere?'

'We have been using Lord Bell's manor, and it's working out well so far. However, many members have decided it's best for both themselves and their families to leave the academy altogether. Things have changed, Arthur, and they will never be the same; we must accept this. Now is the beginning of your true test as leader; this is where you become who you were

born to be. Arthur, the crackdown on personal belief and individual sover-
eignty is being replaced with a forced communal ideological and technological system. This is the beginning of the *great hive*, the merging with the
great beast of darkness; this is the start of the …'

'Coming of the Antichrist,' Arthur interrupts. 'Yes, I am aware of the situation all too well; in fact, I spoke to him face to face in the underworld.'

Julius nods knowingly.

'It's Sickle, isn't it?' Julius asks sombrely, and Arthur nods as they make
intense eye contact.

'You never mentioned to me about the arrival of the Antichrist. You
prophesied almost everything other than it, in fact.'

Julius laughs.

'I shouldn't laugh, but I have already thought about this and the irony
has not gone over my head. All that time my energy was focused on the
prophecies of the fallen books, I had forgotten about the most fallen book
of them all: the Bible. Regardless, it is now confirmed as certain … And all
is following the path as so prophesised.' He pauses for a moment to look
up at a tree in contemplation. 'Oh, and don't worry, the books are all saved.
At least the ones of the highest importance, that is; the chests containing
the 44 fallen books are all hidden safely in Lukas's manor. I also managed
to stockpile some of Jung's books, holy texts and varieties of classical litera-
ture. Books of these sorts will inevitably become rarer and rarer the deeper
we go into the Antichrist age; the authorities will inevitably stop producing
any texts that conflict with the established narrative.'

'That's a relief. I was a bit worried, as I know how much the fallen texts
act as a guide to our community. You truly are their guardian, aren't you?
Amazing work, Julius. Tell me though, did the books themselves give any
clue as to how they might be destroyed?'

'Yes and no. In many volumes it is written that their destruction and abduction are always a danger, but no exact scenarios or times are mentioned.
For this, I have to simply rely on my good old-fashioned intuition, so we
have that to thank for their rescue. It was immediately after your and Jack's
departure that I started to feel a deep anxiety for the books, and then weird
things started to happen in the library. The chests would rattle and the dense
doors would fling open … Something clearly wasn't right; it was almost
as if the books were trying to tell me of the coming danger. So, I took the

initiative and begun moving them to safety. As soon as they were moved, all the strange activities stopped and the books themselves became calm.'

The pair continue to walk through the forest in silence until John's car can clearly be seen through the foliage, parked at the side of a road.

'There he is,' Julius says as John is seen exiting the car.

'Julius, before I see everybody again, I have to ask: You don't seem surprised at all by how I came back alone. Did you know only I would return? Are John and Suzy going to be saddened and surprised by the fact Jack is not with us anymore?'

Julius stops abruptly to face Arthur and then takes a deep sigh.

'I knew ... And it cannot be denied. In fact, you were the only one who did not. Whilst I put great value in truth, sometimes it is best to withhold it temporarily. Your godparents have already mourned, and the news will come as no surprise. Yet I have a feeling you know more than anybody that his soul resides in a place of contentment, am I right?' Julius finishes by giving a knowing look, one that is both warm and even a little cheeky.

Arthur returns a similar glance, and they continue to walk towards John's car.

'Oh, there is some good news to come out of all of this too, you know ...'

Arthur squints at the car as he sees the back doors open. He tries to make out who the two exiting passengers are.

'Welcome back, Arthur,' John says as he leans on the car with crossed arms, smiling.

Arthur smiles vibrantly back as he moves closer. He then turns his focus towards the two who are walking around the back of the car.

Eva and Ishmael.

Eva locks gazes with Arthur, her face bright and glowing, her cheeks flushed. Arthur grins widely as he sees not just his girlfriend but a fully-mobile Ishmael walking next to her. It is true she is helping him by holding his arm as he walks, but his arms and legs are now moving freely and there's not a wheelchair in sight.

'Ishmael?!' He frantically turns to look at Eva, John and back at Julius, who are now all looking at him with great delight.

'Our Sunday sessions may have actually paid off, Arthur,' Ishmael says with a large grin. 'It's either that or all the chocolate orange you've been feeding me ...'

They all erupt in laughter and then embrace one another in loving reunion.